Terry Carr's idea of what a good s-f story ought to be was one that was intellectually challenging, strongly plotted, and gracefully written. There was no particular order of preference to those criteria: he wanted all three. By "intellectually challenging," he meant a story that was built around a strong speculative idea, preferably a scientific-technological one. By "strongly plotted," he meant a story that would hold a reader's attention from start to finish, a story in which you care about the characters and what happens to them. By "gracefully written," he meant just what you would expect.

Terry's criteria for science fiction happen to be mine also, both as a writer and an editor.... I'm quite confident that if he could read the book you now hold, he'd look upon it with pleasure and regard it as an appropriate successor to his own anthologies.

—Robert Silverberg,
from the introduction

UNIVERSE 1

BANTAM SPECTRA SPECIAL EDITIONS

Full Spectrum 2 edited by Lou Aronica, Shawna McCarthy,
    Amy Stout, and Patrick LoBrutto
No Enemy But Time by Michael Bishop
Synners by Pat Cadigan
Views from the Oldest House by Richard Grant
Winterlong by Elizabeth Hand
King of Morning, Queen of Day by Ian McDonald
Points of Departure by Pat Murphy
The Silicon Man by Charles Platt
A Hidden Place and *Memory Wire* by Robert Charles Wilson

SIGNATURE SPECIAL EDITIONS

Mindplayers by Pat Cadigan
Little, Big by John Crowley
Stars in My Pocket Like Grains of Sand by Samuel R. Delany
Desolation Road by Ian McDonald
Emergence by David R. Palmer
Phases of Gravity by Dan Simmons

UNIVERSE

Edited by
Robert Silverberg
and
Karen Haber

 BANTAM BOOKS
NEW YORK · TORONTO · LONDON · SYDNEY · AUCKLAND

1

UNIVERSE 1

A Bantam Spectra Book / published by arrangement with Doubleday

PRINTING HISTORY
Doubleday edition published April 1990

Bantam edition / April 1991

SPECTRA and the portrayal of a boxed "s" are trademarks of Bantam Books, a division of Bantam Doubleday Dell Publishing Group, Inc.

FOR
TERRY CARR,
OF COURSE

CONTENTS

One morning in the summer of 1970, when I was still living in New York City and so was he, my old friend Terry Carr called up to announce that he was going to edit a paperback anthology called *Universe,* consisting of previously unpublished science fiction stories.

"That's nice," I said, or words to that effect, although in truth I wasn't keenly thrilled by the news, because at the time I was editing just such an anthology of my own, called *New Dimensions.* The entrance of a formidable editor like Terry into the field meant that there were going to be that many less outstanding short stories available for me to buy.

"I want you to write a story for me for the first issue," he went on. "I'll pay you three cents a word and spell your name right on the cover and contents page both."

"I'll see what I can do," I said, that day in the summer of 1970, and forgot all about it immediately.

But Terry didn't, which is one reason why he was such a formidable editor. He kept after me and kept after me and finally, the following February, I sat down and wrote a little spoof of a story for him, called "Good News From the Vatican," for which he paid me $90, and when it was published later that year in the first issue of *Universe*, he did indeed see to it that my name was spelled properly.

Very much to my surprise, and Terry's, "Good News From the Vatican" went on to win a Nebula award in 1972. And even more to my surprise and somewhat to my sorrow, here we are seventeen years later and I find that I—in collaboration with my wife, Karen Haber—have replaced Terry as the editor of *Universe*.

What happened, you see, is that whereas *Universe* kept on going strong year after year, outlasting not only *New Dimensions* but all the numerous other original-story s-f anthologies of its era, Terry himself began to suffer from a host of medical problems while he was still quite young. The seventeenth issue of *Universe*, which was published in the summer of 1987, appeared two months after its editor's death at the age of fifty. Shortly afterward, Terry's editor, Pat LoBrutto, asked me—as one of Terry's closest friends, and as someone whose notions of excellence in science fiction were fairly close to Terry's—to continue *Universe* where he had left off. It would be, Pat said, a kind of ongoing memorial to him. I thought about it for a time, and finally said I'd do it—provided Karen, who had had considerable experience in nonfiction editing and now was beginning her own career as a science fiction writer after many years of reading it—could work with me on the project.

And so here it is: the first volume of the revived Silverberg-edited *Universe*.

Our goals in putting it together were complex ones. We wanted, of course, to find stories that would please today's science fiction readers: any editor who sets out to *displease* his readers very shortly finds some other line of work. But there is pleasure and then there is pleasure. A restaurant that serves only cinnamon buns, chocolate eclairs, and cotton candy may indeed please the people who eat there, but to my way of thinking it isn't much of a restaurant.

There are editors who serve up the literary equivalent of bonbons to their readers all the time. Terry wasn't one of them. As the editor of the famous Ace Specials line of novels, he brought such masterpieces as Ursula Le Guin's *Left Hand of Darkness,* Joanna Russ' *And Chaos Died,* Keith Roberts' *Pavane,* William Gibson's *Neuromancer,* and Lucius Shepard's *Green Eyes* into print, none of them designed for lazy readers. The fiction in *Universe* was equally demanding, and provided equally rich rewards—stories like Gene Wolfe's "The Death of Doctor Island," Michael Bishop's "Her Habiline Husband," Bruce Sterling's "Cicada Queen," Kim Stanley Robinson's "The Lucky Strike," Lucius Shepard's "Black Coral," and many more.

Terry Carr's idea of what a good s-f story ought to be was one that was intellectually challenging, strongly plotted, and gracefully written. There was no particular order of preference to those criteria: he wanted all three. By "intellectually challenging," he meant a story that was built around a strong speculative idea, preferably a scientific-technological one (although he was willing now and then to let a little fantasy slip into the book, or a satiric piece like "Good News From the Vatican"). By "strongly plotted," he meant a story that would hold a reader's attention from start to finish, a story in which you care about the characters and what happens to them. By "gracefully written," he meant just what you would expect. I saw him conduct passionate battles with a writer over the placement of a comma, or the careless use of a word.

Terry's criteria for science fiction happen to be mine also, both as a writer and as an editor. Our tastes were formed at the same time, when we were both in our teens, and they moved in parallel directions over the following decades. Sometimes we would disagree on the merits of a particular story, but it was always within a general framework of understanding. And so I felt no hesitation at all about undertaking to continue *Universe* in the mode that Terry had established. I don't doubt that there are two or three stories in this issue that he would not have liked as much as Karen and I do; but I'm quite confident that if he could read the book you now hold, he'd look upon it with pleasure and regard it as an appropriate successor to his own anthologies.

I would have preferred to have more stories in it by writers who had contributed to the seventeen volumes of Terry's *Universe*. But some of those, like James Tiptree Jr. and Edgar Pangborn and Ross Rocklynne, are no longer with us, and others have stopped writing, and some others proved very good at finding excuses. Still, the old *Universe* crew is fairly well represented here: we have Ursula K. Le Guin on hand, Grania Davis, James Patrick Kelly, Kim Stanley Robinson, Barry N. Malzberg, and Bruce Sterling—not a bad turnout. There were a few other old *Universe* contributors we would have liked to have, and they know who they are, and they are on notice now that no excuses will be accepted next time around.

One thing that I know would have pleased Terry is the number of stories by writers who are just beginning their careers. Nearly every issue of *Universe* that he put together had a story or two in it by someone whose name was not exactly a household word—obscure people like Lucius Shepard, Carter Scholz, Nancy Kress, William Gibson, Howard Waldrop, Gene Wolfe, Gardner R. Dozois, Gregory Benford, George Alec Effinger, Pamela Sargent, and John Varley. Their names are somewhat more familiar to us today, as, I hope, will someday be those of Damian Kilby, Leah Alpert, K. Hernández-Brun, Stoney Compton, Jamil Nasir, Francis Valéry, Augustine Funnell, John M. Landsberg, Paul Di Filippo, and Geoffrey Landis, all of them writers who are likely to be completely new to you, or almost so. A satisfying number of those writers are seeing their very first published stories appearing in this issue of *Universe*—which is, though they will probably find it hard to believe, nearly as big a thrill for the editors as it is for them. And there are also a few writers here—Richard R. Smith, M. J. Engh, Scott Baker, and Gregor Hartmann—who have been publishing outstanding science fiction on and off for years, sometimes with long gaps between appearances, and who have not yet managed to establish themselves with the reading public as familiar names. Perhaps their presence in *Universe* indicates that they are moving into new and productive phases. I'm grateful to all of them for making the rebirth of *Universe* possible.

And gratitude is due also to Pat LoBrutto and Lou Aronica of Doubleday and Bantam, whose faith in this project helped to convince its wavering senior editor to take it on; to that extraordinary literary agent Ralph Vicinanza, the inimitable and indispensable, for his help in various significant ways; and above all to my co-editor and collaborator in this and so many other things, Karen Haber, without whom, very literally, the new *Universe* would not exist.

The other person to keep in mind is the gifted and beloved editor, tragically taken from us much too soon, without whom so much that is fine in modern science fiction would never have happened. In all senses of the phrase, this book belongs to Terry Carr.

—Robert Silverberg
Oakland, California
February 1989

$\bigvee\!\!\bigwedge\!\!\bigvee$

The translation machine—that wonderful gadget that conveniently turns the gobbledegook spoken by alien life-forms into nice comprehensible Earthish, and vice versa—has been a staple concept of science fiction for decades. Without it, naturally, first contact with aliens would be ever so much more difficult for our spacefarers to manage, and first-contact stories would be ever so much more difficult for science fiction writers to produce.

Kim Stanley Robinson, the award-winning author of The Gold Coast, "The Blind Geometer," "Black Air," "The Lucky Strike," and a great deal more of the best science fiction and fantasy anyone has written in the last decade, has taken a fresh look at the old translation-machine gimmick here—and has not only managed to provide a searching and thoughtful view of what it would really be like to operate such a device, but has come up with a wickedly funny story in the bargain.

THE TRANSLATOR

KIM STANLEY
ROBINSON

Owen Rumford had a breakfast of postage stamp glue and mineral water. Combination of a rather strict diet and the fact that it was time again to send the bills to all the citizens of Rannoch Station. Rumford himself had had the stamps printed, and now he carefully counted out payment for them and shifted the money from the tavern's register to the postmaster strongbox, kept under the bar. A bit silly using stamps at all, since Rumford was the mailman as well as the postmaster—also the town's banker, tavern and hotel keeper, judge, and mayor. So he would be delivering the bills himself. But he liked stamps. These had a nice picture of Rannoch seen from space, all gray ocean with a chunk of onyx in it. Besides, in a town as small and isolated as Rannoch Station it was important to keep up the proprieties. Good for morale. Must, however, consider upgrading the quality of the stamp glue.

A quiet morning in the empty tavern. Hotel above empty as well; nothing had come in to the spaceport in the last few days. Unusual. Rumford decided to take advantage of the rare lull and go for a walk. On with his heavy orange overcoat. Tentlike. Rumford was a big man, tall and stout. Big fleshy face, cropped black hair, big walrus moustache that he tugged at frequently, as he did now while bidding a brief farewell to his daughters. Out into the stiff cold onshore wind. Felt good.

Down the black cobblestones of Rannoch Station's steep main street. Hellos to Simon the butcher, chopping away at a flank of mutton; then to the McEvoys, who helped administer the mines. Pleasant sound of construction behind the general store, tinsmiths and stonemasons banging and clacking away. Then left at the bottom of the street where it crossed the stream, up the track of hard black mud until he was out of the town and on the low hills overlooking the sea.

All views on the planet Rannoch were a bit dark. Its sun, G104938, known locally as the Candle, cast a pale and watery light. And the hills of Rannoch Island—the planet's only continent, located in subarctic latitudes—were composed mostly of black rock, mottled with black lichen and a bit of black bracken, all overlooking a dark sea. The dirt between stones had a high component of carbon ash, and even the perpetual frost on the bracken had gray algae growing in it. In short, only the white wrack thrown onto the black sand by the black waves gave any relief to the general gloom. It was a landscape you had to learn to be fond of.

Rumford had. Sniffing at the cold wind, he observed with satisfaction the waves mushing onto the beach below the town. All the dories out fishing except the spavined ones, drawn up above the high tide mark. Town sitting above them nice and cozy, tucked into the crease made by the stream's last approach to the sea, to get out of the perpetual wind. Houses and public buildings all made of round black stones, some cracked open to reveal white quartz marbling. Materials at hand. Roofs were tin, glinted nicely in the low rays of the late morning sun. Tin mined here for local use, not for export. They had found deposits of the ore next to the big manganese mines. Easy to work it. Slag heaps inland of the town just looked like more hills, fit in very nicely in fact. Helped block the wind. Bracken already growing on them.

Altogether satisfactory. "A wild and unearthly place," as

the song said. Rumford remembered trees from his childhood on a faraway planet, name forgotten. Only thing he missed. Trees, wonderful things. Would be nice for the girls. He'd told them tales till they'd cried for trees, for picnics in a grove, even though they hadn't the slightest. Flowering ones, perhaps. Grow in the ravines the streams cut, perhaps. Out of the wind. Worth thinking about. Damned difficult to get hold of, though; none native to this star cluster, and they were something traders out here didn't usually deal in. A shame.

Rumford was still thinking of trees when the steep black waves sweeping onto the town beach burst apart, revealing a submarine craft apparently made to roll over the sea floor. Big, dull green metal, lot of wheels, a few small windows. Some of the Ba'arni again, making a visit. Rumford frowned. Bizarre creatures, the Ba'arni. Inscrutable. It was obvious to Rumford that they were as alien to Rannoch as humans were, though he'd never gotten a Ba'ar to admit it. Good traders, though. Fishing rights for plastics, metal nodules gathered off sea floor for refined product, deep sea oddities for machine parts and miscellaneous utensils. Still, what they got from Rannoch Station wasn't enough to sustain an undersea colony. And how start it?

Aliens were strange.

The sea tank rolled above the high water mark and stopped. Door on one side clanked open, becoming a ramp. Three Ba'arni trotted out, one spotted him and they veered, trundled toward him. He walked down to meet them.

Strange looking, of course. The fishermen called them sea hippos, talked about them as if they were intelligent ocean-going hippopotami, nothing more. Ludicrous. The usual fallacy when dealing with aliens: think of them as the terran species they most resemble. Let it go at that. Rumford snorted at the idea. Really only the heads looked like hippos. Bodies too of course, to a limited extent. Massive, foursquare, rounded, etc. But the analogy held up poorly when you examined the fine bluish fur, the squat dextrous fingers on all four feet, and of course the row of walnut-sized excrescences

3

that protruded from their spines. Purpose unknown. Like mushrooms growing out of their backs. Not a pleasant sight.

Then again the pictures of hippos Rumford had seen were none too beautiful. Still, in hippos' eyes, even in pictures, you could see something you could understand. Expression, maybe hostile, but perfectly comprehensible. Not so with a Ba'ar. Faces quite hippo-like, sure. Giant faces, butt-ugly as the fisherman said. The eyes did it—round and big as plates, and almost as flat. And with a look in them you just couldn't read. Curious, that. The fishermen claimed to see them swimming free in the depths, above seafloor mansions of great size. That was after they'd had a few, but still. Obviously alien to Rannoch, nothing more advanced than bracken here. At least on the land. Different in the planet-wide ocean, perhaps; evolutionary advances all submarine, perhaps down in tropics? Impossible to say. But probably visitors, like the humans. Urge to travel fairly widespread among intelligent species. Spaceships filled with seawater. Funny thought.

The three Ba'arni stopped before Rumford. The one on the left opened his voluminous mouth and made a short sequence of whistles and clicks. From experience Rumford knew this was the usual greeting given him, meaning something like "Hello, trading coordinator." Unfortunately, he usually relied on his translation box to make the actual sound of his response, and though he knew what it sounded like he didn't find it easy making the sounds himself. And the box was back at the tavern.

He gave it a try and made the first few clicks that the box emitted when he typed in his usual hello. Then he added another click-combination, meaning, he thought, "Trade, interrogative?"

The Ba'ar on the left replied swiftly. Trade negative, he appeared to say. Something else, well, Rumford had relied too often on the box to do the exact listening, but it seemed to him they were referring to the box itself.

Rumford shrugged. Only one course. He tried the whistle

for translation, added the English words "Rannoch Station," and pointed to the town.

Agreement clicks from the spokesBa'ar.

Sonic booms rolled over the hills. They all looked up; Rannoch's gray sky was split by white contrails. Landing craft, coming down in a very steep descent from orbit, toward the town's spaceport a couple miles inland. Rumford identified the craft by their extreme trajectory. Iggglas.

Then an extraordinary thing happened; all three of the Ba'arni rose up on their hind legs and took swipes at the sky, roaring louder than the sonic booms.

A bad sign. One time it had taken a shotgun blast to get a pack of Iggglas off a lone Ba'ar outside the tavern. Never understood the motive; only time he had ever seen the two species together. Not a good omen. And if the Ba'arni needed translation help—

The three of them returned to all fours with a distinct thump, then more or less herded Rumford down the track to the town. Not much chance of disagreement with them; they were remarkably fast on their feet, and must have weighed a couple of tons each. Drafted.

Rumford entered his tavern and got the translation box from the shelf behind the bar. It was an old bulky thing, in many ways obsolete; you had to type in the English half of things, and it would only translate between English and the alien languages in its program—no chance of any alien-to-alien direct contact. Made for some trouble in the tavern.

Without explanation to his daughters he was out the door. Again the Ba'arni herded him up the street. Quickly they were out of town in the other direction, onto the stony, windswept road leading to the spaceport and the mines beyond.

They were still hurrying up this road, the Ba'arni moving at a brisk trot and Rumford loping, when they came round a hill and ran into a party of Iggglas. A dozen or so of them, flapping about the road and squawking loudly. The Ba'arni froze in their tracks and Rumford stumbled to a halt out in front of them.

He shuddered as he always did on first sight of an Iggglα. They were beyond ugly; they were . . . well, beyond words. Languages, human languages at any rate, depend a great deal on analogies. Most abstract ideas are expressed by sometimes hidden analogies to physical things and processes, and most new things are described by analogies to older things. Naturally all these analogies are to things within human ken. But analogies to the human realm largely broke down when dealing with the Iggglas, for there was simply nothing to compare them to.

Still, Rumford thought. Analogies all we have, after all. Especially for things alien. So the Iggglas were inevitably compared to vultures, because of body configuration. Fine except that their skins were covered by a white mucus substance instead of feathers. And their wings were not so much for flying as for hitting things. And their heads were distinctly fishlike, with long underslung jaws that made them resemble gars. Vultures with gars' heads, covered in whitish mucus: fair enough, only the analogy didn't really do justice to their sickening quality. Because above all they were *alien*, weird and hideous beyond appearance alone. Not even sure they occupied the same reality as other creatures; they seemed to *flicker* a little, as if disturbing the membrane between their physical realm and ordinary spacetime. Yes; disgusting. Next to them the Ba'arni seemed handsome beasts. Almost family, one might say.

Rumford stepped forward to offer some kind of greeting to the Iggglas, make sure the Ba'arni didn't have to. Touchy situation. He had dealt with Iggglas before; they came from the next planet in, and used Rannoch Station as a trade center. Trade again. Remarkable what kind of thing it put you in contact with, out in this stellar group. Certainly had to get used to these creatures. Language of theirs very loud and squawky. Every once in a while they'd spit in each other's mouths for emphasis. Some kind of chemical transfer of information. Box wasn't equipped to deal with that, luckily. Their speech was enough, although it appeared to be an odd grammar. Lacked tenses, or even verbs for that matter. Another indication of different reality.

The Iggglas liked to stick out a claw and shake humans by the hand, maybe to see if they would vomit. But Rumford could do it with hardly a quiver. No worse than a cockroach in the hand, certainly. So he shook hands with the wet claw of the biggest Igggla. Hot bodies, high metabolism. It turned its head to the side to inspect him with its left eye. Foul smell, like asfoetida.

Two of the other Iggglas led a long string of little furball creatures, a bit like rabbits without legs, up to the one Rumford had shaken hands with. Rumford sighed. Probably the high metabolisms, but still. Note the others weren't doing it—

Abruptly the biggest one snapped that gar's head down and devoured the first rabbit-thing in line, swallowing it whole so that it disappeared instantly, as in a conjuring trick. The Igggla would interrupt itself to do the same throughout the rest of the interview. It made Rumford nervous.

The Igggla squawked loudly and at length. "Croownekk-kseetrun-p!" it sounded like. Rumford turned on the translator, switched it to *IgggIas*, and typed in the message, *"Again, please."*

After a short interval the box made a short screech. With a loud honk and a quick drumming of its talon-like feet, the big Igggla squawked its initial message again.

A moment later a message appeared in print on the small screen of the translator box. *"Hunger interrogative."*

The Igggla batted one of the worried-looking rabbit-things forward.

"No thank you," Rumford typed steadily, and waited for the box to speak. Then: *"Why do you come to Rannoch interrogative."*

The head Igggla listened to the box's hooting, did a quick hopping dance, struck one of the other Iggglas in the head, and replied.

The box's screen eventually produced a sentence. *"Warlike viciously now descendant death fat food flame death."*

A typical grammatical artifact produced by the box when dealing with the Iggglas. Rumford pondered it, switched the box to *Ba'arni*, and typed in *"The Iggglas express a certain hostility toward the Ba'arni."*

The box whistled and clicked in the oddly high-pitched Ba'arni language. The Ba'ar on the left, which was not the same one that had spoken to Rumford at first, whistled and clicked in reply. The box's screen printed out, *"Tell them we are ready to (x-click b-flat to c-sharp click sequence; see dictionary) and the hateful poison birds will die in traditional manner."*

Hmm. Problems everywhere. With the Iggglas you got grammatic hash. With Ba'arni, too many trips to the dictionary. Which was a problem in itself. The box was not entirely satisfactory, and that was the truth.

Needed to be seated to type on the keyboard properly, too. So, despite the fact that it might seem undignified, Rumford sat on the ground between the two parties of aliens, called up the Ba'arni dictionary function of the box, and typed in an inquiry. The definition appeared quickly:

"X-click B-flat to C-sharp click sequence: 1. Fish market. 2. Fish harvest. 3. Sunspots visible from a depth of 10 meters below the surface of the ocean on a calm day. 4. Traditional festival. 5. Astrological configuration in galactic core."

Rumford sighed. The Ba'arni dictionary could be nearly useless. Never sure if it was really serious. No idea who actually wrote the thing. Basic programming provided by linguists working for the company that made the box, of course, but in the years since then (and it was a very old box), its various owners had entered new information of their own. In fact this one was jammed with languages that factory-new boxes didn't have. No other box Rumford had seen had a Ba'arni program; that was why Rumford had bought this one when it was offered by a passing spacecraft pilot. But who in fact had added the Ba'arni program? Rather puckish individual, from the look of it. Or perhaps the Ba'arni relied more than most on context. Some languages like that. Impossible to be sure. The box had worked to this point, and that was all Rumford could say about it. Trade a different matter, however. Not quite as delicate as this.

After thinking it over, Rumford typed in another question to the Ba'arni. *"Clarification please. What do you mean by x-click b-flat to c-sharp click sequence, in context of previous sentence interrogative."*

The Ba'arni listened and the one on the left replied.

"Ba'arni and poison birds fight war in (z-click double sequence; see dictionary) cycle that now returns. Time for this ritual war."

Very good. Clear as a bell. Unfortunate message, of course, but at least he understood it. Must have meant definition four, perhaps tied to the timing of three, or five. Add new definition later.

Before he could convey the Ba'arni sentiments to the Iggglas, the chief Igggla ate another rabbit-thing, danced in a circle, and screeched for quite some time. The box hummed a bit, and the screen flickered.

"Fine fiery wonderful this land always again war's heat slag battlefield dead fat food flame death yes now."

Rumford squinted at the screen.

Finally he typed in, *"Clarification please: where is location of ritual war interrogative,"* and sent it to the Iggglas.

The chief Igggla replied at length, howling shrilly.

On the screen: *"Fine fiery wonderful this land always again war's heat slag battlefield dead fat food flame death yes now yes."*

The Iggglas were not much on clarification.

Rumford decided to ask the same of the Ba'arni, and switched the box over. *"Clarification please: where is location of ritual war interrogative."*

The box whistled, the Ba'ar on the left clicked. The screen flickered and printed out: *"Clarification unnecessary as poison birds know every twelve squared years for twelve cubed years ritual dodecimation has taken place on same ritual ground. Tell them to stop wasting time. We are ready for conflict."*

A small vertical line appeared between Rumford's eyebrows.

He switched back and forth from Iggglas to Ba'arni, asking questions concerning this ritual war, explaining that the questions were essential for proper translation. Every Iggglas answer a long string of violent nouns, adjectives, and so forth, with never a verb. Every Ba'arni answer a hunt through the dictionary. Slowly Rumford put together a picture of Ba'arni and Iggglas contingents battling each other. Ritual phrases from the Ba'arni concerned *Air people opposition water people destruction land,* and so on. The Iggglas concentrated on *fat food,* although obviously it was a ritual for them as well—a sort of game, from the sounds of it. The origins of such a curious conflict remained completely obscure to Rumford; some things the Ba'arni said seemed to indicate that they may have had a religious ceremony of coming out onto land in great numbers during maximum sunspot activity, and that for many cycles now the Iggglas had been there to transform this ceremony into a bloody battle. Possibly indicating that the Ba'arni were in fact not native to Rannoch, as Rumford had speculated earlier. But he couldn't be sure. No way of knowing, really. Accident, misunderstanding; no doubt they themselves didn't have the faintest any more.

In any case, ritual war well established, this was clear. And either during or after the battle—sequentiality was difficult to determine, given the lack of tenses in the Iggglas—the two belligerent forces apparently torched, in a kind of sacrifice, the profane land they fought on.

Hmm. Rumford sat cross-legged on the ground between the two groups, thinking. Rannoch Station had only been there for the past thirty years or so. All that carbon in their dirt, sign of great fires in the past. But mining geologists said no vulcanism. Tremendous heat, one said. Solar flares? Or weapons. Tremendous heat. Tin would melt. It was possible. And after all, here they were.

Rumford cleared his throat. Sticky. He hesitated for a bit, and would have hesitated more, but some thirty sets of alien eyes (counting the rabbit-things) stared fixedly at him, and impelled him to action. He tugged his moustache. Sunspots underwater, astrology . . . really a shame he didn't know more about these creatures. Now where was he? Ah yes— Ba'arni had indicated readiness for conflict. We are ready for conflict. The line between his eyebrows deepened, and finally he shrugged. He clicked the box over to *Iggglas* and typed away.

"Ba'arni explain that their priest-caste have performed submarine astrology which contraindicates ritual war this time. Request war be postponed until next scheduled time twelve squared Rannoch years from now in order to achieve proper equilibrium with the stars."

The box honked that out in a series of Iggglasian words. All the Iggglas listeners snapped their big gar jaws as they heard it, then leaped in circles thrashing the dust. Several of the rabbit-things disappeared. The chief Igggla hopped toward Rumford and shrieked for a long while.

On the screen: *"War heat slag death fat food exclamation. Delay impossible war as scheduled astrology stupid exclamation."*

Rumford tugged his moustache. Not gone over so well. The three Ba'arni were staring at him curiously, waiting for him to translate what the Iggglas had just so vehemently squawked. The line between his eyebrows deepened even more. Ba'arni had visited him more frequently in last year. Now what had they been trading for?

He switched the box to Ba'arni, typed *"Iggglas state that they do not want ritual war to take place this time. They note the Ba'arni are suffering famine and therefore population difficulties. Thus ritual dodecimation could lead to extinction of Ba'arni and end of beloved war for Iggglas. They suggest skipping this time and returning to war next twelve squared years."*

A lot of clicks and whistles to convey that. The Ba'arni retreated and conferred among themselves, while the Iggglas

11

squawked derisively at them. Rumford watched anxiously. Ba'arni had been trading rather actively for foodstuffs. Brow needed wiping. He tugged on his moustache. The Ba'arni returned in a new line-up and the one on the left clicked.

On screen: *"Ba'arni completely capable of sustaining their part in (x-click b-flat to c-sharp click sequence; see dictionary). Ba'arni (z-click z-click; see dictionary) insist ritual be carried out as always. Poison birds will die."*

Rumford let out a deep breath, switched the box to dictionary function and inquired about z-click z-click.

"Z-click z-click: 1. (double n-1 click sequence, B-flat; see dictionary). 2. Magnetic sense located in supra-spinal nerve nodules. 3. Eggs. 4. Large bearings. 5. Sense of place or of location. 6. Money."

Nothing there seemed completely appropriate, so he tried looking up double n-1 click sequence, B-flat.

"Double n-1 click sequence, B-flat: 1. (Q-click A-flat; see dictionary.) 2. Honor. 3. Pride. 4. Shame. 5. Face. 6. Molar teeth."

Bit of an infinite regress there, could have you jumping around the dictionary forever. Definitely a prankster, whoever had entered this language in the box. But assume the Ba'arni meant some kind of pride, saving face, that kind of thing. Made sense. Every species must have a version of the concept. Fine. Assume clarification on that front. Now, where was he with the Iggglas? Looking fairly ready for an answer, they were. Rumford pursed his lips so hard that his moustache tips almost met under his chin. Astrologer bit not gone over very far. Iggglas pretty aggressive types. He clicked over to Iggglas and typed away.

"Ba'arni live by submarine astrologer's divine words and intend to decline ritual war. Iggglas insistence will make no difference. Ba'arni have assured this by placement of heat bombs on floor of all seas on Iggglas. Twelve squared heat of weapons used in ritual war. If Iggglas insist on ritual war Ba'arni have no choice but to escalate to total war and annihilate Iggglas seas. Apologies but astrologers insist."

While the box spoke this message in Iggglas (and how was it doing it without verbs?), Rumford pulled a handkerchief from his coat pocket and wiped his brow. Uncommonly warm. Hunger made him feel a bit weak. Have to start eating breakfasts.

The Iggglas began to squawk among themselves very vigorously, and Rumford took a quick glance down at the screen to see if the box was translating their squabble. It was, although apparently it was having problems with the fact that two or three of the Iggglas were always speaking at the same time: *"Lying fat food no meteor shower maybe total war then purpose ambiguous no exclamation one miss translator liar idiot meteor shower no explanation maybe box direct Iggglas fat food why not meteor shower maybe,"* and so on. Rumford tried to direct one eye to the screen and the other to the hopping Iggglas. Looked like the second-largest one might be making the comments about the translator and the box. Yes, even pointing at him as he spat in leader's mouth. Problem.

The Ba'arni were whistling among themselves, so Rumford quickly typed in another message to the Iggglas:

"Ba'arni wish to deal with senior Igggla, suggest that perhaps second-biggest Igggla is one qualified to speak for Iggglas in this matter."

The box squawked this out and Rumford helpfully pointed to the Igggla he had in mind. The chief Igggla took in the import of the message and shrieked, leaped in the air, jumped at his lieutenant, and beat him with a flurry of quick wing-blows. Knocked the squealing creature flat and faster than Rumford could see had the lieutenant's skinny vulture-neck between his long toothy jaws. The lieutenant squeaked something dismal and was allowed to live; it crawled to the back of the group of Iggglas. The leader then strode forward and spoke to Rumford and the Ba'arni.

On the screen: *"Astrology stupid war heat fat food death always compact between Iggglas and fat food change never good annihilation of home planet outside compact realm of total war insistence on ritual war heat fat food death."*

Rumford's brow wrinkled as he read this. Getting nowhere with the garheads. After a moment's thought he switched the box to Ba'arni, and typed in, very carefully, the following:

"Iggglas understand Ba'arni capable of sustaining ritual war and intend no slur on Ba'arni (double n-1 sequence, B-flat)." Possibly it was a mistake to try directly for Ba'arni terms to add power to the message. Box could mess it up entirely, in context of sentence. He typed on: *"Iggglas too have sense of honor and save face by suggestion that Ba'arni weakness is only source of problem in ritual war, but Iggglas also have famine trouble, and demand ritual war be postponed twelve squared years to keep both Iggglas and Ba'arni in sufficient numbers to sustain ritual war in perpetuity. Suggest mutual expression of honor (exclamation) by recognition of ritual promise for next time."*

Clicks and whistles, the Ba'arni listening with their big hippo ears tilted down toward the box. Rumford felt the sweat trickling down the inside of his shirt. Extraordinarily hot for Rannoch. The Ba'arni were discussing the matter among themselves, and again Rumford put one eye to the box to see what it could tell him.

"We must not give (z-click z-click; see dictionary) exclamation. Necessary to (Middle C to high C)."

Surreptitiously he switched over to the dictionary function and looked up middle C to high C.

"Middle C to high C: 1. Stand still. 2. Run. 3. Show interest. 4. Lose. 5. Alternate. 6. Repair. 7. Replace. 8. Subtend. 9. (high C to middle C; see dictionary). 10. Glance through turbid water."

Useful word. Rumford gave up on it.

Finally the Ba'ar on the left, the third one to speak from that position, raised its head and spoke. *"Ba'arni (z-click z-click; see dictionary) satisfied by expression of (n-1 click sequence, b-flat; see dictionary) by poison birds toward Ba'arni and sacred dodecimation ground, if agreed that ritual war should be resumed in twelve squared years at prescribed time."*

Rumford could not prevent his eyebrows from lifting a bit. One down, apparently. Now where was he with the others?

Ah yes. Tricky still, the stubborn buzzards. Entirely possible they might take up his threat of total war and act on it, which would leave the Ba'arni considerably confused. And Rannoch torched. Hmm. A problem.

He thought hard and fast. Each side a different understanding of war. Ba'arni thought of it as religious event and perhaps population control, but couldn't sustain it when population already low from famine. Thus agreeable to postponement, if face saved, and quick to arrange talk when Iggglas seen approaching. Fine, clear. And Iggglas? Food source, population control, game, who could tell? Certainly didn't care what Ba'arni astrologers thought of things. Not big on religion, the Iggglas.

Need to give reasons convincing to receiver of message, not sender. Rumford blinked at this sudden realization. Senders not hearing message, after all—not even sending it in fact. Receiver all that mattered.

He switched the box to Iggglas. *"Ba'arni suffer from famine and fear war would reduce them to extinction, in which case no more ritual wars, no more fat food. Want postponement only."* The Iggglas shrieked at this in derision, but the box's screen included among the printed hash the word *understanding*. Perhaps they now had a reason they could comprehend. Best to press the point. He typed another message to the Iggglas:

"Dodecimation and fat food rely on population existence, as you say. If there is no population there is no dodecimation or fat food and ritual war is ended forever. Ba'arni therefore insist on postponement of ritual war and if Iggglas attempt to wage it regardless of traditional cooperation of the Ba'arni then Ba'arni have no choice but total war and mass suicide for all parties. Suggest therefore postponement. Astrologer's decision necessary given population of Ba'arni."

The box hooted and squawked, the Iggglas leader cocked his head to one side and listened, watching Rumford carefully. When the message was completed, the leader did a little dance of its own, all on one spot. Then suddenly it approached the Ba'arni directly. Rumford held his breath. The

15

Iggglas leader shrieked at the Ba'arni, sweeping one wing at them in a ferocious gesture.

All three Ba'arni opened their immense mouths, which appeared to split their immense heads in half, and whistled loud and high. Rumford had to hold his hands over his ears, and the Iggglas leader stepped back. Impressive sight, those three open mouths. The Iggglas opened his long mouth as if to mock them; lot of teeth in there. Impressive as well. Battle of mouths. All right if it didn't lead to anything. Tense. Need to get a response in squawks from old gar face. Can't seem to intrude too much, however.

A long minute's wait as the two parties stared each other down.

The Iggglas leader suddenly turned and squawked.

On screen: *"Heat death fat food postponement replacement cannibalism for Iggglas assurance renewal of slag heat war fat food in twelve squared years."*

Rumford let out a long breath.

He switched to Ba'arni, typed.

"Iggglas agree to acknowledge Ba'arni honor, promise renewal of honorable battle next time in twelve squared years."

Whistle, click, whistle. The Ba'ar on the left spoke quickly.

"The Ba'arni accept postponement and acknowledgment of their honor."

When Rumford conveyed the news to the Iggglas leader, it too was agreeable. Appeared to like the promise that the conflict would be renewed. But then it squawked on at length:

"Iggglas negative continuance until next ritual war with heat death bombs in Iggglas seas, insistence removal immediate."

Hmm. Bit of a problem, to tell the Ba'arni to remove bombs they didn't know existed. Meanwhile they were looking at Rumford to see what had been said, and to gain time Rumford switched to Ba'arni and typed, *"Iggglas agree to honor Ba'arni and agree to return to ritual war next time."*

A repeat of the previous message to them, but Rumford was too busy to think of anything else, and happily the Ba'arni didn't seem to notice. They agreed again, and Rumford returned to Iggglas.

"Ba'arni state weapons on Iggglas seafloor will be de-activated. All they can do as weapons cannot be relocated."

The Igggla leader shrieked, pummeled the dust. *"War war war total annihilation war fat food heat death unless sea bombs removal exclamation."*

Hmm. Wouldn't do to stop a small ritual war by starting a total war even more likely to destroy Rannoch Island. Rumford quickly got the Ba'arni's assurances that they would return in twelve squared years, then returned to Iggglas:

"Ba'arni state detonator will be given to Iggglas. Detonation wavelength determined by detonator and Iggglas can change this and render bombs inoperative. Demonstration of this on small scale can be arranged in Rannoch ocean. Translator agrees to convey detonator and run demonstration as ritual forbids Ba'arni speaking to Iggglas in between ritual wars."

Could get a good long-distance detonator from the manganese mines, set up an offshore explosion. Hopefully convince them.

After a long and apparently thoughtful dance, the Iggglas leader ate two of the rabbit-things, and indicated his acceptance of this plan. The Iggglas abruptly turned and hopped back down the road to the spaceport. The meeting was over.

Owen Rumford stood up unsteadily, and, feeling drained, he accompanied the three Ba'arni back to the beach. As they got into their seacraft, the one on the left said something; but Rumford had his box in his coat pocket. After the Ba'arni craft rolled under the black waves, he took the box out, turned it on, and tried to imitate the last set of whistles. The box printed it as, *"(Y-click x-click; see dictionary.)"* He switched to the dictionary function and looked it up.

"Y-click x-click: 1. Ebb tide. 2. Twisted, knotted, complex. 3. The ten forefingers. 4. Elegance. 5. The part of the moon visible in a partial eclipse. 6. Tree."

"Hmm," Rumford said.

He walked slowly up toward the town. Y-click x-click.

Those big plate eyes, staring at him. Their half of the conversation had gone pretty smoothly. Very smoothly. And all his assumptions, about the famine, the rituals. Could they be . . . just a little. . . . But no. Language barrier as troublesome in telepathy as in speech, after all. Maybe.

Y-click x-click. If he had gotten the whistle right. But he thought he had. Why have word for something they'd never seen? But Ba'arni had traded with earlier passersby, witness box. Curious.

Tin roofs glinting in the light. Black stone walls, veined with white quartz. Black cobblestones. Very neat. Fine little town. In a hundred and forty-four years, they would have to figure something out. Well, that was their problem. More warning next time. Nothing to be done about it now.

He walked into the tavern and sat down heavily. His daughters had just finished preparing the tables for lunch. "Papa, you look exhausted," Isabel said. "Have you been trying to exercise again?"

"No, no." He looked around with a satisfied expression, heaved out a long breath. "Just a spot of translation." He got up and went behind the bar, started drawing a beer from the tap. Suddenly the corners of his moustache lifted a little. "Might get a bit of payment for it," he told her. "If so—still care for a picnic?"

Geoffrey Landis, who in what he amiably calls "real life" is a physicist doing solar cell research, is one of science fiction's brightest new stars. His first story, "Elemental," appeared in Analog a few years back and earned him a place on the 1985 Hugo ballot and among the finalists for that year's John W. Campbell award. Since then his complex, ingenious stories have appeared in most of the science fiction magazines to general acclaim—most notably the dazzling time-travel tale, "Ripples in the Dirac Sea," which gained considerable attention when it appeared in Isaac Asimov's Science Fiction Magazine in 1988.

He makes his Universe debut with this vivid, tightly plotted account of a high-tech future civilization—an up-to-date variant on the classic theme of Man vs. Machine.

THE CITY OF ULTIMATE FREEDOM

GEOFFREY
A.
LANDIS

The rumor flies, races, *explodes* through the city Vadya: "Miekl has challenged the machine!" It is almost a joke, as if one had said, "Miekl has gone crazy." But no one goes mad in the city (although the standards of "sane" behavior are much wider than what you, perhaps, would consider normal).

And no one ever challenges the machine, the benevolent machine, the wonderful city machine that makes the city of ultimate freedom possible.

Paena, the peace officer, tells it to Edonna, sculptor and composer, who pauses from work to listen: "Miekl has challenged the machine!" Both giggle.

How long has it been, since anyone has challenged the machine? A hundred years? Two hundred? —No, wasn't there that fellow, what was the fellow's name? Forty years back? — Didn't last a day at it, either. —Yes, but that fellow was mad. —Of course, but so is Miekl. They giggle again.

There are other cities on earth, many, but of them all, Vadya is the most beautiful, the most perfect. The citizens are artists and politicians and musicians and flitter-truck drivers, and they run their city with pride, though they know that if they did nothing, the city would run itself. They are happy, but not vacuous;

they are industrious, but not slavish. No citizen ever needs to order another about. If a composer needs musicians to premier a new composition, citizens will surely volunteer; but if none do, why, then the city machine will create them. Robot musicians, to be sure, but ones which look and act and play as well as the best musicians. Whatever one desires to do, one can probably find others in the city to serve as audience or co-workers or critics; but if not, why then the city machine will provide.

Edonna tells it to Jason, the shaper; Jason tells it to Kadja, the star listener: "Miekl has challenged the machine!"

"Indeed," says Kadja with a smile. Kadja has russet fur and a cat's face. Fur was quite the fad in the city, some years back; many still wear it, although the fashion has changed. Kadja thinks it makes lovemaking more sensuous. Once, years ago, Kadja had been Miekl's lover; the memory is part of what makes Kadja smile. Jason has a short prehensile tail, which now switches back and forth slowly, a tuft of brightly colored fur waving at the tip.

How long has it been since anybody has really, seriously challenged the machine? Does anybody remember? Wasn't it a fashion, a fad, four or five hundred years ago? Who remembers that far back?

Even the perfect city grows cloying to some after long enough, and for these citizens, too, the city provides. There is a place—not a fixed physical place, but a place in the city nonetheless—which the citizens call simply "the Primitive." Sometimes it is an Amazon rain forest, sometimes a primordial Midwestern plain, but always it is a place where there is no computer to order around, to satisfy every desire. Anyone can spend time there, but remarkably few ever do, and for decades at a stretch the Primitive lies dismantled, ready to be put together again for a single individual's whim. It is enough for most that such a thing exists. They are too used to the comforts of the city.

It is also a place of exile, if such is ever needed, but it is used for that even more rarely.

Kadja the listener tells it to Kiel, the performer: "Miekl has challenged the machine!" Kiel looks up, smiles, and makes a gesture like holding a stone axe while grunting like a caveman: "Uh! Ugh! Ugh! Ooh-ga!" Both of them giggle.

It is inherent in the very structure of the city that people be free to challenge the machine, but how long has it been since anyone actually *won* a challenge? A thousand years? Ten thousand? Sure, there are the stories—legends, almost—of the great challenges, but that was long ago, when the city was young. The legendary shaper Mandra. The composer Tlastla, who dueled in a single straight session from dawn to dawn, out of whose duel came the "Song of the City" and the "Song of the Human." Legendary Daelus, who invented the Maze. Heroic Tielus, who conquered it.

The challenge is ancient: "Anything you can do, I can do better."

Any citizen of Vadya can order the city around. But who programmed it in the first place? It has learned to program itself; "learned how to learn," if you will. It had to; the city machine is far too complex to be encompassed by a human mind, even a genius. Although any citizen gives it orders, it is unthinkable that a citizen could be allowed to reprogram it. What if a citizen ordered it to shut itself down? What if a citizen ordered it to allow the killing of another citizen? (Although the city will willingly produce sham citizens—robots, to be crude—to be "killed" as often and as violently and as imaginatively as anyone could desire.)

But it is equally unthinkable that *no* one should be permitted to reprogram the city. What if something new comes up? What if there is a problem in the programming?

And so the challenge. To reprogram the city, one must earn the right. One must first prove that there is one thing—anything at all—that one can do better than the city machine.

It is not easy.

There is a penalty for those who challenge and fail. For every day of challenge, a month in the Primitive. This is not so much a punishment as a reminder, a tangible demonstra-

23

tion of what the city does for its citizens. And a way to help insure that challenges are not undertaken frivolously.

Miekl stands, tall and proud in the morning sunlight, looking across the city, contemplating the challenge. Spread out before the challenger, the city is a polychrome panorama, glittering spheres of light and patches of multicolored mist floating slowly past spires which disappear into the sky above. Miekl has chosen to open challenge with the maze, not expecting to beat it on the first try, but intending to get a feel of the machine.

The maze is a huge cube, two kilometers on an edge, gridded with hollow transparent rods like some crazy jungle gym. Inside the maze race three balls. Two—the white ones—are controlled by the city machine. The third, red, is controlled by the challenger. They move with enormous velocity. In five seconds a ball can cross from one side of the maze to the other.

Miekl hovers over the ball, contemplating for a moment, and then takes off. The ball darts through the maze, and Miekl flies after it, suspended by magnetic levitation loops, directing the ball's motion. The challenger's red ball is marginally faster than the city machine's two white ones, and if Miekl can use this advantage to get the ball to a position at least one kilometer from either of the computer-controlled balls, the game is won.

The computer attempts to anticipate the challenger's moves, predict each twist and turn to run its balls along a shorter route, and appear ahead of the challenger. The challenger has an added distraction. Flying along next to the ball, Miekl must dodge the gridwork of rods. The game is not entirely without physical danger. By concentrating too much attention on the ball, Miekl could forget to watch the flight path and run into a grid. At a speed of half a kilometer a second, this would be no minor collision—although the city machine could, and would, resurrect the body, given no prior orders to the contrary.

The center of the cube is laced with obstructions, dead-end paths, confusing interconnections of passages. The outer faces are almost obstruction free. Miekl holds to the outside, racing across the cube at blinding speed, making instantaneous turns seemingly without a flicker of hesitation. The city machine's balls pace along, taking different routes but never more than a few meters distant.

Miekl plays with sure easy moves, with a lazy display of self-confidence, occasionally diving into the maze at the center, flashing through the labyrinthine gridwork, trying to snare the computer into a false trail, before racing back to the surface. Nothing works.

The few watchers eventually drop away. Although the game is an intense struggle of strategy and reflexes, the end is a forgone conclusion. Miekl remains unable to shake the pursuers. In the end Miekl drops out, enervated, exhausted, drained.

No one pays attention.

On the 3D newspaper posters of the city Miekl rates only a corner, showing a loop of action involving a particularly involuted double switchback, where Miekl manages to sidetrack one of the computer's spheres. The other, though, loops around ahead to arrive at the next grid intersection a split second ahead, then pauses, waiting, as if mocking the effort.

There are four billion nodes in the two-kilometer cube. How can one human, no matter how good, compete with the nearly omnipotent city computer? How can Miekl find the one possible combination of randomness and purpose that might frustrate the computer's efforts to anticipate every movement?

In a small performance niche in sector three, Edonna—sculptor, composer, and conductor—pauses from work as Paena tells the news. Ah, so Miekl has indeed failed. It was not unexpected, but Edonna is nevertheless unaccountably saddened. But the sculpture-composition is to premier shortly, so Edonna quickly bends back to work. There is much to do, and little time.

The figure being sculpted stares back with blind eyes, rough-hewn face uplifted to the heavens, stubby wings on its back unable to fly.

In the Primitive, there is no city. The citizen on vacation must plan most carefully, for there is no way to call out to the city machine to return. So, too, the failed challenger. Wander though one might, through jungles, across the dusty plains, over high mountains and down mighty rivers, one can find no edge to the Primitive. Does the city slowly, subtly bend one's path so that one actually wanders in circles, save only that the city machine tears down the jungle ahead, replacing it with savannah? Is it actually a treadmill, so that no matter how one travels, one never leaves the starting spot? Or has the city machine found a way to make it truly infinite in extent? Does it matter?

And yet Miekl persists.

The next day Miekl challenges in symphony. A random jury has been selected. These are people who know Miekl, for the city machine has selected people from sector three, Miekl's own home sector. This, too, gives Miekl an edge—in theory—for he knows these people intimately. But the city machine has pandered to them, pimped for them, procured for them their every pleasure and listened to their most secret confessions. It, too, knows them intimately.

The challenge starts. A randomizer produces a four-note theme, and both machine and human strive to incorporate it into their first movement. The theme is neither melodic nor particularly discordant, merely random, like that produced by a kitten jumping onto a piano keyboard. The random choice ensures that neither human nor computer could have music already prepared for the event, nor stolen fragments of melody from some forgotten composer of the past.

26

The city of ultimate freedom is forever fresh, forever changing, for all that it is thousands of years old. To be sure, some citizens prefer to withdraw, prefer machine-programmed fantasies to the real world, no matter how fantastic the real city may be. And others shun companionship in a different way, preferring never to meet real people at all, acting out their peculiar fantasies entirely in the company of the city's robots. But many live in the real world. They run the city with care and imagination, and take pride in doing so.

If the city machine could be said to have emotions, they would be love and pride. Love for its citizens, pride in their individuality, in each one's accomplishments. It has the records of hundreds of centuries of human culture, and still it glories in the accomplishment of each of the millions of citizens of the city. And it has pride in itself, in its abilities to satisfy the requests and desires of each of those millions, instantly, with maximum efficiency.

Miekl's movement opens with the four-note theme stated plainly, without elaboration, without emphasis. The theme repeats, and each note now splits off into a plethora, a discordant forest, harsh, atonal, chaotic. The four notes appear again, and again, now barely glimpsed through the jungle. Slowly a pattern appears in the chaos, the theme overlaid, not fitting. When the pattern finally resolves, what was seen as chaos is now clearly a complex order, but still the four notes jar, piping in over the ordered background now in high, woodwind sounds, now in low, bassoon tones, trying to find a place to fit. But wait! A shift of half a beat, a jerk in the tempo, and now the theme does fit, it is in fact the last piece of the pattern, whose absence could not even be noticed until it was in place. And the movement resolves with a final chorus of the completed theme, the last note held, a piping voice dying slowly into silence.

Into the silence comes the opening of the city machine's music. A simple melody, elaborated once, then joined in counterpoint by the four-note theme. The two themes dance together, whirling and changing, then returning again as individuals, finally to merge into a single voice. This repeats, then returns in variations, reversed, distorted. Where Miekl's opening formed order out of chaos, the city forms chaos out of order, dissolving into ten, a hundred, a thousand discordant voices, and finally into pure noise.

The movement is complete. Man and machine wait in silence. In the jury, whispered voices discuss the opening, speculating which was Miekl's and which the machine's, until the randomizer rings out three new notes for the second movement.

In the second movement, Miekl weaves the new notes into the theme. After a brief combat they fit in, adding another voice to the texture. In the city's movement, the new voice enters into the jungle of noise, weaving in and out, looking for a place to fit. The first theme returns, also looking, but no home can be found. Confusion remains. The first and second themes link together, making a single voice, but still cannot overcome the background.

And the randomizer intones the final two notes.

With difficulty, forcing the theme a bit, Miekl weaves this, too, into the theme, the whole making a dazzling tapestry of sound. But it is flawed, forced, the third voice not quite fitting in. Now the first, now the second, now the last theme is heard, then they chorus together, a final statement of the theme.

In the city's composition, the final two-note theme enters, a voice crying out against chaos. The second theme, an octave down, comes in almost as an echo, and the first enters yet deeper. Then the chorus, a thousand voices struggling to be heard, struggling to make sense. And slowly it does, a whole begins to take form, a form so huge, so magnificent, that the audience cannot realize how they had been unable to hear it before. The individual voices all were variants of a single theme. They crash together in a final crescendo, a triumphant statement of theme, and then cut to silence.

The vote is clear. Although Miekl had won the first movement, the machine's victory in the final movement was so overwhelming that the decision was unanimous.

And in the newsposter the notice of Miekl's defeat is a little larger. Fragments of symphony, both Miekl's and the machine's, float out across the air of the city.

In Edonna's performance niche, Paena again stops by to tell the sculptor the news. Edonna stops for a moment to listen, then silently returns to work.

But now there is a subdued excitement in the city: "Miekl continues to challenge!" Where the city computer is father and mother and god all in one, this is a pride which surpasses all understanding, a hubris on the edge of madness.

—But Miekl must certainly fail! And spend three months in the Primitive! That is outrageous, that is impossible. Three months outside the city? Three months living as primitive man lived? Can it be done? One month alone is punishment, two torture.

—But what if Miekl succeeds? Then Miekl will be the master programmer for the city, Miekl will be able to nullify the exile.

—But Miekl cannot succeed.

—Nevertheless, think of it! A master programmer in Vadya! What could Miekl not do?

—Don't be silly. What could Miekl possibly want to do, that Miekl, that any of us, cannot do already?

And this is true. The ancient master programmers were wise. The city is programmed to satisfy every desire of its citizens, save only that it cannot allow one to obstruct the freedoms of another, nor will it let one drain the full resources of the city. But the city's resources are unimaginable, and in fifty centuries none has managed to strain them. There is nothing Miekl could do as master programmer that Miekl cannot do as a citizen.

Except prove that man is still the equal of machine.

And in sector three—Miekl's sector—the citizens seem a little prouder, to go about their tasks with just a bit more spring in their step.

—Miekl *continues* to challenge the city!

29

For the third challenge, Miekl has once again chosen the maze. This time Miekl plays without the easy grace of the first challenge, but instead with an intense concentration, a smoldering inward fire. There is nothing in the world except the challenger and the maze, which Miekl thinks of as a being, the personal embodiment of the city. Miekl *zing!*s across the maze with an explosive fury, changing directions instantaneously, diving down into the core and then erupting out into the surface.

If the city computer ever contemplated the game in some stray moment of abstract thought, it would consider the game an analog of its own function. The target ball races through the grid, just as its own citizens move through the city, moving with entirely free choice of action, yet constrained by the three-dimensional gridwork of the cube, by the slowly changing pattern of obstructions, and most of all by the imperatives of their own nature. The city is used to predicting the actions of its citizens in order to be ready with all necessary resources when requested, when needed, without perceptible pause between request and fulfillment. This is the city's pride.

To Miekl it is a game of speed and reflexes, of instantaneous choices and lightning-fast reactions. To the computer, it is a game of calculation: given the target's past behavior, where is it likely to head next, and what is the optimum route for its own markers to get there first?

Miekl sparkles, Miekl flashes and dazzles, Miekl blazes across the maze, darting and weaving in unpredictable patterns. Miekl draws away from the computer's marker balls: five meters, ten, twenty.

As Miekl draws farther away, the range of strategy increases. Now the challenger must dive more often through the tangled center of the maze, seeking to force the other into pathways which are slower, and thus gain yet further. Thirty meters, fifty, a hundred. Miekl seems to stick at a hundred, unable to increase the lead. Up, around, left, down, inward to the center, out to the surface, making choices as fast as Miekl can think, flashing through the maze at incredible velocity.

The city's markers follow tenaciously, a hundred meters away. Miekl cannot gain ground on one without losing to the other. Down, around, across, up. A thousand meters will win the game, but Miekl has only a tenth of that.

In, across, back, up. After two hours of play Miekl knows that it is hopeless. Across, up, across, down, inward, through the center, and out. Conceding, Miekl makes a final race across the top of the maze and, reaching the edge, does not turn, but shoots off into space with a wild cry of exuberance and defiance. A thousand spectators watch Miekl arc across the city and fall.

But, of course, the city will not let Miekl fall. Without altering the arc of Miekl's trajectory, it slows the descent just enough to allow a soft landing.

Miekl lands in front of the largest of the city's newsposters. Even as Miekl lands, it shows, in huge 3D motion, Miekl's arc off the edge of the maze and fall across the sky of the city. The failed challenger bows to the audience and walks away. Miekl walks slowly, but with head still held high.

In the performance niche, Edonna finishes conducting the symphony and bows to the audience. The audience, like the musicians, consists of sculptures. The "real" audience will view the performance only in the 3D recordings. The sculpted musicians and audience form part of the artwork, and the music they play is the wild, atonal music which is the fashion of the time.

Back in Miekl's rooms, the city machine talks softly. "I think you should prepare yourself for your trip to the Primitive, Miekl."

Without looking up, Miekl speaks. "I intend to challenge again, you know."

"I know," says the city machine. "I am looking forward to it. But you must first serve your time in Primitive. You are only permitted three successive days of challenge before your sentence must be served. Unless you claim an emergency requires immediate reprogramming. Is this an emergency?"

Perhaps for a moment Miekl is tempted to lie, but that moment passes. "No," Miekl says. "There is no emergency."

Arriving on duty, Paena stops for a moment to chat with the peace officer from the previous shift, Dai. Paena is humming a small tune, a fragment of Miekl's symphony.

"You're smiling today," says Dai. "There's a bit of spring in your step."

"Yes," says Paena. "I think there is in the step of everybody from sector three."

"Look around," says Dai, and waves at the thronging crowds of the city. "It's not just sector three. It's everybody."

It was true. Around the city, everybody walks with a bit more of a lighthearted walk, a trace more of joy in their expression.

"Miekl will be three months in the Primitive for it, you know," says Dai.

"I know. But, oh! It was worth it! Don't you think so?"

"Yes," says Dai. "Perhaps it was."

If there's any writer in this book for whom the old triteness about Needing No Introduction applies, surely it's Ursula K. Le Guin. Perhaps you don't know that she's been writing elegant, thoughtful, wry science fiction of the highest quality for the past quarter of a century; perhaps you aren't aware that she's the author of the classic The Left Hand of Darkness and a bunch of other books nearly as widely acclaimed (The Dispossessed, The Lathe of Heaven, the Earthsea trilogy, etc., etc., etc.) You may not even know how many Nebula and Hugo awards she's won. (Plenty, the latest being the 1988 spaceship for "Buffalo Gals, Won't You Come Out Tonight.") But in that case why are you reading Universe? Oh . . . you don't know that, either . . . ?

THE SHOBIES' STORY

They met at Ve Port more than a month before their first flight together, and there, calling themselves after their ship as most crews did, became the Shobies. Their first consensual decision was to spend their isyeye in the coastal village of Liden, on Hain, where the negative ions could do their thing.

Liden was a fishing port with an eighty-thousand-year history and a population of four hundred. Its fisherfolk farmed the rich shoal waters of their bay, shipped the catch inland to the cities, and managed the Liden Resort for vacationers and tourists and new space crews on isyeye (the word is Hainish and means "making a beginning together," or "beginning to be together," or used technically, "the period of time and area of space in which a group forms if it is going to form." A honeymoon is an isyeye of two). The fisherwomen and fishermen of Liden were as weathered as driftwood and about as talkative. Six-year-old Asten, who had misunderstood slightly, asked one of them if they were all eighty thousand years old. "Nope," she said.

Like most crews, the Shobies used Hainish as their common language. So the name of the one Hainish crew member, Sweet Today, carried its meaning as words as well as name, and at first seemed a silly thing to call a big, tall, heavy woman in her late fifties, imposing of carriage and almost as taciturn as the villagers. But her reserve proved to

URSULA K. LE GUIN

be a deep well of congeniality and tact, to be called upon as needed, and her name soon began to sound quite right. She had family—all Hainish have family—kinfolk of all denominations, grandchildren and cross-cousins, affines and cosines, scattered all over the Ekumen, but no relatives in this crew. She asked to be Grandmother to Rig, Asten, and Betton, and was accepted.

The only Shoby older than Sweet Today was the Terran Lidi, who was seventy-two EYs and not interested in grandmothering. Lidi had been navigating for fifty years, and there was nothing she didn't know about NAFAL ships, although occasionally she forgot that their ship was the *Shoby* and called it the *Soso* or the *Alterra*. And there were things she didn't know; none of them knew, about the *Shoby*.

They talked, as human beings do, about what they didn't know.

Churten theory was the main topic of conversation, evenings at the driftwood fire on the beach after dinner. The adults had read whatever there was to read about it, of course, before they ever volunteered for the test mission. Gveter had more recent information and presumably a better understanding of it than the others, but it had to be pried out of him. Only twenty-five, the only Cetian in the crew, much hairier than the others, and not gifted in language, he spent a lot of time on the defensive. Assuming that as an Anarresti he was more proficient at mutual aid and more adept at cooperation than the others, he lectured them about their propertarian habits; but he held tight to his knowledge, because he needed the advantage it gave him. For a while he would speak only in negatives: don't call it the churten "drive," it isn't a drive, don't call it the churten "effect," it isn't an effect. What is it, then? A long lecture ensued, beginning with the rebirth of Cetian physics since the revision of Shevekian temporalism by the Intervallists, and ending with the general conceptual framework of the churten. Everyone listened very carefully, and finally Sweet Today spoke, carefully. "So the ship will be moved," she said, "by ideas?"

"No, no, no, no," said Gveter. But he hesitated for the next word so long that Karth asked a question: "Well, you haven't actually talked about any physical, material events or effects at all." The question was characteristically indirect. Karth and Oreth, the Gethenians who with their two children were the affective focus of the crew, the "hearth" of it, in their terms, came from a not very theoretically minded subculture, and knew it. Gveter could run rings round them with his Cetian physico-philosophico-techno-natter. He did so at once. His accent did not make his explanations any clearer. He went on about coherence and meta-intervals, and at last demanded, with gestures of despair, "Khow can I say it in Khainish? No! It is not physical, it is not not-physical, these are the categories our minds must discard entirely, this is the khole point!"

"Buth-buth-buth-buth-buth-buth," went Asten, softly, passing behind the half circle of adults at the driftwood fire on the wide, twilit beach. Rig followed, also going, "Buth-buth-buth-buth," but louder. They were being spaceships, to judge from their maneuvers around a dune and their communications—"Locked in orbit, Navigator!"—but the noise they were imitating was the noise of the little fishing boats of Liden putt-putting out to sea.

"I crashed!" Rig shouted, flailing in the sand. "Help! Help! I crashed!"

"Hold on, Ship Two!" Asten cried. "I'll rescue you! Don't breathe! Oh, oh, trouble with the Churten Drive! Buth-buth-ack! Ack! Brrrrmmm-ack-ack-ack-rrrrrmmmmmm, buth-buth-buth-buth. . . ."

They were six and four EYs old. Tai's son Betton, who was eleven, sat at the driftwood fire with the adults, though at the moment he was watching Rig and Asten as if he wouldn't mind taking off to help rescue Ship Two. The little Gethenians had spent more time on ships than on planet, and Asten liked to boast about being "actually fifty-eight," but this was Betton's first crew, and his only NAFAL flight had been from Terra to Hain. He and his biomother, Tai, had lived in a reclamation commune on Terra. When she had drawn the lot

37

for Ekumenical service, and requested training for ship duty, he had asked her to bring him as family. She had agreed; but after training, when she volunteered for this test flight, she had tried to get Betton to withdraw, to stay in training or go home. He had refused. Shan, who had trained with them, told the others this, because the tension between the mother and son had to be understood to be used effectively in group formation. Betton had requested to come, and Tai had given in, but plainly not with an undivided will. Her relationship to the boy was cool and mannered. Shan offered him fatherly-brotherly warmth, but Betton accepted it sparingly, coolly, and sought no formal crew relation with him or anyone.

Ship Two was being rescued, and attention returned to the discussion. "All right," said Lidi. "We know that anything that goes faster than light, any *thing* that goes faster than light, by so doing transcends the material/immaterial category —that's how we got the ansible, by distinguishing the message from the medium. But if we, the crew, are going to travel as messages, I want to understand *how.*"

Gveter tore his hair. There was plenty to tear. It grew fine and thick, a mane on his head, a pelt on his limbs and body, a silvery nimbus on his hands and face. The fuzz on his feet was, at the moment, full of sand. "Khow!" he cried. "I'm trying to tell you khow! Message, information, no no no, that's old, that's ansible technology. This is transilience! Because the field is to be conceived as the virtual field, in which the unreal interval becomes virtually effective through the mediary coherence—don't you see?"

"No," Lidi said. "What do you mean by mediary?"

After several more bonfires on the beach, the consensus opinion was that churten theory was accessible only to minds very highly trained in Cetian temporal physics. There was a less freely voiced conviction that the engineers who had built the *Shoby*'s churten apparatus did not entirely understand how it worked. Or more precisely, what it did when it worked. That it worked was certain. The *Shoby* was the fourth ship it had been tested with, using robot crew; so far sixty-two instan-

taneous trips, or transiliences, had been effected between
points from four hundred kilometers to twenty-seven light-
years apart, with stopovers of varying lengths. Gveter and Lidi
steadfastly maintained that this proved that the engineers
knew perfectly well what they were doing, and that for the
rest of them the seeming difficulty of the theory was only the
difficulty human minds had in grasping a genuinely new concept.

"Like the circulation of the blood," said Tai. "People went
around with their hearts beating for a long time before they
understood why." She did not look satisfied with her own
analogy, and when Shan said, "The heart has its reasons,
which reason does not know," she looked offended. "Mysti-
cism," she said, in the tone of voice of one warning a companion about dog shit on the path.

"Surely there's nothing *beyond* understanding in this process," Oreth said, somewhat tentatively. "Nothing that can't
be understood, and reproduced."

"And quantified," Gveter said stoutly.

"But even if people understand the process, nobody knows
the human response to it—the *experience* of it. Right? So we
are to report on that."

"Why shouldn't it be just like NAFAL flight, only even
faster?" Betton asked.

"Because it is totally different," said Gveter.

"What could happen to us?"

Some of the adults had discussed possibilities, all of them
had considered them; Karth and Oren had talked it over in
appropriate terms with their children; but evidently Betton
had not been included in such discussions.

"We don't know," Tai said sharply. "I told you that at the
start, Betton."

"Most likely it will be like NAFAL flight," said Shan, "but
the first people who flew NAFAL didn't know what it would
be like, and had to find out the physical and psychic effects—"

"The worst thing," said Sweet Today in her slow, comfort-

39

able voice, "would be that we would die. Other lives have been on some of the test flights. Crickets. And intelligent ritual animals on the last two *Shoby* tests. They were all all right." It was a very long statement for Sweet Today, and carried proportional weight.

"We know," said Gveter, "that no temporal rearrangement is involved in churten, as it is in NAFAL. And mass is involved only in terms of needing a certain core mass, just as for ansible transmission, but not in itself. So maybe even a pregnant person could be a transilient."

"They can't go on ships," Asten said. "The unborn dies if they do."

Asten was half-lying across Oreth's lap; Rig, thumb in mouth, was asleep on Karth's lap.

"When we were Oneblins," Asten went on, sitting up, "there were ritual animals with our crew. Some fish and some Terran cats and a whole lot of Hainish gholes. We got to play with them. And we helped thank the ghole that they tested for lithovirus. But it didn't die. It bit Shapi. The cats slept with us. But one of them went into kemmer and got pregnant, and then the *Oneblin* had to go to Hain, and she had to have an abortion, or all her unborns would have died inside her and killed her too. Nobody knew a ritual for her, to explain to her. But I fed her some extra food. And Rig cried."

"Other people I know cried too," Karth said, stroking the child's hair.

"You tell good stories, Asten," Sweet Today observed.

"So we're sort of ritual humans," said Betton.

"Volunteers," Tai said.

"Experimenters," said Lidi.

"Experiencers," said Shan.

"Explorers," Oreth said.

"Gamblers," said Karth.

40   The boy looked from one face to the next.

"You know," Shan said, "back in the time of the League, early in NAFAL flight, they were sending out ships to really distant systems—trying to explore everything—crews that wouldn't come back for centuries. Maybe some of them are still out there. But some of them came back after four, five, six hundred years, and they were all mad. Crazy!" He paused dramatically. "But they were all crazy when they started. Unstable people. They had to be crazy to volunteer for a time dilation like that. What a way to pick a crew, eh?" He laughed.

"Are we stable?" said Oreth. "I like instability. I like this job. I like the risk, taking the risk together. High stakes! That's the edge of it, the sweetness of it."

Karth looked down at their children, and smiled.

"Yes. Together," Gveter said. "You aren't crazy. You are good. I love you. We are ammari."

"Ammar," the others said to him, confirming this unexpected declaration. The young man scowled with pleasure, jumped up, and pulled off his shirt. "I want to swim. Come on, Betton. Come on swimming!" he said, and ran off toward the dark, vast waters that moved softly beyond the ruddy haze of their fire. The boy hesitated, then shed his shirt and sandals and followed. Shan pulled up Tai, and they followed; and finally the two old women went off into the night and the breakers, rolling up their pant legs, laughing at themselves.

To Gethenians, even on a warm summer night on a warm summer world, the sea is no friend. The fire is where you stay. Oreth and Asten moved closer to Karth and watched the flames, listening to the faint voices out in the glimmering surf, now and then talking quietly in their own tongue, while the little sisterbrother slept on.

After thirty lazy days at Liden the Shobies caught the fish train inland to the city, where a Fleet lander picked them up at the train station and took them to the spaceport on Ve, the next planet out from Hain. They were rested, tanned, bonded, and ready to go.

One of Sweet Today's hemi-affiliate cousins once removed was on duty in Ve Port. She urged the Shobies to ask the inventors of the churten on Urras and Anarres any questions they had about churten operation. "The purpose of the experimental flight is understanding," she insisted, "and your full intellectual participation is essential. They've been very anxious about that."

Lidi snorted.

"Now for the ritual," said Shan, as they went to the ansible room in the sunward bubble. "They'll explain to the animals what they're going to do and why, and ask them to help."

"The animals don't understand that," Betton said in his cold, angelic treble. "It's just to make the humans feel better."

"The humans understand?" Sweet Today asked.

"We all use each other," Oreth said. "The ritual says: we have no right to do so; therefore, we accept the responsibility for the suffering we cause."

Betton listened and brooded.

Gveter addressed the ansible first, and talked to it for half an hour, mostly in Pravic and mathematics. Finally, apologizing, and looking a little unnerved, he invited the others to use the instrument. There was a pause. Lidi activated it, introduced herself, and said, "We have agreed that none of us, except Gveter, has the theoretical background to grasp the principles of the churten."

A scientist twenty-two light-years away responded in Hainish via the rather flat auto-translator voice, but with unmistakable hopefulness, "The churten, in lay terms, may be seen as displacing the virtual field in order to realize relational coherence in terms of the transiliential experientiality."

"Quite," said Lidi.

"As you know, the material effects have been nil, and negative effect on low-intelligence sentients also nil; but there is considered to be a possibility that the participation of high intelligence in the process might affect the displacement in one way or another. And that such displacement would reciprocally affect the participant."

"What has the level of our intelligence got to do with how the churten functions?" Tai asked.

A pause. Their interlocutor was trying to find the words, to accept the responsibility.

"We have been using 'intelligence' as shorthand for the psychic complexity and cultural dependence of our species," said the translator voice at last. "The presence of the transilient as conscious mind nonduring transilience is the untested factor."

"But if the process is instantaneous, how can we be conscious of it?" Oreth asked.

"Precisely," said the ansible, and after another pause continued, "As the experimenter is an element of the experiment, so we assume that the transilient may be an element or agent of transilience. This is why we asked for a crew to test the process, rather than one or two volunteers. The psychic interbalance of a bonded social group is a margin of strength against disintegrative or incomprehensible experience, if any such occurs. Also, the separate observations of the group members will mutually interverify."

"Who programs this translator?" Shan snarled in a whisper. "Interverify! Shit!"

Lidi looked around at the others, inviting questions.

"How long will the trip actually take?" Betton asked.

"No long," the translator voice said, then self-corrected: "No time."

Another pause.

"Thank you," said Sweet Today, and the scientist on a planet twenty-two years of time-dilated travel from Ve Port answered, "We are grateful for your generous courage, and our hope is with you."

They went directly from the ansible room to the *Shoby*.

The churten equipment, which was not very space-consuming and the controls of which consisted essentially of an on-off switch, had been installed alongside the Nearly as Fast as Light motivators and controls of an ordinary interstellar ship of the Ekumenical Fleet. The *Shoby* had been built on Hain about four hundred years ago, and was thirty-two years old.

Most of its early runs had been exploratory, with a Hainish-Chiffewarian crew. Since in such runs a ship might spend years in orbit in a planetary system, the Hainish and Chiffewarians, feeling that it might as well be lived in rather than endured, had arranged and furnished it like a very large, very comfortable house. Three of its residential modules had been disconnected and left in the hangars on Ve, and still there was more than enough room for a crew of only ten. Tai, Betton, and Shan, new from Terra, and Gveter from Anarres, accustomed to the barracks and the communal austerities of their marginally habitable worlds, stalked about the *Shoby*, disapproving it. "Excremental," Gveter growled. "Luxury!" Tai sneered. Sweet Today, Lidi, and the Gethenians, more used to the amenities of shipboard life, settled right in and made themselves at home. And Gveter and the younger Terrans found it hard to maintain ethical discomfort in the spacious, high-ceilinged, well-furnished, slightly shabby living rooms and bedrooms, studies, high- and low-G gyms, the dining room, library, kitchen, and bridge of the *Shoby*. The carpet in the bridge was a genuine Henyekaulil, soft deep blues and purples woven in the patterns of the constellations of the Hainish sky. There was a large, healthy plantation of Terran bamboo in the meditation gym, part of the ship's self-contained vegetal/respiratory system. The windows of any room could be programmed by the homesick to a view of Abbenay or New Cairo or the beach at Liden, or cleared to look out on the suns nearer and farther and the darkness between the suns.

Rig and Asten discovered that as well as the elevators there was a stately staircase with a curving banister, leading from the reception hall up to the library. They slid down the banister shrieking wildly, until Shan threatened to apply a local gravity field and force them to slide up it, which they besought him to do. Betton watched the little ones with a superior gaze, and took the elevator; but the next day he slid down the banister, going a good deal faster than Rig and Asten because he could push off harder and had greater mass, and nearly broke his tailbone. It was Betton who organized the tray-sliding races, but Rig generally won them, being small enough to stay on the tray all the way down the stairs. None of the children had had any lessons at the beach, except in swimming and being Shobies; but while they waited through an unexpected five-day delay at Ve Port, Gveter did physics with Betton and math with all three daily in the library, and they did some history with Shan and Oreth, and danced with Tai in the low-G gym.

When she danced, Tai became light, free, laughing. Rig and Asten loved her then, and her son danced with her like a colt, like a kid, awkward and blissful. Shan often joined them; he was a dark and elegant dancer, and she would dance with him, but even then was shy, would not touch. She had been celibate since Betton's birth. She did not want Shan's patient, urgent desire, did not want to cope with it, with him. She would turn from him to Betton, and son and mother would dance wholly absorbed in the steps, the airy pattern they made together. Watching them, the afternoon before the test flight, Sweet Today began to wipe tears from her eyes, smiling, never saying a word.

"Life is good," said Gveter very seriously to Lidi.

"It'll do," she said.

Oreth, who was just coming out of female kemmer, having thus triggered Karth's male kemmer, all of which, by coming on unexpectedly early, had delayed the test flight for these past five days, enjoyable days for all—Oreth watched Rig, whom she had fathered, dance with Asten, whom she had borne, and watched Karth watch them, and said in Karhidish, "Tomorrow. . . ." The edge was very sweet.

Anthropologists solemnly agree that we must not attribute "cultural constants" to the human population of any planet; but certain cultural traits or expectations do seem to run deep. Before dinner that last night in port, Shan and Tai appeared in black and silver uniforms of the Terran Ekumen, which had

45

cost them—Terra also still had a money economy—a half-year's allowance.

Asten and Rig clamored at once for equal grandeur. Karth and Oreth suggested their party clothes, and Sweet Today brought out silver-lace scarves, but Asten sulked, and Rig imitated. The idea of a *uniform*, Asten told them, was that it was the *same*.

"Why?" Oreth inquired.

Old Lidi answered sharply: "So that no one is responsible."

She then went off and changed into a black velvet evening suit that wasn't a uniform but that didn't leave Tai and Shan sticking out like sore thumbs. She had left Terra at age eighteen and never been back nor wanted to, but Tai and Shan were shipmates.

Karth and Oreth got the idea, and put on their finest fur-trimmed hiebs, and the children were appeased with their own party clothes plus all of Karth's hereditary and massive gold jewelry. Sweet Today appeared in a pure white robe which she claimed was in fact ultraviolet. Gveter braided his mane. Betton had no uniform, but needed none, sitting beside his mother at table in a visible glory of pride.

Meals, sent up from the Port kitchens, were very good, and this one was superb: a delicate Hainish iyanwi with all seven sauces, followed by a pudding flavored with Terran chocolate. A lively evening ended quietly at the big fireplace in the library. The logs were fake, of course, but good fakes; no use having a fireplace on a ship and then burning plastic in it. The neo-cellulose logs and kindling smelled right, resisted catching, caught with spits and sparks and smoke billows, flared up bright. Oreth had laid the fire, Karth lit it. Everybody gathered round.

"Tell bedtime stories," Rig said.

Oreth told about the Ice Caves of Kerm Land, how a ship sailed into the great blue sea-cave and disappeared, and was never found by the boats that entered the caves in search; but seventy years later that ship was found drifting—not a living soul aboard nor any sign of what had become of them—off the coast of Osemyet, a thousand miles overland from Kerm. . . .

Another story?

Lidi told about the little desert wolf who lost his wife and went to the land of the dead for her, and found her there dancing with the dead, and nearly brought her back to the land of the living, but spoiled it by trying to touch her before they got all the way back to life, and she vanished, and he could never find the way back to the place where the dead danced, no matter how he looked, and howled, and cried. . . .

Another story!

Shan told about the boy who sprouted a feather every time he told a lie, until his commune had to use him for a duster.

Another!

Gveter told about the winged people called gluns, who were so stupid that they died out, because they kept hitting each other head-on in midair. "They weren't real," he added conscientiously. "Only a story."

Another— No. Bedtime now.

Rig and Asten went round as usual for a goodnight hug, and this time Betton followed them. When he came to Tai he did not stop, for she did not like to be touched; but she put out her hand, drew the child to her, and kissed his cheek. He fled in joy.

"Stories," said Sweet Today. "Ours begins tomorrow, eh?"

A chain of command is easy to describe, a network of response isn't. To those who live by mutual empowerment, "thick" description, complex and open-ended, is normal and comprehensible, but to those whose only model is hierarchic control, such description seems a muddle, a mess, along with what it describes. Who's in charge here? Get rid of all these petty details. How many cooks spoil a soup? Let's get this perfectly clear now. Take me to your leader!

The old navigator was at the NAFAL console, of course, and Gveter at the paltry churten console; Oreth was wired

47

into the AI; Tai, Shan, and Karth were their respective Support, and what Sweet Today did might be called supervising or overseeing if that didn't suggest a hierarchic function. Interseeing, maybe, or subvising. Rig and Asten always naffled (to use Rig's word) in the ship's library, where, during the boring and disorienting experience of travel at near light-speed, Asten could look at pictures or listen to a story tape, and Rig could curl up on and under a certain furry blanket and go to sleep. Betton's crew function during flight was Elder Sib; he stayed with the little ones, provided himself with a barf bag since he was one of those whom NAFAL flight made queasy, and focused the intervid on Lidi and Gveter so he could watch what they did.

So they all knew what they were doing, as regards NAFAL flight. As regards the churten process, they knew that it was supposed to effectuate their transilience to a solar system seventeen light-years from Ve Port without temporal interval; but nobody, anywhere, knew what they were doing.

So Lidi looked around, like the violinist who raises her bow to poise the chamber group for the first chord, a flicker of eye contact, and sent the *Shoby* into NAFAL mode, as Gveter, like the cellist whose bow comes down in that same instant to ground the chord, sent the *Shoby* into churten mode. They entered unduration. They churtened. No long, as the ansible had said.

"What's wrong?" Shan whispered.

"By damn!" said Gveter.

"What?" said Lidi, blinking and shaking her head.

"That's it," Tai said, flicking readouts.

"That's not A-sixty-whatsit," Lidi said, still blinking.

Sweet Today was gestalting them, all ten at once, the seven on the bridge and by intervid the three in the library. Betton had cleared a window, and the children were looking out at the murky, brownish convexity that filled half of it. Rig was holding a dirty, furry blanket. Karth was taking the electrodes off Oreth's temples, disengaging the AI link-up. "There was no interval," Oreth said.

"We aren't anywhere," Lidi said.

"There was no interval," Gveter repeated, scowling at the console. "That's right."

"Nothing happened," Karth said, skimming through the AI flight report.

Oreth got up, went to the window, and stood motionless looking out.

"That's it. M-60-340-nolo," Tai said.

All their words fell dead, had a false sound.

"Well! We did it, Shobies!" said Shan.

Nobody answered.

"Buzz Ve Port on the ansible," Shan said with determined jollity. "Tell 'em we're all here in one piece."

"All where?" Oreth asked.

"Yes, of course," Sweet Today said, but did nothing.

"Right," said Tai, going to the ship's ansible. She opened the field, centered to Ve, and sent a signal. Ship's ansibles worked only in the visual mode; she waited, watching the screen. She resignaled. They were all watching the screen.

"Nothing going through," she said.

Nobody told her to check the centering coordinates; in a network system nobody gets to dump their anxieties that easily. She checked the coordinates. She signaled; rechecked, reset, resignaled; opened the field and centered to Abbenay on Anarres and signaled. The ansible screen was blank.

"Check the—" Shan said, and stopped himself.

"The ansible is not functioning," Tai reported formally to her crew.

"Do you find malfunction?" Sweet Today asked.

"No. Nonfunction."

"We're going back now," said Lidi, still seated at the NAFAL console.

Her words, her tone, shook them apart.

"No, we're not!" Betton said on the intervid while Oreth said, "Back where?"

Tai, Lidi's Support, moved toward her as if to prevent her from activating the NAFAL drive, but then hastily moved

49

back to the ansible to prevent Gveter from getting access to it. He stopped, taken aback, and said, "Perhaps the churten affected ansible function?"

"*I'm* checking it out," Tai said. "Why should it? Robot-operated ansible transmission functioned in all the test flights."

"Where are the AI reports?" Shan demanded.

"I told you, there are none," Karth answered sharply.

"Oreth was plugged in."

Oreth, still at the window, spoke without turning. "Nothing happened."

Sweet Today came over beside the Gethenian. Oreth looked at her and said, slowly, "Yes. Sweet Today. We cannot . . . do this. I think. I can't think."

Shan had cleared a second window, and stood looking out it. "Ugly," he said.

"What is?" said Lidi.

Gveter said, as if reading from the Ekumenical Atlas, "Thick, stable atmosphere, near the bottom of the temperature window for life. Micro-organisms. Bacterial clouds, bacterial reefs."

"Germ stew," Shan said. "Lovely place to send us."

"So that if we arrived as a neutron bomb or a blackhole event we'd only take bacteria with us," Tai said. "But we didn't."

"Didn't what?" said Lidi.

"Didn't arrive?" Karth asked.

"Hey," Betton said, "is everybody going to stay on the bridge?"

"I want to come there," said Rig's little pipe, and then Asten's voice, clear but shaky, "Maba, I'd like to go back to Liden now."

"Come on," Karth said, and went to meet the children. Oreth did not turn from the window, even when Asten came close and took Oreth's hand.

"What are you looking at, maba?"

"The planet, Asten."

"What planet?"

Oreth looked at the child then.

"There isn't anything," Asten said.

"That brown color—that's the surface, the atmosphere of a planet."

"There isn't any brown color. There isn't *anything*. I want to go back to Liden. You said we could when we were done with the test."

Oreth looked around, at last, at the others.

"Perception variation," Gveter said.

"I think," Tai said, "that we must establish that we are— that we got here—and then get here."

"You mean, go back," Betton said.

"The readings are perfectly clear," Lidi said, holding on to the rim of her seat with both hands and speaking very distinctly. "Every coordinate in order. That's M-60-Etcetera down there. What more do you want? Bacteria samples?"

"Yes," Tai said. "Instrument function's been affected, so we can't rely on instrumental records."

"Oh, shitsake!" said Lidi. "What a farce! All right. Suit up, go down, get some goo, and then let's get out. Go home. By NAFAL."

"By NAFAL?" Shan and Tai echoed, and Gveter said, "But we would spend seventeen years, Ve time, and no ansible to explain why."

"Why, Lidi?" Sweet Today asked.

Lidi stared at the Hainishwoman. "You want to churten again?" she demanded, raucous. She looked round at them all. "Are you people made of stone?" Her face was ashy, crumpled, shrunken. "It doesn't bother you, seeing through the walls?"

No one spoke, until Shan said cautiously, "How do you mean?"

"I can see the stars through the walls!" She stared round at them again, pointing at the carpet with its woven constellations. "You can't?" When no one answered, her jaw trembled in a little spasm, and she said, "All right. All right. I'm off

51

duty. Sorry. Be in my room." She stood up. "Maybe you should lock me in," she said.

"Nonsense," said Sweet Today.

"If I fall through," Lidi began, and did not finish. She walked to the door, stiffly and cautiously, as if through a thick fog. She said something they did not understand, "Cause," or perhaps, "Gauze."

Sweet Today followed her.

"I can see the stars too!" Rig announced.

"Hush," Karth said, putting an arm around the child.

"I can! I can see all the stars everywhere. And I can see Ve Port. And I can see anything I want!"

"Yes, of course, but hush now," the mother murmured, at which the child pulled free, stamped, and shrilled, "I can! I can too! I can see *everything!* And Asten can't! And there *is* a planet, there is too! No, don't hold me! Don't! Let me go!"

Grim, Karth carried the screaming child off to their quarters. Asten turned around to yell after Rig, "There is *not* any planet! You're just making it up!"

Grim, Oreth said, "Go to our room, please, Asten."

Asten burst into tears and obeyed. Oreth, with a glance of apology to the others, followed the short, weeping figure across the bridge and out into the corridor.

The four remaining on the bridge stood silent.

"Canaries," Shan said.

"Khallucinations?" Gveter proposed, subdued. "An effect of the churten on extrasensitive organisms—maybe?"

Tai nodded.

"Then is the ansible not functioning or are we hallucinating nonfunction?" Shan asked after a pause.

Gveter went to the ansible; this time Tai walked away from it, leaving it to him. "I want to go down," she said.

"No reason not to, I suppose," Shan said unenthusiastically.

"Khwat reason to?" Gveter asked over his shoulder.

"It's what we're here for, isn't it? It's what we volunteered to do, isn't it? To test instantaneous—transilience—prove

that it worked, that we are here! With the ansible out, it'll be
seventeen years before Ve gets our radio signal!"

"We can just churten back to Ve and *tell* them," Shan said.
"If we did that now, we'd have been . . . here . . . about
eight minutes."

"Tell them—tell them what? What kind of evidence is
that?"

"Anecdotal," said Sweet Today, who had come back quietly
to the bridge; she moved like a big sailing ship, imposingly
silent.

"Is Lidi all right?" Shan asked.

"No," Sweet Today answered. She sat down where Lidi had
sat, at the NAFAL console.

"I ask a consensus about going down onplanet," Tai said.

"I'll ask the others," Gveter said, and went out, returning
presently with Karth. "Go down, if you want," the Gethenian
said. "Oreth's staying with the children for a bit. They are—
we are extremely disoriented."

"I will come down," Gveter said.

"Can I come?" Betton asked, almost in a whisper, not raising his eyes to any adult face.

"No," Tai said, as Gveter said, "Yes."

Betton looked at his mother, one quick glance.

"Why not?" Gveter asked her.

"We don't know the risks."

"The planet was surveyed."

"By robot ships—"

"We'll wear suits." Gveter was honestly puzzled.

"I don't want the responsibility," Tai said through her
teeth.

"Khwy is it yours?" Gveter asked, more puzzled still. "We
all share it; Betton is crew. I don't understand."

"I know you don't understand," Tai said, turned her back
on them both, and went out. The man and the boy stood
staring, Gveter after Tai, Betton at the carpet.

"I'm sorry," Betton said.

"Not to be," Gveter told him.

"What is . . . what is going on?" Shan asked in an over-controlled voice. "Why are we—we keep crossing, we keep—coming and going—"

"Confusion due to the churten experience," Gveter said.

Sweet Today turned from the console. "I have sent a distress signal," she said. "I am unable to operate the NAFAL system. The radio—" She cleared her throat. "Radio function seems erratic."

There was a pause.

"This is not happening," Shan said, or Oreth said, but Oreth had stayed with the children in another part of the ship, so it could not have been Oreth who said, "This is not happening," it must have been Shan.

A chain of cause and effect is an easy thing to describe; a cessation of cause and effect is not. To those who live in time, sequence is the norm, the only model, and simultaneity seems a muddle, a mess, a hopeless confusion, and the description of that confusion hopelessly confusing. As the members of the crew network no longer perceived the network steadily, and were unable to communicate their perceptions, an individual perception was the only clue to follow through the labyrinth of their dislocation. Gveter perceived himself as being on the bridge with Shan, Sweet Today, Betton, Karth, and Tai. He perceived himself as methodically checking out the ship's systems. The NAFAL he found dead, the radio functioning in erratic bursts, the internal electrical and mechanical systems of the ship all in order. He sent out a lander unmanned and brought it back, and perceived it as functioning normally. He perceived himself discussing with Tai her determination to go down onplanet. Since he admitted his unwillingness to trust any instrumental reading on the ship, he had to admit her point that only material evidence would show that they had actually arrived at their destination, M-60-340-nolo. If they were going to have to spend the next seventeen years traveling back to Ve in real time, it would be nice to have something to show for it, even if only a handful of slime.

He perceived this discussion as perfectly rational.

It was, however, interrupted by outbursts of egoizing not characteristic of the crew.

"If you're going, go!" Shan said.

"Don't give me orders," Tai said.

"Somebody's got to stay in control here," Shan said.

"Not the men!" Tai said.

"Not the Terrans," Karth said. "Have you people no self-respect?"

"Stress," Gveter said. "Come on, Tai, Betton, all right, let's go, all right?"

In the lander, everything was clear to Gveter. One thing happened after another just as it should. Lander operation is very simple, and he asked Betton to take them down. The boy did so. Tai sat, tense and compact as always, her strong fists clenched on her knees. Betton managed the little ship with aplomb, and sat back, tense also, but dignified: "We're down," he said.

"No, we're not," Tai said.

"It—it says contact," Betton said, losing his assurance.

"An excellent landing," Gveter said. "Never even felt it." He was running the usual tests. Everything was in order. Outside the lander ports pressed a brownish darkness, a gloom. When Betton put on the outside lights the atmosphere, like a dark fog, diffused the light into a useless glare.

"Tests all tally with survey reports," Gveter said. "Will you go out, Tai, or use the servos?"

"Out," she said.

"Out," Betton echoed.

Gveter, assuming the formal crew role of Support, which one of them would have assumed if he had been going out, assisted them to lock their helmets and decontaminate their suits; he opened the hatch series for them, and watched them on the vid and from the port as they climbed down from the outer hatch. Betton went first. His slight figure, elongated by the whitish suit, was luminous in the weak glare of the lights. He walked a few steps from the ship, turned, and waited. Tai was stepping off the ladder. She seemed to grow very short—did she kneel down? Gveter looked from the port to the vid screen and back. She was shrinking? Sinking—she must be sinking into the surface—which could not be solid, then, but bog, or some suspension like quicksand—but Betton had walked on it and was walking back to her, two steps, three steps, on the ground which Gveter could not see clearly but which must be solid, and which must be holding Betton up because he was lighter—but no, Tai must have stepped into a hole, a trench of some kind, for he could see her only from the waist up now, her legs hidden in the dark bog or fog, but she was moving, moving quickly, going right away from the lander and from Betton.

"Bring them back," Shan said, and Gveter said on the suit intercom, "Please return to the lander, Betton and Tai." Betton at once started up the ladder, then turned to look for his mother. A dim blotch that might be her helmet showed in the brown gloom, almost beyond the suffusion of light from the lander.

"Please come in, Betton. Please return, Tai."

The whitish suit flickered up the ladder, while Betton's voice in the intercom pleaded, "Tai—Tai, come back—Gveter, should I go after her?"

"No. Tai, please return at once to lander."

The boy's crew integrity held; he came up into the lander and watched from the outer hatch, as Gveter watched from the port. The vid had lost her. The pallid blotch sank into the formless murk.

Gveter perceived that the instruments recorded that the lander had sunk 3.2 meters since contact with planet surface and was continuing to sink at an increasing rate.

"What is the surface, Betton?"

"Like muddy ground—where is she?"

"Please return at once, Tai!"

"Please return to *Shoby*, Lander One and all crew," said the ship intercom; it was Tai's voice. "This is Tai," it said. "Please return at once to ship, lander and all crew."

"Stay in suit, in decon, please, Betton," Gveter said. "I'm sealing the hatch."

"But—all right," said the boy's voice.

Gveter took the lander up, decontaminating it and Betton's suit on the way. He perceived that Betton and Shan came with him through the hatch series into the *Shoby* and along the halls to the bridge, and that Karth, Sweet Today, Shan, and Tai were on the bridge.

Betton ran to his mother and stopped; he did not put out his hands to her. His face was immobile, as if made of wax or wood.

"Were you frightened?" she asked. "What happened down there?" And she looked to Gveter for an explanation.

Gveter perceived nothing. Unduring a nonperiod of no long, he perceived nothing was had happening happened that had not happened. Lost, he groped, lost, he found the word, the word that saved—"You—" he said, his tongue thick, dumb—"You called us."

It seemed that she denied, but it did not matter. What mattered? Shan was talking. Shan could tell. "Nobody called, Gveter," he said. "You and Betton went out, I was Support; when I realized I couldn't get the lander stable, that there's something funny about that surface, I called you back into the lander, and we came up."

All Gveter could say was, "Insubstantial . . ."

"But Tai came—" Betton began, and stopped. Gveter perceived that the boy moved away from his mother's denying touch. What mattered?

"Nobody went down," Sweet Today said. After a silence and before it, she said, "There is no down to go to."

Gveter tried to find another word, but there was none. He perceived outside the main port a brownish, murky convexity, through which, as he looked intently, he saw small stars shining.

He found a word then, the wrong word. "Lost," he said, and speaking perceived how the ship's lights dimmed slowly into a brownish murk, faded, darkened, were gone, while all

57

the soft hum and busyness of the ship's systems died away into the real silence that was always there. But there was nothing there. Nothing had happened. We are at Ve Port! he tried with all his will to say; but there was no saying.

The suns burn through my flesh, Lidi said.

I am the suns, said Sweet Today. Not I, all is.

Don't breathe! cried Oreth.

It is death, Shan said. What I feared, is: nothing.

Nothing, they said.

Unbreathing, the ghosts flitted, shifted, in the ghost shell of a cold, dark hull floating near a world of brown fog, an unreal planet. They spoke, but there were no voices. There is no sound in vacuum, nor in nontime.

In her cabined solitude, Lidi felt the gravity lighten to the half-G of the ship's core mass; she saw them, the nearer and the farther suns, burn through the dark gauze of the walls and hulls and the bedding and her body. The brightest, the sun of this system, floated directly under her navel. She did not know its name.

I am the darkness between the suns, one said.

I am nothing, one said.

I am you, one said.

You—one said—You—

And breathed, and reached out, and spoke: "Listen!" Crying out to the other, to the others, "Listen!"

"We have always known this. This is where we have always been, will always be, at the hearth, at the center. There is nothing to be afraid of, after all."

"I can't breathe," one said.

"I am not breathing," one said.

"There is nothing to breathe," one said.

"You are, you are breathing, please breathe!" said another.

"We're here, at the hearth," said another.

Oreth had laid the fire, Karth lit it. As it caught they both said softly, in Karhidish, "Praise also the light, and creation unfinished."

The fire caught with spark spits, crackles, sudden flares. It did not go out. It burned. The others grouped round.

They were nowhere, but they were nowhere together; the ship was dead, but they were in the ship. A dead ship cools off fairly quickly, but not immediately. Close the doors, come in by the fire; keep the cold night out, before we go to bed.

Karth went with Rig to persuade Lidi from her starry vault. The navigator would not get up. "It's my fault," she said.

"Don't egoize," Karth said mildly. "How could it be?"

"I don't know. I want to stay here," Lidi muttered. Then Karth begged her: "Oh, Lidi, not alone!"

"How else?" the old woman asked coldly.

But she was ashamed of herself, then, and ashamed of her guilt trip, and growled, "Oh, all right." She heaved herself up and wrapped a blanket around her body and followed Karth and Rig. The child carried a little biolume; it glowed in the black corridors, just as the plants of the aerobic tanks lived on, metabolizing, making an air to breathe, for a while. The light moved before her like a star among the stars through darkness to the room full of books, where the fire burned in the stone hearth. "Hello, children," Lidi said. "What are we doing here?"

"Telling stories," Sweet Today replied.

Shan had a little voice recorder notebook in his hand.

"Does it work?" Lidi inquired.

"Seems to. We thought we'd tell . . . what happened," Shan said, squinting the narrow black eyes in his narrow black face at the firelight. "Each of us. What we—what it seemed like, seems like, to us. So that . . ."

"As a record, yes. In case . . . How funny that it works, though, your notebook. When nothing else does."

"It's voice-activated," Shan said absently. "So. Go on, Gveter."

Gveter finished telling his version of the expedition to the planet's surface. "We didn't even bring back samples," he ended. "I never thought of them."

"Shan went with you, not me," Tai said.

"You did go, and I did," the boy said with a certainty that stopped her. "And we did go outside. And Shan and Gveter were Support, in the lander. And I took samples. They're in the Stasis closet."

"I don't know if Shan was in the lander or not," Gveter said, rubbing his forehead painfully.

"Where would the lander have gone?" Shan said. "Nothing is out there—we're nowhere—outside time, is all I can think— But when one of you tells how they saw it, it seems as if it was that way, but then the next one changes the story, and I . . ."

Oreth shivered, drawing closer to the fire.

"I never believed this damn thing would work," said Lidi, bearlike in the dark cave of her blanket.

"Not understanding it was the trouble," Karth said. "None of us understood how it would work, not even Gveter. Isn't that true?"

"Yes," Gveter said.

"So that if our psychic interaction with it affected the process—"

"Or *is* the process," said Sweet Today, "so far as we're concerned."

"Do you mean," Lidi said in a tone of deep existential disgust, "that we have to *believe* in it to make it work?"

"You have to believe in yourself in order to act, don't you?" Tai said.

"No," the navigator said. "Absolutely not. I don't believe in myself. I *know* some things. Enough to go on."

"An analogy," Gveter offered. "The effective action of a crew depends on the members perceiving themselves as a crew—you could call it believing in the crew, or just *being* it— Right? So, maybe, to churten, we—we conscious ones— maybe it depends on our consciously perceiving ourselves as . . . as transilient—as being in the other place—the destination?"

"We lost our crewness, certainly, for a—are there whiles?" Karth said. "We fell apart."

"We lost the thread," Shan said.

"Lost," Oreth said meditatively, laying another massive, half-weightless log on the fire, volleying sparks up into the chimney, slow stars.

"We lost—what?" Sweet Today asked.

No one answered for a while.

"When I can see the sun through the carpet . . ." Lidi said.

"So can I," Betton said, very low.

"I can see Ve Port," said Rig. "And everything. I can tell you what I can see. I can see Liden if I look. And my room on the *Oneblin*. And—"

"First, Rig," said Sweet Today, "tell us what happened."

"All right," Rig said agreeably. "Hold on to me harder, maba, I start floating. Well, we went to the liberry, me and Asten and Betton, and Betton was Elder Sib, and the adults were on the bridge, and I was going to go to sleep like I do when we naffle-fly, but before I even lay down there was the brown planet and Ve Port and both the suns and everywhere else, and you could see through everything, but Asten couldn't. But I can."

"We never went *anywhere*," Asten said. "Rig tells stories all the time."

"We all tell stories all the time, Asten," Karth said.

"Not dumb ones like Rig's!"

"Even dumber," said Oreth. "What we need . . . What we need is . . ."

"We need to know," Shan said, "what transilience is, and we don't, because we never did it before, nobody ever did it before."

"Not in the flesh," said Lidi.

"We need to know what's—real—what happened, *whether* anything happened—" Tai gestured at the cave of firelight around them and the dark beyond it. "Where are we? Are we here? Where is here? What's the story?"

"We have to tell it," Sweet Today said. "Recount it. Relate it. . . . Like Rig. Asten, how does a story begin?"

"A thousand winters ago, a thousand miles away," the child said; and Shan murmured, "Once upon a time . . ."

"There was a ship called the *Shoby*," said Sweet Today, "on a test flight, trying out the churten, with a crew of ten.

"Their names were Rig, Asten, Betton, Karth, Oreth, Lidi, Tai, Shan, Gveter, and Sweet Today. And they related their story, each one and together. . . ."

There was silence, the silence that was always there, except for the stir and crackle of the fire and the small sounds of their breathing, their movements, until one of them spoke at last, telling the story.

"The boy and his mother," said the light, pure voice, "were the first human beings ever to set foot on that world."

Again the silence; and again a voice.

"Although she wished . . . she realized that she really hoped the thing wouldn't work, because it would make her skills, her whole life, obsolete . . . all the same she really wanted to learn how to use it, too, if she could, if she wasn't too old to learn. . . ."

A long, softly throbbing pause, and another voice.

"They went from world to world, and each time they lost the world they left, lost it in time dilation, their friends getting old and dying while they were in NAFAL flight. If there were a way to live in one's own time, and yet move among the worlds, they wanted to try it. . . ."

"Staking everything on it," the next voice took up the story, "because nothing works except what we give our souls to, nothing's safe except what we put at risk."

A while, a little while; and a voice.

"It was like a game. It was like we were still in the *Shoby* at Ve Port just waiting before we went into NAFAL flight. But it was like we were at the brown planet too. At the same time. And one of them was just pretend, and the other one wasn't, but I didn't know which. So it was like when you pretend in a game. But I didn't want to play. I didn't know how."

Another voice.

"If the churten principle were proved to be applicable to

actual transilience of living, conscious beings, it would be a great event in the mind of his people—for all people. A new understanding. A new partnership. A new way of being in the universe. A wider freedom. . . . He wanted that very much. He wanted to be one of the crew that first formed that partnership, the first people to be able to think this thought, and to . . . to relate it. But also he was afraid of it. Maybe it wasn't a true relation, maybe false, maybe only a dream. He didn't know."

It was not so cold, so dark, at their backs, as they sat round the fire. Was it the waves of Liden, hushing on the sand?

Another voice.

"She thought a lot about her people, too. About guilt, and expiation, and sacrifice. She wanted a lot to be on this flight that might give people—more freedom. But it was different from what she thought it would be. What happened—what *happened* wasn't what mattered. What mattered was that she came to be with people who gave *her* freedom. Without guilt. She wanted to stay with them, to be crew with them. . . . And with her son. Who was the first human being to set foot on an unknown world."

A long silence; but not deep, only as deep as the soft drum of the ship's systems, steady and unconscious as the circulation of the blood.

Another voice.

"They were thoughts in the mind; what else had they ever been? So they could be in Ve and at the brown planet, and desiring flesh and entire spirit, and illusion and reality, all at once, as they'd always been. When he remembered this, his confusion and fear ceased, for he know that they couldn't be lost."

"They got lost. But they found the way," said another voice, soft above the hum and hushing of the ship's systems, in the warm fresh air and light inside the solid walls and hulls.

63

Only nine voices had spoken, and they looked for the tenth; but the tenth had gone to sleep, thumb in mouth.

"That story was told and is yet to be told," the mother said. "Go on. I'll churten here with Rig."

They left those two by the fire, and went to the bridge, and then to the hatches to invite on board a crowd of anxious scientists, engineers, and officials of Ve Port and the Ekumen, whose instruments had been assuring them that the *Shoby* had vanished, forty-four minutes ago, into nonexistence, into silence. "What happened?" they asked. "What happened?" And the Shobies looked at one another and said, "Well, it's quite a story. . . ."

Since his debut in 1977 in John Landsberg's Unearth, Paul Di Filippo's stories have been turning up in Fantasy & Science Fiction, Amazing, and various other s-f magazines with fair regularity, and lately some of them have been finding their way into anthologies and onto the awards ballots. Before devoting himself to full-time writing in 1982 he was, he says, "a textile worker, a COBOL programmer, and a snack-bar attendant at a drive-in that featured X-rated films"—all of which seems to have prepared him well for the sort of jaunty, fiercely contemporary fiction that he prefers to write.

ONE NIGHT IN TELEVISION CITY

PAUL
DI FILIPPO

I'm frictionless, molars, so don't point those flashlights at me. I ain't going nowhere, you can see that clear as hubble. Just like superwire, I got no resistance, so why doncha all just gimme some slack?

What'd you say, molar? Your lifter's got a noisy fan—it's interfering with your signal. How'd I get up here? That's an easy one. I just climbed. But I got a better one for you.

Now that I ain't no Dudley Dendrite anymore, how the fuck am I gonna get down?

Just a few short hours ago it was six o'clock on a Saturday night like any other, and I was sitting in a metamilk bar called The Slak Shak, feeling sorry for myself for a number of good and sufficient reasons. I was down so low there wasn't an angstrom's worth of difference between me and a microbe. You see, I had no sleeve, I had no set, I had no eft. Chances were I wasn't gonna get any of 'em anytime soon, either. The prospect was enough to make me wanna float away on whatever latest toxic corewipe the Shak was offering.

I asked the table for the barlist. It was all the usual bugjuice and yeastsweat, except for a new item called Needlestrength-Nine. I ordered a dose, and it came in a cup of cold frothy milk sprinkled with cinnamon. I downed it all in two gulps, the whole nasty mess of transporter proteins and neurotropins, a stew of long-chain molecules that were some konky biobrujo's idea of blister-packed heaven.

All it did was make me feel like I had a cavity behind my eyes filled with shuttle fuel. My personal sitspecs still looked as lousy as a rat's shaved ass.

That's the trouble with the 'tropes and strobers you can buy in the metamilk bars: they're all kid's stuff, G-rated holobytes. If you want a real slick kick, some black meds, then you got to belong to a set, preferably one with a smash watson boasting a clean labkit. A Fermenta, or Wellcome, or Cetus rig, say. Even an Ortho'll do.

But as I said, I had no set, nor any prospect of being invited into one. Not that I'd leap at an invite to just any old one, you latch. Some of the sets were just too toxic for me.

So there I sat with a skull full of liquid oxygen, feeling just like the Challenger before lift-off, more bummed than before I had zero-balanced my eft on the useless drink. I was licking the cinammon off the rim of the glass when who should slope in but my one buddy, Casio.

Casio was a little younger'n me, about fifteen. He was skinny and white and had more acne than a worker in a dioxin factory. He coulda had skin as clear as anyone else's, but he was always forgetting to use his epicream. He wore a few strands of grafted fiberoptics in his brown hair, an Imipolex-G vest that bubbled constantly like some kinda slime mold, a pair of parchment pants, and a dozen jelly bracelets on his left forearm.

"Hey, Dez," said Casio, rapping knuckles with me, "how's it climbing?"

Casio didn't have no set neither, but it didn't seem to bother him like it bothered me. He was always up, always smiling and happy. Maybe it had to do with his music, which was his whole life. It seemed to give him something he could always fall back on. I had never seen him really down. Sometimes it made me wanna choke the shit outa him.

"Not so good, molar. Life looks emptier'n the belly of a Taiwanese baby with the z-virus craps."

Casio pulled up a seat. "Ain't things working out with Chuckie?"

I groaned. Why I had ever fantasized aloud to Casio about Chuckie and me, I couldn't now say. I musta really been in microgravity that day. "Just forget about Charlotte and me, will you do me that large fave? There's nothing between us, nothing, you latch?"

Casio looked puzzled. "Nothing? Whadda ya mean? The way you talked, I thought she was your best sleeve."

"No, you got it all wrong, molar, we was both wasted, remember . . . ?"

Casio's vest extruded a long wavy stalk that bulged into a ball at its tip before being resorbed. "Gee, Dez, I wish I had known all this before. I been talking you two up as a hot item all around TeeVeeCee."

My heart swelled up big as the bicep on a metasteroid freak and whooshed up into my throat. "No, molar, say it ain't so. . . ."

"Gee, Dez, I'm sorry. . . ."

I was in deep gurry now, all right. I could see it clear as M31 in the hubblescope. Fish entrails up to the nose.

Chuckie was Turbo's sleeve. Turbo was headman of the Body Artists. The Body Artists were the prime set in Television City. I was as the dirt between their perpetually bare toes.

I pushed back my seat. The Slak Shak was too hot now. Everybody knew I floated there.

"Casio, I feel like a walk. Wanna come?"

"Yeah, sure."

T Street—the big north-south boulevard wide as old Park Ave that was Television City's main crawl (it ran from 59th all the way to 72nd—was packed with citizens and greenies, morphs and gullas, all looking for the heart of Saturday night, just like the old song by that growly chigger has it. The sparkle and glitter was all turned up to eleven, but TeeVeeCee looked kinda old to me that night, underneath its amber-red-green-blue neo-neon maquillage. The whole mini-city on the banks of the Hudson was thirty years old now, after all, and though that was nothing compared to the rest of Nuevo York, it was starting to get on. I tried to imagine being nearly twice as old as I was now, and figured I'd be kinda creaky myself by then.

All the scrawls laid down by the sets on any and every blank surface didn't help the city's looks any either. Fast as the cleanup crews sprayed the paint-eating bugs on the graffiti, the sets nozzled more. These were just a few that Casio and I passed:

PUT A CRICK IN YOUR DICK.
STROBE YOUR LOBES.
BOOT IT OR SHOOT IT.
HOLLOW? SWALLOW. FOLLOW.
SIN, ASP! SAID THE SYNAPSE.
BATCH IT, MATCH IT, LATCH IT.
BEAT THE BARRIER!
SNAP THE GAP!
AXE YOUR AXONS.
KEEP YOUR RECEPTORS FILLED.

"Where we going, Dez?" asked Casio, snapping off one of his jelly bracelets for me to munch on.

"Oh, noplace special," I said around a mouthful of sweat-metabolizing symbiote that tasted like strawberries. "We'll just wander around a bit and see what we can see."

All the time I was wondering if I even dared to go home to my scat, if I'd find Turbo and his set waiting there for me, with a word or two to say about me talking so big about his sleeve.

Well, we soon came upon a guy with his car pulled over to the curb with the hood up. He was poking at the ceramic fuel cell with a screwdriver, like he hoped to fix it that way.

"That's a hundred-thirty-two-horsepower Malaysian model, ain't it?" asked Casio.

"Yeah," the guy said morosely.

"I heard they're all worth bugshit."

The guy got mad then and started waving the screwdriver at us. "Get the hell out of here, you nosy punks!"

Casio slid a gold jelly bracelet off his arm, tossed it at the guy, and said, "Run!"

We ran.

Around a corner, we stopped, panting.

"What was it?" I said.

"Nothing too nasty. Just rotten eggs and superstik."

We fell down laughing.

When we were walking again, we tried following a couple of gullas. We could tell by their government-issue suits that they were fresh out of one of the floating midocean relocation camps, and we were hoping to diddle them for some eft. But they talked so funny that we didn't even know how to scam them.

"We go jeepney now up favela way?"

"No, mon, first me wan' some ramen."

"How fix?"

"We loop."

"And be zeks? Don' vex me, dumgulla. You talkin' like a manga now, mon."

After that we tailed a fattie for a while. We couldn't make up our minds if it was a male or female or what. It was dressed in enough billowing silk to outfit a parachute club, and walked with an asexual waddle. It went into the fancy helmsley at 65th to meet its client no doubt.

"I hate those fatties," said Casio. "Why would anyone want to weigh more than what's healthy, if they don't have to?"

"Why would anyone keep his stupid zits if he didn't have to?"

Casio looked hurt. "That's different, Dez. You know I just forget my cream. It's not like I wanna."

I felt bad for hurtin' Casio then. Here he was, my only proxy, keeping me company while I tried to straighten out in my head how I was gonna get trump with Turbo and his set, and I had to go and insult him.

I put an arm around his shoulders. "Sorry, molar. Listen, just wipe it like I never said it, and let's have us a good time. You got any eft?"

"A little. . . ."

"Well, let's spend it! The fluid eft gathers no taxes, es verdad? Should we hit Club GaAs?"

Casio brightened. "Yeah! The Nerveless are playing tonight. Maybe Ginko'll let me sit in."

"Sounds trump. Let's go."

Overhead the wetworkers—both private and government dirty-harrys—cruised by on their lifters, the jetfans blowing hot on our necks, even from their high altitude. Standing in the center of their flying cages, gloved mitts gripping their joystix, with their owleyes on, they roved TeeVeeCee, alert for signs of rumble, bumble, or stumble, whereupon they would swoop down and chill the heat with tingly shockers or even flashlights, should the sitspecs dictate.

Club GaAs occupied a fraction of the million square feet of empty building that had once housed one of the old television networks that had given TeeVeeCee its name. Ever since the free networks had been absorbed, the building had gone begging for tenants. Technically speaking, it was still tenantless, since Club GaAs was squatting there illegally.

At the door we paid the cover to a surly anabolic hulkster and went inside.

Club GaAs had Imipolex-G walls that writhed just like Casio's vest, dancing in random biomorphic ripples and tendrils. On the stage the Nerveless were just setting up, it being still early, only around eight. I had met Ginko only once, but I recognized him from his green skin and leafy hair. Casio went onstage to talk to him, and I sat down at a table near one wall and ordered a cheer-beer.

Casio rejoined me. "Ginko says I can handle the megabops."

The cheer-beer had me relaxing so I had almost forgotten my problems. "That's trump, proxy. Listen, have a cheer-beer —it's your eft."

Casio sat and we talked awhile about the good old days, when we were still kids in high school, taking our daily rations of mnemotropins like good little drudges.

"You remember at graduation, when somebody spiked the refreshments with funky-monkey?"

"Yeah. I never seen so many adults acting like apes before or since. Miz Spencer up on the girders—!"

"Boy, we were so young then."

"I was even younger than you, Dez. I was eleven and you were already twelve, remember?"

"Yeah, but them days are wiped now, Casio. We're adults ourselves now, with big adult probs." All my troubles flooded back to me like ocean waves on the Nevada shoreline as I said this konky bit of wisdom.

Casio was sympathetic, I could fax that much, but he didn't have the answers to my probs any more than I did. So he just stood and said, "Well, Dez, I got to go play now." He took a few steps away from the table and then was snapped back to his seat like he had a rubber band strung to his ass.

"Hold on a millie," I said. "The wall has fused with your vest." I took out my little utility flashlight and lasered the wall pseudopod that had mated with Casio's clothing.

"Thanks, proxy," he said, and then was off.

I sat there nursing the dregs of my cheer-beer while the Nerveless tuned up. When the rickracks were spinning fast and the megabops were humming and everyone had their percussion suits on, they jumped into an original comp, "Efferent Ellie."

Forty-five minutes later, after two more cheer-beers thoughtfully provided by the management to the grateful friend of the band, I was really on the downlink with Casio and the Nerveless. I felt their music surging through me like

73

some sonic 'trope. Tapping my foot, wangle-dangling my head like some myelin-stripped spaz, I was so totally downloading that I didn't even see Turbo and his set slope on into Club GaAs and surround me.

When the song ended and I looked up, there they all were: Turbo and his main sleeve, Chuckie, who had her arm around his waist; Jeeter, Hake, Pablo, Mona, Val, Ziggy, Pepper, Gates, Zane, and a bunch of others I didn't know.

"Hah-hah-hah-how's it climbing, molars?" I said.

They were all as quiet and stone-faced as the holo of an AI with its mimesis circuits out of whack. As for me, I could do nothing but stare.

The Body Artists were all naked save for spandex thongs, he's and she's alike, the better to insure proper extero- and interoceptor input. Their skins were maculated with a blotchy tan giraffe pattern. The definition of every muscle on their trim bods was like *Gray's Anatomy* come to life.

Now, to me, there were no two ways about it: the Body Artists were simply the most trump set in TeeVeeCee. The swiftest, nastiest, downloadingest pack of lobe-strobers ever to walk a wire or scale a pole. Who else were you gonna compare 'em to? The Vectors? A bunch of wussies dreaming their days away in mathspace. (I didn't buy their propaganda about being able to disappear along the fourth dimension either.) The Hardz 'n' Wetz? Nothing but crazy meatgrinders, the negative image of their rivals, the Eunuchs. The Less Than Zeroes? I don't call pissing your pants satori, like they do. The Thumbsuckers? Who wants to be a baby forever? The Boardmen? I can't see cutting yourself up and headbanging just to prove you feel no pain. The Annies? A horde of walking skeletons. The Naked Apes? After seeing our whole faculty under the influence of funky-monkey that day, I had never latched onto that trip. The Young Jungs? Who wants to spend his whole life diving into the racemind?

74

No, the only ones who might just give the Body Artists a run for their eft were the Adonises or the Sapphos, but they had some obvious kinks that blocked my receptors.

So you'll understand how I could feel—even as the center of their threatening stares—a kind of thrill at being in the presence of the assembled Body Artists. If only they had come to ask me to join them, instead of, as was so apparent, being here with the clear intention of wanting to cut my nuts off—

The Nerveless started another song. Casio was too busy to see what was happening with me. Not that he coulda done much anyhow. Turbo sat liquidly down across from me, pulling Chuckie down onto his lap.

"So, Dez," he said, cool as superwire, "I hear you are Chuckie's secret mojoman now."

"No, no way, Turbo, the parity bits got switched on that message all right. There ain't not truth to it, no sir, no way."

"Oh, I see, molar," said Turbo, deliberately twisting things around tighter'n a double helix. "My sleeve Chuckie ain't trump enough for a molar who's as needlestrength as you."

I raised my eyes and caught Chuckie sizing me up with high indifference. Her looks made me feel like I was trying to swallow an avocado pit.

Charlotte Thach was a supertrump Cambodian-Hawaiian chica whose folks had emigrated to TeeVeeCee when the Japs kicked everyone outa the ex-state. Her eyes were green as diskdrive lights, her sweet little tits had nipples the color of pumpkin pie where it starts to brown around the edges.

After she was done sizing me up, she held out one beautiful hand as if to admire her nails or something. Then, without moving a single muscle that I could see, she audibly popped each joint in her fingers in sequence. I could hear it clear above the music.

I gulped down that slimy pit and spoke. "No, Turbo, she's trump enough for anyone."

Turbo leaned closer across Chuckie. "Ah, but that's the prob, molar, Chuckie don't do it with just anyone. In fact, none of the Artists do. Why, if you were to try to ride her, she'd likely snap your cock off. It's Body to Body only, you latch?"

"Yeah, sure, I latch."

75

Turbo straightened up. "Now, the question is, what we gonna do with someone whose head got so big he thought he could tell everyone he was bumpin' pubes with a Body Artist?"

"No disinfo, Turbo, I didn't mean nothin' by it."

"Shut up, I got to think."

While he was thinking, Turbo made all the muscles in his torso move around like snakes under his skin.

After letting me sweat toxins for a while, Turbo said, "I suppose it would satisfy the set's honor if we were to bring you up to the top of the Washington Bridge and toss you off—"

"Oh, holy radwaste, Turbo, my molar, my proxy, I really don't think that's necessary—"

Turbo held up his hand. "But the ecoharrys might arrest us for dumping shit in the river!"

All the Body Artists had a good laugh at that. I tried to join in, but all that came out was a sound like "ekk-ekk-ekk."

"On the other hand," said Turbo, rotating his upraised hand and forearm around a full two-seventy degrees, "if you were to become a Body Artist, then we could let it be known that you were under consideration all along, even when you were making your konky boasts."

"Oh, Turbo, yeah, yeah, you don't know how much—"

Turbo shot to his feet then, launching Chuckie into a series of spontaneous cartwheels all the way across the club.

"Jeeter, Hake! You're in charge of escorting the pledge. Everyone! Back to the nets!"

We blew out of Club GaAs like atmosphere out of a split-open o'neill. My head was spinning around like a Polish space station. I was running with the Body Artists! It was something I could hardly believe. Even though I had no hint of where they were taking me; even though they might be setting me up for something that would wipe me out flatter than my eft-balance—I felt totally frictionless. The whole city looked like a place out of a fantasy or stiffener holo to me, Middle Earth or *Debbie Does Mars*. The air was cool as an AI's paraneurons on my bare arms.

We headed west, toward the riverside park. After a while I started to lag behind the rest. Without a word, Jeeter and Hake picked me up under the arms and continued running with me.

We entered among the trees and continued down empty paths, under dirty sodium lights. I could smell the Hudson off to my right. A dirty-harry buzzed by overhead but didn't stop to bother us.

Under a busted light we halted in darkness. Nobody was breathing heavy but me, and I had been carried the last half mile. Hake and Jeeter placed me down on my own feet.

Someone bent down and tugged open a metal hatch with a snapped hasp set into the walk. The Body Artists descended one by one. Nervous as a kid taking his first 'trope, I went down too, sandwiched between Hake and Jeeter.

Television City occupied a hundred acres of land which had originally sloped down to the Hudson. The eastern half of TeeVeeCee was built on solid ground; the western half stood on a huge platform elevated above the Conrail maglev trains.

Fifteen rungs down, I was staring up at the underside of TeeVeeCee by the light of a few caged safety bulbs, a rusty constellation of rivets in a flaky steel sky.

The ladder terminated at an I-beam wide as my palm. I stepped gingerly off, but still held on to the ladder. I looked down.

A hundred feet below, a lit-up train shot silently by at a hundred-and-eighty MPH.

I started back up the ladder.

"Where to, molar?" asked Hake above me.

"Uh, straight ahead, I guess."

I stepped back onto the girder, took two wobbly Thumb-sucker steps, then carefully lowered myself until I could wrap my arms and legs around the beam.

Hake and Jeeter unpeeled me. Since they had to go single-file, they trotted along carrying me like a trussed pig. I kept my eyes closed and prayed.

I felt them stop. Then they were swinging me like a sack. At the extreme of one swing, they let me go.

Hurtling through the musty air, I wondered how long it would take me to hit the ground or a passing train, and what it would feel like. I wouldn'ta minded so much being a Boardman just then.

It was only a few feet to the net. When I hit, it shot me up a bit. I oscillated a few times until my recoil was absorbed. Only then did I open my eyes.

The Body Artists were standing or lounging around on the woven mesh of graphite cables with perfect balance. Turbo had this radwaste-eating grin on his handsome face.

"Welcome to the nets, Mister Pledge. You didn't do so bad. I seen molars who fainted and fell off the ladder when they first come out below. Maybe you'll make it through tonight after all. C'mon now, follow us."

The Body Artists set off along the nets. Somehow they managed to coordinate and compensate for all the dozens of different impulses traveling along the mesh so that they knew just how to step and not lose their balance. They rode the wavefronts of each other's motions like some kinda aerial surfers.

Me? I managed to crawl along, mostly on all fours.

We reached a platform scabbed onto one of the immense pillars that upheld the city. There the Body Artists had their lab, for batching their black meds.

I hadn't known that Ziggy was the Artists' watson. But once I saw him moving among the chromo-cookers and amino-linkers like a fish in soup, if you know what I mean, it was clear as hubble that he was the biobrujo responsible for stoking the Artists' neural fires.

While Ziggy worked, I had to watch Turbo and Chuckie making out. I knew they were doing it just to blow grit through my scramjets, so I tried not to let it bother me. Even when Chuckie . . . well, never mind exactly what she did, except to say I never knew before it was humanly possible to get into that position.

78

Ziggy finally came over with a cup full of uncut bugjuice.

"Latch on to this, my molar," he said with crickly craftsmanly pride, "and you'll know a little more about what it means to call yourself a B-Artist."

I knew I didn't want to taste the undiluted juice, so I chugged it as fast as I could. Even the aftertaste nearly made me retch.

Half an hour later, I could feel the change.

I stood up and walked out onto the net. Turbo and the others reached down and started yanking it up and down.

I didn't lose my balance. Even when I went to one foot. Then I did a handstand.

"Okay, molar," said Turbo sarcastically, "don't think you're so trump. All we gave you is heightened 'ception, extero, intero, and proprio. Plus a little myofibril booster, and something to damp your fatigue poisons. And it's all as temporary as a whore's kisses. So, let's get down to it."

Turbo set off back along the nets, and I followed.

"No one else?" I asked.

"No, Dez, just us two good proxies."

We retraced our way to the surface. Walking along the I-beam under my own power, I felt like king of the world.

Once again we raced through the streets of Television City. This time I easily kept pace with Turbo. But maybe, I thought, he was letting me, trying to lull me into a false sense of security. I made up my mind to go a little slower in all this.

At last we stood at the southern border of T-City. Before us reared the tallest building in all of old Nuevo York, what used to be old man Trump's very HQ, before he was elected President and got sliced and diced like he did. One hundred and fifty stories' worth of glass and ferrocrete, full of setbacks, crenellations, and ledges.

"Now we're going for a little climb," Turbo said.

"You got to be yanking my rods, molar. It's too smooth."

"Nope, it's not. That's the good thing about these old postmodern buildings. They got the flash and filigree that makes for decent handholds."

Then he shimmied up a drainpipe that led to the second floor faster than I could follow.

But follow I did, my molars, believe me. I kicked off my shoes, and zipped right after him. No disinfo, I was scared, but I was also mad and ecstatic and floating in my own microgravity.

The first fifty stories were frictionless. I kept up with Turbo, matching him hold for hold. When he smiled, I even smiled back.

Little did I know that he was teasing me.

A third of the way up we stopped to rest on a wide ledge. I didn't look down, since I knew that even with my new perfect balance the sight of where I was would be sure to put grit in my jets.

We peered in through the lighted window behind us and saw a cleaning robot busy vacuuming the rugs. We banged on the glass, but couldn't get it to notice us. Then we started up again.

At the halfway mark Turbo started showing off. While I was slowing down, he seemed to have more energy than ever. In the time I took to ascend one story, he squirreled all around me, making faces and busting my chops.

"You're gonna fall now, Dez. I got you up here right where I want you. You ain't never gonna get to lay a finger on Chuckie, you latch? When you hit, there ain't gonna be anything left of you bigger'n a molecule."

And suchlike. I succeeded in ignoring it until he said, "Gee, that Ziggy's getting kinda forgetful lately. Ain't been taking his mnemos. I wonder if he remembered to make sure your dose had the right duration? Be a shame if you maxxed out right now."

"You wouldn't do that . . ." I said, and instinctively looked over my shoulder to confront Turbo.

He was beneath me, hanging by his toes from a ledge, head directed at the ground.

I saw the ground.

80

Television City was all spread out, looking like a one-to-one-hundred-scale model in some holo studio somewhere.

I froze. I heard one of my fingernails crack right in half.

"Whatsamatter, Dez? You lost it yet, or what?"

It was the konky tone of Turbo's voice that unfroze me. I wasn't gonna fall and hear his toxic laugh all the long stories down.

"Race you the rest of the way," I said.

He changed a little then. "No need, proxy, just take it one hold at a time."

So I did.

For seventy-five more stories.

The top of the building boasted a spire surrounded on four sides by a little railed-off platform whose total area was 'bout as big as a bathroom carpet.

I climbed unsteadily over the railing and sat down, dangling my legs over the side. I could already feel the changes inside me, so I wasn't surprised when Turbo said, "It's worn off for real now, Dez. I wouldn't try going down the way we came up, if I was you. Anyway, the harrys should be here soon. The stretch for something like this is only a year with good behavior. Look us up when you get out."

Then he went down, headfirst, waggling his butt at me.

So, like I asked you before.

Now that I ain't no Dudley Dendrite anymore, how the fuck am I gonna get down?

A famous passage in a letter from Raymond Chandler to his agent—quoted below—is perhaps the most scathing parody of generic science fiction ever written. Leave it to the mordant and incisive Barry Malzberg, author of Galaxies, Beyond Apollo, and a host of other remarkable and distinctive science fiction stories, to incorporate every single corrosive phrase of Chandler's mockery in an actual story. The result is not only an astonishing technical stunt but also a wildly funny romp, glittering with manic energy. Beyond any doubt Chandler would have loved it.

PLAYBACK

BARRY N. MALZBERG

Did you ever read what they call Science Fiction. It's a scream. It is written like this: "I checked out with K 19 on Alabaran III, and stepped out through the crummalite hatch on my 22 Model Sirius Hardtop. I cocked the timejector in secondary and waded through the bright blue manda grass. My breath froze into pink pretzels. I flicked on the heat bars and the Brylls ran swiftly on five legs using their other two to send out crylon vibrations. The pressure was almost unbearable, but I caught the range on my wrist computer through the transparent cysicites. I pressed the trigger. The thin violet glow was icecold against the rust-colored mountains. The Brylls shrank to half an inch long and I worked fast stepping on them with the poltext. But it wasn't enough. The sudden brightness swung me around and the Fourth Moon had already risen. I had exactly four seconds to hot up the disintegrator and Google had told me it wasn't enough. He was right." They pay brisk money for this crap?

> Raymond Chandler:
> Letter to H. N. Swanson,
> *Selected Letters of
> Raymond Chandler,*
> edited by Frank McShane

I checked out with K 19 on Alabaran III. On the portico, moving slowly against the cracked and ruined spaces of the enclosure, watching the slow, dangerously signatory implosions from the outer ring, I could feel not only the collapse of the project, but my own, more imminent ruin. *Ruin will not be enough,* Google had warned me. *If it were only a matter of ruin, it would have been accomplished a long time ago. They want to smear us, they want us utterly defaced.*

"What is that supposed to mean?" I said. "What do I do now?"

She said nothing looking back at me, the high panels of her face drawn tightly as if to prohibit speech, block it at the source. They will respond to direct questions but are no good on abstractions, on open-ended cries of despair. As I well know. That should have been all right; all my life the abstract has been well lost. "How much longer?" I said, trying again. "Enough time to get clear?"

K 19 shrugged. In this guise she was a tall and intense young woman, her brain packed with deadly secrets which one by one her mouth would promise to impart . . . but no such knowledge would issue, that was not the program and I would hammer again on those panels to no outcome. "I do not understand the concept," she said. "What is time? What is your conception of that?" A horrid precision now to her step, she moved toward an unshrouded viewplate. "Out there, in here," she said, pointing, "no difference."

She froze in that position. I could see the slow enclave of psychic ice glazing her and then she was silent. In my side pocket the heat bar ticked faintly, sent slivers of warmth through the thin fabric; but I was still fixated on K 19, still touched by the possibility that somewhere in her closed and deadly face there would lurk the answer, an answer to take me from the portico, silence the Brylls. Not the heat bar or the poltext, then. A true answer.

"Do you remember?" I said. "You made a promise—"

"I remember nothing. There is no memory, there is only this."

Looking at her so, locked to that lesser desire which still intimated possibility, I could see that this was truth, came to understand in that concentrated moment that all along there had been nothing else, no imminence, grandeur, possibility or disclosure, only this denial. And knowing that at last, I felt the beginnings of release, the snap of that fine and tensile emotional rope that bound us. Testing the force of that insight, I moved away from her, ducked under the refractory bands cast by the high binding rings, *and stepped out through the crummalite hatch,* seized instantly by the vacuum that snapped and skulked at the perilous enclosure.

Now, against the blurred firmament itself, undefended by the thin expanse of the dome. I could feel the half-forgotten swaddled in those caverns we make, I could feel the awful power of the heavens, understand that what stood between us and retrieval was little more than a set of assumptions, assumptions which at any time could be blotted as thoroughly as K 19 had destroyed whatever compact we had. Knowing this did not strengthen nor change a thing but the acceptance was in itself a kind of control. The Brylls have come a long way, worked hard, dedicated themselves, applied all of their awful technology, but that cunning of effort has not yet succeeded in taking from us all recollection. So we are sport for the trajectory of the Brylls' conquest.

Now and then there are these pure moments of recovery, and outside the enclosure, K 19 still behind, I had another, turned the power *on my 22 Model Sirius Hardtop,* watching the sheaves of light curl from the element, now drawing pure solar heat at reversed amperage, seeking the internal source that we had dragged from the vacuum.

What joys we had from the cosmos before the Brylls! Our Sirian hardtops, galactic entertainments, bustling travel, our dolefully cosmic cries: oh, cascades of stars, nebulae of grandeur thus informing our spirit and possibilities until those Brylls came to show us the real force of universal law and to illustrate the limitations of our own condition. Crammed in the vehicle, feeling the tremors of the engine, I thought too of the easy, gliding weight of the hardtop when it had made fast passage from Peking Festival to the port of Macon, the wharfs of Brooklyn to the Empyrean Tower. Times when I had chanted mantras of speed to the hardtop, before the change,

85

the emergence, the debarkation of the Brylls . . . and these shards of memory were knives, slaughterhouse of memory. *I cocked the timejector in secondary* and felt the rush, the sense of distances opening and then as the hardtop lifted—

I waded through the bright blue manda grass toward the beckoning Bryll, feeling the pull of the mud as I tried to clamber away, retain balance. This more than anything else they enjoy, taking our dignity, making us cartoons, yanking from us the solemnity of our distress and placing us on a flat and colorful map where we deal with pale, exploded forms who may or may not be representative of the Brylls themselves. We do not know if it is submission or some parody of conquest. *My breath froze into pink pretzels* as I squeaked.

Beyond the rise, the ape snickered and pointed; the Sirius fell with a whoop and I could hear the ape's chuckling. "So little," it said in that mechanical voice, as refractory in its burning as the fire beyond the portico. "So little and so strong, so ugly and so nice, so nice and so distressed. What do you want?" They toy with us; if this is our vision of purgatory I think that it must be theirs of transcendence. Here is where they want to go when they die, one might have said, and now all of them through the eons are dead. "Nice!" the ape said and I bounced, then fell to ooze. Stumbling for balance, *I flicked on the heat bars.* They had not plundered before the transfer; in their eagerness to bring me to the pink pretzels they had left weaponry behind and suddenly it was in my hand, the feel of it steady and reassuring.

Yes, I thought. I can at least take the ape. If this is my purgatory, then perhaps I can block their transcendence. We live in small snatches, now and then we are granted a glimpse of recovery. The ape waved with a scanty claw, winking, and then there were others, jolting presences. No longer alone. *The Brylls ran swiftly on five legs* from all directions.

It was as if in my focusing of the weapon I had panicked them, made them show their true aspect. Ringing me on all sides, almost offhandedly, they attacked. I could feel the imminence of their horror and then, once again, the darkness.

"They are treacherous," one said.

"No," I offered. "Listen to this. We are not treacherous. We are driven. You gave us no choice, you gave us at the end no dignity." But having spoken, knew it was unheard, knew that there was no way in which connection could be made, was locked once again in that place so well known to K 19 from which there was no emergence.

"Using the other two to send out crylon vibrations," the ape said, and this time I could see, in the flooding light I could see the bowl of roof, beyond that transparency the stricken and venomous sun, and I tried to move but found myself locked into place. At the edge of vision the ape was talking to something else, oblivious. "They die," one said, "they die and they die and it is not enough."

"Of course it's enough," I said, as if they could hear me. "It's always enough, it was a sufficiency when we began," and tried to wave, tried to show them through the intensity of movement the thorough nature of my distress, but they wouldn't acknowledge me, I might have indeed been dead and they large solemn demons, blank devil and primate, assessing larger goals. "It wasn't enough for Google," it said again, "and it's not enough for you."

The strangulation, as if an arm were laid across my throat. *The pressure was almost unbearable* but the heat bar was there, they still had not taken it through all their insistence. Somehow, yanked to a seated position, I felt the pain seize me like a fist *but I caught the range on my wrist computer* and said, "Listen here! Listen to me! You must not turn away from this, we suspire, we are creatures, we live and suffer. *Through the transparent cysicites* of the atmosphere I felt as if I had caught their attention, told myself that I had their attention at last, could somehow break through.

"You've broken us," I said. "You've done it now."

"It's never enough—" The gorilla moved deliberately, its companion turning now.

The Brylls were coming.

I pressed the trigger.

"Now what?" K 19 said.

She lay against me in terrain like knives, ice and slice sending tender, necessary slivers of pain, the two of us stretched one by one on heavy mesh like metal. We were in an enclosure; the air stale *and heavy, and the thin violet glow was ice-cold against the rust-colored mountains* in the distance.

"I don't know," I said. Her skin lay damp and open under my fingers, rising in small response as I clutched. "We're somewhere else now. We've been taken away."

"What did we do?"

"We were taken. They turned our breath into pink pretzels."

"Yes, but what did we *do?*" Once we had lain together in transaction, hovering, mild connection, but now, even as I felt her stillness, it was as if this had not happened. Far from me, distilling loss with every breath, K 19 said, "You have destroyed us."

"We were already destroyed."

"My name is Linda. Call me that, give me my name."

"It was over, Linda. Wherever we are, whatever has been done, it was over."

I could feel the stirring and then there were many sounds, perspective cleared, breath again began to pretzel. Looking toward the sounds, I could see the little forms, could see them scuttle, *could see the Brylls shrank to half an inch long*, hopping, scuttling. They ringed us with the eagerness of their necessity, showed us their incessancy.

"What is it?" Linda said. "Where are they?"

I pointed, drew the line of her attention, and then with her breath, her first frozen and intense knowledge, I reacted instinctively, did what some of us had tried at the beginning, *and I worked fast, stepping on them,* lunging somehow to a

standing position. Linda screamed as she saw what I was doing, pointed at the rust-colored sky, and I ignored the heat
bars, consigned them to darkness along with the rest of my
life, no transaction left now, and began to fight *with the
poltex;* the small rubber flange opening like a petal as I beat at
them. If this was to be the final battle (and it was, my time
was over, I knew that now), it would be as deprived of dignity
as the rest but at least I could right the balance, struggle on.
Even as Linda tried pathetically to crawl away, I found myself
pitched against them, grunting, heaving with that sole
weapon left, seeing them pulp, listening to their brisk and
intermittent cries as some—but not too many—of them died.

But it wasn't enough.

The sudden brightness swung me around and Linda, the
mask clamped tightly, was holding the heat bar, aiming at me,
maniacal and concentrated laughter pouring through.

Pouring through as fuel of my destruction.

And it was at that moment, then, and not an instant earlier
nor a flash later, that I came to understand what had happened, the true nature of the Brylls, the deadly and insistent
nature of their circumstance and plans.

"And the Fourth Moon had already risen," the thing in the
mask said, "and it was time then, time for us if not for you
and it would always in that extreme be enough."

If I had understood what was happening, I might have *had
exactly four seconds to hot up the disintegrator* of the heat bar.

But even then—

"Google had told me it wasn't enough," I said. I believe I
had lost control. I believe I had really lost control. That flush
of abandonment, the surge of separation, the conviction of
utter disaster—

"Not for you," the thing that had been Linda K 19 said.
"Not for you, perhaps. But it is for us."

He was right.

New Jersey, 1987

M. J. Engh's striking first novel, Arslan, *appeared as an undistinguished-looking paperback original in 1976, to practically no acclaim. But against the odds it established and maintained a loyal following for many years, and finally achieved an improbable apotheosis a decade later when it was republished in hardcover, something that happens to perhaps one book out of ten thousand. She has since written a second novel,* Wheel of the Winds, *and a handful of short stories, of which this—a strong, uncompromising, beautifully told account of prehistoric epiphany—is one of her finest.*

MOON BLOOD

M. J.
ENGH

When the moon begins to empty, moon people go into the house. Moonlight is different from sunlight, and moon blood is different from wound blood. Inside they sing, and outside the others sing. It is a bad time, because the moon people are inside—all but the mothers with babies on their hips—and wild things are hunting. It is a good time, because of the singing and the blood.

In the house, there is more than singing. I have been in the house, and I know.

When the moon is filling, we take grass and sticks and make the house ready. We can all help do that, putting new grass and new sticks where old ones have fallen or broken or blown away. But only moon people can go inside.

When the moon people come out, sometimes one of them is still full. She does not go into the house next time, not for many times. When she is ready, she makes a new house. She goes into it with one of the aunts. And when she empties, there is a baby in the blood. After that, we take down the new house.

We were playing in the grass, I and my friend. There was a lioness hunting in the grass, but we were playing and did not see her, and did not smell her because of our own smell. The moon people were digging, and they called to us. My friend ran. I ran, but the lioness caught me. The moon people threw their digging sticks at her and roared, and some of them poked at her with sticks, and they pulled me and carried me, and we came home. They licked my wounds and sang to me. When the others came home from hunting, my father gave me a fat lizard, but I was too hurt to eat it.

Home is a good place. There are big rocks. There are trees, not many, but enough for all of us to climb at once. The leaves are good for shade, but not to eat; they make us hurt inside. But sometimes the trees make flowers, which are sweet and good, and later they make good fruit. Birds come to eat these things too, and sometimes we catch a bird. There are good branches to make sticks. Toward the sunrise is grass for a long way, good digging, good hunting. Toward the sunset is a good water place. Farther that way is where the trees are— many trees together, not like our home trees. Hairy people live there.

We can see a long way from home, we can hear and smell, we can hide among our rocks or in our trees, we are near to good digging and good hunting, we know where the water places are. When the digging is good, when the hunting is good, when we have plenty of things to eat, we hide them between the rocks. The big rocks are warm to lie on in the night. When it rains, we go under our trees. When it rains harder, we go under the rocks. It is a very good place.

But when I was little, we were in a different place, nearer to the trees, and that was a good place too. We went under the trees and ate fruit. There was always fruit there. But there were many hairy people, too many. They fought each other, troop against troop, and they fought us. I had a mother then. One time we were fighting hairy people and they chased us. My mother turned to fight, and they caught her and hurt her. After that we did not go under the trees so often. We licked my mother's wounds, but after a while she died. Then most of us left that home place and came here. We do not get much fruit now, except when we sleep. When I sleep, I eat fruit, play with my friend, snuggle with my mother. But the lioness is still hunting. Sometimes she catches me in my sleep, and I wake up and cry. Then my father snuggles me, or one of the aunts.

When the moon people go to dig, the others go hunting. I used to go sometimes with my father, before the lioness. Hunting is when we go a long way and find things to eat and carry them home. When we come near to wild things, we throw sticks at them, and good stones, and chase them, unless they are too big, and sometimes we catch them. Mostly we catch lizards, mice, running birds, fawns, turtles. We find snails, eggs, nests of young things. When the water is low in the water places, we go in and catch fish along the edges. We eat some things, we carry some home. We find termites, fruit, good leaves, bugs. Mostly we eat those where we find them. We walk a long way, going and coming. When the sun is high, we sit down. We scratch and pick each other and eat bugs. Some of us play, some of us sleep. I liked to pick in my father's hair. He would reach up and rub my hand with his hand while I picked. That was before the lioness.

When the sun is low, the others come home. The moon people have been digging in the digging places. They have the babies with them, and the little ones too young to run fast or walk far. Young ones like me and my friend go sometimes with the moon people, sometimes with the others. The moon people give roots and bulbs and grubs and many good things, and the others give what they have carried home.

That was before the lioness, and before the dry time. After the lioness, I could not go far. My father still brought me things to eat. But when the grass began to die, the bad time began. In the water places, the water was very low. First that was good, because many wild things came to drink, and because we caught fish. I could still catch fish. But it was bad, because many lions hunted at the water places too, hyenas, other wild things that kill. Then most of the water places were dry, and the grass died. Wild things began to go away. The ground was hard—hard for the moon people to dig. When the others went hunting, they went farther away. Some days —many days—they did not come home. My father is a good hunter. When he came home, he always brought me something. But when the grass was dead and most of the wild things had gone away, sometimes what he brought me was only empty snail shells, bright rocks, bones.

We are different from wild things, because we bleed moon blood. A lioness is strong, she can kill, she can make cubs, but she does not bleed. We bleed; we fill and empty like the moon. The others do not bleed, except from wounds, but they are us too, they are our friends and our fathers. We play together and eat together, we pick each other and snuggle each other and give each other things. When the moon people dig, the others hunt. When the moon people sing, the others sing. When the moon people make digging sticks, the others make throwing sticks. They are not wild things. But I was afraid when they would not let me eat.

The sky was bright. There was no rain. The grass was dead. Most of the others went hunting and did not come back. Some of the moon people went with them. Nobody came back, not for many days. My father did not come back to snuggle me and give me things. I could not go far, since the lioness. Everything smelled dusty. The water was very low in the good water place. All the other water places were dry. A few of the others had stayed. Wild things were easy to catch, because they were weak, but not easy to keep. The lions had gone away, but there were still hyenas. Sometimes there were dogs. I was not much good, and there was not much to eat. The others would not give me anything. There was one with a crooked arm, who had not gone away. My father could throw a stick better, but this one was strong. One of the aunts gave me a gourd with grubs in it, and the crooked-arm took it away from me and hit me and ate the grubs. He wanted to hit me more, but the moon people put me in the house.

Nobody goes into the house except moon people, and they only go in when the full moon begins to empty. I was too young, I did not bleed yet, and it was not emptying time. I was afraid in the house, because there was nobody there. It smelled wrong, and I could not hear much or see much, because of the walls. The house is made against the rocks, so one side of it is all rock. The rest is sticks and grass, and sunlight comes through in little bits, like sunlight coming through many trees. To go inside, moon people lift up some of the grass and crawl under. When the wind blew, it made a different noise. I sat in the house and watched the shadows. One of the moon people brought me a gourd with water in it, and some dry roots, but she did not stay. The moon was empty.

Inside the house there were many sticks. When moon people are singing in the house, that is when they make digging sticks. There were unfinished sticks, broken sticks, pieces broken off to make the right shape. I tried to dig, but it was not good digging there. The ground was hard, with rocks in it, and little stones. I took a stone in my hand, and that felt good.

When the light died, it was very dark in the house. In the dark time, when the moon is empty, is a good time to snuggle. After we scratch and pick each other, we lie close together. Babies snuggle with their mothers, mothers and fathers snuggle together and play, aunts lie together, the others lie together or one by one, and we young ones lie together. In the house there was nobody.

I wanted to bleed. I would be one of the moon people then, the moon would be full and emptying and so would I. The house would be full. I wanted so hard, the wanting hurt me inside. I squeezed the stone in my hand, I rocked back and forth and cried and began to sing. I sang all alone. That was a bad singing.

When the sun was going up, there was noise outside. I looked between the sticks. A troop of hairy people was coming. Hairy people are not wild things because they bleed, they go in troops, sometimes they use sticks, they play, they make babies. But they are not us. They do not make a house. They do not sing. They do not use gourds to carry things. They do not make digging sticks. They are hairy all over. Their hands go on the ground when they walk. I go like that, since the

95

lioness. But I am not hairy, and I will bleed by the moon. Hairy people bleed, but not by the moon.

The others roared at the hairy people. The moon people roared. The hairy people roared, and some of them hit the ground with sticks.

Good throwing sticks are for hunting, not fighting. Sometimes the others fight with sticks, but not their good throwing sticks. So I knew this was a bad fight. Everybody threw everything, hit with everything, bit, tore. I had a stone in my hand. But nobody came to the house. They all ran toward the sun, fighting and roaring and crying. There were many hairy people, more than us.

Nobody came back. When the sun was high, I came out of the house. There was no water left in my gourd, so I took it and went down to the good water place. But the water was gone. I saw where wild things had dug, and moon people. I licked inside my gourd.

Everything smelled dusty. Everything smelled hot. I had a stone in my hand, and I hit the ground with it. I was hurting and I did not know what to do. I was afraid to sing loud—afraid of wild things, afraid of hairy people, afraid of the crooked-arm who would not let me eat—but I rocked myself back and forth and hit the ground and the rocks around me and sang very softly. It was bad to sing alone, but not so bad as not singing.

There was a round stone on the ground there, smooth and dark and dusty. I hit it with my stone, and it broke open. Inside, it was bright like water. I touched it. It was smooth like water running over my fingers, smooth as sleek hair, smooth as a fish when I rub it the right way, smoother than any stone I had ever touched. I put down my old stone and took the broken pieces, one in each hand. That felt good. One of them was curved just so, like a piece of gourd or eggshell, but thicker, with a knob on one side. They were good to hold, and good to look at. The edges where they broke apart were sharp. I rubbed one edge against my gourd, and the stone bit

96

the gourd—bit through it like a sharp tooth, fast and smooth and easy. I laughed.

There was a broken digging stick, where the moon people had been digging for water. I bit the stick with my new stone. I bit the ground with it. Then I began to dig.

It was better than a digging stick—sharp and hard and curved, sharper and bigger than any tooth. I dug and scraped the ground away. Once the stone bit me, and my fingers were wet with blood. Then I dug more, and they were wet with water, too. Then there was water in the bottom of where I was digging, so I took some in my gourd and drank. That was good. But there was not much water. I dug more, but my stone was not so sharp now. I dug with the other piece, but it broke.

I looked for more good stones. There were some that looked right—smooth and dark like my biting stone before I broke it. But I smelled people and heard people coming. I was glad, but I was afraid, because of the crooked-arm who had hit me. I took the pieces of broken stone and went behind a tree. Some moon people came. They saw the water and the digging, and they called. So I came out.

They were glad, because I was there and because of the water. I showed them my biting stones and how I dug. We drank, and we laughed, and we called for the rest of us. They all came then, and drank, and they picked in my hair and snuggled me. I showed them what I did; I took a stone and hit a round stone until it broke, and we all laughed. I showed them how to use the new biting stones. Then we went home. We carried our new stones, and we sang together. That was a good singing.

But there were not many of us now, only my friend I used to play with, one of the aunts, a mother with her baby, a mother with little ones—one that was hers and one whose mother had died. None of the others had come home.

The moon began to fill. Every day we went to the water place and dug. I found more stones that looked right. Some of them we broke to make new biting stones. Some of them we took home, and the moon people put them in the house.

We were hungry all the time. But we were glad because of the biting stones. We bit the ground where it was too hard for digging sticks, and found more grubs and more roots, and ate them. First the aunt did that, then we all did it. My friend climbed a tree and bit off little branches with his stone, and we laughed.

We saw hairy people a long way off, but they went toward the sunset. We chewed old bones and little branches, and ate leaves from our trees, and we hurt inside. Then one of the little ones died—the one whose mother had died before—so for a while we had enough to eat. We cracked the new bones and ate the marrow inside. That was good.

The moon was almost full. We bit through the skin of the trees with our biting stones and ate the inside skin. I ate, but I hurt inside, worse and worse. The aunt smelled me and laughed.

When the moon was full, the moon people went into the house, all but the mother with the baby on her hip. They took me with them. I was afraid to go into the house again. I remembered the smell and the way the wind sounded and how dark it was in the nighttime. But the moon people would not let me stay outside.

We were not many in the house, only me and the aunt and the other mother. When we sang, it was not a loud singing. Outside, there was nobody to sing but the baby's mother and my friend and the little one, who was too young to know how to sing much. The moon people began to bleed, first the mother and then the aunt. I did not bleed yet, but I was full, I felt it inside me.

The aunt had brought many stones from the water place. We sang, and we worked. We sang and made digging sticks. We sang and made biting stones. Biting stones are harder to make. Sometimes the stones break wrong, sometimes they do not break, sometimes we hurt our hands. For the biting stones, we sang new songs. The moon people bled. The moon was emptying. Then it began to rain.

It did not rain much. This time we had not put new grass on the house, but no rain came in. It made a strange noise on the grass over our heads, different from the noise of rain on trees. I looked between the sticks and saw my friend in the rain, licking his hands and laughing. I wanted to go out and play with him in the rain, but the moon people stopped me.

At night it was very dark. I looked between the sticks, but I could not see the moon. It rained again, and this time water came through the grass in places. When the sunlight was bright again, we sang and worked.

Outside, they were not singing. We heard them climbing the trees outside, and then we heard them calling. I looked out between the sticks, and after a while I saw some of the others coming home—my father and another.

I went out. The moon people did not go out, because they were still bleeding, it was still house time for them. But I had not bled yet, and the moon people did not stop me. We called and laughed, I and my father, and we came together and touched each other and laughed. He gave me his empty gourd, because he had nothing else to give. I showed him my good biting stones. I showed him how we bit the ground, how we bit the trees to find bugs and grubs inside and the sweet inside skin. The baby was still alive. Some of the grass looked green in places. My friend came to me. It was different now, because I had been in the house in the emptying time. I smelled of moon blood.

Then the other one came near to me. It was the crooked-arm who had not let me eat, that time before. He looked at me and he looked at the cracked bones of the little one. He laughed. I took a piece of bone to chew on. He took a stone in his hand and hit me. People fight with sticks sometimes, but when they hit with stones, that is for killing.

My father is a good hunter, but that one was stronger. I heard fighting, but I could not see much for a while. There was blood in my eyes, and when I tried to see, it was like

looking at the sun, and my head hurt very much. Something
fell on me and lay across me. It was my father. His breath
made a loud noise in my ear. His arm was over my arm.
Through the blood, I could see the other coming at us. He
had a big stone in his hands, a stone to pound and break with.
I felt my father move, and I moved too. There were biting
stones there, the ones I had been showing to my father. I got
one in my hand. And when the big stone came down at us, I
lifted my stone and it bit his crooked arm and he cried very
loud.

Wound blood is what comes when wild things bite, when
claws tear, when stones scrape or sticks poke very hard. But
my stone was different. It did not scrape skin or pound it. It
bit like a wild thing, like a lioness, like a hunting lioness that
kills.

My father took another biting stone and began to hit with
it. I hit too, but I could not do much. All the rest of us roared,
and the other cried and fought and died.

Wound blood is different from moon blood. My head was
bleeding, but the crooked-arm bled more. The smell of the
blood was very strong. My head hurt, and I felt something
change inside me. I put my hand between my legs and found
moon blood. I looked at it for a while.

Moon people were looking out from the house. I was one of
them now. I would go back in to finish my bleeding. I took
my biting stone and touched its edge with my fingers where it
was already wet with blood. So now there were two kinds of
blood on it together.

My friend and the baby's mother were already pulling at
the dead one. My father gave them his biting stone and they
began to use it. So now we would not be hungry.

I showed my father the moon blood on my hand. We
looked at each other, I and my father, and then we began to
sing. That was a different singing.

John Landsberg describes himself as "a practicing family physician, an avid drummer, an amateur filmmaker, and a not-quite-ripping body boarder." He is also, I think, the only contributor to this Universe *who once published a professional science fiction magazine himself: the short-lived and estimable* Unearth, *which he founded in 1977 with Jonathan Ostrowsky.* Unearth *billed itself "the Magazine of Science Fiction Discoveries," not an inaccurate cognomen, considering that among the writers it discovered were James P. Blaylock, Somtow Sucharitkul, and William Gibson.*

Now Dr. Landsberg makes his own bid to become a science fiction discovery. He has already had two short stories published in Fantasy & Science Fiction, *and now he makes a distinguished debut in the longer lengths with this crisp and searching novelet of alien contact and inner conflict.*

AND OF THE EARTH, A WOMB

JOHN M. LANDSBERG

McManus hears the creak of leather behind him as Marc rises from an armchair. In front of him, the window chatters and hums under the onslaught of a freak rainstorm that slashes across the Arizona landscape, obscuring the boxy military buildings that comprise his usual view.

"Too bad it hasn't cooled things off," Marc says.

"I know you hate having this mission postponed," McManus replies. He stares into the rain, but his thoughts soar far above it, and suddenly, in the brief pause before Marc can answer, in the space of a single indrawn breath, he is captivated by an image of the creature they will capture. Beyond the rain, beyond the somber clouds, beyond even the farthest reaches of blue sky, he sees it suspended in orbit: a mottled brown globe.

But a *living* globe, twice as large as a human—and now it is falling. Still outside the atmosphere, aflame with the unimpeded rays of the sun, the faceless, purposeful sphere burns a path Earthward through the black vacuum. On all sides it is flanked by thousands, millions, of its kind—scaly brown globes that crowd the skies around the much larger blue globe beneath them, a planet where billions of humans have stood siege for years under this alien rain, seldom witnessing it directly, but always sensing its inexorable, malevolent weight above their heads.

"It'll be clear tomorrow," Marc says. "And then I'll nab one for you."

Marc's words draw McManus back. His eyes shift focus and catch sight of himself in the window, his reflection floating on waves of dark rain. Do I always wear such a serious expression? he wonders. He forces his still-black eyebrows upward to a more relaxed position and combs both hands through the gray at his temples, then pauses a moment to press his hands over his eyes. When he releases the pressure, he feels a momentary, artificial sense of relief, but the window still mirrors the same pensive look in his slate-colored eyes.

He swivels his chair around. Standing in front of his desk is a tall young man with the easy stance and eager grin that were once his own.

"Good luck, Marc," he says.

"No luck needed, Dad, but thanks."

McManus rises and steps around the desk. Clasping his arms tightly around his son, he is gratified to feel the embrace warmly returned. The irony of living so close together, he thinks, is that there are too few excuses for doing this.

Marc breaks off the hug. "Say there, General, you aren't thinking there's something special about this mission, are you?"

McManus smiles and shrugs. "I just can't believe it's finally happening. Too bad I can't fly this one myself."

"Sorry, Dad," Marc says on his way out. "But I'll tell you all about it tomorrow night. You and Mom are coming over for dinner."

"I suppose you expect me to eat your cooking," McManus calls as Marc disappears behind the closing door. His vision blurs for a moment, as if trying to focus through the wooden barrier into the hall where Marc is walking away. He feels his smile fade.

Returning to his chair, he swivels away from the empty office to stare again into the charcoal clouds. His eyes narrow against the flash of a nearby lightning bolt. Seconds later, thunder rumbles through the room, and his thoughts ride the sound back through the years to his final combat mission:

The sonic boom bursts in his ears as one of the chase planes moves ahead and peels off to assume a flanking position.

McManus tenses his right arm, pitting the muscles against one another. Agonist and antagonist are now locked in perfect isometric balance. Thus he controls the hand that controls the fiery scream of the jets.

Modulating the flow of energy, he shifts the muscular balance away from equilibrium: He charges the extensors marginally more than the flexors, easing the throttle stick forward a few millimeters, firing the jets still hotter.

Just below his line of sight, caught now in his lower peripheral vision, lies an array of numbers and letters—a glowing green computer display suspended on the inner surface of his closed visor. The data seems to float in midair. To the right of center he sees: AIRSPEED 2057 KM/HR. Below that: TARGET RANGE, telling the distance at just over twenty-one kilometers. The range reading is accurate to within one meter, although the last two numbers change so rapidly they are only a blur. The target, still unseen, helps to close the gap by adding its own velocity to his; their combined speeds fling them together at nearly one kilometer every second.

His flight path a true vertical, McManus is in effect lying on his back in the contoured seat, peering straight upward into nothingness, the nothingness of a blank screen of white clouds. Just behind that screen, hundreds of alien beings plunge toward Earth. They are the target. In seconds, he will face them alone.

He narrows his eyes and clenches his teeth in anticipation, and an icy shock jolts the space below his heart when he sees the aliens pierce the clouds. As if magical, they suddenly fleck the entire sky above, pinpoints of blackness blossoming beneath the featureless white blanket. Seen this way, they mimic a photographic negative of the heavens at night: black stars against a white sky.

His stomach leaps, wrenched by a blend of anger, fear, and *yearning*. Every one of his missions against the aliens has been colored by this feeling, this confused stew of emotions that rises in response to a deadly, implacable unknown, and yet demands answers, demands discourse, demands to understand who these creatures are and why they have come here to kill instead of communicate—curses them for crossing the stars in hatred rather than to help answer the great questions of existence. The feeling hits him frequently, disrupting his thoughts during the day, jerking him out of the deepest sleep at night, but it is always strongest at this moment, this crucial point in a mission, just when there is no time to ponder it. No time to think. *But this time*—

—this is the last scheduled mission of his career.

Pushing the stick forward, he races ahead to meet the aliens.

"Colonel! What's wrong?"

"Nothing, Max," he radios to his wing man. "Don't break the pattern. Just getting a closer look, then I'll hook up again."

"But, Zan—"

"Don't tell me. It's dangerous."

And then he is among them, among hundreds of aliens filling the sky. It is the first time he has ever seen a group from within. Few humans have ever been this close to the huge, tumbling brown globes they have chosen to call Orbs.

Reversing direction, he joins their downward plunge to Earth . . . and for a sudden frozen fraction of a heartbeat, as he sees nothing else in the world but the Orbs around him, his mind empties of human thought, and he feels something *joyous* in their fall—*and he becomes one of them.*

In almost the same instant, before it can attain any meaning, before it can grow into a *vision*, the feeling passes.

There is no time to do more than gasp a quick breath, no time even to wonder what happened. Accelerating downward, he speeds ahead of the Orbs, shrinking them to black pin-points behind and above him once more. Turning, he resumes his climb, to face them again.

"Melpomene, begin arm mines end," he says.

Melpomene, his on-board computer, prints a red answer on his visor as it intones the words into his ear: MINES ARMED.

Relentlessly falling, the alien black pinpoints have again swelled into brown globes overhead. McManus throttles back, then yaws and rolls away from his vertical climb, deforming his flight path into a tight horizontal spiral. One wingtip now points down at the ground, the other up at the Orbs. Centrifugal force crushes him into his seat, but he knows it will fade as he widens the pattern, riding farther and farther out the arm of the spiral.

To his left, the Earth spins dizzyingly, far below. To his right, the Orbs drop like stones.

"Melpomene, begin deploy mines end," he says.

Behind the plane Melpomene strings a floating spiral of mines, each ejected with the exact velocity to stop it dead in the sky. They hang almost motionless in midair.

MINES DEPLOYED, the computer says at last.

He rolls ninety degrees and clears to a safe distance. Hovering, he gazes at the mines suspended in the sky like buoyant pearls the size of beach balls. Above, the Orbs tumble down-ward like spherical brown meteors. As always, he is amazed that they can fall so peacefully, even though they *must* be aware of their fate. And as always, he marvels at the strange beauty of this frightening ballet.

The sky catches flame as the rain of Orbs ignites the prox-imity-fused mines. Tongues of fire lick the clouds. Seconds later the shock waves, with a roar like the yell of a giant, buffet his plane. The hull temperature peaks at nearly one hundred eighty degrees, then gradually slides down to a more normal fifteen.

McManus takes his first deep breath in ten minutes. The

Orbs are gone—disintegrated. A few mines still dot the sky. He blasts them with his lasers.

ALL ORBS AND MINES DESTROYED.

"Thanks, Melpomene." The blue words blink off. "Melpomene, did I ever ask if you understand why I named you after the Muse of Tragedy?"

QUESTION NOT FORMATTED.

"No, I guess not."

How many this time? he wonders. Melpomene could give him a body count, but as usual, he hasn't the heart to ask. The answer would not help him anyway, because his real question is *why?* On such questions, the kind for which he most needs answers, Melpomene has nothing to offer.

A second flash of lightning only partially wakes him to the present. Ghostly images of exploding Orbs overlay the office that has delimited his professional world since he assumed command of the base three years ago. Trailing thunder, not quite as loud this time, jolts him, and the walls adorned with his linguistics and philosophy diplomas, his Distinguished Flying Cross and his Purple Heart, gradually solidify and come clear in his vision.

Four years, he thinks ruefully. Four wasted years. Just look at us: We have been so conditioned by our disastrous attempts to capture an Orb on the ground, and by the eventual perfection of our air defenses, that we have been lulled into thinking we only had to keep mining the skies until they got tired of it and went away. So what if we can't understand why they would travel across the universe to commit suicide above our planet? If that's what they want to do, why not let them?

We think we know these creatures, but all we really know is not to let them land: They are too deadly, and too hard to kill, once they touch ground. And once killed or captured, they simply dissolve.

But tomorrow that will change. Once we get an Orb into that room, we may be able to take our first real step toward understanding them.

Restless with anticipation, he punches a button, and for perhaps the hundredth time runs the tape of Luna's last transmission. Over the years he has been drawn again and again to stare, incredulous and bewildered, at these images of wanton destruction:

The spherical brown aliens, raining down from their orbiting battle cruisers, crash into the moon's surface unharmed, then unfold to become horizontal cylinders. Sprouting from each end, dozens of pseudopods fling the creatures toward the colony, then serve as brutal weapons. Luna's meteor-resistant walls shatter like papier-mâché under their bullwhip attacks.

Once inside, the Orbs race down the walkways, flinging people aside like dolls, or crushing them as they pass. In the frenzy of killing they emit a shrill, warbling shriek, an eerie keening that raises the hairs on the back of McManus's neck. And when all the air has been sucked into the void, and people without spacesuits suffocate and die, the Orbs go on killing the suited ones in airless silence.

McManus knows every frame, every burst of static, every splash of blood, but still he watches until the last camera is knocked aside and the tape lurches to an abrupt end in a screen full of hissing snow.

On his way out, he glances into the tracking room. The radar displays hundreds of gargantuan battle cruisers orbiting Earth about one hundred forty kilometers up. Occasionally one of them, apparently having discharged its entire contingent of Orbs, pulls out.

He knows without looking that another always takes its place.

II

Megan kisses him on the tip of the nose and shoves a vegetable peeler into his hand. "If you want dinner, you can get to work on those," she says, waving a paring knife at four small potatoes on the kitchen table. "So. How was the meeting today?"

"Terrible. Boring." He flicks a piece of potato peel onto the floor accidentally. "We've been over the same ground a dozen times. But it *was* our last briefing before we get our hands on the Orb. It's just . . ."

"It's just what?"

He thinks of the meeting: his entire Intelligence team crowded into their largest conference room, each member of the team merely reiterating established data and plans. Net effect: a final, superfluous assurance that the containment room is ready, and that every procedure for establishing contact is detailed on an elaborate schedule.

"It's just what?" Megan says again.

"It's just marking time, and I've had too many years of that." He puts aside a peeled potato. "How was your day?"

"Got a letter from Jessamyn," she says.

"Oh? How's she doing?"

"Not bad. Except still no tenure. They claim they can't give it to her because of budget cutbacks, which they blame on the war, as usual."

"Well, it will come eventually."

"That's right. I keep telling her to be patient. She's only twenty-six."

He smiles. "We were never patient at that age."

"Mmm, I guess not." Her knife clicks against the counter as she trims a pork chop. "And I talked to Marc. He said something about a scoop."

"Right. I told you about it—I guess a while ago. We built a scoop under an F-181C. It leads into the bomb bay."

"I remember. But I was wondering—once he scoops up this Orb, won't it just dissolve?"

"Good question. Norma's theory is that if we catch one falling, before it hits the ground, it will be in a different phase of its life cycle, and might not be able to dissolve. We're just hoping."

"But is it really that important to talk to an Orb?"

"Important?" He is stunned. "I can't believe you're asking

me that. Don't you wonder what they want from us, why they keep coming—why they won't *talk* to us?"

"Of course I wonder," she says. "I only mean it's been four years, and it seems like if they wanted to talk they would have done it by now. I just can't imagine they're ever going to."

"They have to!" he says, and without warning a deeply buried memory surfaces. "Megan, when I was two years old" —and he realizes he has never remembered this before, has never told anyone about it—"when I was two, I looked up one night and saw the stars, and—and they were the most beautiful thing I had ever seen—the most beautiful thing I *have* ever seen. And I put my hand up, and it wouldn't reach. I couldn't touch them. I closed my fingers and my hand was empty. And I cried all night. My parents couldn't understand why I was crying, and I couldn't explain." He hesitates. "My God, I can't believe I never—never told you that."

She crosses to the table and takes him in her arms. He is amazed to feel himself trembling, but she strokes his hair and he begins to relax.

"I can't believe they don't wonder, too," he says softly.

"Wonder about what?"

"About everything."

On the walls around them, shadows leap and dance. "What's that?" she says. "Lightning?"

He searches the sky through the kitchen window. "Not lightning," he says, and they run out into the backyard.

High overhead, the stars themselves seem to be exploding. A group of Orbs is falling toward the woods around their house, and the Air Force is wiping them out. Hundreds of flashes of light pierce the sky, obscuring the sight of any actual stars.

Scattered among the brilliant white blasts of the sky mines, scores of smaller flashes color the gaps. McManus watches in awe. From his plane, in battle, it never looked like this. He never perceived, through the blinding flames of the sky mines, this rainbow display of burning Orbs.

111

He looks down at Megan. The delicate angles of her up-turned face seem to tremble in the splashes of light.

"Don't worry," he says, "they won't come near us."

She turns to him with wide eyes, and he realizes that, for the first time, she has some understanding of what he felt when he flew beneath the rain of Orbs, what he still feels in his need to talk to them. But there is something more in her expression.

"Megan," he says, "what is it?"

"I don't know why, but somehow I just suddenly got the feeling that you want to go in there, don't you?"

He is startled. A human being entering the containment room with the Orb is not in the plans, not yet. But it has been in his mind.

"We—we're going to have to do whatever it takes."

She looks searchingly into his eyes. "And there's no way I could talk you out of it. There just isn't, is there?"

"Megan, we're not even planning . . ."

"Zan," she says, "tell me everything will be all right. I just want to hear it."

He pulls her into his arms. "It will."

"It will," she repeats tonelessly. He knows from the sound of her voice that she doesn't believe him, but there is nothing he can say to alter that. All he can do is hold her.

In the night, as in so many other nights, he dreams.

He stands alone in the ruins of Pluto Colony, surrounded by the mangled bodies of the colonists. A whirlwind of Orbs shrieks and roars around him. Some leave the circle and fling themselves at his face, threatening to crush him, but even though they fly toward him faster and faster, they never come close, never within reach of his straining, outstretched hands.

He awakens to find the bedroom flickering in the light of distant explosions. He watches, transfixed by the play of light and shadow until it dies.

When the last of the lights has gone, he still stares, looking at a place far beyond the dark walls, until at last the light grows again, and becomes dawn.

III

In the late morning, the containment room waits.

McManus stares into it through a window of luxon. Twenty centimeters thick, the dense plastic could easily withstand the onslaught of a wrecking ball. Inside the room, metal walls gleam softly in the subdued light. Directly across from the window, a smooth, featureless door fits almost seamlessly into the wall. Outside the door, the molybdenum-titanium-steel alloy box that has held the Orb since its capture is being bolted into place.

An army of people surround McManus, mostly members of his team, augmented by visiting scientists and interested observers. The jumbled conversations are deafening, then suddenly even louder as a cheer goes up. He turns to see his son entering the observation room.

"Looks like you did it," someone calls out.

"Sure did," Marc replies. "The scoop worked like a charm."

McManus smiles, unable to suppress his pride. As Marc approaches, McManus claps him on the shoulder. "They're about to make the transfer. Any second."

They turn to the window. McManus steps closer, nearly touching the thick plastic with his nose.

The door opens. Anticipation silences the crowd.

The spherical Orb rolls lazily into the room and comes to rest near the center. The mass of human observers, as if it were a single breathless creature, leans closer.

McManus raises his palms to the window, leans gently against the cool plastic.

The Orb explodes through the air and slams into the window, splashing across it like a huge lump of putty. The wall thunders and quakes like a huge drum. The crowd recoils, gasping, but McManus presses his fingertips against the luxon

113

barrier, riding the vibrations as the Orb hammers its body against the transparent shield.

Three times it tries the window, then it retreats to the middle of the room. It jerks from side to side, as if searching frantically for an exit. It has not assumed the typical cylindrical shape of Orbs that have hit ground; nevertheless, it extrudes whiplike pseudopods which lash out, slamming each wall, the ceiling, and the floor in turn, then all parts of the room at once.

But the walls hold, and as abruptly as it started, the tirade ceases.

Again the Orb is motionless, but it is no longer spherical. It has become a thick horizontal cylinder, thicker at the middle, with a fat, round plate on each end; it resembles an axle between two wheels. The "axle" is about a meter thick and three meters long. The "wheels" are about three meters in diameter. On the axle and inner sides of the wheels, a mottled blue-green color oozes across the surface. On the outer surface of the wheels, the skin is brown and scaly, the familiar outer covering of a spherical Orb. Apparently the wheels can stretch into pseudopods, or fuse to form a protective brown sphere.

If this is the same cylindrical form that he has seen in tapes, wreaking havoc on Pluto, Mars, and the moon, there is no hope of holding it for long. But if it is different, the Orb will still be here later.

He pushes away from the window. He has seen his Orb. For now, that is enough.

IV

"Okay, what have we got?"

"Roughly speaking, Zan, four weeks of absolutely nothing."

"Not absolutely nothing, Norma. At least your theory was right. The Orb hasn't disintegrated."

Norma Friedlich pushes her glasses back up her nose. "Oh, great. That's roughly enough information to advance the field of exobiology into the next century."

"All right, all right," McManus says. "I realize we're all frustrated."

"Frustrated?" exclaims Gunderson. "It would be easier getting answers out of the Sphinx."

A few members of the group chuckle weakly. Randolph, the CIA liaison, tosses a dart at a huge wall photograph of the Orb.

McManus turns to Yamamoto. "Anything on the latest scans?"

Yamamoto shakes her head. "We repeated the magnetic resonance imaging just for the heck of it, but got zilch." She ticks off fingers: "Plain X rays, CT scans, augmented no-dose positron emission scans, whatever! They all say the same thing. There is no internal structure."

"Or some type of random structure," Friedlich suggests.

"Random structure?" asks Bajuraman, the geneticist from Sri Lanka. "How is that possible?"

Friedlich shrugs. "How is *no* internal structure possible? How is anything possible with this creature? I think unless we break down our preconceived notions about what we're likely to find, we may not find anything at all."

McManus nods. "I know exactly what you mean, Norma. Sometimes this feels like looking for X rays with the naked eye."

"That," Randolph says, "might be a much more successful endeavor." This draws another laugh, but with even less enthusiasm.

McManus knows they are deeply dispirited, and with good reason. Aside from their fruitless attempts to analyze the Orb's structure by every means short of surgery, their attempts at communication have been equally barren. They have spoken to it—never in person—in every known language. They have offered it thousands of mathematical patterns—pictorially, audibly, and by vibrating the floor. They have displayed photographs of stars and diagrams of atomic structures. They have dispatched waves of changing air tem-

115

peratures, variable magnetic fields, shifting electrical currents, and pulses of gravitonic fluxes.

None of these things has elicited any response.

They have played music, animal noises, and in desperation, recordings of natural disasters. They have even shown it the tapes of Orbs destroying Luna.

No reaction.

They have placed objects in the room, from a grain of sand, to a mirror, to a small satellite—and then living creatures, from an amoeba up to a gorilla.

But through it all, the Orb has remained impassive. As far as they can determine, it does not even produce any waste products, or else it can store them in its body indefinitely. Its only activity is the ceaseless shifting of colors on its skin. They have analyzed the colors but can make no sense of them because no pattern has ever been repeated.

After four weeks they know only one thing: Its body temperature is four degrees Celsius.

McManus pushes his chair back and steps into a morning sunbeam that slants through an east window. He stares across the dusty compound to the building where the Orb is imprisoned. "I'm going in there," he says simply.

For a moment, the entire team is too stunned to react. It is the next logical step, known to all, but they are startled to be facing the reality of it at last.

"Zan," Friedlich says, "I agree everything else has been tried, but that only means everything we can think of so far. Just give us a little more time. We'll think of lots more, I guarantee it."

"No," McManus says. "Enough has been tried. It's time to try direct contact."

"How do we know it will work?" Bajuraman demands. "You are risking your life on an action with a low probability of success."

McManus turns to face them. "Obviously, we don't know it will work. But we all know it's something that deserves to be tried. It's not the ultimate step. It's just one more method of trying to break through. We'll probably have to try a hundred more ideas afterward but unless anybody has any better suggestions right now, *this* is our next step."

He scans the blank faces. Everyone looks around, as if hoping someone else has another idea, but there are no suggestions.

"Right. So let's not waste any more time. The last three days had such a light schedule that they could have been compressed into one morning, and not one thing on the schedule was new. Nothing but repeats."

"But why you?" Yamamoto asks. "I don't think you should be the one to take the chance."

"Number one, I subscribe strongly to the old cliché that I wouldn't ask anyone to do something I'm not willing to do myself. Number two, quite frankly, I've been dying to get a chance like this for four years. Number three, since I'm in charge of this project, I'm not planning to accept any other volunteers. And number four, it has to be someone, so why *not* me? Okay?"

No one says anything. A few people nod.

"Okay," he says. "End of argument."

Three days later, the team is in agreement: He should carry no weapons into the room. If the Orb decides to kill, no hand weapon will stop it, so there is no sense risking any provocation.

That evening, he is ready. Outside the Orb's prison, he brushes fingertips against the smooth metal door, stares into its reflective depths, and thinks of Megan. The feel of her delicate body cradled in his arms each night as they go to sleep. Her voice in the darkness, one night last week, asking him not to tell her when he will go into the room, but only to say when it is all over.

The door slides back, slicing through his thoughts. A wave of tension traces his spine upward to the base of his skull, spreads into his jaw, forces his teeth to clench.

He steps into the access hall. The door whooshes into place

behind him. Tiny whirring noises, like electric hummingbirds, fill his ears as the locks are set and checked. The noise stops, then the inner door glides to one side. He steps through and the door whisks shut.

Palms wet, the roar of blood in his ears, he stares at the immobile alien. His left ankle itches maddeningly, but he doesn't move, doesn't breathe. A faint crackle of static seeps through one of the walls, and his eyes involuntarily dart toward the cluster of tiny holes that betrays a buried speaker. Quickly his gaze returns to the Orb, just in time to see it move.

Moving. After weeks of paralysis, the Orb is moving. It is a slow alteration in shape, barely perceptible, but when it is finished, he is certain the alien has turned to observe him. He is stunned to become, so suddenly, living proof that what he hoped for is true. The Orb has been waiting for a human.

As it was moving, every inclination of his consciousness was devoted to it. Now, having turned, the Orb is once again motionless, and McManus has a chance to become aware of his unblinking eyes, his galloping heart, his ice-bound intestines. His lungs scream with the need to breathe.

Slowly, he exhales, letting the air hiss between his teeth for a second until he hears himself—and finishes exhaling silently.

What do you want? he calls mentally. He does not expect a reply, but perhaps . . .

The Orb does nothing.

His peripheral vision records an image: the luxon window crowded with people, their faces alive with anticipation. He wishes they had agreed on what actions he should choose, but what some of them think might open a channel of communication others suspect might get him killed. Aside from a few simple gestures, he will need to improvise.

Gradually he raises his right hand and displays it palm forward beside his face. A universal symbol of greetings. *But no,* he realizes, *perhaps not universal, perhaps only on Earth.*

No response.

"Wha—" he says, as his throat constricts around the at-tempted word.

Nothing.

"Why won't you talk?" he whispers fiercely.

Still nothing.

Suddenly the years of frustration well up within him, and he is poised to yell for the Orb's attention, but before he can, the alien rises. Ponderously, like a creature far more vast, it stirs itself, and grows. Stretching its side plates into thick pseudopods, it flows toward him.

A commotion erupts outside the window, but McManus stabs an open hand sideways into the air, spreading his fingers to subdue the crowd. Something is happening—after long weeks of futility the Orb is reacting—and whether he can understand it or not, he is determined to experience it. One thing is certain: This is not the way the Orbs move when they intend to kill.

Growing still larger, the Orb expands like a strange balloon. Its pseudopods lengthen until it towers over him. Then slowly, by immeasurable degrees, it descends. The touch of its skin is frigid and rough, and he feels the weight of the crea-ture behind it.

"What?" he says, raising his hands, pressing back against its powerful bulk, feeling his arms tremble with the effort of not striking out in fear. *"What . . . do you want?"*

Moving so gradually it seems almost gentle, it forces him downward. Before he even realizes the floor is near, he feels it come up beneath him. Flowing, shifting, oozing around him, the Orb envelopes him.

All at once he realizes he cannot see, hear, move, or even breathe, and panic explodes inside him. His muscles tense and swell with pain. Every cell in his body shrieks in agony and in terror of being crushed. Starry bursts of color jolt his mind and send it jabbering down a long tunnel to blackness.

And then his world changes.

He loses contact with his body and its burden of pain. Aimlessly, weightlessly, his consciousness drifts through a vast fog. The entire universe takes shape incrementally, as if by condensation, but the image fades in and out of the swirling mist.

Within this murky vision swim planets. Their inhabitants are various: delicate winged hunters, sluggish rocklike burrowers, fierce reptilian warriors. Orbs rain from their skies. Many explode overhead, others spring up from the ground. These ground-risen Orbs are clearly different, though none are clearly visible. On each planet, the native creatures fight fiercely, but they all die.

Earth coalesces out of the fog. Its fate is the same. And when every human has been obliterated, the Orbs move on, relentlessly, throughout the universe.

And then his world changes again, begins to fragment and dissolve. He spins, and collides with sundered pieces of himself. He screams.

He is on the floor outside the room. He vomits. Hands hold him, inject drugs into him, and he sleeps.

He realizes he is awake.

Monitors—intravenous lines—he is reclining in bed in an intensive care unit. His entire body hurts, but at least the pain is a reminder that he is still alive.

A pressure against his rib cage. Looking down, he sees Megan slumped forward in a chair beside the bed. Her head is nestled on her folded arms, nudging his side.

"Megan?"

She startles, head jerking upward. Her pupils shrink, her eyes focus. "Zan," she says quietly. She stands, takes his face in both hands, and kisses it lightly all over.

"How long was I asleep?" he asks.

She turns to the clock. "Almost thirty hours." Smiling, she strokes his forehead. "Marc is outside."

"Let me see him."

As she steps out, he pulls back the covers. Most of the skin he can see is swollen and deeply bruised.

"Dad!" Marc says as he follows Megan into the cubicle. "How do you feel?"

"Resurrected." He smiles weakly. "Unless I'm not actually alive."

Marc chuckles. "We weren't betting on it, but you are."

"Tell me what happened."

"You're supposed to tell *us* that."

Already he feels himself fading. "First tell me what it looked like to you."

Marc scratches an ear. "Well, it wasn't much. The thing came down on top of you for about a second or two, then skipped back into a corner before we could even get the door open. It hasn't moved since."

"Only a second or two?"

"That's all."

McManus presses the heels of his hands against his closed eyes. "I saw the entire life of the universe in those seconds," he breathes. He feels extremely tired. Marc is speaking again, but he is asleep before he can hear the words.

V

"A lot of this data came right out of your head," Friedlich says. "Once we tracked down all the procreation images, we had most of what we needed. All we had to do was flesh it out in the field."

Three weeks after his encounter with the Orb, McManus is no longer surprised by the wealth of images telepathically implanted in his mind. Although most of what he saw was vague, masses of buried information have been unearthed by hypnosis, drugs, and electroneural stimulation.

"I can't believe," he says, "that all this time we thought we were *killing* them."

Friedlich turns her palms upward. "What else *could* we think?"

McManus shakes his head. "But—scattering their cells around," he says incredulously. "Helping them reproduce!"

121

"That's roughly the case," Friedlich says. She pushes her glasses back up on her nose and beams with scientific enthusiasm. "Amazing, isn't it?"

McManus rubs his chin thoughtfully. "This also explains why we couldn't figure out their internal structure, doesn't it? A collection of one-celled creatures doesn't have any organs big enough to show up on X rays."

He peers into a luxon box on the lab table. "How many cells are in there?"

"Roughly three hundred million. That's about how many it takes per cubic meter of air to start a colony." She pats the top of the box. "Tomorrow morning, none of these cells will be suspended. They'll all be joined in a single colony on the bottom of the box."

He stares. The box looks empty, but it is full of microscopic Orb cells floating in midair.

"Of course," she goes on, "a lot of factors probably influence colony formation—atmospheric composition, ionic distribution, who knows what?—but we haven't worked those out yet. All we know for sure is that colonies get started at a certain cell density. I figure it would take upwards of five hundred billion Orbs to reach that density worldwide." She frowns. "That's a very rough estimate, of course."

"You mean," he says, "if we blew up five hundred billion Orbs, that would leave enough cells floating around to start forming colonies, which would then settle to the ground, burrow into the dirt, and begin to grow?"

"Well, yes. That's roughly it. But don't say 'floating around.' Their specific gravity keeps them in a small range of altitudes, roughly two kilometers up. They inhabit a narrow zone of air, like a sphere all around the Earth." Her hands illustrate: a gesture like caressing a basketball. "And the colonies don't need dirt. They can burrow into almost anything."

"Before we knew it, Orbs would be springing up all over the place." McManus climbs onto a tall stool and leans on the lab table. "But what kind of Orbs? What do the colonies become when they're big enough to break out of the ground?"

"You mean what's a mature Orb like?" She cocks her head to one side. "Unclear. We couldn't get a good picture out of your mind, and we haven't completed a life cycle either, so we've never seen an adult Orb. We're under orders not to grow colonies past two billion cells—"

"You *are?* When did that happen?"

"About ten days ago. You were still on sick leave."

He shakes his head, disappointed in himself. "I thought I'd caught up with everything that happened while I was out."

She smiles. "Apparently not quite everything. Anyway, it's the rule worldwide. Everyone's worried because they get too big too fast. The cells don't replicate at a fixed rate. The rate *accelerates*, and not just by squares, but by *cubes*. Before we were told to quit, we had a colony that went from half a billion cells to twenty billion in a few hours, and who knows what would have happened after that?"

"We should let one mature."

Her eyes widen. "Would *you* be willing to take that risk?"

"Maybe," he says, his features darkening. "Someone will have to."

"Well," she replies, "even if you think you could control an adult Orb, I don't think you'll find anybody else who cares. Except me and a bunch of scientists around the world, but we don't count. Our bosses only want to get this war over with. So nobody's being allowed to grow an Orb, and that's that."

He ponders this. It fits with everything else he has learned. The world seems satisfied with what it knows about the Orbs. Enough to kill them, once and for all. New defensive plans are already in effect.

"Norma, how do they reproduce on their own planet? They couldn't have evolved in a place where someone was blowing them up with sky mines all the time."

She shrugs. "Who knows? According to your psychic contact, they can explode themselves. Is that part of their normal reproduction? I can't say. If they normally explode themselves, why didn't they do it on Pluto, or Mars? Not enough atmosphere?" Another shrug. "I have no idea. But they let *us*

123

blow them up here on Earth. Probably just because it conveniently fits their life cycle."

"Or maybe," he says, "because it fools us into thinking we have an effective defense." But no, he thinks, I can't believe that. If they've been deceiving us, then why communicate even once? Merely to brag that they will conquer the universe? Simply to threaten us? I *know* it wasn't a threat. It didn't *feel* like that. There was something more, something the Orb was trying to explain, something it wanted to tell me but couldn't.

"If," he says, "this is all true—"

"Oh, it is."

"Well, if it is, it seems like we've been planting the seeds of our own destruction."

"Yes," she agrees. "That's actually a very apt way of putting it." She removes her glasses and waves them at the sky. "But so far they've only got roughly thirty million cells per cubic meter. That's not enough for colony formation, and the individual cells never replicate until they're part of a colony."

He nods. "So with the one-oh-ones in place . . ."

"One-oh-ones?"

"The new sky mines. The ones that burn hotter."

"Oh, yes," she says, "hot enough to kill the cells. As long as everybody keeps using them, the Orbs will never have enough cells to reproduce. And the individual cells already in the atmosphere will eventually just wither away and die."

"How do you know they won't live forever?"

"Well, if they can't form colonies, it doesn't matter, does it?"

McManus sighs. "Add that to the list of questions we still can't answer." He turns to go, then hesitates. "By the way, Norma, who initiated the order to keep the colonies small?"

"It was signed by Caldwell herself."

124

"President Caldwell?"

"The same."

McManus raises his eyebrows for a moment, nods, and leaves, pondering his next move.

Every night as he lies on his back in bed, staring at the ceiling, an image of the Orb comes to him. He sees it rising above him, then slowly swallowing him. He feels its thoughts pushing into his head, bursting in his mind like a series of exploding balloons, one inside the other.

Sleep is becoming only a memory.

His thoughts race. Do they intend to kill us all and populate the Earth with Orbs? Aren't they curious about us? How do they account for their existence in the universe? What is their theory of creation?

And why did the captured Orb respond to nothing except me?

The questions ricochet inside his skull until he wants to scream. He is the only person ever to make meaningful contact with an Orb, yet so much meaning eludes him. It rankles him to feel messages buried in his psyche, inside his own head, but still out of reach.

And to make it worse, there is no one else who even cares. All over the world, governments and militaries are spending their energies producing, implementing, and deploying one-oh-ones, and gloating over the results as more and more Orbs are completely disintegrated every day.

As for the scientific community, their only concern seems to be competing for more Orb cells to study; they are practically trampling each other's lab coats in the process.

And the whole world is racking its brains for a way to destroy the invisible alien miasma that encircles the Earth, just in case the low concentration of individual floating cells can somehow become a threat.

They don't care that no real communication has been achieved, that no *important* questions have been answered. They don't know what it is like to touch an alien mind and come away thirsting for more—they don't understand that it cuts much deeper than never having made contact at all.

He will have to do something about it. In these long sleep-

125

less nights, as the one-oh-ones sear the skies overhead, he begins to give shape to a plan.

On the eleventh day, construction is nearly complete. Having satisfied himself that the work is up to spec, McManus is returning to base. The site is accessible only by air, and he is glad he has always maintained his pilot's rating. It means he can visit alone when he wants to.

He is receiving clearance to land when he hears it.

"General McManus, do you hear—?" says the air traffic controller before being drowned out by the noise. McManus lowers the gain and listens.

In the tower, the controller yanks his headphones off. "Damn!" he yells, clapping his hands over his ears and rubbing vigorously. "What in the name of . . . ?" He flips a switch to activate a wall speaker, and a piercing shriek assaults his ears. His hand jumps to turn it down.

"If that isn't the strangest damn thing I ever heard . . ." His voice trails off as the shriek warbles up and down the frequency spectrum, accompanied by the boom of distant thunder and waves of shrill, rapid-fire coughing. He picks up a phone to call the officer of the day.

He does not know that every radio on every frequency in the world is receiving the bizarre noises being broadcast by the Orbs, and every line to the OD is already busy.

A young sergeant in the tracking room has gotten through to the OD first. "They're leaving, sir!" he is yelling into the phone. "They're pulling out! I show no Orbs falling, and their ships are pulling out of orbit!"

McManus has been listening to the radio noise with mixed emotions. He is sure he knows what it means, but he is not sure it pleases him. The one-oh-ones have been in worldwide use for nearly six weeks. Now the Orbs truly and irrevocably die when they meet the sky mines, and they have finally recognized it. They are admitting defeat.

He is gratified and relieved that the war seems finally over, but he feels troubled and unfulfilled that the Orbs are leaving before contact has been made.

Minutes later, it is over. The "noise"—only the second transmission ever sent from Orbs to humans—has ceased.

McManus decides not to land. He radios the tower that he is going to do a little more flying, and begins to climb. Pushing the throttle forward, he hurtles through an empty sky. Soon he is high enough to see the horizon curving away, and stars winking through the thinning blue. For the first time in years, the heavens threaten no Orbs. He does a barrel roll. He wants to feel exhilarated, but something is missing.

A few hours after he lands, the tracking room reports that all the spaceships are in one vast formation. The ship nearest Earth is six hundred kilometers away, and they are all receding rapidly.

Now, he knows, only one Orb is still on its way to Earth.

The "womb," as he thinks of it, lies hidden in a secluded mountain spot. It is a dishlike depression in the earth, seventy meters across and ten meters deep. Twenty meters below its surface lies a thick bowl, fashioned from the same alloy that comprises the walls of the captured Orb's prison. The sides of the bowl rise up through the earth and above it to a height of two meters.

He scans the rim of the bowl, where twelve evenly spaced one-oh-ones stand guard. Their proximity fuses have been disabled. They now contain receivers keyed to a radio detonator switch.

He checks the safety cover on the switch, which is located in Station One, one of twelve elevated bunkers which look down into the womb from a hundred meters away. Each bunker contains a backup detonator switch, hard-wired to the mines. Five airmen are stationed at each post: one for communications, one for the backup detonator, two for the laser cannon, one as an emergency reinforcement, and all for observation.

With binoculars, he stares down at the layer of dirt and

127

rock comprising the center of the womb. Buried within this layer is a small aluminum canister. Inside the canister are over three hundred million living cells collected out of thin air. Soon they will grow large enough to disrupt the canister and thrive on whatever they can glean from the soil. Seismic monitors will keep watch on their activity, and when the amount of movement in the center of the womb reaches a critical level, an alarm will sound through McManus's pocket communicator, in all the guard posts, in the air control tower, and in the base operations office.

Eventually the cells in the ground will create an Orb, but not the kind that falls from the sky. This will be the kind that grows from the ground of a planet the Orbs once meant to conquer.

But will this ground-risen Orb be any more capable of communicating than the one Marc scooped up in midair? If Norma Friedlich is right, it may be. She believes the captured Orb is an immature form; a colony of cells in the ground should produce an adult.

This time things should be different.

In any case, he has done his part. Now it's up to the growing alien in the womb. He returns to his plane, does a vertical lift-off, and points the nose back toward base.

It has taken a tremendous amount of work, all under his orders, to create the womb. So far he has managed it without having to actually forge Caldwell's signature on any orders. That does not, however, change the fact that everything he is doing is in direct contravention of presidential edict.

When this is over, he thinks, as the mountains give way to red and yellow sands far below his streaking jet, he will be court-martialed.

It is, at this point, his only certainty.

VI

He is in the shower, the white tiles reddened by dawn seeping through the window. Lying next to the sink is his pocket communicator. The alarm is shrieking, bouncing echoes off the tile.

The womb is bursting open.

He leaps out and throws on his clothes without toweling off. Megan is still asleep.

It is usually a ten-minute drive to the base but he makes it in three. Seven minutes after the alarm, he is in his plane, lifting off. Four minutes later, he has covered the one hundred and sixty kilometers to the womb.

Hovering over it, in the company of four heavily armed helicopters, he sees the ground cracking. His breath scrapes his throat in quick bursts, and his heart rakes claws around the inside of his chest.

Setting his plane down near Guard Station One, he jumps out and runs to unlock the safety cover on the detonator switch. One of the airmen on guard hands him a pair of binoculars. "Nothing to see yet, sir."

Through the narrow luxon window he focuses the binoculars on the center of the dish.

For almost five minutes the ground trembles and shakes. "What the devil—?" one of the airmen mutters, but other than that everyone is silent, staring at the unsettled earth. Cracks appear, scarring the dish and sending up puffs of dust. Clods of dirt dance and quiver across the chapped surface.

McManus remains poised with one hand clasping the binoculars to his eyes and the other over the detonator. His legs, arms, and back begin to ache from being held so rigid for so long.

He is just shifting his weight to the other foot when, at the center of the dish, a huge geyser of dirt shoots into the air. He jumps; his hand twitches near the detonator, almost setting it off. He peers anxiously into the cloud of dust, his fingers trembling over the switch.

When the dust settles, an Earth-born alien is standing at the center of the womb.

Its overall shape is triangular. Three thick cylinders form the sides of the triangle, linking three large globes, one at each

129

point. Only the globes touch the ground. He can't be sure of its size from this distance, but he estimates each side of the triangle at about four meters, and the globes perhaps two meters in diameter.

Throughout the interior of the triangle runs an intricate meshwork of twisting fibers. A smaller globe hangs suspended at the center of the mesh.

The mesh and the central globe appear smooth, but the outer cylinders and globes are covered with thousands of densely packed tentacles. The tentacles sway in rippling waves. The creature has no one predominant color; instead, a prismatic riot of subtle hues—claret and jade and tangerine, silver and sienna and saffron—surges through the forest of tentacles, and across the mesh and central globe.

Its beauty staggers him.

A probing, tickling sensation touches his mind. Eagerly he waits. An itching, distant hum coruscates through his brain, like a memory just out of reach, as if his synapses were being tested but not stimulated enough to fire.

After some minutes, words crystallize inside his head: I-this if kill you-that.

The Orb is speaking to him telepathically.

And it seems to be threatening to kill him.

He feels the urge to take an awestruck step backward, but he cannot afford to be stunned by what is happening; he must try to respond.

Why do you want to kill me? he thinks, hoping it can hear.

You-that want this, it responds.

I want this? he thinks. I want—you mean, I want to die?

No answer appears.

"Come on, Orb—" he mutters, and is immediately cut off by a word echoing inside his head.

Ocean, it says.

Ocean? he thinks.

Not Orb, it says.

You are an ocean?

We-they Ocean. I-this we-they joined. I-this Ocean.

Their name, he thinks. Their name translated into English. But how did it pick "Ocean"?

He stares through the binoculars at the rippling tentacles. It's trying to make sense out of my language, he thinks, trying to pick out words to fit its concepts. Trying to understand and speak an entire alien language in just a few minutes!

Explain "Ocean," he thinks, and realizes he is straining, in some indefinable way, to *aim* his thoughts at the creature.

Ocean, comes the response. Close word, *closest* word, say one-entity-makes-many-makes-one, and gives mother, and always life, and source, and other . . . concepts. Many concepts. All combined make Ocean. We-they. Ocean.

And *you*—individually—are also called Ocean?

I-this Ocean we-they Ocean.

This one alien is Ocean, and the whole race is Ocean—it sees itself as part of an all-encompassing mother race. And those combined pronouns: "we-they," "I-this"—they must have to do with the relationship between the individual and the whole.

And it dawns on him, with a prickling sensation of awe that threatens once more to paralyze his thoughts, that he is actually communicating with an alien. He is the first human being ever to talk to a member of another intelligent race.

You-that must speak, Ocean says. I-this translate concepts difficult and you-that make many concepts. Speak to choose.

Speak? he thinks.

Voice, it says.

Voice? he thinks. He coughs, unconsciously clearing his throat. "Voice? You want me to speak aloud?"

Good. You-that not organize thought. Speech organize.

Suddenly he becomes painfully aware of the sound of his own thoughts as they tumble over one another. To the alien, it must be cacophony. But speaking helps—it must create a mental emphasis that helps Ocean recognize the thought he wants to send.

"Okay, I'll speak. Is that better?"

Better.

131

"Sir, are you all right?"

"What?" McManus yells, whipping around. "Oh. Oh, yes, airman. It's—it's what we were hoping. Telepathic communication. Except it wants me to speak aloud."

"Yes, sir."

He turns to look again at Ocean through the binoculars.

"Okay, back to step one. You said I wanted to die."

Yes.

"But—I *don't* want to die."

You-that *want* to die. Ocean explain now. Once, you-that fall in sky with Ocean. Make *first* mind touch.

Yes. His epiphany, his moment during a downward plunge with the aliens when he felt as if he were one of them.

"I thought that was just my imagination!"

Much imagination. Yes. Also much . . . empathy. Also first mind touch. You-that, McManus, yes?

"Yes. That was me."

Next, you-that capture sibling-seed-Ocean. Yes?

"I—" He hesitates. "No, I didn't. My son Marc captured one of you. Not me."

You-that, yes. Sibling-seed-McManus.

They recognized Marc as . . . as part of him. In their understanding of things, Marc was a part of him the way the captured Orb was a part of Ocean.

"Yes. I—I captured one of you."

You-that then *large* touch mind sibling-seed-Ocean. Ocean learn some of McManus mind when first touch, learn more of McManus mind when then touch sibling-seed-McManus mind.

"You 'touched' Marc's mind? Did he—?"

No. Sibling-seed-McManus not aware. One-direction touch.

"But you found out more about me then?"

Yes. And much more when you-that large touch mind Ocean. Ocean learn *much* mind you-that. You-that then, and now, ask to die.

"But I still don't understand. You read my thoughts, and

you determined I want to die?" *Maybe it's a misdefinition of "die."* "Can you explain what 'die' means?"

To join we-they in love.

"Love!"

Yell? I-this do not understand.

My God, he thinks, lowering the binoculars and leaning against the wall to steady himself. This is too complicated. I'm trying to deal with concepts that have no bearing on anything I understand, while this alien tries to shoehorn those concepts into words that just don't fit. Who am I to make sense of it? Who am I to be talking to an alien?

He looks upward through the window. He sees clouds. He notices a high, thin streak of silver, a scratch against the sky, racing to the north. In a flash of imagination, he flees this desperate, fractured conversation, and places himself there. Suddenly he feels clouds whipping past his shoulders. He is slicing cleanly through the air, moving at supersonic speeds into the teeth of the problem, pressing the right buttons, obliterating any difficulty in the flash of an exploding sky mine. He is nothing if not efficient. He is a warrior.

No.

He *was* a warrior.

And he is not flying a jet fighter now. He is earthbound, caught in a web of words. Tendrils of fear and frustration tickle the edges of his mind.

Not only warrior, says the alien.

"What?"

McManus was warrior, yes. But more. More than warrior.

"Am I?" he whispers.

The alien ignores the question.

Now explain, Ocean says. Die is love. Yes. Die is love. But this upsets McManus. Explain.

"Explain," he murmurs, raising the binoculars. "Explain," he repeats with a sigh. "Well, 'die' and 'love' are not synonymous to us. You must mean something else. You've got to give me a better idea of what you mean by love."

Love. Best kindness most regard learn-teach-learn into all Ocean.

Wait, slow down, I almost got it. "Wait—uh, could you explain a little more?"

Learn-teach-learn. Give strongest best admiration for all we-they. Go into mind of we-they.

He sits back onto a rock, bewildered. Ocean is telling him that "love" is the best word it can find for a process that includes mind fusion, learning, teaching, and *death*, along with who knows what else. It is too confusing. Perhaps he can decipher their definition of love by approaching along a different tack.

"Ocean, *why* do you love?"

Love gives knowledge.

"Then . . . explain knowledge."

Knowledge is understanding. Ocean. Universe. All. Best. Life.

Suddenly connections are forming. "Yes," he says excitedly.

Ocean goes on: Knowledge is reason to exist in universe.

He can't help smiling. It is like hearing an echo of his own thoughts from beyond the stars. But he still can't quite understand the link between knowledge and love.

"So you 'love' to gain knowledge. Okay, then—*how* do you love?"

Love by death. With death, many go into the mind of Ocean. The mind of Ocean will *fill* if enough ones go into mind. The mind of Ocean then can become knowledge.

McManus pauses, suddenly impressed anew. Ocean's use of the language is growing more sophisticated by the second.

"You love by dying, and when you die, you 'go into the mind of Ocean.'"

Join the mind of we-they. Love. Die.

So that's it. The first step on their path to knowledge is death, in order to join their group mind, a mind that somehow *equates* with all knowledge. And so they think I want to die because I want knowledge.

I-this can kill you-that. You-that want to die. You-that are the only human who still wants to die.

"None of us want to die," he says. A pang of despair strikes him as he begins to see how vast the gap may be between their two ways of viewing the universe. "*I* don't want to die. It doesn't mean the same thing to us, don't you see?"

No, Ocean does not understand. Humans once showed much love, helped Ocean to die, but then stopped. Instead of loving, they began helping Ocean *end-disconnect*.

"I know. You mean the one-oh-ones. You're saying that when we started using the new mines, we didn't just send you into your group mind, or whatever it is. We terminated you permanently."

Yes. I mean that. But Ocean does not want to end-disconnect. Ocean helped the humans on Pluto, Mars, Armstrong Station, and Luna die, but they were not enough. The mind of Ocean is not filled. Humans are not becoming knowledge. But the dead ones are waiting. We-they are willing to help enough of you die, enough with we-they someday to become knowledge. We-they do not understand why humans would first help us die and then force us to end-disconnect.

McManus is stunned. Ocean thought the humans were helping them in their "loving," their liberation of the mind through one kind of physical death, and they couldn't understand why they had suddenly been rejected.

"We didn't understand what you were doing. We thought you wanted to kill us. I mean, end-disconnect us."

I have always wanted, and I still want, to help humans become knowledge. Ocean, however, believes that humans do not want to become knowledge. Ocean has now destroyed all its Earth cells except me.

"You mean there's nothing left of Ocean anywhere on Earth except you? Even the one I—Marc—captured? And the cells floating in the air?"

All have been disintegrated. I alone am here.

"Why?"

I feel that human beings may have much that can expand

and enrich the entity of universal knowledge, and help carry us toward our goal of *knowing*. But Ocean feels the human race has shown it does not want to pursue this endeavor, and although that is regrettable, it is your right. However, I have brought myself into this body because I feel there may still be a chance for humans to share in our quest.

"You have brought yourself into that body?"

It is no problem to shift locations of consciousness throughout ourself.

"But why—why you? Why me?"

McManus receives an impression of benevolent amusement.

You have an intense desire to know, to understand the universe and the meaning of life, a desire stronger than any other we have detected within your race. Your yearning to know, and specifically to understand Ocean, drew me to you. I possess similar desires, in their strongest manifestation within Ocean. It was I who tried to contact you years ago. That first time was only out of a desire to communicate with one who shared my feelings so deeply. I tried again, when we touched physically, inside the containment room. Unfortunately, I was utilizing immature forms, as you surmised, and I'm afraid the physical body does influence the telepathic process quite a bit. I apologize for the incomplete, and possibly startling nature of the messages.

"No—" McManus hesitates, stunned by what he is learning. "No—" he repeats, shaking his head, then at last finishes the thought: "No apology necessary."

Thank you. But now, this communication, this discussion we are having, is not like the first, not a matter of pleasure. It is of overwhelming importance.

"But—" He pauses. "My God, I'm lost. I don't know what to say. I don't even know what questions to ask."

You need no more questions. I offer you all possible answers. Listen to me: I present myself to you because you share so many of my feelings. You share the burning desire to explain, to understand, to *make sense*. We can do it together. If you tell me there is a chance to cause this to happen, I can signal Ocean. We can return. Many more of you must die. You must fuse with the universe. Don't you see? The universe *is* knowledge. Matter is only an aberration, less than one one-hundredth of one percent of the true universe, the extent of which your race has not even begun to suspect. Please tell me we can become knowledge together.

" 'Become knowledge together.' You don't know how strange that sounds."

But it should not be strange. It is the way.

"The way?"

Yes. And I want you to see it, so much so that I have deeply . . . dishonored . . . and—I can't find the word—in my language it is *ghalyinggred*—I have done this to myself, and to Ocean, by pleading your case. I think this concept has no equivalent in your mind. If it helps you understand, I can explain what I have done only by saying it is metaphorically as if I have buried my own soul in the mind of an enemy. This is the most terrible thing one can do, and so, if your answer is no, my only path is that you end-disconnect me.

"What? How can that be? If your whole race lives in search of knowledge, how can there be anything wrong with what you are doing now?"

It is simply not our way.

"That's not much explanation."

It is all the explanation that exists. If you do not wish to follow our path, it is extremely—*incorrect-improper*—to ask you to do so. But I *must* ask. I can't leave you behind without at least trying to help you understand. You deserve at least this much, because you are reasoning creatures.

There is a pause, then:

Please.

McManus lowers the binoculars. A wrenching feeling twists through his chest. The alien is reaching out to him, trying to forge a link between two races. It has coalesced its identity into this body, just to give humankind one last chance to know its truth.

But what is its truth, and is it possible for humans to comprehend it? Does Ocean *know* the true nature of the universe, or does it merely *believe* the universe is a group mind simply because it possesses telepathy?

How could any human, he wonders, not be doubtful of this concept of the path to knowledge? Ocean has a cycle of "death" in the sky and "rebirth" from the ground. They have "dying" and "end-disconnecting," and maybe still other kinds of death, other kinds of life. How can they understand what life means to beings who die, or at least believe they die, only once?

Ultimately, it all comes down to this: Only one representative of Ocean remains, one who feels that Zan McManus might be the only human who still wants to *understand,* who still wants knowledge. It is asking him to join with a race of creatures from beyond the stars in a quest for revelation.

And if he joins, how many will die—and will it do any good? What if there is no group mind, no higher plane of existence where living creatures somehow *become* knowledge? Or worse, what if there is such a higher existence, but human beings *cannot reach it,* no matter how many die?

But what if Ocean is right, and this is the path to understanding? What if he is being offered the chance to uncover the meaning of existence, the answer to the greatest of the questions that have troubled humankind throughout its history: "Why are we here?"

To his right, jagged rocks dot the mountain as it climbs into the clouds. To his left, the ground descends into a dry valley. It is all real, all solid, part of the same Earth that has nurtured billions of human beings, cradled them in their journey through an unforgiving universe.

Beyond the womb, to the east, the sky is aflame with the red light of the rising sun. He thinks about his children. In Phoenix, his daughter Jessamyn is probably pondering the lesson she will try to impart today to her undergraduate philosophy students. And Marc, an Air Force pilot at age twenty-two; at this moment, he seems hardly more than a child. He hasn't sailed a small boat alone to Europe, or seen the sun rise over the Himalayas, or written a bunch of ridiculous sonnets to a woman who makes his heart carry on from one beat to the next. What chance has he had to create his own ideas about life? He hasn't *lived*.

They are so young. They have so many years ahead to learn about the world, to push their minds against the questions that haunt humankind.

Maybe in some way Marc and Jessamyn will bring the world closer to an understanding of human existence, and maybe they won't, but there will be meaning in their attempts. They will live, and they will love—in a human way—and one day they *will* die. But whenever that day comes, it will be too soon.

Ocean speaks into his mind again. He raises the binoculars to stare at the triangular alien. In its words he can feel its desperation.

The time has come for humans to leave this womb. Zan McManus, please. Think what awaits you.

"No!" he cries. "This can't be the only way! We must talk. We must share our ideas about the universe."

You will know the universe only when you are the universe.

"How can I believe that? Give me a way—"

You want knowledge. Become it with us. There is no other way.

"But how do you know?"

Know? I have explained that. We do not know until we know. It is our way. We . . . simply do not doubt.

They don't know.

"You don't really *know*, do you? You don't really have any way to prove to me that what you say is true."

He waits. He has become so used to immediate responses that he is unnerved by the pause.

How can you ask for proof? The only proof is in the doing. There *is* no other proof. It cannot be discussed in any other way! There *is* no such thing as proof! There *is*—

"Stop! Please stop it." McManus is shaken to have suddenly felt such a burst of emotion from the alien, an emotion nearly identical to his own desperation in battering the brick wall of indifference that the universe holds up against his questions.

Forgive me, Ocean says.

McManus pulls the binoculars away from his eyes. The alien shrinks to an indistinct blur of color.

He squeezes his eyelids shut, feels the sting of tears. After all the fear, all the wondering, all the combat missions, all the sky-ripping explosions, all the years of life under an alien rain, all the longing to know the mind of these creatures—at last it is over, and at last he knows—with a certainty that grips his soul like the ice of a thousand winters—at last he knows that he cannot know. His struggle for understanding has come up against a truly impenetrable barrier, a place marked with only one statement he can understand: Until you die, you will never know if they were right—and perhaps not even then.

A hollowness is inside him. He tries to fill the cavity with a deep, ragged breath.

Very quietly he says, "It is not *our* way."

Zan McManus, then I pray you, give me end-disconnection.

"No," he whispers. "No. You must stay here. We have to try—" He stops, knowing that there *is* nothing left to try.

Zan, give me end-disconnection. It is in your power.

"I know! But I can't do that!" He wants to say that he loves this creature—or perhaps he wants to say that he *wants* to love Ocean, in Ocean's way—but in the agony of his conflicting desires, he is not even certain he would know what he meant if he said it.

You do not think unheard, Zan.

"I . . ."

Zan, I thank you deeply for your thoughts—for the inclinations of your heart—but you have said no, and you *must* give me end-disconnection.

Though he struggles against admitting it, he does understand this. All that is left for this alien, this stranger who is so like him, who may for all he knows be more like him than any other being in the universe, is an honorable death.

He stares at the circle of one-oh-ones, pearly globes so similar to the mines that he once sowed like seeds of destruction in the sky. Now they ring Ocean like a halo, and wait silently to perform their final sacrament.

Goodbye, he thinks—

—and flips the detonator switch.

The twelve mines flare at once, hiding Ocean, and the dish in the Earth, in a blinding flash. The shock wave rattles the guard station. Thunder pounds his ears. A cloud of dust and rock billows outward, raining dirt all around him a minute later. It takes three endless minutes for the dish to come back into view.

The deep metal bowl is empty; its upper edges have been atomized, and the rest is pitted and charred.

Ocean is no more.

It is over. A hundred questions have gone unasked. Perhaps *every* question will now go unanswered. If so, then he has robbed the human race of meaning.

A wave of self-perception washes over him; suddenly he is uneasily adrift in an awareness of that to which he has clung as an alternative to Ocean's belief. It is the fragile hope—the gossamer, unsupported hope—that the answers lie not at the end of the quest for understanding, but somehow in the quest itself.

Behind him sits a jet fighter, an elegant and cruel masterpiece of human reason, a killing machine that will rescue him from this place of death and return him to the things he cherishes.

Turning toward the plane, he takes his first faltering step back to the world he knows, the answers that elude his grasp, the quest he can believe.

141

Scott Baker is a sly, playful, and soft-spoken man from Illinois, who for reasons best known to him decided some years back that Paris might be a better locale for conducting a literary career. Now he and his ebullient wife Suzi live in a romantic top-story flat within walking distance of a thousand wondrous restaurants and twenty thousand delightful cafés. But nevertheless he finds the time to produce the occasional story—such as the extraordinary "The Lurking Duck," which was legendary years before it finally saw print in Omni, and "Still Life With Scorpion," which won the World Fantasy Award in 1985—and also the sly, playful, and soft-spoken item we offer here. Its subject—what else, from a man who lives in Paris?—is food. But there's a startling contribution to speculative economic theory here too, and, since economics is certainly a science, albeit a dismal one, there can be no question that what we have here is s-f of the purest sort.

ALIMENTARY TRACT

SCOTT
BAKER

It was 3 A.M. on a Thursday morning when they came for me. They were unable to find the concealed door leading into my private dining room, so they broke through a wall and caught me red-handed enjoying a solitary turkey dinner.

I was dragged up in front of the appropriate judge and the charges were read: Corruption of Public Officials, Illegal Diversion of World Government Food Stocks, Subversion of a Universal Larder (#598934623221), Receiving Stolen Goods, Hoarding, and Gluttony. The turkey carcass with its bones almost picked clean was shown, as was what remained of the broccoli in hollandaise sauce, the creamed onions, scalloped potatoes, and endive salad, with as pièce de résistance the as-yet untouched two-kilo charlotte aux baies mauves. The holoscan of my stomach's contents with attached medical report was presented, proving conclusively that I had not only eaten the meal, but had eaten all of it, and alone.

The judge found me guilty and sentenced me to nine months alimentary charity and humility, the sentence to commence immediately.

I tried to protest but before I could say anything they hit me with a jet-spray somnifere. I woke up lying on my back in the Luna Penal Clinic with a skeletally thin doctor looking down at me with the utter, fanatical contempt of an alimentary tither. Probably a forty percenter, to judge by the look of him.

"When are you going to do it?" I asked, forcing myself to remain calm.

"We already have."

I couldn't feel anything. I tried a few experimental swallows, poked myself as hard as I could in the stomach, made myself burp. Everything seemed normal.

"I don't feel any different," I told him.

"What did you expect—some sort of clumsy plastic glove from the back of your tongue down to your anus?"

Which actually was more or less what I'd been expecting.

"What is it, then?" I demanded.

"We've merely modified the tissues of your alimentary tract so as to render you incapable of assimilating nourishment. Otherwise, your digestive system functions much as it always did: You secrete the same acids; most wastes pass through the tract just as they normally would. The teleport filter blocking your large intestine strains out the nourishment you've prepared for assimilation and sends it on to your beneficiaries. . . . Here."

He handed me a holo of a vaguely Oriental-looking family standing in front of a crude hut made out of broken fragments of wood, dried fronds, and odd pieces of junk. Four bloated-bellied children with matchstick arms, the parents, and ancient, stooped grandmother looking more like parchment-covered skeletons than like living human beings.

In the distance far behind them I could vaguely make out a nondescript cylindrical tower of pink and silver glass rising from a vivid green jungle.

My father had raised me Eugenicist: Any human being incapable of providing him or herself with the food necessary for life doesn't deserve to eat or reproduce. But I was repulsed despite myself. "What happened? Who are they?"

"We can't tell you that."

"Why not?"

"Some of our benefactors develop rather pathological cases of hostility toward their beneficiaries."

I started to protest, saw the way he was staring at me, as if daring me to tell him that I'd had no intention of hurting them, that I'd only been treating myself to some of the just rewards my considerable achievements entitled me to.

"How much are you tithing?" I asked instead.

"Fifty percent." Another superior smile, before he went back to his lecture. "When the sensors on your teleport filter register enough calories to keep your family nourished for the day, they activate that device on your wrist—" He gestured and I noticed for the first time that what I was wearing on my left wrist was no longer my normal multimodem but something of only vaguely the same shape and form. "It will release the minimum daily requirement of vitamins, minerals, and nutrients directly into your bloodstream. You'll be required to get your dosage adjusted at your mandatory weekly alimentary reeducation classes."

"What if I don't eat enough for all of them?"

"Then you don't get any nourishment." Another tight, nasty smile. "According to your records, you vote Eugenicist. That's what your principles teach you should happen, isn't it? No work, no food. Plus, you risk getting your sentence extended."

"What if I eat more than the minimum they need?"

"You think you're capable of eating more than enough for seven people with severe dietary deficiencies?"

"I've made a habit of it for years," I told him, and was pleased to see from the self-righteous horror on his pinched face that I'd finally gotten to him.

"Any charity above and beyond your sentence will of course be taken into consideration at your quarterly reviews. If you show yourself generous enough, your sentence may be reduced."

Which actually sounded wonderful: the more I ate, the sooner I'd have purged my sentence. A punishment inappropriately appropriate to the crime, like back when they'd picked up starving homeless bums and sentenced them to warm jail cells and hot meals for vagrancy. More proof the government still didn't have any idea what it was doing.

"Where am I supposed to get this food?"

"Your universal larder has been modified. You can order all the food you want—subject, of course, to the principles of Alimentary Humility."

"Which are?" I asked suspiciously.

"You can eat your food in secret, the same way you were convicted of consuming it, but never in public eating places. You can't invite anyone in for dinner or a snack . . . unless, of course, you ask them to take whatever they eat out of their own allotments."

"What about alcohol?"

"It's filtered out and sent directly to the city fuel tanks. You don't get drunk, your beneficiaries don't get nourished, and you don't get any credit toward your personal nourishment."

I nodded.

"We've reserved an aperture for you on the 19:45 wormhole to Chicago. Your clothes are in the closet behind you. Do you have any further questions?"

"Just one. How did anyone as obviously incapable of dealing with the public as you get this job?"

"Because they couldn't find anyone else who *wanted* to talk with people like you." He started to go, then stopped and looked back. "By the way. If you think *this* is bad, you don't even want to imagine what we've got in store for attempts at alimentary murder."

"Meaning what?" I wasn't going to let him intimidate me.

"Meaning that anything else you ingest—arsenic, acids, finger bombs, or rusty nails—all gets routed through the police analyzer and back into your system. And if it isn't enough to do the job, we add enough excess bulk so you pop like a blister."

146

I calmed down a little when I got back to my apartment, even cheered up when a little playing with my universal larder showed me the quantitative limits had all been removed. I called up the regulations pertaining to my sentence and saw that the price scales were three times what I was used to paying for legal food, but still far cheaper than the black market. Things weren't all that bad. I'd always eaten for the taste, not for the uncomfortable bloated feeling a too-heavy meal gave me. And now I wouldn't have to worry about my waistline or keeping my mass-reading below the point where it would alert the police when I used a wormhole. Pretty soon I'd be skinny as a tither.

I ordered myself a turkey dinner just like the one I'd been arrested for, then canceled the order. I was no longer limited to what the black market had to offer; for a fraction of the cost I could obtain the rarest and most exotic delicacies the larder had to offer—hummingbird tongues in aspic, candied Samoan jellyfish, lunar viral cheeses. . . .

Still, I liked the idea of turkey. A transition from my old to my new culinary habits. So I punched up a turkey with chestnut stuffing, preceded by a selection of hors d'oeuvres—caviar, three-snake soup, boudin blanc truffé, oysters—which didn't really go together, either with one another or with the fabulous selection of side dishes I ordered to accompany the turkey, but which each and every one demonstrated my newfound freedom.

As I ate, I tried to detect the teleport filter in my large intestine, but except for a slightly unsettled feeling—due, no doubt, to nervousness—I couldn't feel anything.

It was wonderful at first. I could eat and eat without even approaching that threshold after which another bite becomes not a pleasure, but an impossible task. Yet, there was no satisfaction in it. Or rather, there was satisfaction of a sort but no . . . satiation. No appeasement. I was still as jangled as I'd been before I began, with none of that thick comfortable fuzziness a full meal had always given me, even without the additional muddled warmth that alcohol lent. And without

147

that feeling, my dream meal seemed to have solidified inside me, like some hard-edged mass distending the frail membranes of my stomach, threatening to split it open.

I tried to distract myself with some correspondence I'd brought home, but couldn't concentrate on it, so turned on the 3D. But I couldn't get interested in that either, so I finally ended up taking the East African wormhole to Nairobi and hiking around the park there.

Yet the fresh air and exercise only made things worse. I began to develop a paradoxical appetite. The more I tried to concentrate on the walk, on watching the herbivorous-modified lions slinking bewilderedly through the tall grass after the herds of zebra and gnu their programming prevented them from attacking, the worse the conflict between the sensations got: I was starving, yet at the same time so bloated it was as if I had some sort of malignant growth expanding inexorably through my entrails.

I felt better after retching my guts out: even hungrier than before, but this hunger was normal, reassuring.

Returning to my apartment, I found there'd been a surcharge for the food I'd thrown up, because it wasn't going to my beneficiaries. Since I was still hungry, I decided to content myself with a meatball sandwich. I ate it, felt neither more satisfied nor sicker, and began cautiously nibbling pastries and other things that seemed like they'd be relatively rapid and easy to digest.

By pacing myself I was able to keep from getting sick again. The tastes of the eclairs, custards, and fruit tarts were as exquisite as I could have imagined them—and yet there was curiously little pleasure to my eating. Or rather, the pleasure was there, but distanced, almost like the sensuous excitement I sometimes felt watching beautiful women undressing on 3D: I could appreciate it, even enjoy it, but it never became real for me.

I remembered something from a Japanese novel I'd read once, about how the height of refined pleasure for the nobility of one period had been getting together to sample incenses. It must have been the same sort of pleasure.

At 2:20 in the morning I felt a sharp jab in my left wrist, a momentary blood-sugar exaltation. I had been nibbling a baba au rhum and the sudden, perfect conjunction of its taste and texture with the satisfaction of my body's hunger was almost enough to make me forget the horror of my homecoming turkey dinner.

By the time I was ready to go back to work Tuesday, I'd learned to eat constantly, small quantities of foodstuffs rich in easily digested sugars but containing enough fats and proteins to provide my Southeast Asian beneficiaries, whoever and wherever they actually were—if, in fact, they really existed at all—with their basic minimum. When I felt my intravenous feeder's jab I ate as fast as I could, stuffing myself so the two forms of satiation would coincide long enough to allow me to take pleasure in my meal. But even that was ultimately unsatisfactory: with normal digestion the satiation spread from my digestive tract outward to my whole body in thick, warm waves, but now the whole process was aborted, leaving me only a feeling of loss, a vague dissatisfaction. . . .

That first day back at work I took a spare suitcase full of sweets and sandwiches with me. Nora, my new assistant, was twenty-three, pleasingly plump, and highly attractive: I'd invited her out to dinner once or twice, and had hoped that things would develop further, but I'd obviously have to come up with another approach now. I sent her off to a neighboring department while I cleared out the top right-hand drawer of my desk and put the food there, nibbling on something whenever I was alone, then returning whatever remained to my desk before anyone else entered the office.

The first week went smoothly. I pleaded overwork to avoid lunching with my co-workers, and when Thursday evening came and the week's work was over, I went home having actually accomplished more than usual.

The following Wednesday I had an important luncheon with a client interested in investing in surgical futures, but I pleaded a gastric disorder which required a special diet and so had left me without even the allotment necessary to spring for so much as a round of drinks. He was far from pleased, but it was too minor a matter to affect our negotiations.

Back at the office, I was eating lionfish sashimi and making vague plans to develop a long-term gastric disorder which would excuse me from ever eating and drinking in public, when Nora burst into my office with what, I later learned, she thought was extraordinarily good news about an exclusive deal with a Buenos Aires organ bank that had already been hanging in the balance for over three years when she'd joined the firm.

My mouth was full of raw fish, and when I tried to gulp it down whole so I could yell at her to keep out, it caught in my throat. I couldn't even get my desk drawer closed in time to keep her from glimpsing the two-kilo cheesecake with boysenberry topping, the half-dozen pastrami sandwiches, and the bowl of chopped chicken liver.

Her incredulous stare unnerved me. I swallowed twice, finally managed to choke the fish down, and tried to regain my dignity.

She was still gaping at me. So rattled that I forgot she was a tither, even if only a token three-percenter, I yanked the drawer open again and, grabbing a pastrami sandwich, thrust it at her.

"Here. Have a sandwich. A friend with a dietary disorder couldn't use his allotment this month so he gave it to me and—"

I'd forgotten about the alimentary humility which was part of my sentence. As Nora reached hesitantly for the sandwich, an alarm went off. Immensely loud, and coming from my stomach: another modification they'd made in my digestive tract, but one they'd neglected to inform me about.

A moment later the alarm cut off and a baritone voice started shouting from my insides:

"WARNING TO ALL CITIZENS! JONATHAN HOLLAND IS UNDER

SENTENCE OF ALIMENTARY CHARITY FOR CORRUPTION OF PUB-
LIC OFFICIALS, SUBVERSION OF A UNIVERSAL LARDER, HOARD-
ING, AND GLUTTONY. JONATHAN HOLLAND IS FORBIDDEN TO
SHARE HIS FOOD WITH ANYONE OTHER THAN HIS BENEFI-
CIARIES. ANY PERSON ACCEPTING NOURISHMENT OF ANY SORT
FROM HIM WILL BE SUBJECT TO PROSECUTION UNDER ORDI-
NANCE 11780847A WHICH STATES . . ."

The recorded voice went on for at least ten minutes, citing
the entire ordinance—then, adding insult to injury, repeated
the message. By the time it had finished, the whole office was
gathered around my desk or jammed into the doorway, staring
and listening.

From then on I was a pariah, shunned even by the most
die-hard Eugenicists: when success is your only criterion of
judgment, getting caught for something, even something
nonreprehensible, is just as bad as doing something reprehen-
sible in the first place.

They couldn't fire me . . . in fact, I could have fired most
of them. But I knew the news would be getting back to the
board of directors within a few hours. And though the board
couldn't fire me, not without a lengthy battle in the World
Labor Court which would only bring them far more adverse
publicity than keeping me on ever could, I knew my chances
for further advancement were finished.

For the next few days I redoubled my security efforts, doing
my best to make sure no one caught me eating. Then, when I
saw their attitude remained unchanged, I started flaunting my
consumption, calling people into the office and making them
wait while I gorged myself, all the while apologizing for the
fact that I was forbidden to offer them anything. I had trouble
refraining from doing it in front of clients, though I managed.
Otherwise, labor courts or not, I would have been out of a job.

By the time I returned to my former secretiveness, the
damage had been done. Everyone around me, and especially
Nora, regarded me with a curious mixture of envy and contempt.

One day I returned from one of my mandatory alimentary re-education meetings—a lot of 3D pictures of hungry children and lectures by self-righteous tithers about how they'd found a new sense of self-worth through their donations—to find one of the coffee eclairs I'd left in the desk was missing. At first I was afraid I'd be punished or publicly humiliated for the loss, as I'd been for offering Nora that sandwich. But nothing happened, and when, three days later, an apricot tart disappeared, I realized that the AI they'd implanted in me had to be too limited to deal with anything more complicated than the simplest person-to-person situations.

I started leaving food on my desk when I left in the evening, cautiously at first, just a pastry or a half sandwich, in case there was some sort of overall accounting of my food consumption going on; then, when that drew no reaction, whole trays of pastry and cold meats. The food was always gone by the time I got to the office the next day.

Though I suspected Nora, I was never able to catch her, nor learn whether the stolen food was shared or hoarded. And though I hoped at first that my surreptitious generosity would be rewarded by improved relationships with those around me —bread cast upon the waters—it seemed, if anything, to have the opposite effect: I was treated with even more disdain than before.

Which was, on the whole, acceptable, because to their public contempt I could oppose my private knowledge that not only were they stealing from me, and so breaking the same laws that I was, but that they were being hypocrites about it as well, so were worse than I was.

Some weeks after my office situation had stabilized in mutual contempt, I arrived home to find a dove-gray, hand-addressed envelope waiting for me. There was no return address. I opened it and read:

Dear Mr. Holland:

It has come to our attention that you might be a suitable candidate for membership in the L-5 Gourmet Club. We are a select group of charity-minded connoisseurs of

fine food and drink with unlimited personal ration allot-
ments who enjoy meeting for our mutual enjoyment far
from the teeming billions of small-minded people who
infest . . .

The letter continued on in much the same vein. The gist
was obvious: only spend the enormous sum demanded and I
could indulge myself in the convivial company of other convicted gluttons, far from the prying eyes and certain censure
of those still forced to live within their ration allotments.

The letter concluded with an invitation to discuss matters
with the club's membership secretary if I thought I might be
interested. I called, found he was free, and took the wormhole
to the club's private aperture.

Yoshi, the membership secretary, met me in the lounge,
whose walls were covered with holos of those whom the club's
members had eaten back from starvation to glowing health.
He opened the door to the dining room and allowed me to
peer through—though I was not, of course, allowed to actually
enter the room, as I was not yet a member. Even the waiters
were club members, serving on a rotating basis.

It was everything the dining room of a private club was
traditionally supposed to be: rich wood decor, beautifully embroidered white linen tablecloths and napkins, exquisite silver
and china, waiters in white coats. An artificial gravity field,
seven-tenths earth normal. Each table had a modified larder
in its center, and the whole dining room had a wraparound
view of the blue-green Earth turning below.

The only thing seemingly out of place were the thirty-six
pillars ringing the dining room. Most of them were simply
cloudy crystal, but a number of them contained 3D images of
fanatical-looking tithers in black staring around disapprov-
ingly. One of the tithers caught my gaze and held it, staring
fiercely at me, as if daring me to enter the room.

"Who's that?" I asked Yoshi, gesturing.

Yoshi snorted in derision. "The Alimentary Surveillance
Committee. All volunteers, maintaining a vigil over us to

153

make sure we never forget that we're miscreants stealing from the public trough."

"It doesn't seem to have discouraged anyone."

"The whole Alimentary Charity program's a sham. Government public relations. It's just a way of paying lip service to the law while letting those of us who are too rich and powerful for anyone to prevent us from eating what we want go on doing so."

"But what about the surgery?"

"That's what makes the whole thing work, don't you see? It scares people who haven't had it, even though it's just a more extreme form of what the tithers do to themselves. And it's a great political gesture—the poor get their revenge on their rich oppressors by stealing the food right out of their stomachs. And when we do get our nourishment, we get it through a painful jab in the wrist instead of through the teleport filter, as though it were just more punishment. See?"

Yoshi's voice held the same fanatical conviction that the tithers at the weekly re-education meetings had, but what he was saying sounded plausible. I nodded, not altogether convinced.

"Besides, this club alone pays nine percent of the Alimentary Charity Program's operating expenses, and there are twenty other clubs. So they operate the whole thing at a tremendous profit, and get a lot of propaganda value out of doing it at the same time. That's all they really care about, not punishing us."

I waited until the tither in the pillar opposite me looked at me again and grinned at him, then told Yoshi I'd be proud to be a member. As soon as I transferred the first installment of my dues to the club account, I was allowed into the dining room, where I was welcomed with a celebratory feast.

My initiatory meal lasted nine hours. The club's services, I soon learned, included on-call medical supervision; special treatments enabling one to digest one's food (and thus pass it on) faster; discreet, under-the-table, AI-supervised stomach massages; special cooking facilities; and foods not registered in the universal larder's recipe banks. Though women were not allowed in the clubhouse, there was a dating service in conjunction with the various similar women's clubs.

The club, however, had only one activity.

Eating.

The club's one activity, however, gave rise to a host of variations: bake-offs and pie-eating contests, creative cookery and cake-decorating competitions, wine tastings . . . The conversation helped dull the visceral contradiction between my stomach's contents and its nutritional yield; the various treatments and medicines available lessened my discomfort.

Still, some of the other members gave me pause. Tonante, for example, would stuff himself with tasteless nutritional supplements and bland custards, rice and other inexpensive foods until he received his nutritional shot, then start in on the more refined foods he loved . . . only to retire to the washrooms and vomit up every course as soon as it was finished.

"No point in giving the little bloodsuckers anything more than they need," he said at least once an evening.

He was a skeletally thin man, so gaunt that even among us he stood out, with teeth worn to brown nubs from their daily doses of stomach acids, though he had new ones implanted every few months. He was serving a life sentence for reasons he refused to talk about, though the rumor was that he'd tried to bribe a surgeon at the Luna Clinic to undo his bypass in such a way as to allow him to keep his unlimited access to the universal larder.

Luckily, most of the other members were more sympathetic, though when I tried the club's dating service, the scrawny crone from one of our sister clubs that the AI set me up with proved to be so truly ghastly that I never made another attempt.

At my first quarterly review session the committee—all of them, thankfully, civil servants and not tither volunteers— gave me a new holo of my beneficiary family. They all had

155

some flesh on their bones; the children's bloated bellies were less swollen.

The garbage-and-frond hut was the same. I looked up to see the review board studying me as intently as I'd been studying the picture.

"They don't seem to have used the opportunity your charity provided them to better their condition, do they?" one slightly plump young woman asked me.

"Why do you say that?" I asked guardedly.

"Because that's what all you Eugenicists think when you see your second holo."

"You were the one who said it, not me. I'm not a fanatic. I'm glad they're healthier."

"Good."

"But what's the point of all this?" I demanded. "This kind of punishment?" At the club, opinion was divided between the people who agreed with Yoshi and those who thought the treatment was to condition us out of any desire for food by removing our pleasure in it. Like Pavlov's dogs, only we were being conditioned to find the food we were salivating for no more rewarding than the ringing of a bell.

I'd already tried asking at the weekly re-education meetings, but the tithers who ran the things thought of the whole process in terms of evildoers being punished for their sins. These people looked more reasonable.

"The road of excess leads to the palace of reason," the plump spokeswoman stated, obviously quoting somebody, but she refused to make herself any clearer. I looked it up on the 3D that night before I went to the club, but was no more enlightened than before.

At the club I had a reproduction of the new holo made and put up on the wall beneath the original. Then I went up and down the displayed holos, comparing the beneficiaries shown in their successive poses. For the most part, I found myself agreeing with the words the woman had tried to put in my mouth: the beneficiaries seemed to have accepted our involuntary charity without using their good fortune to improve their condition or avoid falling back into the same situation afterward.

And yet, I wondered if I would have come to that conclusion if the woman had not primed me with it. In which case, why had she done so?

Still, I found myself avoiding Tonante as much as possible. There was too much bitterness in the way he ate. It was impossible to share a meal with him and tell myself I was enjoying it.

My life had settled into a stable pattern. I did my job well, since there was nothing at work to distract me. My former friends avoided me and I avoided them: my free time was divided between solitary activities and the club.

At my second quarterly review session I was told that a provisional decision had been made to reduce my sentence, though the exact amount of that reduction would be dependent upon the extent of my continuing generosity.

In other words, they were trying to encourage me to eat even more. Why?

But suspicious though I was of the board's motives, I found myself looking forward to the office hypocrites' reactions when they found their food supply cut off.

A week later there was a special luncheon banquet at the club to celebrate Hawkin's return. Our champion trencherman, he had disappeared after having had his sentence commuted for successfully feeding a group of seventeen Yugoslavian Gypsies back from near starvation to near obesity. Two weeks after his departure, and twenty kilos heavier, he returned, to tell us that this time he was serving out a ten-year sentence for a third offense.

I went to the office directly from the banquet and for once didn't think to bring any extra food with me. That evening, returning from a negotiation with the Buenos Aires organ bank people that concluded earlier than I'd expected, I caught Nora desperately going through my briefcase in search of the pastries she could no longer find in my desk.

I didn't say anything about it to her, then or later, just

pretended I thought she was looking for some papers we needed. The next day I made sure I filled my desk drawer with sweets again, but the food remained untouched. I replaced it with fresh pastries.

Three days later food began disappearing again.

From then on I started varying the kinds and amounts of food I left in my desk, leaving far too much food for one person to eat one day, then nothing for two or three days, followed by the remains of a half-eaten sandwich, then a more normal meal, nothing the next day, and so on.

It all disappeared.

I began amusing myself by bringing in and leaving things that would be almost impossible to smuggle out of the office without being seen: tureens of turtle soup, ten-kilo wheels of the greenest, strongest-smelling viral cheese I could find, half a suckling pig. . . .

Other than that, work went on as usual. I got thinner and thinner, Nora grew plumper and plumper.

Seven and a half months after I'd been sentenced, the same two policemen who'd arrested me came for me at the office, accompanied by seven ragged but well-fed Southeast Asians. My beneficiaries. Somehow, instead of seeing the humiliation of the thing, I couldn't help noticing how healthy they seemed, and couldn't help thinking that, for whatever reason, I had at least fed them for seven and half months, while the hypocrites around me had only been feeding themselves.

It was one of the days when I'd brought in enough food to feed my family for a week. I took a special pleasure in leaving it in my desk when I left work that evening, imagining the staff fighting over their last free feast at my expense.

When I returned home from the Luna Penal Clinic later that night with my digestive apparatus returned to its original condition, I found that, bizarrely, my ration allotment for the coming month had had added to it everything I would normally have had the right to eat during all the months I'd been outside the normal system.

I started to order up a gargantuan meal, hesitated. If the

authorities were letting me do so, they had to have a reason. Out of sheer contrariness, to defeat their purpose, I ordered a meal that was almost tasteless by comparison with anything the club had ever offered: mock tuna and celery salad, some fresh vegetables and fruits, a vanilla custard.

Bland though it all was, there was a real physical satisfaction in eating it . . . as though I could continue to taste it long after it had left my mouth, all the way down my alimentary tract. And yet, oddly, I didn't finish my meal, trivial though the quantities involved were. I was . . . not satiated, but satisfied with so little now that it surprised me.

My seven and a half months had served to sharpen my hunger, to give me so much unsatisfactory "satisfaction" of what I had thought to be my real desires that now, at the slightest hint of true satisfaction, I could at last recognize it for what it was.

They'd made an incense sniffer out of me after all.

I felt suddenly furious at the way the government had dared manipulate and condition me. The same fury that Tonante must have felt, that must have been behind Hawkins's triumphant return to the club. It didn't matter whether they were right or wrong, what mattered was that they were trying to force me into something, trying to change me into someone else, against my will.

I ordered up the same turkey dinner I'd been sentenced for, began tearing my way through it, accompanying it with one of the wines I'd learned to appreciate at the club. Felt my satisfaction become satiation, my satiation give way to torpor, a thick dull anger as I continued to choke the food down, showing them all they couldn't—

Like Tonante vomiting in the bathrooms, replacing his teeth every few months. Punishing myself to get back at them.

Like a rat that has been conditioned to push a lever to get food pellets and that keeps on pushing the lever even though all it gives him now is an electric shock. Except, I realized, that my laboratory analogy was wrong. I hadn't been condi-

tioned, I'd been deconditioned. And with the excessive allotment they'd granted me for this month I was free to choose
for myself whether I wanted to return to my old ways, or
remain an incense sniffer. I could always exceed my allowance
and return to the club if I wanted to.

I started to put the remains of the turkey, the untouched
two-kilo charlotte aux baies mauves, back in the refrigerator to
wait until I was hungry enough to enjoy it.

I might even *enjoy* my food more if I became a three- or a
five-percenter tither, so I could satisfy my palate without satiation or torpor—

A three-percenter. Like Nora. I suddenly stopped dead, the
refrigerator door open and the charlotte in my hands, remembering the hypocritical loathing with which Nora had regarded me the day the alarm in my stomach went off.

If the police raided her apartment today, they'd undoubtedly catch her with all the food that I'd left in my desk.

I put the charlotte and the rest of the food away carefully,
then called the police's anonymous denunciation service, and
accused Nora of Alimentary Theft, Illegal Hoarding, and
Gluttony. I hadn't used either of the two anonymous denunci-
ations I had been allotted for that year, so I only had to pay
for the third one.

Tomorrow or the next day, when she got back from the
clinic, I would call her, invite her over for dinner, and she'd
come. Maybe not that first night, but sooner or later, when
she realized how cut off from everyone else she was, she would
come.

And when she did, I'd be able to sit there, acting understanding and oh so sympathetic, as I watched her gorge herself ineffectually while I controlled myself, and ate just
enough to please my palate.

And there, at last, would be *real* satisfaction.

∿∿∿

Grania Davis, that world-traveled raconteur and ebullient denizen of California's notorious Marin County, was a frequent contributor to Terry Carr's Universe, and has contributed fiction and semifiction to a wide assortment of other publications over the years. Her novels include The Rainbow Annals, Moonbird, and the recent Marco Polo and the Sleeping Beauty, written in collaboration with her former husband, Avram Davidson.

Here, in characteristically lively fashion, she provides us with some of the most seductive alien life-forms to head our way in a long while.

THE SONGS THE ANEMONE SING

GRANIA DAVIS

I felt like *merde*, as I stumbled out of the Translocator on Ta2. "Gracias . . . thanks," I said to the tech who schlepped me to my feet. Bouncing through the DenseG Translocator Network is never ding-dong, and rumors say that some mench never get back on synch—though that's never mentioned in The Company contract. Snag it. I'd be maharaja as soon as my synapses stopped swirling.

Neo-terre, neo celeste to goggle. Not the muddy-madre Earth sky, and the old-crone constellations. Nova night sky of Ta2, with alien astral clusters and the mucho-macho Ring Nebula, looking like a grande gleaming smoke ring from my padre's pipe.

Never see my padre again, nor my madre. They went pow in the epidemic. I'm solo now, but never solitary on mucky-madre Earth; cram-jammed with mench and more mench, subsisting in vast multiethnic bunk-lofts—one family per bunk—sleeping and working in twenty-four-hour rotating shifts, and babbling in polyglot pidgin. Never solitary on madre Earth-ball; that's why I Translocated to Ta2.

My family was bourg. We leased our own cube, and had cold running agua four hours a day (except Sunday). We had gelt for goodies—like school. So I became a mining engineer, sifting through the rubble and crud of the past. Then the protein deposits were discovered on a remote ice-ball named Ta2.

Protein. Edible protein growing mucho-macho in underground caves. Free protein for millions of mench to munch. The Greed-Corps jostled, and contracts were signed. The mines went Ready with hi-gelt volunteers. Who scrawls up for Ta2? Solos who want out of the global village bunk-lofts . . . loners who want to be *alone.* Moi.

An ice-blonde femme named Sub-Supervisor Lara schlepped me through the metallic-gray tunnels to the barren cubicle which would be my bower—all mine. Aesthetics don't Translocate, but no snag. I had my own bunk, illuminator, even a WC unit, all in metallic gray; Company must've salvaged a gray-glop stash.

"Achtung! Briefing in the meeting-mess," announced Lara, as she guided me to an overheated salon painted metallic gray (surprise!). She punched some codes in a chef unit, and out came something vaguely hot and munchable, made of Ta2 protein. Merde-cuisine.

Then something never-never entered the metallic gray port of the meeting-mess. It looked like an undulating flower arrangement, whose rainbow petals blinked my orbs with prismatic tendrils of light.

"Goggle that?" I asked, though I already snagged it—I'd seen them in the illuminator on Earth-ball.

"It's a delegation of Anemone," said Lara. "Bounced here to orb the protein harvest."

"I'll stash one in a vase to blink up my cube," I said, making a minor hoo-ha which my ice-mentor passed.

But ding-dong, I'd never orbed live Anemone before. The treaty blips them from Earth because they might riot up superstitious mench-mobs. My synapses swirled. Here I was at the butt-end of the galaxy, sipping hot ersatz caffeinated protein, and goggling a fiesta of Anemone undulating across the metallic gray deck.

The Anemone are the first sentient-form we've met in the

Translocator net. That makes them numero ichiban, and they are so primo; more veggie than critter, by homo-standards. They are pensive, pax, and bonny, like sophisticated flowers.

We tag them Anemone because of the meld of flora-form and sentient-synapses. They nosh off trace nutrients in agua, and their home-ball is a terre of marshes and muck, where they sprout half-dunked. Thus the obvious tag after the extinct anemone of murky-marine Earth. Their own tag for their species sounds like a snore.

"Aloha," hailed Lara, and they hummed and undulated toward our bench. There were five Anemone, ranging from waist to chest height, with concentric rings of petals, like agua-lilies pulsing tendrils of light. They had a ding-dong dulce scent, and hues ranging from red to purple to blue, with cobalt orb-spots at the petal tips. One was tall as my shoulder, with bouffant rings of violet petals veined with neon-blue, and restless magenta light-strands. I goggled and blinked and stared. Maybe aesthetics *can* translocate. Primo ichiban!

"Achtung! Meet David Arnson," said Lara. "He'll monitor the protein harvest—he just bounced through the Translocator."

Sympatico humming from omni Anemone, then Big-blue's tones resolved into clear homo-speech. Nothing too profound, I think it said: "Banzai, David Arnson, ichiban to meet you."

When flowers greet you, it snags that you are very far from home-ball.

When the briefing was pow, we plunked down into the mines. The Anemone ganged along to orb the mature protein cells preharvest. The protein mines were maharaja. We schlepped in protective blubbles, down schwarz and barren shafts, to underground igloos of icy gravel. There the protein cells endlessly grow and multiply like a mucho-macho replicating organ. They form a grande fleshy carpet which noshes off the minerals of the cavern walls. As each cell divides, it blinks phosphorescence, so the igloos twinkle like a ding-dong galaxy. It was an ichiban show. The Anemone in their blubbles, radiating neon-crimson tendrils, schlepping through the maze of blinking protein caves. Murky-madre Earth felt very far away.

The blubbles snag sound, so we could hear the constant drone of the Anemone as they blarneyed among themselves, and a crackling which Lara tagged as the shifting pressures of the frozen walls.

"Are they stable?" I asked.

"Randomly there are Taquakes," said Lara. "We can usually seismic-tech them, and evacuate the igloos chop-chop."

Usually. Another kvetch The Company recruiters hadn't tagged.

The protein caves are primo, but harvesting the multiplying cells is a slave-labor sentence. The blubble-tech activates cutting and scraping blades that meticulously slice the mature deposits, and pack them into enviro-tins. If multi-cells die, the shipment will be pow. The blades must slice like a lover's touch, and the tins must snag the igloo milieu of Ta2, or the Earth-mench who unseals the Translocator port will find a rotting glump of malodorous cells. My coolie was to check and recheck omni. Wunderbar, nespah?

As Lara showed me the controls, I heard a cracking roar. Our blubble waltzed around, and a void appeared in the galaxy of blinking cells as the ice-wall went loco.

"Avalanche!" kvetched Lara, as she tried to chop-chop the cavorting blubble back through the maze.

Fissures opened omni, and a maharaja boulder of iced gravel, covered with winking protein cells, kerplunked onto the blubble which held the big blue-veined Anemone. I heard a hum which sounded like a sob, as the creature plopped with helpless petals pulsing dolorous pink light.

I subbed the scraper, so the Anemone could schlep onto the blade. We were blipping around so much that I kvetched about blitzing the beast. But merde, neh? The unprotected Anemone would soon be pow in the frigid milieu, with ice boulders spritzing like meteors.

The Anemone snagged the scraper blade with strands of

lavender light, which seemed to cling like a spider's web, as I drew it toward the blubble. Lara opened the port and hauled the fluttering creature inside. Then we bounced among ker-plunking boulders, and through the maze of tunnels, followed by a babbling bouquet of flipped flowers.

Ding-dong; omni escaped the Taquake. Big-blue was battered but not pow. Two petals were grunched, but they could be pruned off and would heal over.

"It should siesta in its tank," said Lara. "It needs time to mend, and the tank's temp and munchies must be monitored. You said an Anemone would blink up your cube. We'll plunk the tank with you for a few cycles to orb it."

"That was just a hoo-ha," I said. "This flower has synapses —it voxes and synchs. It would be more amigo with the others."

"Niet. The Anemone can't snag the manual controls on their tanks, and they hum and blarney endlessly. You should learn to tech the tanks—and it would blink up your cube." An arctic smile.

"Affirmative," I kvetched. I didn't want a vita-veg in my cube. I wanted to be solo. But the creature needed to be goggled during its siesta—and it was just for a few cycles.

So we schlepped the tank of nutrient-enriched agua into my tiny gray bower, which no longer looked angst. Now it looked like a belle greenhouse for a nodding violet sans two clipped petals. I was no longer solo. I was nursing a grunched Anemone.

"Aloha! Are you taking siesta, David?" asked the low hum.
"No, just nodding."
"Merci for plucking me from the mine."
"No snag."
"Where did you sprout?" asked the blue-veined Anemone.
"I sprouted from Earth-ball."
"Do your petals droop for your home-pond?"
"Niet. It's ultra crowded and murky."
"What about your comrades . . . clan . . . mate?"

"I'm solo," I said.

"But mench are social organisms, with tight emotional ties to their tribes," hummed the Anemone.

"Not me. I'm the exception."

"The exception, neh? Then your function is to prove the rules."

"Are you studying us?"

"Merely goggling homo-forms . . . and the protein harvest."

"You're very scholarly—for a flower. What's your home-ball like?" I asked.

"It's warm and wet and pax, and we dunk together in the marshes and hum harmonious blarney. Soon I'll have a neo song about the protein harvest, the first since I sprouted off my parent."

"Sprouted off . . . ?"

"We shed our mature petals, which float in agua and sprout into nova Anemone . . . as you tag us. The two petals that went pow in the mines were my two buds. They would have become separate Anemone, but sharing my hues and memories."

"You xerox your parent's memories?" I asked.

"Si, since we were once joined," hummed the Anemone.

"So you have clans, but nil mates."

"We don't need mates. But mench have a maharaja need to mate. Sub-Supervisor Lara is a suitable organism. Will you mate her?"

"That frosty fish . . ."

"Fish? Aren't fish extinct aquatics? Is Lara an aquatic fish?"

"Niet, that's just a tag. I prefer to be solo, and Lara is Xerox . . . or she wouldn't be here."

"Am I clogging your solitude?" asked the Anemone, its light-filaments turning pale pink.

"No snag; it's just for a few cycles while you siesta. How's the temp in your tank? Petal stumps causing any grunch?"

"I'm ding-dong," hummed the Anemone. "So what's the difference between mench tags *alone* and *lonely?*"

Lara said they liked to blarney, and Big-blue was clearly rehearsing its home-ball musical debut. But *I* needed some pax and silence, not an anthropological interview. "Alone can be plus," I replied coolly. "Some homos amour solitude. Lonely is minus . . . missing multi-mench. Do Anemone get lonely?"

"Niet. We are never solo. Omni dunk together in fiestas."

"Never solo! You should snag it sometime—it can be very pax." (Right now it would be ding-dong pax).

"Who would I blarney with?" asked the Anemone.

"Sometimes you can be sans blarney."

"What would I *do?*" The Anemone's light filaments abruptly turned scarlet.

"What else do Anemone do?"

"That's what we do. We dunk together and sing stories."

I began to synch. The Anemone home-ball supplies all their needs, and they have no hands to manipulate tech, yet they are HI-Q. So what else would they do but dunk in the warm and nourishing muck milieu . . . and lieder and blarney and hum?

"I'll sing a story for you," hummed the Anemone. In a sympatico drone, it sang about ancient Anemone who met fiend-forms from the stars that attacked with bristly claws and dents. But the Anemone sang ichiban lieder until the fiend-forms schlepped away.

Sans much of a plot, yet the song was hypnotic. And Big-blue looked so belle, with violet petals laced with cobalt that matched its orb-spots, and magenta light-tendrils that flicked a rhythmic beat. I lay on my bunk and goggled and blinked. How gauche and bristly mench seem—like fiend-forms from the stars.

Then I felt angst. A graceful creature was singing just for me—but it wasn't homo. If I met a femme as bonny as this plant, I could feel amour for her . . . and I wouldn't be solo anymore. My synapses swirled . . .

There was a loud grump on the port, and Sub-Supervisor

Lara entered. "Achtung! You're a unit late for coolie in the mines!"

"Mea culpa. I fugued the time. I was listening to an Anemone historical opera."

"Punctuality is de rigueur in the mines," she kvetched.

"D'accord. I'll schlep presto. Will you be pax while I'm gone?" I asked the Anemone.

"Si. I'll siesta now, David . . . but I'll sense the presence of your absence . . ."

My coolie-cycle in the mines seemed endless. Apres, I declined to join the techs for a hot ersatz protein nosh in the salon. I bounced back to my cube, eager to aloha my Anemone. I found it humming gently in its tank.

"Banzai, David. I missed you."

"I missed you too," I burbled. "Your singing is ichiban, and your hues are too. You're more amigo than most mench I know."

The Anemone's light tendrils snapped neon-pink. "You're a primo homo," it hummed.

"Neh? I'm a gauche tan hue, and covered with bristles, and can't chop-chop a tune."

"You can babble ichiban stories. Tell me about yourself as a bud, David, and tell me about your clan."

I plunked onto my bunk, orbed the hypnotic weaving tendrils . . . and began to babble . . . and babble in polyglot pidgin about moi as a niño, and as a student. I kvetched about losing my madre and padre in the epidemic, and about the cram-jammed yet lonely global village bunk-lofts of Earth-ball. Neo-vox drained my brain. The Anemone in its tank hummed a soft sympatico drone, waved those enchanting magenta tendrils, and mercilessly plucked swirling synapses from me as no mench could. Multi-units later I fell silent and kaput. I also felt wunderbar. "If you were a homo-femme, I could . . . love you. Loco, nespah?"

"I love you too, David," hummed the Anemone, its streamers deepening to maroon.

170

"But we're mismatched life-forms . . . we can never mate." I kvetched in a voice tense with angst.

"We are sans need to mate," droned the Anemone. "We can just be together."

"Voila. *Be* together, neh? I feel more ding-dong being with you than with omni before—and I can't even pronounce your tag!"

The Anemone and I epoxied. It shared my blubble in the mines and my bench in the salon. We spent siesta-cycles at the illuminator, orbing the eerie ultra-violet sky of Ta2, glowing in the blaze of the amethyst star within the maharaja ring nebula. And we babbled . . . and blarneyed . . . and hummed.

So my amigo wasn't homo-form, no snag. (Don't look a gift flower in the . . .) My Anemone was ichiban, and I didn't care if omni thought I was loco. Lara dropped multi-therms, and the Anemone bouquet flared scarlet shock-volts when we continued to share my cube.

Cultural exchange. That's how we voxed it. Anemone were blipped from Earth, so we could only goggle each other on Ta2. Omni mench should bunk with Anemone. Lara should invite one into her cube—it would blink up the gray decor. That grumped them; nil would siesta with an alien-form. Merde cultural exchange.

But the truth was ultra-loco. Big-blue and I were toujours together. Voila; we were in love.

Then the hex happened. A fanatic mench-mob on Earth snagged a Translocator, which was bouncing a petit Anemone from a secret botanical meeting back to its home-ball. They plant-napped the poor creature as hostage over obscure political grumps. The howling and verminous mench-mob schlepped the wailing Anemone from the Translocator port, and powed its petit petals one by one.

Omni on Ta2 met in the mess and babbled in polyglot pidgin as we orbed the images on the illuminator in shocked oy vey. The goggling Anemone gang in the mess flashed wan strands of palest pink, and keened a dolorous kvetch. Ta2 Mining Company immediately ordered omni Anemone to bounce back to their home-ball.

The bouquet droned with audible relief and regained a slurp of color—except Big-blue, who flared pure white lightning. "I can't leave you solo, David," it hummed to me.

"I'll be pow if you go—stay here! I'll be your guardian . . . and your gardener," I said.

"Achtung! The Translocator is ready," announced Lara.

The Anemone bunched around Big-blue, who pleaded to transplant to Ta2. Their light tendrils flicked like restless red serpents, as they grumped in growling tones. Then those tendrils became whips of startling white voltage that spider-webbed Big-blue in a luminous trap.

My Anemone kvetched and struggled, but the floral arrangement schlepped purposefully out of the salon, and down the metallic gray tunnels to the Translocator—hauling Big-blue. I'd never orbed those creatures move so presto, nor use any force. My synapses swirled, but I could do nil except follow. If I tried to fight, it would prove that homos are bristly fiend-forms from the stars—and how could I blitz strands of light, neh?

"Sayonara, David!" wailed Big-blue, as the tech sealed the Translocator port.

"Bon voyage," I cried. Then my Anemone was kaput. I would never goggle it, nor hear its song again.

"What's this angst all about?" demanded Lara, as I fled back to my dolorous cube . . .

The cycles swirled and blurred as I tried to coolie, nosh, and siesta, without exposing my ennui to omni. I made mis-techs in the mines and powed multi-tins of protein. I twitched and jittered in my barren cube while orbing the maharaja smoke-ring nebula in my illuminator—solo.

172

I could only synch on Big-blue . . . such an ichiban creature . . . such primo songs. How gently it plucked at my synapses. I was ding-dong with my Anemone. Now I knew what *lonely* meant.

"Achtung! Please vox with The Company psycho-tech; you may be suffering post-Translocation-trauma," said Lara. "Your addiction to that flower is grunching omni. The creature has you bewitched with ersatz emotion. Try to fugue it, David."

But I could never fugue Big-blue, and no psycho-tech would rehab me. Although it was ultra-taboo, I determined to follow my cher Anemone.

I slipped through metallic gray tunnels to the Translocator. It was siesta-cycle, but the port was always guarded. I had my Luller, and the first guard was no snag. But the second guard voxed an alarm before I could stun him with Lull. The alarm summoned Lara and a fiesta of mine-mench, grumping in polyglot pidgin. I stood at the port with the Luller raised like a gun.

"Neh?" asked Lara, still wearing siesta-sweats.

"Adios," I said with a courteous bow.

"If you want to bounce back to Earth—why not scrawl up a trans-form?" she asked.

"Niet . . . not Earth-ball."

"Merde! Not the Anemone home-ball—that's taboo. Please blarney with the psycho-tech . . . or with me, David. You seem fermished with this idea fixe."

"I'll blarney with nil . . . I want to orb my amigo."

"You never try to amigo with mench on Ta2. And you're sans Translocator training. How will you bounce there, David? It's not facile. You'll schlep to vacuum-balls or ice-balls or fire-balls. This is Kamikaze," said Lara.

"I know the basic Translocator tech . . ." I began. Then in a sudden slurp of motion, one of the miners snagged a Luller. Enough kvetching. I spritzed them one by one. Lara was last. Sweet siesta, Lara.

They crumpled like grunched sweats. Now I was solo with the Translocator—my only hope of snagging Big-blue. But Lara was right; I was sans training. The DenseG Translocator networks across the galaxy like a maze of lethal mine shafts

173

that can bounce you anywhere—or nowhere. If you mis-tech, you're pow.

Was Lara right . . . was I suffering post-Translocation trauma? Should I ask the psycho-tech for euphoriants . . . and try to fugue Big-blue? But I wanted to epoxy with my Anemone again, and merde the risk. Could I synch the Translocator-tech? I sealed the port and tried to set the coordinates. Time and space are teachers sans mercy . . . pass and fail are the only grades.

A sensory tsunami engulfed me. In the illuminator, the maharaja ring nebula of Ta2 blurred into static. My synapses swirled into timeless static . . . perhaps I kvetched. Flame geysers blinked on the illuminator . . . fire-ball! I set the coordinates again . . . vacuum-ball . . . ice-ball . . . agua-ball . . . nil-ball . . . how long could my synapses contra the stress?

Then the illuminator blinked warm and pax magenta dawn-light . . . on the bayous and billibongs of the Anemone home-ball. But would the creatures aloha an amigo—or veto a bristly fiend-form from the stars?

I unsealed the port onto dank and damp. The humidity hugged me like a sweaty womb. Agua spritzed from the dense dome of zoftig fern-trees and vines, and melded with miasmic mists over mossy muck. I was in a spongy lavender rain-forest . . . sans edifice . . . sans Translocator-tech to sayonara . . . for Anemone are sans homo-skills.

I schlepped through the bush, scented with purple puff-balls, until it opened onto a murky pond. There I orbed my first bouquet of Anemone, with pink petals and light-strands, dunking and munching nutrients, and humming in their matey way. Their song blinked up my hopes. Big-blue was nearby—somewhere.

But were they amigo? I tried to camouflage behind a scrubby shrub. The bouquet sensed my presence pronto, and blared a shrill siren song. Their light tendrils grew ruddy and restless as serpents snagging prey . . . and I recalled what those mobile webbing streamers could do.

But I was an amigo . . . why should I lurk? I stepped into the clearing with a manic hoo-ha—and was instantly cocooned in cool rosy light. I could hardly twitch, and they didn't synch my aloha kvetch . . . or perhaps they didn't care. Time-units passed as the cycle dimmed on Anemoneball. Soon I'd be pow like a gnat in a web. Sweet siesta, David. *Merde.*

Suddenly I was whipped away in a slurp of magenta light, that schlepped me through the tangled bush to a pond in a distant clearing . . . and there I orbed Big-blue, hauling me like fishermench once hauled extinct fish. I was libre, and I sputtered and smirked on the slimy shore.

"Banzai, David! Aloha!" hummed Big-blue. "I sensed your presence and tried to snag you. That pink bouquet misgoggled a fiend-form from the stars. Do you want to siesta . . . do you want to nosh?" Big-blue snaked a magenta tendril into the bush and hauled a fiesta of iridescent fruit. Adios Ta2 protein cuisine!

But I didn't want to siesta or munch just then. I wanted to synch the bouquet of Anemone that dunked in the pond with Big-blue. A dozen identical Anemone, with xerox cobalt-veined petals and orb-spots, and magenta light strands.

"We've budded," sang Big-blue proudly. "We *all* remember and love you, David. Stay with us . . . lieder with us . . . blarney with us."

"We all remember and love you, David," hummed the fiesta of xeroxed blue-veined Anemone, waving their hypnotic streamers of light. "Stay with us . . . lieder with us . . . blarney with us . . ."

I goggled the dusky lavender rain-forest, and the slime-pond alive with caressing magenta light.

"Omni love you, David . . . why be solo? Stay with us . . ." crooned Big-blue.

"Omni love you, David . . . why be solo? Stay with us . . ." echoed the chorus of xeroxed buds.

My synapses swirled. I wanted to epoxy with Big-blue . . . not with a flower arrangement! What should I do? Should I

175

try to schlep back to the Translocator, and bounce across the treacherous DenseG Network . . . to murky madre Earth-ball or icy gray Ta2? Or should I squat beside the slime-pond and munch dulce fruit, and sing stories with the ding-dong Anemone . . . my cher Anemone. A fiesta of my cher Anemone.

"Stay here . . . we love you," sang bewitching Big-blue.

"Stay here . . . we love you," chorused the Xerox of buds.

I noshed on a piece of syrupy fruit and orbed the pond . . . at least I would never be solo again.

$\longleftarrow\!\!\!\!\bigwedge\!\!\!\!\bigwedge\!\!\!\!\longrightarrow$

Which writer in this issue of Universe, *they asked slyly, has had the longest career in science fiction?*

Silverberg, you say? Well, yes, his first published material goes back to antediluvian 1953—but he doesn't have a story in the issue. Just stick to contributors. Well, then, you say, it must be Le Guin. And indeed the bibliographical references show that her work began appearing in the s-f magazines in 1962.

But it's a trick question, of course. The senior author in our ranks is Richard R. Smith, whose first s-f story appeared in the September 1954 of long-forgotten Fantastic Universe, *and was followed during the next few years by contributions to such equally nostalgia-provoking titles as* Planet Stories, Thrilling Wonder Stories, Infinity, *and* Science Fiction Adventures. *After which he took a lengthy sabbatical from science fiction, during which he managed to produce, under some twenty pseudonyms, thirty novels in an assortment of other fields, hundreds of short stories for men's magazines and mystery/detective publications, and a great deal of nonfiction material.*

Science fiction seems to be an incurable virus, though. His long hiatus is over, and here he is again—writing once again under his own distinctive name—with this wacky one-of-a-kind item, a headlong tale of unlikely adventure in implausible places that manages to break every editorial rule we've been handing out to would-be contributors—and somehow to get away with it.

178

This time it looks like Smith has returned to science fiction for a lengthy stay, and is keeping up with recent developments in the field. He reports that he's working on two trilogies.

ALIEN USED CARS

RICHARD R. SMITH

I have this particular vice that I have by long habit kept hidden in some ways— not that it's particularly bad or evil or anything like that, but just the kind of little vice that most people want to keep private . . . perhaps inwardly I think of it as a kind of weakness, bordering on sinful . . . my first wife did not exactly approve but then she did not exactly disapprove since some men had much more hazardous vices such as alcohol or women. My vice— I guess it started when I was a teenager and bought my first and became hooked: used cars. I loved to buy them years before astronomers discovered the Rich Galaxies with their thousands of alien races. Then, when the races started visiting Earth and their used vehicles began showing up in used car lots all over the world, I became a kind of fanatic, trying to look at every used alien car, buying a large number, sometimes reselling them or trading them in on other cars. . . . I don't want to take the time to tell you about all of them, it would take too long, but I would like to tell you about three alien used cars I bought . . . *four*, actually. I bought the first of the four when my first wife was still alive. (She died of natural causes; I never remarried—not *exactly*—but I'll explain that later, and even before I met the woman who became my second wife, sort of, I used to say, "My first wife," and it was a good line because sometimes a beautiful woman would say, in effect if not the exact words, "What about your second wife?" and I'd say, "I haven't met her yet. Maybe." And then I'd give the woman an appraising look and my smile that has been called charming when at its best and the woman would just *melt*, you know, smile and melt.) Well—I'm sorry if I digressed, I'll try not to do it again but maybe you found it interesting—anyway, I heard about this alien used car and went to see it and went crazy with desire. . . . You've heard of double-decker British buses? This was a *triple-decker* alien bus-motorhome . . . a vehicle as large as a small mountain . . . well, a small hill, at least . . . (from a world called Yakkayamma) and it was one of the first times that I learned aliens do not *think* the way we do. No. They really *don't*. I became very aware of that when, at a point in my life I'll describe later, I became interested in alien literature and began reading it and became fascinated by one race that never wrote in short choppy paragraphs the way some Earthlings do, most I suppose, but wrote in long continuous paragraphs, sometimes telling a whole story in one paragraph and I found it so fascinating I began trying it myself—*Darnakians* their name was. Darnakia, the world—Darnakians, the people. I'd never been there at the time this story starts, but I'd read a lot of their books. Sorry if I digressed again, but it is marginally relevant. Anyway—this thing . . . this used car, used bus-motorhome, was one of the first indications to me personally that aliens do not think the way Earthlings do, because the car dealer explained that on Yakkayamma, the world where the triple-decker bus-motorhome originated, the bus driver lived on the bus with his family. No kidding. A section of this enormous triple-decker vehicle, a portion of all three levels, was allocated to the bus driver and his family—about one-ninth of the bus, I guess. And that was their home, most rooms sealed off from the main part of the bus, for privacy, but one certain room open to bus passengers so they and the bus driver family could mingle socially on occasions. If that's not *alien*, I don't know what is. How many times have you gotten on a bus and the driver has given you that cool, *cool*, aloof look as if saying, *This is my bus, you're a stranger, I'll be glad when you're gone, where's your money?* Sorry to digress. I guess I acquired that habit partly from Darnakian literature. You know, Earthling literature is so often right to the point that, when you see a backflash and especially a backflash *within* a backflash, some people tend to think, *Hey, what's this guy trying to pull?* as if he's violating some kind of federal law. Anyway, this triple-decker bus-motorhome *wouldn't run* and nobody on Earth had the slightest idea how to repair the engine, so I bought it real cheap (with forty-eight wheels underneath) and had it moved to this property we'd bought in Maryland. Shortly after we married, my first wife and I bought some summer cottage property in Maryland, a place called Chesapeake Landing, our piece of land had its own little forest, so I cut down some trees and had this bus-motorhome put plunk in the center. As a kid (and later as an adult) I'd always had the desire to build a treehouse and, strangely, this alien bus-motorhome, the top level, was taller than the trees in our little forest, so you could look out over the treetops. It was like having bought a kind of alien treehouse. My first wife's eyes bulged when she saw the thing. Later, as she saw me walking around inside (it was much larger than most houses) and saw me grinning from ear to ear, she began to suspect the degree of my used car disease. Another alien used car I bought was an amphibious thing from Phlipphlocklov, a thing I used more as a boat than a car— went fishing in it umpteen times, and when it somehow started floating *above* the water rather than riding *on* the water, I parked it at our summer property as a kind of huge combination ornament/weather vane (tied it to a tree). It attracted a lot of attention and because the thing was as large as a yacht, it became the largest weather vane in the county. Another alien used car I purchased was from the Pym and Lizdon races on a world called Traurig. (A masterpiece of alien engineering, the Pyms did the assembly while the Lizdons supplied the parts.) The car was about the size of a motorcycle for two, but you were completely enclosed; air-

181

conditioned interior, very comfortable in the heat of summer, and comfortably warm in the winter—and the thing ran on water. *Water.* *WATER.* When the used car dealer first told me, I could hardly believe it but he said the Traurigian races had developed a technology for extracting the hydrogen from water and exploding it for energy, he thought. He wasn't sure. But anyway, the thing had a kind of grilled rain-catcher on the top that caught rain and funneled it down into its fuel storage tank which was, I suppose, only a couple of gallons in size, but after a heavy rain you could run for a month or two, a few thousand miles normal driving. A spoonful of water would take you about five hundred miles in heavy city traffic, the dealer said, but I never found a way to check that. Some things I did have a chance to check, however: he said it could burn anything with *liquid* in it and laughingly said that if I ever ran out of gas I could spit in the tank (it also had a fill pipe on the side) or urinate in it, or borrow a cup of water from a stranger. It had some kind of purification system so the engine took what it needed and discarded everything else—I don't want to tell you about *all* my adventures in the thing but I would like to say that once, when traveling cross-country with my friend, Veronica, we were crossing a long dry desert road and ran out of fuel (no fuel gauge), and I managed to get us another ten or fifteen miles on a few drops of Dad's Diet Root Beer left in a can. Then Veronica said she had to go to the bathroom, and as I politely looked the other way, she gave the thing enough fuel to take us to Las Vegas, where we filled the tank with unleaded gas just for the hell of it, although ironically, the thing got less mileage on *gas* because it had less hydrogen than water! You may think these vehicles were strange, but I encountered some others . . . one I'll always remember I found at the rear of a used car lot. I liked the looks of it. Sleek lines. No windows. Not real windows—there were a couple of narrow slits to look out, slits with tinted glass —no one could see in—and when I say *narrow,* I mean *narrow,* about three quarters of an inch high and a foot wide; but the inside had radar and video screens to show the driver the road ahead (but the things didn't work). . . . I loved the color. Orange. You don't see many orange cars. My first wife said, "It looks like an orange Easter egg" . . . I asked the dealer about it and he just shrugged and said, "It doesn't run and we don't know how to fix it." He paused and lit a cigar and added, "Good interior . . . and I think the radio works." So . . . I sat in the thing and the dealer wandered off and I closed the door and fumbled around and turned on the radio, which was actually more than a *radio*—it sent music into your mind telepathically—the music was fascinating— the seats were as soft and comfortable as anything in this world, or out of it, so I bought the thing and put it in some bushes on our property at Chesapeake Landing, and whenever I wanted to escape from this world for one reason or another, I'd go to that car that didn't run—and turn on the radio, the only thing that worked, and I'd turn up the volume and listen to that alien music (from a world that translates as Nikki-Rikki-Nokki-Tikki) pouring into my ears, my mind, into my *soul*, and after a short time I'd feel refreshed and feel like going out into the world again, conquering whatever came my way. Another alien used car I bought (from a world with the name of Oooh Ahhh Oooh Ahhh [so-named because the fa- mous intergalactic explorer Sam Breckenridge was about to officially name the planet at a ceremony, with thousands and thousands of the inhabitants present, on a world with a double sun, where everything was always extremely hot, and although Sam had been careful to wear sunglasses and lightweight clothing, he'd not realized the microphone would be ex- tremely hot . . . and took hold of it as he was about to say the name he'd decided on, and burned his hand, saying, "Oooh Ahhh Oooh Ahhh!"—and the inhabitants sent the *Oooh Ahhh Oooh Ahhh* flashing around their world, record- ing it everywhere as their new official name. When Sam Breckenridge heard the news while still nursing his burned hand, he said, "What the hell, I can't stick around this damned place any longer," and left to discover other worlds.]), the dealer said was stuck in gear. I said, "Stuck in first or

183

second or third?" and he said, "Stuck in *up.*" We went for a test drive, he showed me the one lever that worked, pulled it, and we went *up*—hundreds of feet—then came back down and I bought the thing as soon as we touched the ground. I had it moved to our summer cottage property and when I felt in a certain mood I'd get in that thing and push the lever and go up-up-up . . . up so high I could see for miles and miles, up into the clouds sometimes, above the clouds other times, and on a few occasions into the upper atmosphere where it became hard to breathe (toyed with the idea of taking an oxygen mask and seeing just how far the thing would go, but never got around to it—always seemed too busy with other things to fool around that way) and. . . . I've described more alien used cars than I intended to, I'm sorry, but I guess you get the idea I was really enthused about used cars, especially *alien* used cars, the bizarre, the unique, the whatever, and over the years I'd become a steady customer at a place in Philadelphia called Foolish Rajah's. The name came about because Rajah, the owner, an individual from a world named D'Gobba-D'Lama, thought names such as Crazy Eddie (for car dealers) were very clever, but didn't want to be too much of a copycat and didn't want to imply he was completely bananas, so he came up with *Foolish Rajah's* as a name for his new and used car lot. He sold most makes of new cars but also had a collection of used Earthling cars and used alien cars. I liked Rajah's cars and deals, but I didn't like Philadelphia, and every time I went there, I always had this creepy feeling at the back of my neck as if something awful was going to happen. Philadelphia—called "The City of Brotherly Love" . . . I don't know where it got that name—one of the highest crime rates in the country with the teachers and garbage collectors on strike almost constantly, it always seemed to me one of the dirtiest cities in America, if not *the* dirtiest—sorry if anybody from Philadelphia is reading this and it offends you, but hey, it's just my personal feelings. And what always puzzled me, *aliens* liked Philadelphia for some reason or other. Strange, isn't it? It's in the statistics—when aliens began coming to

184

Earth to live, they began settling more in Philadelphia than in Washington or New York or Los Angeles or Smallsvilleburg, Idaho. So, ironically, Philadelphia became a treasure chest of alien used cars, with Foolish Rajah's the largest outlet. Rajah. Maybe I should describe him. He was about one foot tall and looked like a teddy bear. Like those creatures from *Star Wars*, but smaller. Superintelligent but superweak. All his salespeople were human, for one reason or another. (I collect alien stories the way some people collect Polish jokes and I've always liked the story that when Rajah disappeared once for a year—his staff kept the business running during his absence—he'd actually been kidnapped by a six-year-old girl who threw him in the trunk of her parents' car, thinking he was just a play teddy bear, and then kept him hidden in her room for some months—once her mother saw him and he tried to explain who he was but his voice was never very strong and he got in only a few words before the girl's mother said, "Oh, that's a cute talking bear, Nancy, but do you think it's nice to keep him chained to your toy box?" and then left the room before Rajah had a chance to explain. I've thought about writing a short story or novel about it someday.) Getting back to the point—I received a phone call one day from a new salesperson at Foolish Rajah's, she said her name was Sandra, and would I be interested in looking at a new used car they'd just taken in inventory? I asked her if she could describe it and she said she'd rather show it to me, so I drove up to Philadelphia, to Foolish Rajah's and went in the office and found Rajah sitting on the knee of a gorgeous blonde. *EXCUSE ME*, I said. And started to leave. The blonde said, THAT'S ALL RIGHT. RAJAH WAS JUST DICTATING A LETTER. MY NAME IS SANDRA, I'M DOUBLING AS SECRETARY UNTIL HE FINDS A REPLACEMENT. (We weren't really shouting at each other as it may appear here. In Darnakian novels, dialogue of the main character or narrator is always in italic capital letters and dialogue of other characters is in plain caps, I began trying it after reading Darnakian novels for forty years—but I'll explain that later.) Getting

185

back to my entry into the office, Rajah said something—hello or something else, I couldn't hear what, his voice was so weak. Meanwhile, Sandra put Rajah back on top of his desk and put down the steno pad she'd been writing in and I realized it *had* been innocent: Rajah had been sitting on her knee because his voice was so weak she couldn't have heard him if he'd been farther away. *Lucky Rajah,* I thought, following Sandra out into the lot, getting a good look at her shape, legs, etc. THIS IS THE CAR I WAS TELLING YOU ABOUT, Sandra said, opening the passenger door for me, sliding into the driver's seat, handing me her card which I read, noticing the name, Sandra-Brooke Shields-Watson. *UNUSUAL NAME,* I said. MY FATHER WAS A BROOKE SHIELDS FAN, she said. MY MOTHER WANTED TO NAME ME SANDRA, DAD WANTED TO NAME ME BROOKE, SO THEY COMPROMISED ON SANDRA-BROOKE. MY LAST NAME IS REALLY SHIELDS-WATSON, WITH THE HYPHEN. SOME PEOPLE CALL ME SANDY BROOKE TO BE CUTE. *WHICH DO YOU PREFER?* I LIKE ALL THREE—SANDY, SANDRA, SANDY BROOKE. HOW DO YOU LIKE IT? *DO YOU MEAN YOUR NAME OR THE CAR?* I said with a grin. EITHER, she said with a smile. *I LIKE YOUR NAMES AND I LIKE THE CAR. DOES IT MOVE?* We had closed the doors and I knew more about her name than I knew about the vehicle. I WAS AFRAID YOU'D ASK THAT, she said, frowning prettily. *SORRY,* I said. *WRONG QUESTION, HUH?* The interior of the car was very nice—beautiful upholstery and impressive dashboard. In fact, half the interior of the car seemed to be a dashboard with little square buttons all the colors of the rainbow and some I'd never seen before—some that no rainbow had ever seen—some buttons with combinations of colors, some with symbols although most were plain colors—and the buttons extended from one side of the car to the other, they wrapped around the *doors* and the *headliner*—which reminded me of the cockpit of a Boeing superjet, but aside from little chrome bars here and there, there was nothing except

186

buttons. Zillions of them—and some were now blinking in a more or less pleasant way—they hadn't been blinking before we got into the car, but they were blinking now and the blinking alarmed me deep inside somehow, something deep inside me saying, *Get out of here.* And with unexplainable fear creeping up my back and shivering down my spine, I looked out the windshield, which was approximately normal size, and then looked at Sandra-Brooke, who was looking at me, and she smiled again and said nervously, DO YOU LIKE IT? DO YOU WANT TO BUY IT? NICE, HUH? She crossed her legs and accidentally or deliberately her skirt skidded back to reveal some lovely thighs. *WHAT'S THE CAR'S NAME?* She consulted a thick sales book. IT'S A SAM BRECKEN-RIDGE. IT— *A WHAT?* IT CAME FROM THE WORLD THAT SAM BRECKENRIDGE THE EX-PLORER NAMED AFTER HIMSELF. ACTUALLY, AL-THOUGH SOME PEOPLE CALL THIS A SAM BRECK-ENRIDGE CAR, IT WAS REALLY MADE BY PYM AND PIPJIK COLONIES ON SAM BRECKENRIDGE, MADE FOR THE MILLITORIAN RACE ON AN-OTHER WORLD WHO DIDN'T HAVE THE TECH-NOLOGY TO BUILD THEIR OWN CARS, BUT HAD ENOUGH MONEY TO BUY IMPORTS FROM OTHER WORLDS. WHILE SOME PEOPLE CALL IT A SAM BRECKENRIDGE, OTHERS CALL IT A PYM-PIPJIK AND OTHERS CALL IT A MILLITORIAN SINCE IT WAS MADE FOR MILLIES. *I UNDERSTAND.* YOU DO? *DOES IT RUN?* I inquired. YES, she said. And acciden-tally or deliberately exposing more thigh, added, RAJAH SAID I COULD LET IT GO TO YOU FOR NINE THOUSAND, NINE HUNDRED NINETY NINE, NINETY FIVE. *IF I BUY IT, I'LL WRITE YOU A CHECK FOR TEN THOUSAND AND YOU CAN TELL RAJAH TO KEEP THE CHANGE.* DO YOU WANT TO WRITE THE CHECK HERE OR BACK AT THE OF-FICE? *I SAID IF.* THIS IS MY FIRST WEEK HERE AND I HAVEN'T SOLD ONE OF THESE ALIEN CARS.

RAJAH GAVE ME YOUR NAME AND NUMBER, SAID TO CALL YOU ABOUT THIS ONE. HE SAID YOU'RE A LITTLE CRA—SAID YOU'RE A RICH WRITER. *A WRITER BUT NOT AS RICH AS I'D LIKE TO BE.* WHAT DO YOU WRITE? *SCIENCE FICTION RECENTLY.* OH. I DON'T REMEMBER SEEING YOUR NAME BUT THEN I DON'T READ MUCH SCIENCE FICTION. MY FATHER USED TO READ A LOT OF SCIENCE FICTION. HE SAYS NOW WE'RE LIVING IN A SCIENCE FICTION WORLD WITH SO MANY ALIENS VISITING EARTH FROM OTHER GALAXIES, NOW HE READS STORIES ABOUT THE OLD WEST AND PIRATES. FUNNY, HUH? *FUNNY,* I agreed, debating if I should tell her I'd had some bestsellers under my pen names, wondering if I could work it into the conversation gracefully, wanting to impress her for some reason, she was beautiful, I hadn't impressed her so far, and even while these thoughts were going through my mind, I reached for the door handle and opened it a couple of inches, something creepy in the back of my mind saying, *Get out, get out, get out,* an eerie feeling also in the back of my neck as if I'd sat down on a keg of dynamite accidentally. *DOES IT MOVE?* I asked, nodding at the car around us. Sandra-Brooke smiled at the dashboard. NICE DASH, ISN'T IT? *YES. WHAT ARE THE CHROME BARS FOR?* THEY WERE FOR THE PREVIOUS OWNERS, WHO HAD SIXTEEN TENTACLES . . . THEY OPERATED THE CAR BY PUSHING THE BUTTONS WITH THE TIPS OF THEIR TENTACLES, THE CHROME BARS ARE TENTACLE RESTS. *OH.* And after a moment of silence, I asked for what seemed the third time, *DOES THIS THING MOVE?* RAJAH SAID YOU OFTEN BUY ALIEN CARS THAT DON'T MOVE. *TRUE. I BOUGHT ONE CAR THAT'S AS BIG AS A THREE-STORY HOUSE. IT DOESN'T MOVE. THEN I BOUGHT ANOTHER ALIEN CAR IN WHICH ONLY THE RADIO WORKED. SITTING IN IT IS LIKE SITTING INSIDE A RADIO.* OH? she said, and I noticed she opened the door on her side as if suddenly leery of me, thinking I might be some kind of nut or something. *IT'S NOT AS STRANGE AS IT MAY SOUND. THE MUSIC IS WONDERFUL, MORE THAN STEREO, IT'S TELEPATHIC, COMES INSIDE YOUR MIND.* THAT'S NICE, she said, her eyes widening as she looked at me, opening her door wider. *YOU WANT TO SELL THIS CAR, DON'T YOU?* YES. UH . . . MY BOYFRIEND AND I BROKE UP LAST WEEK. I'VE BEEN VERY LONELY. IF YOU BUY THIS CAR I'LL HAVE DINNER WITH YOU. AND COCKTAILS. AND WE CAN GO DANCING. THEN WE CAN STOP AT YOUR PLACE OR MY PLACE FOR A NIGHTCAP AND SEE WHAT DEVELOPS. YOU'RE SORT OF CUTE. *DOES IT MOVE?* IT HAS THIS FEATURE OF HAVING BOOKS RECORDED IN ITS COMPUTER. HUNDREDS OF DARNAKIAN BOOKS. SEE? YOU PUSH THE TOP GREEN BUTTON AND A BOOK STARTS. . . . She pushed the button and the windshield became an opaque screen. I read the first few lines of introduction—a Darnakian book translated into English by so-and-so. *I THOUGHT YOU SAID THIS WAS A SAM BRECKENRIDGE CAR . . . OR A PYM-PIPJIKS . . . OR A MILLITORIAN . . . IF THAT'S THE CASE, WHY DOES IT HAVE DARNAKIAN BOOKS IN ITS COMPUTER?* BECAUSE THE MILLITORIANS DON'T HAVE A LANGUAGE OF THEIR OWN . . . THEY RENT THE DARNAKIAN LANGUAGE. *OH.* Smiling prettily, she said, ISN'T THAT A NICE FEATURE . . . HAVING BOOKS IN THE CAR'S COMPUTER? *NICE.* She turned the book off and the windshield was once more just a windshield. *I'LL BUY IT.* OH, GOOD. *BUT I AM INTO MOVING USED CARS THIS YEAR. I'M JUST CURIOUS. DOESN'T IT HAVE A STEERING WHEEL? NO ACCELERATOR?* She blinked, leaned forward. THESE BUTTONS TAKE THE PLACE OF STEERING WHEEL AND ACCELERATOR. I DON'T KNOW ALL THE BUTTONS. RAJAH TOLD ME SOME OF THEM.

I SHOULD HAVE TAKEN MORE NOTES. She took a notepad from a skirt pocket and squinted at it, then pushed a button experimentally. The window went up on my side. Another button, the window went up on her side. *THE WINDOWS WORK. THAT'S NICE.* IT'S A BEGINNING, she said, frowning over her notes and the buttons. HERE. She pushed another button and the vehicle started to move. Slowly. Very slowly. We were creeping across the lot. SMOOTH, ISN'T IT? *YES, BUT WE'RE GOING AS SLOW AS A THREE-LEGGED TURTLE.* More frowning at her notes. THIS BUTTON IS FOR FASTER, I THINK. OH. SORRY. THAT BUTTON WAS UP. We had risen above the other cars, still moving as slow as a three-legged turtle, but then a sudden breeze caught the vehicle and moved it faster. I THINK . . . THIS BUTTON . . . HERE . . . MIGHT BE THE DOWN BUTTON. . . . She pressed it. We came down on the street outside the sales lot. She turned to me and smiled. Beautiful teeth. Beautiful smile. So satisfied with herself, like a little girl partly winning a game. *Beautiful person,* I thought. Somebody behind us started honking their horn. *WILL IT GO FASTER?* She gnawed her lower lip as she bent over her notes once more, frowning. Beautiful frown, beautiful gnawing. *I WILL,* I said. YOU ALREADY SAID YOU'LL BUY IT. *I MEANT I WILL HAVE DINNER WITH YOU. THANKS FOR THE INVITATION. MIGHT BE FUN.* OH. HERE. I THINK THIS BUTTON IS FASTER. AH! She gave m͟ another triumphant smile as we began doing something like thirty miles an hour. She pushed another button. The vehicle kept picking up speed. *YOU'RE PAST THE LIMIT NOW,* I said. I KNOW. She turned to look at me and her pale face told me more than words could have, but she gave me some words anyway, RAJAH SAID THE CAR PICKS UP SPEED AUTOMATICALLY UNTIL YOU PUSH THE RIGHT BUTTON TO STOP IT. I JUST REMEMBERED. THAT'S WHY I DIDN'T WANT TO GO FOR A TEST DRIVE. BECAUSE I FORGOT WHICH BUTTON STOPS IT

FROM GAINING SPEED. IT'S WAY OFF TO ONE SIDE. RIGHT? LEFT? GREEN? YELLOW? I CAN'T RE-MEMBER!! She pushed a button on the far left, a button with what looked like a purple asterisk. The seat—a single unit—contracted upon itself, narrowed, leaving a large empty space on each side where a pretty pink but inscrutable mist appeared, Sandra-Brooke and I were thigh-to-thigh, then thanks to invisible mysterious forces, she was lifted in the air, placed gently on my lap, the seat stopped adjusting, she pushed another button and the windshield wipers activated—not mechanical, but some kind of energy bar flashing up to evaporate the rain not only on the windshield but some feet before it struck the windshield, I'd seen that type on other alien cars. We were roaring down the highway, no speedometer to tell how fast but it seemed a hundred and twenty. The car must have had some sort of automatic radar because it swerved to avoid collisions, Sandra-Brooke screamed and flung her arms around me, squirming frantically on my lap. WE'RE GOING TO DIE! IT'S YOUR FAULT!!! YOU HAD TO SEE IT MOVE!!! *EXCUSE ME,* I said, enjoying the feel of her warm body so tightly against mine and on my lap—enjoying the softnesses and her warm breath on my cheek but hating the way her fingernails dug into my back, not liking her screaming in my ear and positively disliking the way the car got up to some hundreds of miles an hour and a big truck blocked the whole road—the car sped off the road—a computer will solve a problem one way or another—through a yard, through somebody's house, in one door, out the rear door, taking a big chunk of door frame—computer selecting the largest opening it could find, I guess—into a forest, zooming around trees, gathering speed, zooming, zooming, out of the forest, headed straight *up,* to the sky . . . stars . . . the stars blurred . . . zoom . . . zooom . . . zoooom . . . zooooom . . . Sandra-Brooke fainted . . . I fainted . . . and came to with Sandra shaking me, shouting, WAKE UP! WHERE ARE WE? TELL ME, WHERE ARE WE? I opened my eyes and we left the vehicle and looked around.

Vegetation. Green mostly, but it didn't look like anything on Earth. There were trees not too far away but their trunks were as wide as a house, wider, and they weren't tall like redwoods. WE'RE ON ANOTHER PLANET! Sandra shouted up at the sky, her arms flung wide. IT WORKED UP ITS SPEED UNTIL IT TOOK US THROUGH SUBSPACE OR SOMETHING. *OR SOMETHING*, I agreed. *IS THAT IN-VITATION TO HAVE DINNER WITH YOU STILL OPEN?* She came at me then, hissing like a cat, trying to scratch my face, I grabbed her wrists, we fell to the ground, we rolled, wrestled, rolled some more, wrestled some more, and somewhere in there we started kissing. We had nothing else to do. She relaxed. I relaxed. One thing led to another. And it was great. We didn't find our way off that planet for forty years. We had children. Our children had children. I read a lot of Darnakian books on the ship's computer—which is how I picked up the Darnakian style of literature. It grows on you (like a fungus?) and you really start to like it because it's so different, I've written a whole novel in the Darnakian style . . . but—that's getting ahead of my current story. . . . We thought the car was dead and besides, we were afraid of the damned thing, so we didn't go near it for thirty years and even then we did so just to raise and lower the windows on what we called our wedding anniversaries when half drunk. The planet didn't have any other intelligent life and we may not have been too intelligent, but at least we had half a brain between us and built a home and provided for our children. The planet had no carnivorous creatures, no dangers really, only a bad storm now and then—lightning, heavy rain, but no tornadoes or hurricanes, or anything like that, the most peaceful planet I've ever heard of. I wrote a book about our adventures there—wrote it on the car's computer/word processor . . . and one day, when we were both in our eight-ies (in our eighties we felt as most people do in their fifties—which we attributed to clean living, no cigarettes, and the planet's food, which seemed chock full of vitamins) celebrat-ing a wedding anniversary, we climbed in the car and, drunk as lords, began pushing buttons like crazy, and the damned car started moving. It moved faster and faster and faster and teleported us back to Earth. We wound up in Foolish Rajah's used car lot and the first thing Rajah said when he saw us, he said, THAT'S THE LONGEST TEST DRIVE I'VE EVER SEEN. So . . . my money in the bank had earned a lot of interest. We bought a house, settled down, and someday we'll figure out how to operate that damned car, travel through subspace again, and visit our children and grandchildren. One complication—when we emerged at Foolish Rajah's, we were as young as the day we'd left, which made us younger than our children, but being young again is such a good feeling I'm reminded of the adage, *If it works, don't try to fix it,* so we are not analyzing why it worked the way it did. Meanwhile—I decided what I wanted to do with the rest of my life—I decided to take all my savings and borrow as much as I could—and open my own alien used car business.

Gregor Hartmann is not quite forty years old, lives in San Francisco, and has been writing long enough to have had a story in New Dimensions 8 (1978), which your senior co-editor was producing in that far-off decade. His science fiction has also appeared in Fantasy & Science Fiction, Galaxy, and Galileo; and he has contributed to literary magazines such as The Iowa Review, Antioch Review, and Ascent.

This story, he tells us, was conceived one tropical day off the coast of Baja California, while he was crewing on a seventy-two-foot yacht, which was anchored, at the time, near a cliff of red sandstone. The mesas seemed straight out of the Southwestern canyon country, the water looked Mediterranean, and he had just been reading a copy of Borges' Ficciones—the combination would have been enough to make anyone feel adrift in space and time. And out of that moment of dislocation in sultry climes came this beautifully executed fantasia of a world breaking loose from its moorings.

TIME YOUR PYRAMIDS

GREGOR
HARTMANN

Vincent Winslow stared at the island, afraid to go ashore.

They were anchored about a hundred meters from a cliff of reddish stone. The island was bare as a brick, tolerating only a few cacti and some withered shrubs. Winslow had worked at Los Alamos so he was used to an arid landscape, but this little island in the Sea of Cortez was the most desolate place he'd ever been to. It was prehuman, inhuman. He felt as if he'd been swept back in time to the primitive Earth, to gaze upon raw new elements actively hostile to life.

Ecker must have sensed his reluctance to leave the ship, for he draped his arm over Winslow's shoulders and gave him a paternal squeeze. At the same time he nudged Winslow forward, shoving him toward the rail. "I'm counting on you, Vince. This is your big chance. If anyone can do it you can."

Winslow smiled gamely and clambered down into the dinghy. All the scientists were watching, which made him nervous. He was a plump man with stubby legs and a weak city body; he felt awkward and ineffectual around macho things like dinghies. The crew knew this and teased him mercilessly. Before Winslow could sit down, the sailor/chauffeur put the engine into gear and the dinghy leaped forward so abruptly that Winslow almost fell overboard.

Grinning, the brute ferried him in to the "beach," which had not one grain of sand. Rather, it was a jumble of red and purple rocks the size of baseballs and larger, a treacherous heap eager to break his ankles. Winslow cautiously waded ashore and the sailor gunned the outboard and roared back to the ship, away from the forbidding island.

With a sigh, Winslow began to lug his body up the rocks. He found a faint trail and followed it up. It was so steep he went on all fours, like a goat. The white ship looked smaller and smaller as he climbed. Ecker was on the bow, lying in the shade of a sail and observing Winslow's progress with field glasses. Two sailors sat nearby, respectful, ready to serve. Winslow admired and envied his boss's social prowess. Scientists, sailors—Ecker could dominate anyone. No one ever made fun of Ecker.

While he was looking at the ship, Winslow slipped and slid toward the edge. He hit the ground, flattening himself against the dirt, clawing at rocks. Heart pounding, he watched a clatter of pebbles bounce and arc into the cobalt sea. Automatically he counted the seconds: one thousand one, one thousand two . . . Matter kissing matter at an acceleration of 9.7 meters per second-squared.

Gravity was Winslow's baby. For nine years he'd studied the constant G. Was it really constant, or was it decreasing as the universe expanded? Winslow had invented a clever way to tweak data from distant quasars. Since data from quasars was data from the past, he was able to demonstrate that G had not changed appreciably over the life of the universe. G was indeed a fundamental constant, rightful colleague of c and h. The week he figured that out was the happiest week of his life. One night he lay on the roof of his apartment and stared out into space, in the direction where his quasars hid, feeling their sweet black gravity lift him out of his tame academic life.

Of course, that was three years ago. Before the Strange. Before the fundamental constants began to flicker and twitch. Before the fabric of the universe began to ripple and billow ominously, as if monsters prowled behind the curtain of unknowing. Nowadays when physicists used the word "constant," they sounded either nostalgic or pleading.

Sweating and puffing, Winslow reached his goal: a shallow cave or deep niche about seventy meters above the surface of the sea. He peeped over the edge and found Dr. Sharon Ferris sitting cross-legged on a faded blue flotation cushion. Her legs stuck out of shorts, thin legs mottled with brown bruises. She wore a cotton workshirt too big for her and a red cap with a long bill. Her dark curly hair had been cut short. She sat against the back wall, motionless except for alert eyes focused on her visitor.

"Do I pass inspection?" she snapped.

"Sorry to stare." Winslow scrambled over the edge, relieved to be on flat ground. "The last time I saw you, you were showing some people from DOE through Building 70. You were wearing a business suit, a silk blouse, and jade earrings."

"It worked, too. I got the grant." The faint smile flicked off as she scrutinized him. Despite his doctorate and publications and professional success, Winslow felt the same fear and unworthiness he'd felt nine years earlier when he first knocked on her office door and asked her to be his physics advisor.

"How'd you find me?"

"I don't know. Ecker tracked you down, somehow." He tilted his head toward the ship. "He's here."

"I knew I smelled something bad. I thought it was a dead seal on the beach."

Her lair was a deep niche, not a cave. She had a white wooden table with a bucket turned upside down for a chair. There were some torn pieces of canvas for rugs, and on them a sleeping bag. To hold her physics books and journals she'd built shelves from scraps of lumber. Empty shelves were filled with bodies of dead fish. Dozens, maybe a hundred spiky yellow fish, preserved by the dryness, blank eyes gaping in astonishment. Winslow had a similar expression as he took in her crude camp. He'd always known Sharon Ferris as a tough, self-reliant woman, but that she was capable of this . . .

"How do you like my apartment?"

"It's . . . Spartan," he said diplomatically.

She smiled. "You should try it sometime. You'd be amazed how much thinking you can do without distractions. No committees, no gossip, no news. Nothing but mind and time. I sit up here and pretend I'm Aristotle, perched on an island overlooking the Aegean. The world is new and I'm the first to think about it."

Ferris closed the book in her lap and opened a can of grapefruit juice. While they drank, passing the can back and forth, he brought her up to date on events in North America. The Strange was getting worse. At first the fluctuation in physical constants was so subtle it could only be detected by instruments. Now it had reached a level where people could sense it. Since it was strongest in the most advanced nations, some people believed that scientists were *causing* the weirdness. Labs had been attacked, computers destroyed. The religious fanatics were going wild. At least the TV preachers were off the air; TV transmitters and receivers, like most sensitive electronics, were unreliable.

"Did you try the experiment I suggested with atomic clocks?"

"We managed to do that before they quit working. You were right. Time is flowing at different rates in different places."

She laughed and clapped her hands. "What did I tell you? Quantum universe, quantum time. But would they listen? Noooo. Ecker said I was nuts. I hope he chokes on his causality violations."

"Well, you showed him. Now's the time to come back and rub it in."

Her happiness vanished. She lit a cigarette and sucked on it till the tip glowed like a torturer's brand. "They cast me out, Vince. They rejected my research, cut off my funding, took away my staff. I was willing to debate and be debated by my peers but they treated me like a germ. Now they expect me to come running home so they can pick my brains?"

"Look at it this way. Here's your chance to make a grand entrance. Sharon Ferris returns from exile. You could have anything you want. Money, computer time—well, computers aren't much good now, but if there's anything else . . . Sharon, they're scared."

"Who isn't? I can feel the Strange down here." She stood and stretched and stepped to the brink of the ledge. "I talk to fishermen about it. Mexicans call it *El Cambio.* The Change. Do you know what they're doing, down at the fishing camp? They already had a little shrine to Jesus and Mary. Recently they built a little pyramid for Tlaloc, Aztec god of storms."

"Does he handle time storms too?"

"I hope so. Tell you what. Why don't you toddle back to the ship and have Ecker start building an altar to Tlaloc? When it's done, I'll be happy to climb down and cut his heart out."

Winslow plugged away, arguing with her until the sun went down. Another disturbing sunset. Bolts of green and purple fire. The disk of the sun changed shape—a diamond, a coin emblazoned with cryptic symbols, a swarm of red bees—before it finally subsided, bubbling, into the ocean. There it seemed to move about underwater, until the entire sea glowed and faces appeared in the water, muttering in unintelligible tongues.

When it was dark, Ferris gave Winslow a flashlight and led him down the path. They veered off before the rocky beach and walked across a rise to the fishing camp on the lee side of the island. Winslow was shy, but the fishermen knew Sharon, who joked with them in Spanish. She traded a deck of cards for a kilo of fresh shark, two avocados, and some oranges.

Winslow felt out of place among these short, dark, ragged men. When the shopping was concluded he was ready to go, but Ferris put her purchases aside and sat at the fire with the fishermen. They were drinking Oso Negro, a cheap gin they mixed with soft drinks. Winslow took one sip and decided it was the vilest thing he'd ever tasted. He tried to pretend he liked it, but the fishermen weren't fooled. They laughed and nudged each other as tears rolled down his cheeks.

A man in tattered green pants and nothing else opened the deck and began to play a gambling game for cigarettes. Ferris insisted on being dealt in. Winslow didn't understand the rules, and smoke from the fire made his eyes hurt, so he went off to explore the camp. The huts were built of driftwood and scrap lumber. He peeked into one and saw that the men slept on blankets on the sand. Again he had a flash of being adrift in time. Neolithic settlements were probably a lot like this. Primitive huts and clothing and food—Winslow wouldn't have been surprised to see skulls hung on poles with garlands of flowers.

Back at the fire, Ferris and Green Pants were playing the same hand. Her laughter soared above the men's like a frigate bird above pelicans. Winslow stood outside the ring of fire and light, biting his lip. He couldn't find that path by himself, but he didn't want to be a killjoy. Finally he went for a walk. On this side of the island the beach was sandy and smooth. In the night it shimmered like a vague magic road, leading into the unknown, where a dark figure waited. . . .

Ecker had come ashore in the dinghy. Alone. He didn't need someone to drive the boat, not Ecker. The Institute's associate director was a bull of a man, physically and psychologically imposing. Next to him Winslow always felt smaller. During the trip south the sailors set up poles and fished. They caught yellowtail and wahoo and mahi-mahi. When the fish were hauled aboard, flopping and fighting, Ecker seized a winch handle and clubbed them till there was blood on his knees, the mast, other people. . . . Winslow felt sorry for the fish. He'd seen Ecker do something similar at staff meetings.

The older man clamped a meaty fist on Winslow's upper arm as if to keep him from running away. The only sounds were surf and the distant laughter of the fishermen. Ecker got right down to business. "Have you convinced her?"

"I'm making progress. She misses the comforts of home. In a few days—"

Ecker squeezed his arm like a tourniquet. "You're wasting time, Vince. Persuade the bitch to come along nicely and you'll be a hero. If you can't, we'll do it my way."

"I need more time."

"Time is what we're running out of. We've lost contact with the Institute."

"What about the tube radio?"

"It still works. We can hear Mexico City and Panama. But the States . . . God only knows what's happening up there."

Overhead, a faint pink ripple moved across the sky from north to south. Where it passed, the stars smeared into red and blue whirlpools, slowly spinning.

Winslow plodded back to the fishing camp. He felt duplicitous, torn between loyalty to Ferris and the desire for Ecker's approval. Obviously it would benefit his career at the Institute if he talked her into returning. But even apart from politics he sincerely wanted to please the man. Why was he so subservient to people with power? Men, women—he was just a puppy dog, fetching for anyone who deigned to pet him.

The card game was still going strong, but Ferris and the fisherman in the green pants were nowhere to be seen. The men grinned at Winslow, yellow teeth flashing in dark faces. He called for Oso Negro and drank. Mixed with warm Pepsi it wasn't half bad. He polished off a jar and like a good scientist began to experiment with other mixes.

The last thing he remembered was throwing rocks at the ship and screaming of gravity, of hyperbolic vectors pulling down obsidian bolts from Tlaloc's storms.

Morning found him lying on the beach, shivering at the water's edge, his clothes stiff with salt. He vomited and washed his mouth in the ocean, and spat to clean out the salt taste. The beach was covered with an astonishing number of dead fish: grayyellow blobs of translucent skin and nubby spikes. Puffer fish, he remembered the name. This must be where Ferris found them.

He climbed the red cliff. Sharon wasn't there. He threw a stone into the sea and counted the seconds. G, his old friend, was still on the job. With a piece of charcoal he wrote its value on the flat red wall of rock: .00000000006673 Newtons-meter-squared per kilogram-squared. The traditional value, pre-Strange. This display of scientific precision made him feel better. So what if he was a fat blob incompetent at politics? He had known gravity to fourteen significant digits. Sitting in the sun, he contemplated the number and felt content with his life.

Sharon came up around noon. Moving slowly, as if in pain. He noticed she no longer shaved her legs. The bruises irritated him.

"Look at you," he burst out. "You're killing yourself."

She hobbled over to the sleeping bag and collapsed into a fetal curl. "Canteen," she whispered.

Winslow brought it. Instead of handing it over, he held it above her head and poured water on her face. Her only reaction was to close her eyes. Immediately he felt humiliated.

"Vince." She patted the canvas mat beside her.

He sat down, careful not to touch.

She was silent so long he thought she'd fallen asleep, until she licked her lips. "The ship. Who else is on it?" she rasped.

"Nicholas, McLaughlin, Penrose . . . Karen Moss and Tamara. Some people from Group 12. They've been measuring fluctuations in the Strange as we sailed south. Why do you ask?"

He waited, but now she was asleep. Winslow remained sitting beside her, like a sentry, nailed to the rock by slow hot waves of gravity.

That evening the numbers on the wall began to flicker. Not all of them. Just those to the right of the tenth decimal place. A six became a seven, then six, then five . . . Winslow was too shocked to speak; he tapped Ferris on the shoulder and pointed.

She gazed at it curiously. "Amazing. I believe we're seeing time tear loose. It must be really bad in the States."

"How can you be so blasé? This isn't an experiment in heat transfer. It's our universe melting down."

"According to the Aztecs, the world has been created and destroyed four times. We're due for a fifth meltdown, they say."

"Since when do you practice Aztec physics?"

She shrugged and began to arrange stones in a square. "I know you think I'm nuts, living down here like this, but the old girl still has a few brain cells firing. We desperately needed new ideas for coping with this crisis and I couldn't get them sitting around the Institute listening to everyone munching on the latest scraps from CERN. It's so damn noisy there. I couldn't even pick up my phone without it beeping at me and saying I had thirteen messages. You'd be surprised how much you can learn by staring at the sea and listening to the wind."

"So what have you figured out?" he demanded.

"Lots of things." She nodded at the shelves. "That red notebook is full of ideas. I think we're seeing quantum fluctuations of a time field."

"Wow. What started it?"

"Beats me. It would be logical to assume they've been occurring all along, on a very small scale, but why the amplitude would increase now I don't know." Concentrating, she began a second level of rocks atop the first. "We're poking around with finer and finer slices of time. Maybe somebody's femtosecond experiment split the smallest unit of time and started a chain reaction. Or maybe we've injected energy into a tuned system and it's oscillating. My math fits a lot of physical systems. But the bottom line is there's nothing we can do about it. First of all, I don't see how we could 'fix' something that subtle, and secondly, any attempt that failed would only make things worse. So we have to wait till the fluctuations or vibrations or whatever die down."

A third level of stones. She was building a pyramid, he realized. A little throne for Tlaloc.

She opened the red notebook and they worked through some of her ideas until his head was spinning. Winslow said he needed a walk. He took the flashlight and picked his way down the trail. The sky was lit by geometric patterns of phosphorescence. Stars moved in groups, like schools of tropical fish. The cacti around him seemed to be rustling and moving their arms. He wasn't sure because he was afraid to look too closely.

On the rocky beach he stripped to his shorts and walked into the water, trying not to think of all the poisonous or sharp or slimy things he could step on. As soon as the water rose to his waist he lay down and started to swim, awkwardly paddling toward the ship.

Ecker was in his cabin. He looked over Winslow's shoulder, and his face cooled. "Where is she?" he demanded.

"On the island."

"Then what are you doing here?"

"I came to tell you it's not going to work. Even if she comes with us she won't cooperate." He told Ecker about Tlaloc and the pyramid, omitting the irony and whimsy. He made her sound like a demented hermit, mind turned inside out by the sun, rock, loneliness.

Ecker didn't care. "She's coming with us. The situation is critical. We need her insights."

"But she's crazy!" Winslow wailed.

"Let me worry about that. Get her ready. Her and any notes she may have written."

"There aren't any."

"In that case we'll take all her books and journals. There may be marginalia we can use. Tomorrow. We sail as soon as it's light." With that the scientist turned back to his desk, ignoring the younger man.

Old reflexes made his legs twitch obediently, but Winslow overrode them and stood his ground. "I'm warning you. It won't work."

"Out."

Winslow climbed up on deck and stood at the rail, ignoring the glances of the sailors on watch. The sky was a kaleidoscope of bizarre images, a good match for the swirl in his head. I'm failing everyone, he thought, sick of being the man in the middle. Ecker and Ferris were two powerful personalities, and he was caught between them like a phonon echoing inside a crystal.

Winslow stepped over the side and swam back to shore. He couldn't find the flashlight, but he didn't need it. Climbing to the niche, he could see for miles. The northern sky was lit by a giant bonfire: a vast swirl of color and geometric patterns. At regular intervals spikes of light shot down, as if cosmic picadors were driving flaming lances into Earth's shoulders.

Ferris sat facing the ocean. Behind her the numbers changed. The Strange was up to the fifth decimal place. Staring at it Winslow imagined he felt lighter and heavier as G fluxed.

"You have to hide," he said. "Ecker is coming for you tonight. Is there anyplace on the island where you could go?"

She laughed. Her little pyramid was complete. Around it she'd arranged the dead fish in columns and rows, like a welcoming committee.

"Come on. Let's try. There must be someplace . . ." But it was already too late. When he looked over the edge he saw the dinghy had already been launched from the ship. By the time they reached the foot of the cliff, Ecker and his men would be waiting. They were trapped.

He looked about wildly, and stared at her pyramid. "Are there any big rocks we could drop on them?"

She shook her head. "Relax. It's time I had a chat with Dr. Ecker."

So they sat, watching the turmoil in the sky, until the big man clambered over the ledge. So arrogant that he'd come alone, confident in his ability to dominate the other two. Ignoring Winslow he settled on his haunches, staring at the woman. They were about the same age—two graying senior scientists—but he looked like the Minotaur confronting the latest sacrifice from Athens.

"Having a nice sabbatical?" he asked her jovially.

She crossed her arms. "Published any papers lately? Or have you run out of grad students?"

Even in the gloom Winslow could see muscles cord in Ecker's neck. His voice became harsh. "Vacation's over, Dr. Ferris. Time to get back to work."

"Is there anything left to work on?" She motioned to the wall of numbers. Everything beyond the fourth decimal place was a blur.

"It's obscene," Ecker hissed. "Come back to the Institute. We'll put an end to this nonsense."

She lit a cigarette and stared at him shrewdly, like a wily old administrator sizing up a flaky research proposal. Winslow bit his lip. Had he gone out on a limb for nothing? Maybe she was bored with this island and ready to go back. If she showed him the red notebook and Ecker realized how he'd lied . . .

"Isn't it time to drop the cover story?" she asked.

Ecker's face went blank. "What cover story?"

"You're not going back. You have a low-tech sailing ship that doesn't depend on electronics, so you're going to take your crew and supplies and personnel and head south. Down where the Strange is less intense. When the coast is clear you might slink home but when the shit hits the fan Jack Ecker is going to be safely over the horizon."

Winslow looked from one to the other. Ecker's neutral expression spoke volumes. Suddenly everything clicked into place. Rescue, hell. They were refugees.

Ecker licked his lips. "Come with us, Dr. Ferris. Your knowledge of physics, your Spanish—you'd be a valuable addition to the team."

"You're a fool, Jack. And I wouldn't set foot on a ship with you if it was the last ship in the world."

A series of booms caught their attention. Far out to sea, giant glowing clouds cracked and spat lightning. Swelling and sinking lower. Where they touched water the ocean exploded.

Impossibly tall waves, twisted into weird shapes, fought each other and collapsed and rose again.

Ecker produced a syringe and needle from his pocket. "Hold her arm," he ordered Winslow.

The young man hesitated, looking from one to the other.

"Don't be stupid, Vince. Just hold her arm."

Winslow shook his head. "No," he said, feeling ludicrous, heroic, foolish.

The needle swung to bear on him. The big man took a menacing step forward. The ground rippled, and he fell back, crouching to keep his balance.

"Here we go," Ferris said to Winslow. "Time has broken loose and space is adjusting itself to the changes."

Her calm impressed him more than anything he'd ever seen. She sounded like a high school physics teacher about to drop two weights for the ten-thousandth time. Winslow tried to match her mood. "What do we do?"

She blew a puff of smoke and watched the wind eat it. "Observe this fascinating phenomenon. Monitor our thoughts and feelings and sensations. We will be our own instruments, like Galileo timing with his pulse."

They groveled on the ledge. Ecker clung to a spur of rock, positioning himself between them and the path, as if to prevent escape. The wind pounded with terrible force. Wind alternately hot and cold, mixed with strange shrieks and smells and faces. Sound came from inside the island too: grinding and pops and clatters and booms. Ferris had to cup her hands to Winslow's ear to make herself heard as they huddled against the wall.

"How do you feel?"

He shouted back, "Don't say. Independent observations. Compare later."

She nodded, pleased.

Winslow felt awful. His body seemed to be expanding and contracting, his arms and legs growing longer and shorter. Maybe his nerves were transmitting impulses at different speeds? His head felt like a Rubik's Cube. His thoughts were

207

glass bubbles swirling in a space larger than his head. He half expected to see them drift by in front of his eyes.

The wind swirled through the crevice, picked up Ferris's notebook, and batted it against the wall. Ecker saw them stare at it and focused on the notebook with keen interest. "What's that?" he yelled.

"Nothing," Winslow yelled back, preoccupied with keeping his grip on the rock. He didn't trust what he felt so he was watching his hands to make sure the fingers obeyed orders.

The wind clawed at them, a solid force, irresistible. Winslow and Ferris wedged themselves into the angle of the rock. The wind snatched Ferris's notebook and flapped it toward the ocean. Ecker grabbed at it, and suddenly the air was filled with an explosion of rocks and puffer fish, battering them all. Winslow and Ferris dug their faces into the soft trembling rock, but Ecker was pounded by the whirling debris. They heard him scream, a scream swallowed by the sky. . . .

Winslow came to gradually, mind pouring into his body like sand into the bottom half of an hourglass.

When he opened his eyes, Ferris was already awake, sitting on the ledge, feet dangling over the ocean.

Not trusting his legs, Winslow crawled to her and looked over the edge.

Island and sea. That much was the same as before. But the island seemed to have changed shape, as if giant hands had squeezed wet clay. And there were new islands out there. And the horizon went too far. And the sky was gray and green and burned with dozens of bright spots.

Winslow buried his face on his arm. Ferris patted his shoulder and spoke soothing words until he stopped trembling.

Finally he sighed and rolled over and forced himself to stare into the strange sky. "Well, at least we're alive."

"That's better," she said. "Let's go see how the fishermen did. They can give us a ride to the mainland."

"Do you think there is one?"

208

She shrugged. "We can't stay here forever. Let's go find out what happened to the world."

Winslow conceded that was reasonable. Inspired by her calm, he pulled himself together and sat up. "OK. But first I want to do an experiment. The first scientific experiment in the new world."

He found a loose stone and threw it toward the glittering slate sea. One thousand one. One thousand two. A white spurt, followed by a distant plash.

"G?"

"Roughly the same, I think."

They started down the cliff. On the way he stumbled and kicked some pebbles into space. Observing their graceful arcs, Winslow realized that the big ones fell faster than the small ones.

He smiled, thinking of all the new constants he could measure.

‌᷋᷆‌〜〜〜

Anybody's list of the top new science fiction writers of the 1980s would have to include Bruce Sterling. In truth he arrived on the scene longer ago than is generally suspected—he wrote his first novel, the strikingly original Involution Ocean, *in 1974, when he was just twenty-two years old—but it is in the past half-dozen years that we have had such significant works from him as* Schismatrix, Islands in the Net, *"Swarm," and "Cicada Queen." At last report he was collaborating with William Gibson on a novel called* The Difference Engine.

Sterling is married, lives in Texas, and when not writing fiction occupies himself as critic, polemicist, and all-around gadfly of science fiction, restlessly urging s-f writers to avoid the familiar and stale and venture constantly into unfamiliar territory. Certainly he is his own best example, unpredictable and unpigeonholeable—a writer whose byline has come to mean the unexpected, the challenging, the unusual. As herewith.

Rodolphe sat on the edge of his feather bed and cradled his favorite clock in his hands. The clock was made of polished black walnut and inlaid mother-of-pearl. It was handsome and cleverly made, and assembled with care and precision.

But at some time in the night, the clock had broken.

Gently Rodolphe tried the windup key. The key turned loosely in its socket, with a dry, useless clicking.

Rodolphe felt a harsh sadness. He set the unhappy clock aside, then threw off his pajamas, and shrugged into an embroidered dressing gown. He unlocked the lowest drawer of a massive bureau, and withdrew a calf-skin schedule book.

He dipped a goose quill and began to write, with quick, precise strokes. *The alarm clock has ceased its function. Its gearwork seems broken, and no longer responds to the key. Reason unknown.* Rodolphe found his pocket watch, which hung by its gilded chain from the bedside watchstand. *I have failed to rise at seven o'clock,* he wrote. *I have overslept an hour, and violated my daily schedule!*

Rodolphe paused, thoughtfully stroking his stubbled chin with the quill feather. *Yet another dream of*

THE SHORES OF BOHEMIA

BRUCE
STERLING

flight, he confessed at last. *I flew with strange winged beasts, high above the city.*

He blew the ink dry, then locked the book back securely in the drawer. He was afraid his wife, Amelie, might glance into the book. After their years of married life together, Amelie knew his failings well enough. But Rodolphe did not want her to learn the disturbing nature of his recent dreams.

Rodolphe sponged his face and armpits over a brass basin. He stropped a razor and shaved. Then he dressed: trousers, undershirt, suspenders, shirt, waistcoat, dress coat, handkerchief, throat tie, socks, boots, stickpin, cane, and hat.

Amelie had left him some money. A stack of six gold coins gleamed ostentatiously on the corner of the bureau.

Amelie took pride in being a good provider. She had just been paid, Rodolphe recalled—she had finished sewing the upholstery for her latest steam car. Steam cars were fine things. Rodolphe envied her the pleasure she and her girlfriends took in building them.

Rodolphe flung open the linen window curtains, and studied each coin carefully with a powerful hand lens. Two of the coins had been minted in Syria, brought in by the caravan routes. The third came from glamorous Las Vegas, by the shores of America's great inland sea. The fourth coin was from China, a lovely little artifact with the ancient symbol of a television.

The last two were domestic coins from southern France; a disappointment. The French coins were nicely crafted, but nothing special; they were not even antiques. Rodolphe wondered why Amelie had accepted them. Sometimes he suspected that his wife simply didn't understand the true allure of money.

There was no time now for the comforting ritual of breakfast. Rodolphe left his apartments, clumped loudly down the wooden stairs and into the cobblestone streets of Paysage.

212

It was a crisp winter morning, under a pale pine-scented sky. Paysage's young citizens went about their business, heads held high, faces sober, eyes set straight ahead. Rodolphe returned their respectful salutes with brief smiles and crisp gestures of his cane.

Rodolphe made it a point to show courtesy to all. The stewardship of a public trust was a delicate matter. It required the creation of a general consensus; the studied garnering of public goodwill. After thirty years' hard work on his great project, Rodolphe knew that, to many people, he *was* the Enantiodrome; any personal failing of his own was somehow a reflection on the merits of the great construction.

As he did every day, Rodolphe walked downhill past a bakery, a flower shop, and a piano store. He paused on a street corner, awaiting a break in the jostling flow of horse-drawn traffic.

Rodolphe was joined in his wait by the city's mayor. The mayor was a thin, gangling man, in spare, elegant dress, with a hawklike profile. The mayor was a hundred years old, and something of a bore.

"Good morning, Henri," Rodolphe said.

"Yes, a lovely day," the mayor agreed, gazing critically at the uniformed policeman guiding traffic. "It seems to get a bit cooler every year now. . . . It might even snow this winter." The mayor's tone suggested that this meeting was less than coincidence.

The mayor took Rodolphe's elbow, in apparently friendly fashion, as they crossed the street. "Are you prepared for that, Rodolphe? Snow?"

"We need no further construction grants," Rodolphe said. "We'll be finished very soon—well before the worst of winter."

The mayor chuckled. "The Enantiodrome is never *truly* finished! To be sure, there will be a hearty celebration, as the latest *phase* is completed. You and your gallant work crew deserve every credit! And yet . . ."

They reached the far side of the street. The mayor still held Rodolphe's arm. "Trust my experience, Rodolphe. Of course we are pleased with your success. But eventually the city will get restless again. Though the Enantiodrome *seems* com-

213

pleted, we always find room for expansion. Another minaret, another set of buttresses . . ."

"My plans are very nearly fulfilled," Rodolphe said.

"But the Enantiodrome is no mere *blueprint*, Rodolphe. It's a tradition. A symbol. An incarnation of our civic spirit . . ."

"It's a building, Monsieur Mayor. It's a physical object. It has to stop growing eventually."

"Perhaps it's simply your *personal role* in the Enantiodrome that is near completion." The mayor smiled evasively, to lessen this wounding remark. "It's time you found a new vision, Rodolphe. You should direct your praiseworthy energies toward another career in Paysage. Architecture is not the only worthy pursuit, you know. There's banking, perhaps. Or law. Or politics—and politics has no illusion of finality!"

"Yes." Rodolphe nodded tactfully. "You were wise in your choice of vocation. Good day, monsieur." He walked on.

The man aroused an instinctive distaste in Rodolphe. The mayor, a hundred years old, was very young indeed for an old man; but he was far too old for a young man. The mayor had lived too long in this City of Youth. Now there was a musty air about him, something of the pressed flower, something brittle and dry. Or stale, and bottled-up . . .

Rodolphe himself was fifty-one years old. He had walked this route to work for thirty years. He'd gone eagerly, willingly. People had been able to set their watches by his progress. This was only proper, for a man of civic responsibility.

But now it struck Rodolphe—not for the first time—how dreadfully easy it would be simply to *keep walking*. Straight down the street, out past the city walls of Paysage. Out past the plowed fields, out where the highway dwindled: first to a dirt track, then to a mere mule path through the endless tangled wilderness of Europe. A savagely thriving world, without boundaries, without direction, without constraint.

The thought struck his imagination with a deep, perverse thrill. To walk, naked and alone, into that vast ruin-spotted forest—that mystically seething realm . . .

It might be better to be dead. Rodolphe, with confused surprise, felt a sudden muddled uprush of deep love for this place, for this beloved city. His home. This sweet and settled landscape, every humble cobblestone set by someone who had cared for it, someone who had struggled to put meaning and structure into human existence. The buildings around him, the very pavement under his boots, seemed to vibrate suddenly with an essence of civilized purpose.

Rodolphe's eyes were watering. Ashamed of his weakness, he walked on with careful dignity, his face and shoulders set. Despite himself, his thoughts wandered. He remembered the fate of his old friend, Charles.

Charles was the former chief architect of the Enantiodrome: "poor old Charles," as Rodolphe had used to call him. Nothing solid or coherent could explain the poor fellow's distress, and yet Charles had become a haunted man.

Sometimes, when he and Rodolphe found a moment alone together during a day's hard work, Charles would confess his inner turmoil. Some senseless tormented babble about "transcendence" and "dissolution."

Rodolphe would listen with a show of patience, then go home, satisfyingly sore and tired, and covered with mortar and stone dust. "Poor old Charles was at it again today," Rodolphe would tell his wife. And Amelie would shake her ringletted head in remorse and disdain.

Something had driven Charles to give up his life here, his status, his material comforts, his satisfying routines. But now Rodolphe could feel the lure of it; the lure of the Conventions, preying on his mind. He had never realized how vastly subtle and strong Conventionality was; that it would flood into the cellar of one's mind, like black water. . . .

Rodolphe rounded a familiar street corner, and saw the great clock minaret of the Enantiodrome. His reverie broke and his heart shed its unhappy weight. Perhaps Charles' life, perhaps Rodolphe's own life, perhaps the human condition itself, was somehow inherently redolent of this creeping ambiguous tragedy . . . but did that really matter?

215

After all, there was still the Enantiodrome. This great stone monument, this Cathedral to Youth, this soaring and splendidly useless edifice that defined the heart of Paysage. Rodolphe had fallen in love with it the first day that he saw it. Its defiant beauty had enchanted him.

He entered the spire-topped iron gates. Today workers swarmed across the site, over two hundred of them. Glaziers, painters, gargoyle sculptors, rooftop lead pourers whose smelters belched a picturesque black smoke across the city.

The Enantiodrome's coming "completion" had never been officially announced. Nevertheless, Paysage seemed to sense the approaching climax. The city's people felt the truth in the marrow of their bones, and it drew them to the site. Most of these volunteers would never be paid for their efforts here; even the highly skilled regulars received only token pay. They didn't care; the pay was not their motive. Rather, they all wanted, with a deep unspoken yearning, to know they had *been there*. To know they had *lived the life*.

Rodolphe left his hat, coat, and cane at the gate, and assumed his customary leather working apron, boots, and hard hat. Cheerful supply workers passed out free sugared pastries and tiny cups of strong Algerian coffee. The chaffing and gossip of the crowd sounded shriller than usual, to Rodolphe's ear. As if they were doing all this for the last time, and saving nothing for the morrow.

Despite the impressive scale of the work, most of this was cosmetic: painting, trimming, adornment. There remained two vital structural activities: the completion of the fifteenth anterior buttress, and the sealing of the Great Dome.

Rodolphe, munching a pastry, went to inspect the buttress. Rooted in bedrock and surrounded by trampled mud, the great structure was lashed in a towering framework of tarred cordage and graying lumber.

All last month there had been a critical shortage of decent brick. It had slowed work on the buttress, which had to be completed before the Great Dome could be trusted to bear the weight of its capstone.

Mysteriously, today there were several hundredweight of bricks, heaped carelessly nearby, on the muddied grass. Rodolphe studied them, nonplussed.

"Where is the night watchman?" he called.

A foreman sent a messenger to fetch the man. The night watchman came slithering downward from the heights of the buttress, on a knotted rope. He leapt from a final catwalk, landed in the mud with a splash, and capered barefoot to Rodolphe's side.

The night watchman wore a thick moldy coat and baggy trousers, gone ragged at elbows and knees. A puckered leather cap was slung over his dented, shaggy head. He was almost dwarfish, his spine oddly bent; but his huge hands and feet were gnarled and muscular.

"Good morning, Hugo," Rodolphe said.

"Good morning to you, Monsieur Rodolphe!"

"Who brought these bricks last night?"

"Bricks?" Hugo growled. He stared at them, rubbing his chin, his ugly head cocked sideways.

Rodolphe waited patiently. The unfortunate Hugo had never been quick, but even a man of subhuman, childish intelligence could win his way to an odd kind of wisdom, in a lifespan of centuries.

"I don't know," Hugo confessed at last.

"Come now," Rodolphe said. "Nothing within this building site escapes your notice, Hugo! You must have seen someone arrive last night. Look, there are cart tracks."

Hugo yanked up a brick from the heap, weighed it in one hand, sniffed it, touched it to his tongue. "These are city bricks," he pronounced. "They have the smell of Paysagè." He looked up, blinking. "It is demolition work. Fresh."

"Well, that's helpful information," Rodolphe said. "If we find an injured building in the city, then we have our unwanted benefactors. But I ordered no demolition, and expected none. I fear some mischief was committed to obtain these bricks. Why didn't you see these people, Hugo?"

Hugo jerked his dirty thumb toward the distant scaffolding

ringing the Great Dome. That was where Hugo stayed, most nights; high above Paysage, crouched under a flapping tarpaulin.

"Last night there were screams," Hugo said. "Strange noises in the sky, the sound of many wings." Hugo reached into one vast pocket of his baggy trousers. "And this morning I found this, Monsieur Rodolphe!" He pulled out the limp corpse of a large bird.

A closer look showed it was not a true bird, but some kind of feathered animal. This dead creature had sharp conical teeth in its beak, and scaly claws at the joints of its wings. Its green and yellow feathers were loosely socketed in a tough gray hide.

It seemed to have broken its long snaky neck, colliding with a scaffold pole, in the darkness. Blood had clotted at its yellow nostril holes, and it stank like a snake, a sharp reptilian reek.

"What on Earth is this creature?" Rodolphe said.

Hugo shrugged. "I have never seen one."

"Never, in your long life? Then they must be rare, Hugo."

"There was a large flock of them, monsieur. They were very loud in their cries and rustling. They stopped here to roost. Then they flew off—south, I think."

"It's some queer beast from the deep wilderness," Rodolphe said. "A creation of the Conventions. What are they resurrecting now, I wonder?" He looked at Hugo sharply. "Were there machines inside it?"

Hugo shook his head. "I did not cut it open to look, monsieur. It smells very bad."

"Well, it's no use looking for devices now," Rodolphe said. "If they wanted to hide their cunning little nano-gnats, we would never find them. We would never know . . . the Conventions are mysterious. It is the nature of Conventionality, I suppose. But I don't like mysteries, Hugo. Not here, within our very walls!"

Hugo smiled shyly, as if it were all somehow his fault. "This has happened before, monsieur. We have had other birds. I remember, when the third minaret was completed . . ."

218

"When was that? How many years, Hugo?"

"I don't count years, Monsieur Rodolphe. But Paysage was happy that night. We lit great fireworks in celebration. Many ducks flying from the wilderness were dazzled and blinded. . . . We gathered them in the morning and made fine pies from them." Hugo rubbed his stomach with a leer.

Rodolphe sighed. "I hate it when things like this happen. I like things to make proper sense."

"You are young," Hugo observed. He stuffed the creature back into his pocket. "May I go now?"

"Yes, very well. . . . Wait a moment. What's all this now?"

There was a sharp disturbance near the gate. Raised voices, an angry scuffle. Frowning, Rodolphe hurried toward it.

A supply table suddenly flew upward, coffee tureens and pastry plates catapulting through the air. Rodolphe broke into a run.

The work crew were struggling with an intruder. Five of them had tackled him and flung him to earth, and an angry crowd was quickly gathering, clutching shovels and brick hods.

A tremendous bestial roar rang out, echoing from the Enantiodrome's stone walls. Another table flew into the air with a tumbling lurch and a smash. Workers backed away, stumbling and dropping their impromptu weapons.

A huge furred monster reared up above the crowd, jaws agape and roaring. It sat on its haunches, its long clawed arms swiping loosely at the air. Its teeth were like ivory chisels. It was a great brown bear.

Rodolphe ran headlong through the crowd, shouting and waving his arms. "Let him go, you fools! Release that man!"

Shouting orders, Rodolphe fought his way into the struggle. He wrenched their hands away from the invader's gaunt naked limbs. The man collapsed, trembling.

He was a Wild Man. A hairy, filthy Conventional, a savage of the woods.

The crowd was trying to keep the Wild Man's bear at bay,

219

feinting at it timidly with shovels and crowbars. "Leave it alone!" Rodolphe shouted. "Can't you see this man *belongs* to that creature?"

The crowd protested. "But he's a savage!" "A dirty spy!" Rodolphe saw that the loudest shouter was Mercier, one of his most trusted foremen. Mercier's face, normally placid and sensible, was beet red now, congested with instinctive hatred.

Rodolphe was loath to touch a Wild Man, but he forced himself to act, and hastily dragged the disgusting wretch to his feet. "I'll take care of this matter personally!" he shouted. "Clear a way for us there! Mercier, get a grip on yourself, for God's sake! You must take charge here, in my absence."

Mercier blinked. As Rodolphe had hoped, the sudden weight of responsibility brought Mercier to his senses. "All right, Rodolphe."

Rodolphe turned away. "Be careful of that beast, you fools! Don't try to annoy it!"

The Wild Man half flung his stinking arm over Rodolphe's shoulder, sagging against him. Rodolphe, wincing, hauled the Wild Man away toward the gate. The bear shambled up quickly at their heels, growling and pausing to snap at a hoe handle. Rodolphe looked over his shoulder; Mercier was calming the crowd.

"You disgust me!" Rodolphe hissed at the Wild Man. "What are you *doing* here?"

"Sorry," the Wild Man muttered.

"It's bad enough when we see one of you people in the common street! Don't you know this building is a special place for this city? You have the whole outside world for your demented wanderings. . . ." Rodolphe hauled the stumbling Wild Man through the gate and into the street.

A few of the angriest workers followed them past the gate, shouting and waving their tools. Most of them stopped within the site, gawking, and even laughing nervously, now that the trouble was over.

Rodolphe hustled the hobbling Wild Man half a block down the street, then dashed across it, into an alleyway.

They staggered down the alley, and past a turn, out of public sight. Then the Wild Man's legs seemed to give out; he sat in a doorway with a groan, and cradled his tangled, shaggy head in his hands.

The bear shouldered its way past Rodolphe, slinking up with its huge blunt skull hung low. The bear sniffed at the Wild Man's bruises, and licked at a bloody scrape.

Rodolphe wiped his hands with a kerchief. "There are laws here, you know," he said. "We could arrest you! Throw you out—or even put you in prison!"

The Wild Man looked up pitifully. "Rodolphe! It's me."

Rodolphe stared at him in horrified alarm. *"Dad?"*

"No, I'm not your *father*, you fool! It's *me*, your old friend, Charles!" The Wild Man brushed his tangled hair back from his cheeks. "Look!"

"Charles!" Rodolphe said. "So it is! But you're so . . . so thin and filthy. . . ."

"You get used to it," Charles muttered. He wiped his mouth, and spat. "I didn't know you would make such a fuss! When I ran the Enantiodrome, we used to let Wild Men in to see the work. Why, we were *proud* to show it!"

"That was *years* ago, Charles!"

Charles shrugged his bony shoulders. "I suppose it was. . . ."

"We simply can't let you in there *now*. The Enantiodrome is almost *finished*. It's *important.*"

" 'Important.' Yes, that's just what I used to think." Charles sighed. "I couldn't believe it was almost *done*, though. *Completed*, at long last. . . . I had to *see* it, Rodolphe, see it with my own eyes."

Rodolphe nodded slowly. Despite himself, he was touched. Even in his pathetic indecent exile, poor Charles was still drawn by the fine old loyalties. "How did you learn the news?"

"A little bird told me," Charles said, without any trace of irony. He got shakily to his feet, which were wrapped in hairy moccasins. "And it's true, Rodolphe—it's almost done! It's

221

beautiful, isn't it? And I'm such a mess. Sorry. This isn't easy for me, you know."

"We must get you away from here," Rodolphe said. "Out of the public street. We'll go to my apartments."

Charles shuddered slightly. "I'd be just as happy to stay in the open air. Walls and roofs are so confining."

"Nonsense. We'll take the back streets. . . . Can you walk? Are you badly hurt?"

"No," Charles said. He looked at a swelling bruise with indifference. "It's all right."

The bear suddenly spoke up. Its lips writhed and a long chain of guttural muttering came from its hairy throat. Rodolphe stared at it, his skin crawling.

"This is Baltimore, my domestic," Charles said. "He says not to be frightened. You can ride on his back if you like."

"No thank you," Rodolphe said.

Charles climbed lithely onto the bear's shoulders. "Don't be upset, Rodolphe. You've seen domestics before."

"Of course. My old parents had domestics," Rodolphe said. "But those were *horses.* Normal-looking creatures." He paused. "It still bothers me to see a wild animal talk."

"He's not an animal," Charles said, without rancor. "He's an instrument of the Conventions. The Conventions sent me a bear, once my inner mind had . . ." Charles seemed to choke on his words. "I mean, after I left this city. It might have been a horse instead, but a bear better suited my . . . my 'temperament,' is the term you might use." Charles shook his head in confusion. "It's hard to explain to you, in a way you can understand. But Baltimore looks after me. That's all. He won't hurt you, Rodolphe."

"Good," Rodolphe said.

"It's not so strange," Charles said vaguely. "A bear, I mean. There's a very old man in China whose domestic is a *bed of ants.* He has a . . ." Charles paused and swallowed, his eyes gone distant. "He has a *very big soul.*"

"That's just fine, Charles," Rodolphe soothed. "Come along with me now. Quickly."

"I *can* talk, you know," Charles said. The bear carried him easily, lumbering along at Rodolphe's heels. "I just have trouble speaking in a manner you can understand." They left the alley, and dodged across a street lined with shops, to the frowning alarm of passers-by. "My ways of thought have changed so much. . . ." Charles continued blithely. "That's what we *do*, Rodolphe. Talk about thinking. And think about talking."

"I know, Charles. That was always what most disgusted me about Conventionality."

Wild People were rare in Paysage. There were always a few of them, blundering in for their own inscrutable reasons: nostalgia perhaps, or some silent urge to make their obnoxious presence felt. Those who lingered were thrown out of town by the city police. And the same would soon be true of Charles, if he wasn't hidden somehow.

Rodolphe did not bring up the topic, however. He knew it would not be much use. It was always hard to talk straightforward common sense to the wretches. Decent people simply shunned them. It saved a lot of trouble, all around.

Rodolphe hurried home, trying to maintain his dignity under the accusing stares of fellow citizens. It embarrassed Rodolphe to be seen publicly with a Wild Man, but he had little choice. The repute of the Enantiodrome was involved.

At last, Rodolphe urged Charles and his monstrous escort up his apartment stairs. Two of the stairs cracked loudly under the beast's great hind paws.

Rodolphe managed to get the bear settled into a corner of his sitting room, where the floor joists groaned ominously under its weight.

Charles sat wearily on a canary yellow chaise longue. "Get up!" Rodolphe snapped. "Look what you've done to that upholstery . . . my wife sewed that herself!"

"Sorry," Charles muttered, brushing ruefully at the stained fabric. "I don't mean to make any trouble. You should have left me at the building site."

"Not in your condition. It's simply impossible!"

"I want to see it, Rodolphe. I gave years to the great work. I have a right."

"We can talk about that, when you look like a decent human being again," Rodolphe said. He marched Charles into the bathroom.

Rodolphe lugged in towels and a tin kettle of steaming hot water. On his second trip, the bear addressed him, from its den behind the card table. "Rodolphe," it said. "May I ask you some questions?"

"No!" Rodolphe shouted.

"They are well worth thinking about."

"I'm not listening!" Rodolphe said.

After an hour's determined scrubbing, Charles was clean and shaved. He sat on a settee, wearing Rodolphe's second-best houserobe, while Rodolphe snipped at his hair with his wife's sewing scissors.

Without its thicket of hair, Charles' face had a fiercely compelling asceticism. His pale eyes glowed with weird intelligence, and his gaunt weatherbeaten arms and legs were all tendon and leathery sinew. He sat calmly on the settee, his hands folded. His quietude, in contrast with the obvious whipcord strength of his lean body, was almost frightening.

"Doesn't this feel better?" Rodolphe asked. "To be clean and decent again?"

"I suppose it does. Yes." Charles cleared his throat. "The sensations are different. And it does bring the old memories back." He smiled, with a shadow of his old charm. "You're too kind to me, Rodolphe! You have done me a service; you were always a good friend."

"That's better. You sound much more like yourself now, Charles."

"Perhaps. I often remember my days here in Paysage." He blinked. "It does have some meaning, Rodolphe. What we do here; the work, and the sweet little rules of daily life, and all that baggage. Even in the great outside world, looking back on this little enclave . . . The effort isn't wasted; it's a necessary process."

"Don't patronize me," Rodolphe said.

"I just felt you should know that, Rodolphe! Someday it will be a comfort to you."

"Don't take that tone with me!" Rodolphe said. "You're a fine one to talk about 'wasting effort.' What have you done, since you left this place, that has made the world one whit better?"

Charles sighed. "It depends on your definitions. You don't have the terminology, Rodolphe."

"Words!" Rodolphe said. "All words, and airy nonsense! You've lost your mind, Charles. You've lost your purposes. You're nothing better than that shambling beast of yours."

"Oh but I *am*," Charles said. "Baltimore is *intelligent*, but he has no *consciousness*. He's . . . he's really a cybernetic-organic incarnation of the former industrial urban environment. The megatechnic infrastructure has miniaturized, and woven itself on a cellular level into the ontological informa-tion-processing structure of what was once the natural realm. The Conventions are a global data system that has assumed the function of an Immanent Will."

"What?" Rodolphe shouted.

Charles sighed. "It's not as strange as it sounds. You get quite used to it, once you . . . well . . . give up, and be-come Conventional. The Conventions have their own kind of beauty, Rodolphe. Not at all like the simple beauty here but . . . the Conventions do have a place for human beings. We have a role there, a true function. We . . . we *personify* the Conventional world, Rodolphe! We are its soul!"

"My God, it's hopeless," Rodolphe said. "You've become a babbling lunatic."

"No, I don't think so," Charles said patiently. "Once you live the life outside, you learn to see matters differently. To read the patterns of immanence, smell it almost . . . the very way you might read your own dreams, or understand the clouds. Storm fronts of meshed intelligence ripple through the living fabric of the Earth. Perceptions become data, data be-

225

comes thought, thought becomes . . . I think you might say 'spirit,' though that term doesn't really—"

"Shut up, for God's sake!" Rodolphe flung his scissors to the floor. "I don't *need* that, do you understand me? I have a world here in Paysage, a world I can understand, a world I can work within, a world that *makes sense!* I won't become some empty puppet of your vast inhuman system—"

The door slammed downstairs. Rodolphe's wife had arrived; he heard her familiar footsteps, plus a lurch and a yelp of pain as she missed her footing on a cracked stair.

Amelie hurried in, whipping the bonnet from her hair. "Rodolphe!" She stopped short with a swish of skirts and stared in horror at Charles. "So! It's true, then!"

"Please don't be frightened, Amelie," Charles said.

Amelie put her fists on her hips. "I'm not frightened of you, you worthless layabout!"

"I meant the bear," Charles said, pointing at the corner. Amelie turned, went white, and shrieked aloud.

"He won't hurt you, dear," Rodolphe said.

"Rodolphe, what have you done? My God, think of the scandal! Rodolphe, what *is* this *creature* in our house? What will the neighbors think?"

"Calm down, dear," Rodolphe said. "I don't like this situation any better than you do! But let's discuss it like civilized beings."

"Oh, don't give me any of your Monsieur Architect calm rationality!" Amelie shouted, stamping the carpet. "Of course we're 'civilized beings'! That's exactly why we abhor persons of his sort!" She glared at Charles. "Why we shouldn't *look* at such people, much less invite them into our drawing room with their vile snorting animals!"

"I'm not an animal, Amelie," the bear said.

"You stay out of this, you walking hearth-rug!" She turned to Rodolphe, folding her arms. "Have you gone mad, Rodolphe?"

"Dear, this is Charles. Our old friend. You remember. We used to have him to dinner."

"This miserable personage is not what I call 'our old friend Charles,'" Amelie said. "He has betrayed us. He has joined the oppressor gerontocracy. He is our class enemy!"

"Oh no," Rodolphe begged. "Not politics, Amelie!"

"It's the truth," Amelie retorted. "Why won't you face it? You, with your head-in-the-clouds masculine construction schemes! I always told you, Rodolphe: you mustn't get *mystical* about your business! It's just stones and mortar, Rodolphe: *stones* and *mortar!* Otherwise it turns your head, and you end up . . . well . . . like one of *them!* Just like *he* is now!" She drew a breath. "Is *that* what you want?"

"No!" Rodolphe said. "You know that's not so!" The accusation stabbed him with anxiety. "It would mean the end of everything," he said. "The end of our marriage. And our home. The end of everything I've built here—that *we* have built here, together! You know I don't want that, Amelie!"

Amelie was silent a moment, biting her lip. She was moved by his distress. "Well, if that's so," she said, "then why do I find you in this person's company?"

Rodolphe sat down. His legs felt weak. "Perhaps I did make a mistake, dear. But it seemed the best way to avoid an even larger scandal. There was a nasty stir at the Enantiodrome. It seemed best to . . . well . . . get Charles out of sight."

"You should have summoned the police."

The bear spoke up again. "That action would have engendered an unfortunate complexity."

"Let me speak," Charles told it. "Amelie, I know my presence is unpleasant to you, but please try to understand. A . . . a vital transition is about to occur in this place. I had a hand in creating it. I have a right to witness it. You owe me this."

"Oh, so *that's* it, is it?" Amelie said. "You barge in here with this horrific instrument of brute authority, and then try to appeal to our better natures. A typical power play of the coercive gerontocracy!"

"I haven't done anything," Charles said meekly.

"Don't pretend you're not implicated," Amelie said.

"Maybe you don't oppress us, directly and obviously. But you profit by everything that's done to confine us here, and disrupt our lives, and rob us of a normal, civilized existence!"

Charles winced. "What a strange mode of discourse . . ."

"Be fair, dear," Rodolphe urged. "He doesn't understand what you're saying."

Amelie walked across the sitting room to the chaise longue. She noticed the stain on it, but sat there anyway, her lips tightening. "Oh, it ought to be clear enough," she said. "After all, most of the world belongs to him, and his antediluvian friends. All we have of it is little ghettos and caravan routes. We could civilize the whole world again, if we were allowed to. We could have hot water, and meals three times a day, and books, and art, and decent clothes, and roads, and rules . . . and *families,* too." Suddenly she burst into tears.

Rodolphe sat beside her, and took her hand. "Try not to take it so hard, dear."

She looked up, wiping her eyes with a kerchief from her bodice. "Oh no," she said, "I don't suppose I should be *allowed* to take it hard, should I? Perhaps I should simply *sublimate* my feelings, in piling stones on stones, instead of giving care and love to other human beings!"

She turned on Charles fiercely. "I'm a grown woman! I may not be two hundred, or three hundred, or four hundred years old, but I have the wants and needs of a normal human being. I want a child! And *you* won't let me have one."

"But you're not old enough," Charles said.

"That's your answer to everything," Amelie said. "Of course I'm old enough! Women used to bear children at forty, or thirty, or even younger!"

"Yes, but that was when people *died* young," Charles said. "You can't expect to live for centuries, and bear hundreds of children! Earth would be overwhelmed."

"Don't put words in my mouth," Amelie said. "That's not what I said." She pointed at Rodolphe. "I'm not being selfish. It's very simple. I love this man! I want his child, I want a true marriage with him, with a family! But you tell me I must wait for that fulfillment until I'm a strange old crone. Are Rodolphe and I supposed to wait out centuries, while the dust slowly settles on our souls? No, we'll surely drift apart, and our love will be nothing but an episode." She wrung her hands. "Every day of my life, thanks to you, I have to taste my own sterility."

"I'm sorry for your distress," Charles said. "But at least you don't have to taste your own approaching *death*. And other people have lived through this situation. Your own parents, for instance!"

"I never really *knew* my parents," Amelie said. "None of us do. How can we, in this world? They were always *patient* with me, and I think perhaps they loved me in their own strange way, but I never really saw *them*, did I? I just saw the facade that very old people create to show to the very young. We can't love each other simply and directly; there's too much distance between our hearts. The situation isn't humane, it's not natural. It hurts!"

"There's no other way to manage, though."

"All that means is that you don't *want* another way." She glared at Charles. "Why don't you get out of here? Leave this place, and go back where you belong. Paysage belongs to us! We built everything here, with our own ideas and our own hands. We never used your help; we owe you nothing, we reject you totally. I want you *out of my house!*"

There was a ringing silence. "Amelie," Rodolphe said at last. "This isn't some stranger. This person used to *be* us."

"That only makes it worse," she said. "You ought to throw him downstairs!"

"That would scarcely be polite, would it?" Rodolphe said, with a sidelong glance at the bear.

She noticed his look. "Oh yes," she said. "For a moment, I forgot that he holds the whip hand of authority over us. I suppose, if we gave him the hiding he deserved, this great brute of his would reduce our home to matchsticks!"

"I thought, if we made Charles seem presentable," Rodolphe suggested, "we could leave without him creating a public stir."

"Are you going to shave the bear, too?"

"We can't help the bear, dear. Perhaps, if Charles looks fairly normal, people will forgive him that eccentricity."

"Well, I suppose that's something," Amelie admitted. She stood up, shakily. "I suppose I could help you, if it comes to that. His hair looks dreadful."

"Thank you, dear. I knew I could depend on you."

Rodolphe chose a suit of clothes, while Amelie set to work, reluctantly, on their guest.

Charles was too short for the trousers, so Amelie took in the hems. With his hair trimmed, and the proper accoutrements, Charles looked almost human.

At Rodolphe's suggestion, they treated Charles to a proper home-cooked lunch. Charles had trouble with the silverware, and the flavors of the food seemed to startle him, but he did well enough. The bear devoured two loaves of bread and apparently went to sleep.

When the domestic ritual was over, Amelie seemed mollified.

"Perhaps I was a bit overwrought earlier," she said. "I don't like to talk about my grievances—after all, there's not much I can do about the oppressive power structure, is there?—but sometimes it simply overwhelms me. And it makes me feel quite wild." She looked at Rodolphe, troubled. "Are you angry with me, Rodolphe?"

Rodolphe smiled indulgently. "No, sweetheart. Truth to tell, I feel much the same way sometimes."

"You don't show it. Not to me, at least."

"I try to be reticent. I depend on you for solid common sense."

Amelie sighed and looked at the clean tiled floor. "I broke your clock last night, Rodolphe."

"You did?"

"I couldn't listen to its ticking any longer—it was like a reproach." Amelie was fighting tears.

"That's perfectly all right, dear," Rodolphe said numbly. "We can get another clock."

Charles rose cheerfully from the table, wiping his mouth on his coat sleeve. "This was charming! I feel quite fit now. Perhaps we should go."

After the dishes had been scrubbed, and arranged in the china cabinets, they went to the drawing room.

"Can you come with us, dear? It's worth seeing today; quite a hubbub. Might cheer you up."

"Later tonight, perhaps," Amelie said. "I don't want to walk in public with a bear."

"I'll stay here," the bear remarked. It opened its jaws in a horrific yawn.

A nano-gnat the size of a horsefly emerged from its gullet. The little mechanism flew silently across the room and landed on Charles' lapel.

"Will you be all right here, dear?" Rodolphe said.

"I won't be staying home either," Amelie said tartly. "I have work to do at the garage. This beast can stay here by itself."

Rodolphe and Charles picked their way down the fractured stairs. "This will help matters a great deal, Charles. Though I'm surprised that your bear is willing to stay behind."

"Baltimore doesn't have a 'will,' " Charles said. "The nano-gnat will link us. Baltimore can move very quickly should I need his services."

They walked together into the afternoon streets. As two respectable gentlemen, they did not attract a second glance. Charles walked a bit stiffly, as if the clothes chafed him, but he was not so odd as to be an anomaly.

"Why do you call him 'Baltimore'?" Rodolphe said.

"Baltimore was a city," Charles said. "An ancient city on the shore of America. But when the seas rose, the waves came and claimed Baltimore. It is submerged."

"So 'Baltimore' was a city from the age of industrial mortality?" Rodolphe shrugged. "Interesting. But not at all like our modern civilization."

Charles grunted.

They paused on a street corner. Traffic was snarled. Cordons had been erected half a block down the street. A gang of men in work clothes were tearing the great marble facade from the City Bank.

"I don't like the look of this," Rodolphe said. He led Charles up the street.

A circle of onlookers were admiring the action. Rodolphe noticed the president of the Bank, a portly gentleman of great dignity whose name was Gustave. They exchanged greetings. "What's all this?" Rodolphe said.

"It is the future capstone of the Enantiodrome, of course," said Gustave in surprise. "Surely you knew."

"I gave no such orders," Rodolphe said. "Besides, we already have a capstone! Fifty years ago the capstone was hewn from Carrerra marble, and transported here from over the Alps by mule team. It was then decorated by a generation of artisans, and now lies safely in the basement of the Enantiodrome, awaiting the great moment of its installation!"

"Oh *that*," Gustave said. "Apparently they broke that one. They're going to chisel out a new one, from out of the front of my Bank."

"They *broke* it?" Rodolphe shouted. "My God! How did it happen?"

"Don't alarm yourself," Gustave said. "We at the Bank are more than pleased to help you out. It's a civic honor for us, really. Why, they dug a ton of bricks out of City Hall last night; in comparison, we in private enterprise are getting off cheaply!"

Rodolphe backed away into the crowd, disguising his horror. "Someone is flouting my authority," he said to Charles. "It's a conspiracy, clearly. Come, we must hurry."

Within minutes they were at the Enantiodrome. The great building was the scene of near-riot. The crowd of workers had swollen from mere hundreds to a large fraction of the city's whole populace. Men and women swarmed across the grounds, hauling boards, shoving wheelbarrows, arguing, eating, laughing, sitting around bonfires of scrap lumber. It was like an army of occupation.

"What is this outrage?" Rodolphe said. "Have they all gone out of their heads?"

"They're working very hard," Charles observed, his eyes gleaming.

"With no efficiency at all," Rodolphe said.

"They work like ants," Charles said. "Small individual actions, some even counterproductive, yet adding up to an unspoken emergent whole."

"Spare me," Rodolphe said. He plunged into the crowd. People waved at him cheerily, clapped him on the back, and shouted incoherent congratulations. It took him a long time to find Mercier.

"What happened?" he asked the foreman.

"Isn't it wonderful how the people have responded in our time of need?" Mercier said. He grinned politely at Charles, clearly failing to recognize him. "It's a bit of a muddle, but we'll get it up by tonight, all right. Imagine that, Monsieur Rodolphe! Finished by midnight! It makes you want to weep with joy!"

"Who specified this so-called deadline?" Rodolphe asked.

Mercier looked startled. "Well . . . I don't know. But we're finishing today! I mean, ask anyone—everyone knows it is the truth!"

"Some irresponsible rumormonger," Rodolphe grated. "This is grotesque! Look at this blundering amateurism. It's mob hysteria!"

Mercier looked cowed. "But, sir—everyone's having such a good time—"

"You've all fallen for some sort of stupid prank! This will set our schedule back by months! Tomorrow, we'll have to dismantle and repair all this botched work—not to mention apologizing to City Hall and the Bank!" Rodolphe wiped his brow with his kerchief. "My God, think of the damage to our credibility! To my reputation! This is what I get for abandoning my project, even for a few short hours—"

233

Charles took his elbow gently. "Rodolphe?"

Rodolphe yanked his arm away. *"Now* what?"

"This is a building, Rodolphe. It's not you. It doesn't belong to you."

"What do you mean? It's my responsibility; everyone knows that!"

"But the Enantiodrome doesn't *care,* Rodolphe. It was here before you and it will be here after you. You can't *be* this thing, Rodolphe. It has its own momentum. You have to let it go."

"That's nonsense," Rodolphe said, sweating.

"Look at the people, Rodolphe. They're *doing* it. Not exactly as you wanted it, perhaps, but in a way that . . . well . . . suits the innate purposes."

Rodolphe hesitated, stunned. Then he rallied. "No. I can still restore order here. I'll fetch the mayor, I'll summon the police. . . ."

"Some of these people *are* the police, my poor friend." Charles smiled angelically. Rodolphe felt a strong urge to strike him.

Mercier spoke up. "Sir? I think I saw the mayor here earlier —he was here with the City Council. He went inside."

"Then there's still a chance to settle things!" Rodolphe said.

He ran quickly across the site and through the gigantic double doors of the Enantiodrome. The doors had been hung in an earlier century, and were weatherstained, their massive hinges eaten with verdigris. But they were still stout, and even beautiful, with bas-reliefs of bats and angels.

Rodolphe hurried up the cavernous entrance hall, with its flanking rows of vast peaked windows. Men and women thronged the galleries, slopping soap buckets, polishing the colored glass. Some were even singing.

Beneath the echoing vastness of the Great Dome stood a group in dark suits and dresses—the mayor and his City Council. The late afternoon sun cast a vast column of dusty light through the open apex of the Dome, splashing in a loz-

234

enge shape against the stair railings ringing the fretted interior.

The politicians were examining a heap of fresh rubble in the center of the great circular enclosure. Their muttering echoed with ghostlike authority.

Rodolphe saw that it was the great capstone. The huge marble lid had slipped through the hole it was meant to seal, and fallen, end over end like some vast stone coin, to shatter against the rain-stained tessellations of the Dome's hard floor. Rodolphe's heart constricted. Years of careful work and preparation, smashed and cast aside. . . .

"Monsieur Mayor," Rodolphe began.

"Ah, Rodolphe," the mayor said, offering his hand. "It seems we were both mistaken, my dear fellow. We shall finish even sooner than we hoped."

"Henri, I need to have a word with you," Rodolphe said.

"If you mean *this,*" the mayor said, gesturing at the rubble, "well, these things happen, eh?" He paused, staring at Rodolphe's companion, who had just arrived. "Charles," he said. "Charles, is it not?"

"Yes, Monsieur Councilman," Charles said.

"I'm now the mayor, Charles."

"I always knew you were meant for great things, Henri," Charles said with a smile.

Rodolphe picked up a piece of marble rubble with the broken face of a horned cherub. "I presume you realize, by this striking evidence of incompetence, that none of this is proceeding according to my plans."

"Yes," the mayor said, "somehow I gathered as much, by the fact that you were absent and the place was full of a mob."

"Well? What are we to do about this?"

"It's a politician's dream," the mayor said, smiling. "A genuine popular movement, Rodolphe! You ask what I should do? I'm their leader, aren't I? I run in front of the marchers and wave a flag! So here I am."

235

"But it's senseless, Monsieur Mayor. There's no point to it."

"The people are not required to 'make sense'—not to you, at least," the mayor said. " 'The Voice of the People is the Voice of God.' "

"You'll regret this, when you see the mess they make of things," Rodolphe said.

"It's *their* mess," the mayor said. "Not yours, Rodolphe. We're not the public. We only serve it."

"Well said," Charles remarked.

Rodolphe put his hands to his head. "What am I to do then?"

"Lead, follow, or get out of the way," the mayor suggested. He looked upward suddenly, and prudently stepped sideways. A chunk of marble a foot across came plummeting from the summit to smash to dust nearby.

A tiny head with waving arms showed at the daylit hole. "Hey! You lot be careful, down there!"

"Let's go," Charles murmured, clapping Rodolphe across the back. "One last time, eh? To the heights!"

The hours that followed were a sweaty nightmare of sledges and levers and pulley work. The vast unwieldy slab of stolen marble came foot by foot, sometimes inch by inch, around, under, and through the maze of scaffolding. Men rushed back and forth with crayon and tape measures, chopping the slab to fit with mauls and chisels. Cranes were raised, timbers set, as the incomplete Dome itself squeaked and shuddered under the strain.

Toward the end they worked by torchlight. In the grounds below, a vast crowd swayed, singing in unison.

The workers were in a cheerful frenzy. Both Rodolphe and Charles found themselves struggling to keep a rudiment of order; trying to keep the crew from injuring themselves in enthusiasm. Everyone wanted to contribute *something*, even something without apparent meaning of any kind. The restless energy could not be brooked. Those who could not help with the capstone were stripping away the scaffolds and cat-walks. As the gangs flung the lumber down, end over end, people scattered below, scrambling, laughing, and cheering.

Then the last wedge was hammered loose and the capstone sank into place with a shrill grinding. One man lost his crow-bar; another lost the end of his finger, and held up the bloody stump in white-faced glee, like a badge of honor.

They stood around for a moment, expecting some epiphany that no one seemed able to define. "Why aren't they cheering down there?" someone asked dazedly.

"They don't know yet," Charles said patiently. "They see no vital signal of consummation."

"Well, let's tell them, then!" Mercier shouted joyfully. He glanced around the top of the Dome, in the wind-whipped torchlight. "Wait a moment—where's our catwalk?"

The scaffolding of the Great Dome was gone. People had been disassembling it wholesale and flinging it down, cleaning the building of it, in thoughtless haste. "My God, we're trapped up here!" Mercier said.

The night watchman, Hugo, spoke up. He had a length of tarred rope around his shoulder. "No," he said. "There is still a way for you; I know it." He knotted his line to the tripod crane at the summit, and began to pay out rope, hopping downward across the curve of the Dome with a strange and crooked grace.

Rodolphe hustled the work crew into a proper order. "Show some dignity," he told them. "Remember, the eyes of the people are on you. Behave in a way that matches the majesty of this great moment."

They nodded, and followed the rope down, hand over hand, to a shaky catwalk. But when they reached earshot of the people below, their dignity broke and they began shouting wildly.

Then the celebration began.

Amelie was amid the turbulent crowd, waiting. She had the bear with her. No one seemed to mind its presence.

She embraced him. "I'm proud of you, Rodolphe."

237

Rodolphe laughed. He was light-headed with fatigue and triumph. "I don't deserve the credit," he said. "It wasn't really my idea."

"Whose idea was it, then?"

"I don't know. It seemed to come out of the air somehow."

"Take the credit," Charles advised. "Who knows who deserved it? Who knows who really started this thing, so many years ago?"

Rodolphe paused. The idea of final credit, of origination, had never really struck him before. "I don't know how it started. But it can't have been much to begin with, can it? Some poor fool, I suppose, piling a stone on a stone with his bare hands, while the rest of the world was wrapped in its strange transformation. His motive is lost in time."

"It was defiance," Charles said. "Stubbornness. The act of someone who wouldn't—or couldn't—join the Conventional world."

"You think so, Charles?"

"I know it."

Rodolphe laughed again. "Well, that would fit, wouldn't it? The central impulse at the secret heart of our milieu. I hope he's happy today, if he's still alive somehow. I'd dearly like to shake his hand."

Amelie was looking at him strangely. Rodolphe shrugged. "Or *her* hand, of course. It might very well have been a woman!"

Amelie said nothing. She was wide-eyed, looking into his face. Rodolphe touched her shoulder gently. "You're not angry with me, are you, dear?"

"No," she said. "It's just that I've never seen you like this before."

Rodolphe spread his hands. "You mean, now that it's all done? Have I changed so very much?"

"I don't know. . . . But I've never seen you before, as the father of my child."

Rodolphe started. "What's that, dear?"

238

Amelie smiled. A slow, secret, radiant look. "It will happen, Rodolphe. We will be parents together. Someday."

"What makes you think that?"

"I don't *think* it, Rodolphe. I know it."

Rodolphe stared at her in alarm. "Oh dear. You haven't been talking to the bear, have you?"

"You're wrong about the bear, Rodolphe. It's not a personality, like us. It's just an intelligence—a repository of much vaster forces. It knows things without understanding them."

Rodolphe was stricken with despair. He barely heard her next words. "But *I* understand them, Rodolphe. Someday you and I will meet again, in deep futurity. And we'll have a true marriage then. Something strange and profound, that we can barely imagine now."

"Well," Rodolphe said. "I suppose that's very good news, dear. In the meantime, you and I can. . . . Well, you can be the belle of the ball tonight, can't you? We can share the acclaim. Let's enjoy ourselves."

She shook her head. "No, Rodolphe. You do understand, don't you? In your heart, you know how this changes things between us. We can't play the game of young lovers, now that we know the truth. There's no point in it, darling."

"But you can't simply leave me! Not here. Not like this!"

"There will never be a better, truer time, Rodolphe. I know you'll remember me always, if we part at this very moment. But it's not goodbye. Only au revoir." She turned her back on him.

In a moment she had run gracefully into the depths of the crowd.

"Oh my God!" Rodolphe cried. He turned on the bear. "This is your fault, you stupid beast! I should kill you for this!"

The bear nosed at his knee with a snuffle. Rodolphe looked into its eyes. There was nothing there—just an animal blankness.

"Then it's *your* fault!" he shouted at Charles.

239

"I haven't done anything," Charles pointed out.

"I'll rush home, then, and find her. She'll never leave me, without taking her favorite things."

"She won't need 'things' where she's going," Charles said.

Rodolphe gasped. He braced himself to plunge into the crowd in pursuit; to find his wife somehow, tackle her, chain her down if necessary. But then the mayor and a crowd of celebrants emerged, blocking his way.

The mayor offered Rodolphe an open bottle of sparkling wine. "Fireworks!" he shouted. "Fireworks soon! What a fete, my dear fellow! The ball will last till dawn!"

A timber fell nearby, cascading end over end to splinter on the turf. The crowd billowed away in alarm. "What's this?" the mayor shouted, staring at Rodolphe. "My God! The whole thing's not going to fall on us, is it?"

Rodolphe, stung, drew himself to his full height. "Get a grip on yourself, Henri," he said sternly. "Of course it won't fall! It's only poor old Hugo, the night watchman. He's flinging down the last of the scaffolding, from high up on his Dome."

"Ah," said the mayor, "the final touch. Yes, I had a feeling there was something missing yet. Some final climax." He paused. "Good old Hugo, eh? It's a pity! You know, he's been at it for ages! He must be the oldest and most faithful worker we have! The poor old wretch should be down here for this. We should honor him. Yes, honor him—that's it."

"We can coin him a medal," a city councilman suggested.

"Capital idea. Medals all around."

"You're drunk," Rodolphe realized.

"There will never be a better time for it," the mayor said, forcing a bottle on him. "You look too sad, Rodolphe. It's not proper. Dignity's well enough in its place, but if you want to live within the walls of Paysage, you have to share the living heart of the people. There's no other way, my friend."

Charles tapped the mayor's shoulder. "Henri, forgive me if I phrase this question poorly, because the assumptions behind it are a little odd to me. But now that the Enantiodrome is finished, *what are you going to do with it?*"

"It doesn't need any purpose," the mayor said loftily. "It's entirely sufficient merely unto itself."

"There must be more to it than that."

"Yes . . . I suppose it is, for instance, beautiful." He paused. "Why ask me, anyway? I only voted the funds. *You* built it, not me. Why did you work on it?"

"I don't really know why I did it when I did it," Charles said naively. "But I think I *know how it did itself now*—wait, that didn't come out right."

"All right," Rodolphe interrupted. "Just tell us, Wild Man, if you know so much. Tell us what it's for, then. Tell us all about it."

Charles blinked in the carnival torchlight. *"It refreshes the soul of the world."*

"And what on earth is that supposed to mean?"

"I don't know," Charles confessed. "I know something ought to happen, but I don't think it's fully emergent yet."

A mass of cordage and lumber came slewing off the side of the building, caromed from a buttress, and fell in a heap. The crowd scattered, whooping. "He's still busy up there," Charles observed.

"How are we going to get the poor idiot down again?" the mayor asked.

"Oh, he lives up there," Rodolphe said. "He's used to it. He'll be fine." Suddenly he burst into tears.

"Brace up, Rodolphe," the bear told him kindly. "This transition won't take long. Your suffering will be brief."

Rodolphe stared at it. "You dare to speak to me?"

"Only to you, Rodolphe. The others can't hear my speech —they hear only an animal muttering. But I know the structure of your perceptions."

"Ah, of course," Rodolphe said in disgust. "Conventionality has always had its little spies, within my very body, eh? Nano-gnats. I suppose they must know my blood by heart, and every thread of my nerves. . . ."

241

"They keep you alive and youthful, Rodolphe. The secret structures of Conventionality support and sustain you, deep beneath your notice."

"I defy you and your secret structures!" Rodolphe shouted.

The bear nodded. "I'm proud of you, Rodolphe." The look in its eyes faded at once.

Then the fireworks began.

There were a surprising amount of them. Great scarlet rockets and sky-scratching yellow sparklers. The city, it seemed, had kept a happy arsenal in stock. The fireworks lasted almost till dawn.

At dawn, the sky began to answer them. Vast blazing streaks of light, skipping in from over the horizon. Meteors with blazing comet tails, flaming ensigns of powdered crystal.

Above the city they unfurled their red-hot wings, with vast shattering booms. There they circled, like a flock of glowing kites, over the heads of the people. Vast cooling things, with angular crystalline heads and wings like woven auroras.

They circled for a long moment, their eyeless faces twisting back and forth, like living pendulums. They seemed to search out some point of unspoken equilibrium.

Then, one after another, they swooped down in sudden arcs of heart-aching precision. Straight through the open doors of the Enantiodrome.

"What are they, Charles?"

"They have come to refresh the soul of the world," Charles said.

"Come from *where*, for heaven's sake?"

"The Moon, I think," Charles said. He paused, seeming to listen to an inner voice. "Yes, the Moon, Rodolphe." He smiled. "Convention's farthest-flung machineries. They are roosting in the Great Dome. Come, let us go inside and witness them."

"*You* go," Rodolphe suggested. Charles needed no urging. He was borne along into the building through the worshipful rush of the crowd.

242

Rodolphe turned away. He began to walk around the building, trampled earth littered with the sad debris of spent celebration.

Someone had collapsed. The mayor and a small group of citizens were gathered by a fallen citizen, who lay beneath a blanket.

It was Hugo. Rodolphe knelt quickly by his side.

"He fell," someone offered.

"He jumped," the mayor said. "From the edge of the Dome." He wiped at tears. "No one noticed. We were distracted by the glory."

Rodolphe looked at Hugo's battered face. Someone had already closed his eyes. He was quite dead. As Rodolphe watched, a tiny mechanism, no bigger than a pinhead, emerged from between Hugo's lips. It spread minuscule wings and took flight.

"They are inside us. They've always been inside us."

"We are inside *them*," the mayor said.

"What consolation is that?"

"We are their image. We are their antonym. We are their complement." The mayor lifted his head. "It's not a bad death, Rodolphe. Some of us never find it in ourselves to leave this place. I'll die here too someday, I swear it!" He raised his hand, and his voice. "We cannot be defeated! Even if Paysage itself were demolished, street by street, there would still be places like it in spirit. Our immortality is no less than theirs. Our life is the glow of renewal in the secret heart of age. It is the shadow of dissent, cast from resignation, in the restless light of hope!"

"Even to talk about ourselves, you have to talk just as they do," Rodolphe said.

The mayor's face twisted in anguish. "Yes . . . *but it's still the truth!*"

"We have to bury this poor man," a woman said.

"It is my youth that is buried," Rodolphe said. He turned on his heel and began to walk.

Sometime later, as he was picking his way through the wilderness, a great black raven appeared, and settled on a branch above his head. It followed him, cawing. At last came to roost on his shoulder. After that they began to have a long talk.

$\sqrt[]{\wedge\wedge\wedge}$

James Patrick Kelly is a dapper New Englander whose work has appeared in virtually all science fiction publications since his first sale in 1975 and lately has been showing up consistently on awards ballots and in best-of-the-year anthologies. Among his most highly acclaimed pieces are the stories "Solstice," "Glass Cloud," and "The Prisoner of Chillon," and his 1984 first novel, Look into the Sun.

Here he offers a powerful little vision of the hallucinatory universe that lies beyond the speed of light.

246

THE PROPAGATION OF LIGHT IN A VACUUM

JAMES
PATRICK
KELLY

*Women have served all these
centuries as looking-glasses pos-
sessing the magic and delicious
power of reflecting the figure of
man at twice its natural size.*

> Virginia Woolf,
> *A Room of One's Own*

Maybe you think I'm different, but I've got the same problems everyone has. Just because
I'm on a starship traveling at
the speed of light doesn't mean
my feelings can't be hurt. I still
get hungry. Bored. I lust like
any other man. When a bell
rings, I jump. I don't much like
uncertainty and I have to clip
my toenails every so often. I
want my life to have a purpose.

(You're nattering, dear. This
is about us, so go ahead and tell
them.)

Ah.

Yes.

My imaginary wife and I are
much happier these days, thank
you. We've come through some
tough times and we're still together. So far. But we still have
a way to go. Exactly how long,
I'm not sure. When you attempt to exceed 299,792.46 kilometers per second, here and
there are only probabilities. Relative to you, I am no place. I do
not exist.

I used to think that she was a hallucination, my sweet imaginary wife. Proof that I'd gone mad. Not any more. If I ask her whether she exists, she just laughs. I like this about her. We often laugh together. She keeps changing though; I'm afraid she aspires to reality. I had a real wife once but it wasn't the same.

(You're an artist. She didn't understand you.)

I don't want to paint too rosy a picture. Like any couple, we have our ups and downs. Then again, down and up are relative terms which vary with the inertial frame of the observer. Einstein warned that c is the ultimate limit within spacetime. Exceed it and you pass out of the universe of logic. Causality loops around you like a boa; the math is beyond me. Of course, logic and causality are hardwired into our brains. It makes for some awkward moments.

I was a hero when I began this grand voyage of discovery. Like Columbus. In his time, the world was flat. People believed that if you sailed too far in any one direction, you would fall off the planet. My imaginary wife informs me that we have sailed off the edge of reality. Perhaps that explains our predicament.

(Predicament? *Opportunity*. Nobody has ever had a chance to invent themselves like this.)

The problem was that the theoretical framework supporting faster-than-light travel stopped at c. No one really knew what was beyond the absolute. Oh, there was extensive testing before any humans were put at risk. The robots, unburdened by imagination, functioned exactly as expected. The design team accelerated an entire menagerie: spiders and rats and pigs and chimps. They all came back; the ones that weren't immediately dissected lived long and uneventful lives. So I suppose there's hope.

(What he hasn't told you yet is that it wasn't just him. He's embarrassed, but it's not his fault. There were fifty-one people on this ship. Crew and colonists. His real wife was one of them. Her name was Varina.)

I remember once Varina made a joke about it. She said that

science ended at c. The other side was fiction. It's not so funny any more.

I don't know what happened to the others. All I can say is that when the ship warped, I blacked out. I have my theories. Perhaps there was a malfunction. I could be dead and this is hell. Maybe the others had reasons for stranding me here—maybe they had no choice. When I woke up, there was no one else but her and she's imaginary.

I have no idea how to save myself, or indeed, if I even need saving. My grasp of the technology that surrounds me is uncertain at best. Do any of you understand the dynamics of a particle with a mass of 10^{19} GeV? You see, most of us were specialists. Aside from the crew, there were programmers, biologists, engineers, doctors, geologists, builders. Only the least important jobs went to people with multiple skills. I'm down on the organization chart as Nutrition Stylist, but I'm also in a box labeled Mission Artist. Corporations pledged money, schoolchildren sold candles, and the arts lobby worked very hard to create a place for me on the roster. Of course, it didn't hurt my cause to be married to a civil engineer. My speciality has always been dabbling. I've spent a lot of time in front of image processors. It says on my résumé that I throw pots but I haven't spun a wheel for years and who knows if there'll be clay where I'm going. I write my own songs for the voice synthesizer and can even pluck a few chords on the guitar. I do some folk dancing and tell stories and can juggle four balls at once. And now I style food. After I got into the starship program they sent me on a world tour of cooking schools. Budapest, Delhi, Paris—more dabbling. You know, I used to hate to cook; now dinner is all that matters. What's the point to doing art when you have no audience?

(You've uploaded some beautiful vids. Your stills were hanging in galleries.)

They were on late at night on back channels. All right, I'm better than some, but not as good as others. A journeyman. Yes, that sums up my condition nicely.

My condition. Should I describe a typical day? But then the

notion of day is another fiction. The laws of science do not distinguish between past and future. Here the arrow of time spins at random, as in a child's game. I'm never sure when I fall asleep whether I'm going to wake up tomorrow or yesterday. Fortunately, the days are very similar. For purposes of sanity, I try to keep them that way. Artists make patterns; we impose order even where there is none. Maybe that's why I'm still here and the others are gone.

Today, then. She snuggles next to me as I wake up. Her warm breasts nudge my back. Her breath tickles my neck. I roll over and we kiss. Her hair is the color of newly fired terra cotta. When she opens her eyes, they're green. She has wide shoulders and I can see unexpected muscle beneath her pale skin. She can appear to be any woman I can imagine. Today she is large. Magnificent. There's a kind of music to her voice. When she talks, I hear bells. She's not perfect, though: the skin under her jaw is loose, there's a mole on her temple. Clever touches. Another time she may be petite. She could have big hips. Long fingers. I think the reason she keeps changing is that, like so many women, she has a poor body image. She's far too critical of her appearance. But no matter how she looks, she can't help but become herself.

We make love. That shouldn't surprise you. Sex mostly happens between the ears, not between the thighs. Sometimes I lose myself and skip ahead in time to find I'm caressing a different body. But today she remains the same; it's what we both want. I take pleasure from the way her lips part, the bloom on her cheeks. At the end a moan catches for a moment in her throat, and then she draws breath again.

(And you?)

I can't help but love her. That's the biggest problem with our marriage. I love her even though she wants to separate from me—don't deny it! Go her own way.

I hold her until the blood stops pounding; she plays with the hair on my chest. Finally I kiss her and get up. I'm hungry. There's French toast and orange juice. As always. Just once I'd like to serve her breakfast in bed but she doesn't eat. The high price of being imaginary. She watches, though.

Afterward we visit the fx lounge. She chooses Trunk Bay on St. John: bone white Caribbean beach, palms tilting toward water the color of the sky. This is part of our imaginary past. Our honeymoon, I suppose. She keeps the temperature set at 29° Celsius. Invisible fans waft a breeze laden with her own homemade brew of coconut oil, female pheromones and brine. She's convinced that the way to a man's heart is through his nose. The floor looks just like sand except it doesn't sift between the toes, more's the pity. We spread blankets and soak up UV in the nude. Sometimes I wish she'd program the surround to show other people on the beach, but we're alone. Always alone.

(Other women kept staring at you. You were so handsome and everyone knew you'd be famous someday. I didn't like the way you looked back. I wanted you to see me. Only me.)

I never stay in the fx lounge very long. I want to relax but I can't. I hear things, even over the ocean soundtrack. The hull creaks under the stress of whatever is outside. If I rest my head on the floor, I can feel the vibration of the ship in my molars. My imaginary wife tries to make conversation, divert me with her memories of what might have been. But somewhere on board a thermostat clicks and a vent opens. What machine makes a sound like a cough? I have to get up and see. Either the ship or my imagination is haunted. I miss Varina.

(I can be her for you. Anyone you want. Where are you going? *Wait.* At least get dressed first.)

Here's a theory. Say you're traveling at 299,792.46 kilometers per second and for some unknown reason you want to go faster. You would then exceed the speed of light propagated in a vacuum. But what if spacetime does not yield up its absolute so easily? You attempt to accelerate beyond c to, say, $c + v$, the smallest, the most infinitesimal increment in velocity you can imagine. However, there's still a little infinity lurking between c and $c + v$, no matter what value you assign to v. What if it takes forever to achieve $c + v$? What if the speed of light is not a limit, only a barrier? You could spend all time crossing it—probability's revenge.

(But that doesn't explain where everyone went.)

Maybe they realized what was happening. That we were trapped. So they step into the airlock, cycle through and leap into eternity.

(All of them? What about you?)

I see them going one by one at first. Later in groups. They ask me; I can't bring myself to make the leap. Because I have you. Obviously. I'm traumatized; I blank it out. And I only am escaped alone to tell thee.

(Very dramatic; it fits you. You've always had a bigger ego than you cared to admit. But please don't go in there. It always upsets you.)

A typical day, my sweet. This is the control room of a starship. The bridge between reason and the irrational. Not what you expected? Every surface here is a screen, just like in the fx. I can black the entire room out or put on a light show of instrumentation. From here I can access the computer, view just about any corner of the ship, cook pizza for fifty-one, fiddle with the internal gravity, even vacuum-flush the toilets. If there were a god in this machine, that couch would be his throne. Once I cranked up the humidity until the air was just about saturated and then dropped the temperature twenty degrees in two minutes. My own rainstorm. A one-time miracle, though. Hell of a mess.

Unfortunately, while I can examine the inside of the ship in almost microscopic detail, I have no idea what's outside. Try the sensors and what do we get? Blank screen. Here's external telemetry . . . every readout is flat. It's maddening. I actually used to punch the walls after I brought this display mode up. *Wham,* just like that. The cursors jump into the red for a second before dropping back. Most of the time I don't even know what's being measured; all I want is a reaction. It must have shaken them, the scientists and engineers and programmers. No data across eternity—nothing but the uneasy play of imagination. Well, it took a while but I'm resigned to blindness now. Whatever's out there can't be observed from in here, at least so long as reason holds its tenuous sway. It has to do with the Uncertainty Principle, I think. The only way to truly understand is to participate in the phenomenon, become one with the event itself. Through the airlock, what do you say? The leap of faith.

(There's no way of knowing.)

No, I suppose not. Sometimes I wish the screens would show Varina's ghost or burning babies on meathooks or Jesus Christ transfigured. I could accept any of those. Because I don't believe that there's nothing out there. Maybe the instruments aren't sensitive enough to register the absolute, but that doesn't mean it doesn't exist. We have to find a way to go beyond our limitations.

But first, let's eat.

(Will you put some clothes on? You shouldn't be walking around naked. They'll get the wrong impression.)

Yes, my sweet. See how she clings to convention? But I love her anyway. We can stop by the room on the way to the galley. I do feel a chill.

Dinner is always the highlight. Stimulate the senses with food stylings and the mind with sharp wit. I allow myself two meals a day, breakfast and dinner. I have to watch my weight; I really don't get enough exercise prowling around the ship. Since she doesn't eat, my imaginary wife usually tells funny stories during dinner. My favorite is the one about the white-water canoeing course we took. She laughs about it now, but apparently we were almost drowned. What a disaster! And then there was the time she played that joke on her sister with the wasps' nest.

(I don't think she ever forgave me for that one.)

I'm going to make my specialty again. I hope you like meatloaf. I can't remember, have I shown you my room yet? It's not as big as the project manager's, not as tech as the captain's quarters. I suppose I could move, but this place has sentimental value. Besides, maybe they'll come back someday;

253

I wouldn't want you to think I doubted them. I still keep
Varina's clothes in the locker. And this is a picture of us on
our fifth anniversary. Let's see, I was thirty-four then, which
would make her thirty-eight. We married late. And the bed
that we never slept in. When I look at it now, I wonder how
we both could have fit. We would have been at each other's
throats before long; I like to stretch out at night. All right.
Shirt, pants, I'm even wearing slippers. Satisfied?

(You look wonderful.)

I'll run ahead and start cooking then. Keep them busy for a
few minutes, will you? I'll see you all in the mess.

(How does he seem to you? I'm worried about him. He's
been brittle lately, like a glass angel. Nothing I do makes him
happy. Not like before. He was very upset at first, but at least
he'd let me comfort him. When he stopped trying to remember what happened, I thought that was progress. He wanted
to accept our situation—make the best of it. But month after
month passed and there was no relief. I know that depressed
him. And then he lost control of time. He started swinging
back and forth, skipping ahead to see if anything had
changed, going back to the moment he woke up alone and
reliving it all again. I don't know what he needs anymore. I do
my best to keep smiling. I tell him how wonderful he is. And
it's whatever he wants in bed. Sometimes I worry he takes me
for granted. It's not easy for me, either. I have nightmares,
you know. About them. Her, especially. The real one. There's
a beautiful chef's knife in the galley, twenty centimeters long,
high-carbon stainless, forged in Germany. It's his favorite.
Uses it for everything; he probably has it in his hand right
now. In the nightmare I'm holding his knife, prowling the
halls. The handle is blood-hot. When I listen at doors, I hear
them breathing. I rub the flat of the blade across my lips and
think of her kissing him. They all have reasons for being on
board. Important things to accomplish. Why am I here? To
chatter, to amuse? Any one of them could tell stories and still
do something worth doing. Sleep with him? She did it and
had responsibility for water distribution and sewage treatment

254

besides. I think she was cheating on him. I know she took him for granted. It would have killed him to find out; he was in love. In my dream the knife is long and hot. I can hear her breathing. My throat feels thick. That's all.)

Are you still here talking? I swear, there's no keeping you quiet. Come on then, come on. Dinner is on the table!

Funny that the mess should seem so empty now, because before it wasn't big enough to seat everyone at once. We were supposed to go in shifts. Those little pasta things are spaetzel. From Switzerland. They're great with butter, or try them with gravy. And here's salad, produce fresh from the tanks. And this is the famous meatloaf, my very own culinary master-piece. In fact, it's about the only work of art I've created since the ship warped.

(Except for me.)

Would you like the recipe? It's really good eating.

FASTER-THAN-LIGHT MEATLOAF

> *500 grams ground meat*
> *2 grams salt*
> *1 gram pepper*
> *1/2 small onion, chopped (about 50 grams)*
> *50 grams powdered ovobinder or 1 egg, beaten*
> *30 grams stale bread, crumbled*
> *1/2 green pepper, chopped (about 50 grams)*
> *200 grams creamed corn*

Preheat oven to 190° Celsius. Mix all ingredients, holding back half the creamed corn. Form into loaf and bake 50 min-utes. Heat extra corn and pour over finished loaf.

SERVES TWO.

255

You can substitute whole corn if necessary but then you lose the topping. Creaming the corn is well worth the extra trouble, in my opinion. You know how memories attach themselves to certain aromas? I smell creamed corn and I'm in Grandma's dining room at Thanksgiving and I'm a happy little kid again. I missed creamed corn in my first marriage; Varina used to say it looked like vomit. Ground meat is, of course, rather hard to come by on this side of c. Luckily, there was an ample supply on board.

After dinner we usually go back to the fx and run simulations; sometimes we put on one of my vids. My imaginary wife enjoys them, or pretends to. Then we go to bed.

(Why don't you show them *Mr. Boy?* It's so layered. Every time I watch it, I see things I'd missed before.)

Truth to tell, I'm awfully sick of my old stuff, so why don't we just skip to the bells? It's an advantage I have: I don't necessarily have to stick around through the boring parts. From my inertial framework, I can clearly see that sequence is an illusion. At reasonable speeds, time's arrow appears to travel in one direction only, from the past to the future. But I'm moving at an irrational velocity.

So the bells wake me. I thought I knew every noise the ship could make but I've never heard this before. My imaginary wife is confused too. We query the computer from bed. It responds that all internal systems are green; it detects no unusual sounds. The blood stirs within me as I listen to the bells contradict its dry report. I can feel neurons firing in my fingertips; tears burn my eyes. You don't realize what this means: after all the deadening sameness, a life-giving mystery! I roll out of bed and run naked to the control room. Nothing here has changed. The external screens are still blank. The instrumentation is conspiring with the computer. I notice that the bells are harder to hear on the bridge. They're coming from elsewhere on the ship. The ringing reminds me of church bells that call the faithful to service.

My imaginary wife wants us at the airlock. You don't have to wait for me, I'll get there as soon as I can.

(It's not my fault. When he imagined me, he did better work than he thought. Exceeded his limitations. He needed

256

more than a mirror, so now I love him for my own reasons. I do love him; you must understand that. It's just that we can't go on like this. He's afraid to change because that might unblock his memory. But he wants me to change—and I have to remember. It wasn't just him, they did it to one another. The halls reeked of blood. At the end he was able to pull back from the madness. He found a way to survive. I have to do the same.)

What have you told them?

(Listen.)

This is the place, isn't it? The bells are ringing just outside the hull.

(Do you understand what they're saying? They're calling me to become real. I can't stay any more. I've reached my destination.)

I wonder if this is how the others went. Varina. They answered the call of the bells. The bells. The bells are very loud here. You can't ignore them.

All right, I'll admit I'm scared. But when she turns her face up toward me, it doesn't matter. I love her. I don't want to lose her too.

(Will you come with me? I can't live without you.)

The ship seems different; the computer must have missed something. I'm sure of it. I can feel a stillness in the deck beneath my bare feet. The vibrations have stopped. I'm shivering, as if the cold of space has breached the seals of the airlock.

(It's not space out there. It's nothing you can imagine. That's why we have to go. To see for ourselves. It's why they went. Maybe they're waiting out there for us.)

Varina, waiting. How will I explain my imaginary wife to her? What will they think of one another? It's impossible.

(Everything here is impossible and yet you've created it. Make me another, a better world. I believe in your abilities.)

257

She reaches up and cycles open the exterior hatch. Now there's only the interior hatch left. A single barrier between me and the absolute. The bells are deafening. The ship's hull rings like a bell.

(You can do whatever you set your mind to.)

I watch my finger extend toward a flashing blue button. I no longer control my actions. Her trust sings down my arm. My muscles twitch with her faith in me.

But you, you've already decided what's beyond the hatch. Majority opinion wants me to pull back. *Don't touch that button,* you say, *don't kill yourself.* But what if you're wrong? You're seeing this from a different point of view; you're still locked in the logic of spacetime. String theory tells us that the dimension of the observer is all important. How can you possibly hope to know what is happening outside a starship that has exceeded the speed of light? You can't hear these incredible bells. And despite everything I've said, you still don't accept my imaginary wife. Has anyone ever believed in you as much as she believes in me?

When I press the button, the hatch irises open. My imaginary wife and I go together.

At first, I don't understand what's happening. I'm sprawled flat on the floor of my room and I'm disoriented, groggy. I must've fallen out of bed. I can feel the ship's vibration in my cheekbone. It's as if the decks were ringing, except there's no sound. Something's wrong.

"Varina?"

She's not where she's supposed to be. My face is stiff, as if I've been crying. I notice the scratches on my wrist. Four sticky scabs that look like bad body makeup. Blood hammers in my head as I pull myself back onto the bed. I toggle the intercom. Silence.

The rooms on either side are empty. No one in the library or fx. The control room: abandoned. There's an odd animal stink in the air. I race through the ship, bouncing off walls like a madman.

(You're not crazy.)

I find her standing beside the airlock. I don't recognize her at first. She's pale. Dazed. Her chin trembles and she comes into my arms.

(Please, please tell me you're not crazy.)

I always hated it when Varina cried. She used her tears as a lever to move me. I wouldn't be here if she hadn't sobbed. Now I realize that if I don't help this one, she'll fall apart too.

"Who are you?"

She pulls away from me and sniffs. I've said the right thing.

(Who do you want me to be?)

She smiles then and I fall in love. It makes no sense, but there it is. Impossible things happen, she tells me. There's a kind of music to her voice. When she talks, I hear bells.

$\sim\!\!\wedge\!\!\wedge\!\!\wedge\!\!\sim$

The Arctic background of this impressive and rugged story is not something that its author got out of the *National Geographic. Stoney Compton lives in Alaska. He has served in the U.S. Navy, and has worked as a gandy-dancer on the Alaska Railroad, as a film editor and cameraman for a Fairbanks television station, as a free-lance graphics artist, as art director for Juneau's Public Broadcasting System station, and these days, is the operator of Ptarmigan Ptransport and Ptours, which boasts the only Bristol Double-Decker bus in Southeast Alaska.*

Those long Alaskan nights, I suppose, leave him some time for writing science fiction, a craft that he's been pursuing for the past few years, with—at last—success. Here is Stoney Compton's first published story, a harsh and impressive portrait of telepathy and survival in the far north.

WHALESONG

STONEY
COMPTON

The pod of leviathans moved north, great muscles undulating to the DNA command from past generations. Their numbers had increased in the past seasons. Usually solitary, they had formed pods directed by some whim of nature.

The toothed ones had fought among themselves and thus spared the pod much of the tearing death. They were few now and did not wait for the pod in the far reaches of the open water. Only near the edge of the world did they lurk, but even there they were much fewer.

In the center of the pod, now angling up to the top of the world to fill their lungs once more, was one whose eyes watched with a quiet intelligence, one who was aware. Thinker felt the minds of those around him; comforting, serene, content, the green and blue thoughts rolling over in their brains like gamboling calves. But only Thinker was aware of how many there were, of the lesser creatures that surrounded them in their world and above it. He could touch their minds and feel the hunger/feed/mate/nurse/protect/ dive thoughts that constituted their entire universe. From the tiny minds of the spiny backs around them to the bits of feather-covered flesh that swam in the world above theirs, all of the minds were basically the same. Except his.

Thinker's mother had been sick when he was born. He had been aware of the cellular collapse and the pain she endured. Sometimes he could not nurse because of the intensity of the anguish she was undergoing. Thinker felt it all. Her death heralded comprehension of his awareness, for that was when he realized that none of the others in the pod were able to touch with their mind, as he could. Her death was noted by them only in the abstract.

Had his mind not been unlike those of the others of his kind, Thinker would have perished without his mother. She had died when he was still a nursing calf, only halfway to that point when he would have fended for himself. He watched the adults, learning by example how to surround the krill with bubble nets and spiral up to the top of the world, filtering his sustenance through the baleen in his large maw.

Thinker knew that the middle of the pod was safest from the toothed ones and from the ones that waited above. When the pod moved with unknown purpose through the vast reaches of a now truly pacific ocean, his mind would turn over the imponderables that tormented him while his companions sang the migration song. Thinker searched for reason in a universe of liquid geometry and wordless melody, but reason eluded him. He continued his search as the pod moved north into waters that grew colder and colder, closer and closer to the remaining toothed ones.

2

Simon Manaluk sat balled against the wind in an effort to deny the elements his body heat. A pair of binoculars hung around his neck uselessly. They had insisted he take them for whale watch even though he didn't need them. The pack ice had retreated under the spring sun and tides until the

Chukchi Sea glistened with a sparkling blue for miles while errant floes dotted the frigid water.

Since the time the gusiks made war on themselves the whales had been on the increase. No longer were the factory ships from Russia and Japan plying the northern seas and taking his people's traditional sustenance. No longer was there a Russia, and as a result, the new Japan had richer fields to harvest. Simon moved his mind to more important thoughts. Where were the whales?

Motion caught in the edge of his eye off to the left. Ben Adams was running along the shore toward Simon, nimbly skipping over upthrust chunks of sea ice with practiced feet. Simon cast out in an attempt to sense the presence of anything other than young Ben. There was nothing.

"Simon! Simon!" Ben's breathless shout could be heard at fifty yards even with the wind blowing the sound away to their left. Ben skidded to a stop in front of the seated man.

"I saw." Ben gasped for breath, his twelve-year-old chest heaving. "I saw a whale!" He turned and pointed back the way he had come. "Out there, more than one, I think!"

Simon squinted up at the boy quietly. The wind snapped the wolverine trim of his cloth parka out in front of his face.

"I don't feel them. How far out were they?"

"Bout a mile 'n' a half, maybe two." Ben squinted back at Simon, trying to fathom the mind hidden in that bald skull. How could he not believe him?

Simon let his gaze wander back out to sea. "That's a good distance out for me to pick them up," he said carefully as he looked back at the boy. "But if you're sure they are out there go tell my brother and the other men."

Ben's smile flashed. He whirled and sped toward the village spread along the low hill behind them. Simon concentrated as he searched for a quickening in the sea. Still nothing.

Simon looked over his shoulder toward the village. Men were already emerging from houses and running toward the umiaks waiting at water's edge. His eyes flicked around the horizon, focusing as a medium-sized gull caught his attention.

He probed it for a moment before dismissing it from his thoughts.

Voices reached out to him from the village. Whale hunters were arriving at the skin boats, eyes sparkling and faces flushed with excitement.

"Have they come yet, Simon?" asked Nicholas Manaluk, senior umialik, captain of the largest umiak and Simon's older brother.

"My mind has yet to touch them, Nicholas. But if Ben is correct they will be here soon. With his eyes you really didn't need me out here to find them for you."

"Simon." Nicholas's voice was slightly reproving. "Please remember that we all do what we can for our people, some more than others. We didn't need you to find them, but we need you to bring them to us." The whaling captain walked away toward his boat.

Simon sat looking after the solidly built Nicholas for a moment and then grunted stiffly to his feet. He was small even for an Eskimo. His body was spare and hairless. Even with a constant coating of seal fat on his skin, he was cold all the time. For years he had been convinced that he had been born to the wrong place and the wrong people.

His father had been one of the last of their people to fly in the gusiks' airplanes. The plane had been the last to leave Fairbanks before nuclear weapons vaporized that city of many thousands. Simon's father thought he had escaped the modern storm of death, but he died two months later, his hair gone and his pale blood spinning uselessly in his veins.

While still in her grief, Simon's mother quickened with life and rejoiced at this final gift from her husband. But the last son of Solomon Manaluk was scrawny, hairless, pale, and whined in a thin parody of a healthy child's cry.

264

The technological world faded quickly from the day-to-day life of the village. Soon the supply of hydrocarbon fuels was depleted with no way of obtaining more. As a result the village generators stopped making electricity.

Aircraft didn't arrive on a schedule any longer. All ground vehicles soon gasped and stopped, forever. Even the snow machines sat idle and began to rust in the moisture-laden air.

When all the electrically and mechanically generated noise stopped, many of the People looked at their physical environment for the first time in years. They saw that things had to change once again.

Many of the old ways reemerged and the People maintained in most years and even prospered in some. As a small child, Simon was treated with great deference by his mother. He thought it was either because he was not as strong as the other boys of the village or because he needed his mother and his older, self-sufficient brother didn't.

Actually she thought him special. He was always thinking. She tried to point it out to others but all thought her words those of a mother making allowances for a difficult child. But he was so good at predicting things!

Then, some days after his twelfth birthday, his mother's brother came to their house.

"I come to take Simon on maupok. He must learn how to take a seal."

Simon's mother was excited, much more excited than Simon was.

"Get yourself ready, my son! Do not keep your uncle waiting, he is doing you an honor."

"Mother," he whispered. "We won't even get to eat any of it, we'll just have to give it all away."

"No. Simon! Every boy of this village is honored by his mother's brother in this way. You're already too walled off from the people. You're going to go with your uncle and bring back your first kill as a hunter."

Simon had never seen her so unwavering. He could feel the strength of her convictions as they radiated out from her. Her immovable stance made him angry.

"What kind of seal would you like, Mother?" There was an edge to his voice.

"Don't insult me or the animal you are about to kill! If we

could choose which animals to take we would soon run out of them. We take what is offered."

Her admonishment had no effect on him. "Tell me what kind of seal you want and I will bring it back to you!"

"All right, Mighty Hunter!" she whispered sharply, "Bring me an oogruk!"

Simon smiled. He knew she would say that. He knew that when he did bring back a great bearded seal, he would be spared further expeditions of this sort.

When a boy or young man of this village killed a bearded seal for the first time, it was a great event in his, and the village's, life. A young man's first kill of any species which the Real People depended on for subsistence was considered an important step toward adulthood. But in killing a bearded seal, one became an adult.

Simon sat patiently through the demonstrations and explanations presented by his mother's brother. After a long lecture the uncle asked Simon, somewhat smugly, where he thought they would find a seal.

"Follow me," Simon replied. He rose and led his uncle far out onto the ice pack. The boy walked in an unerringly straight line. Even after negotiating small mountains of stacked pack ice he did not lose his direction.

At a point four miles from the village, Simon and his uncle came around a particularly awesome cliff of ice rising far above their heads. Simon pointed to a seal breathing-hole in the ice.

"There, my uncle, is where I will kill oogruk."

The uncle looked at the large hole in the ice. "An oogruk could fit through that hole, Simon. And it is located on the protected side of the ice wall. But how do you know it is an oogruk rather than a smaller ring seal?"

Simon looked at his uncle with eyes that seemed to glow. "I just know." Taking the kakivak, Simon walked down to the breathing hole.

". . . and as he stood there the oogruk came shooting out of the water and landed on its sunning shelf! And Simon killed it!"

Simon's uncle looked around at the other men in the sweatbath. The men regarded the hunter, knowing he would not say these things if they were not true. This was an important thing that had happened, and at this of all times!

This was the final and most important day of the Bladder Feast. All of the men who had killed sea mammals over the past year had carefully inflated and painted each creature's bladder. For that was where the animal's inua, or spirit, lived.

After final purification in the sweatbath the men would perform the most important ritual of the Bladder Feast. The bladders would be returned to the sea, deflated and pushed under the ice, so that the inuas could return to their home. They would then create other sea mammals for the Real People to consume.

"This one is a shaman, surely," Uncle said through the steam.

"How is one to know? Who among us can remember the last shaman?" an elder asked.

"My uncle told me there was such a one here when he was a boy," a second elder announced. "But the gusiks sent their doctors to us. The old ways began to die when they made little gusik doctors out of our young men."

Steam wrapped about the men. All was quiet save for appreciative grunts as the heat did its work and the pores cleansed themselves.

"We need ones who can speak with the inua of our world," Uncle said. "This one can speak easily with the animal spirits. He can summon the beasts and make them understand that they are needed for the Real People to continue living."

The first elder moved toward the door to leave. He stared into the steam where Simon's uncle sat. "Then let us regard him as a special one. What have we to lose?"

So Simon was treated with even more than normal courtesy. He was one to respect and fear. For a few years the village ate well as Simon located or summoned the creatures of land and sea. Then the wife of a whaling captain fell ill and the seventeen-year-old shaman was summoned.

Simon edged into the house and looked down at the woman's sweating face, glassy eyes, and trembling limbs, and listened to her tortured breathing. He felt uneasy. He felt death in the small room and the woman's total surrender to it.

Without once touching her, he turned to the husband and said, "Your wife is dying." And he left the grief-stricken man without comfort or apology.

The captain hated the shaman, not realizing that the young man simply did not understand most of the social amenities. Being special and different could be a double-edged knife. But the captain spoke to the other villagers in malice and they listened.

After that Simon almost starved. There were no more frozen fish left in the passageway between his door and living space by those wishing him well. The people no longer left him portions of fresh seal or walrus. The people did not speak to him when he passed.

So a bad thing came to be. He began to hate the people. Simon had never felt comfortable with them. He had not felt he was really one of them. Although the motions had been gone through and he had tried, he had been different. Always. The few times Simon had looked upon the available women of his generation he had been rebuffed by the fear, or worse, mockery, in their eyes.

As the people shunned him, he began to push the game away with his mind. Hunters came back to the village empty-handed. The snowshoe hares avoided the snare, seals ceased appearing at breathing holes in the ice if men waited. Even the polar bear was not to be found.

When hunters from Sheshalik visited and saw the people of Point Hope near starvation, they were amazed. "Game is more plentiful than ever! Have you offended an inua?"

The people examined their consciences and decided that

268

Simon had been wronged. The whaling captain Nicholas Manaluk and two old men sat outside Simon's house and called for him to come out.

"Simon Manaluk, we would speak with you," Nicholas called to his brother.

Simon's bald head gleamed moonlike in the shadowed opening as he pulled back his door.

"You wish to speak to me or to kill me?"

"We wish to speak with you, Shaman," the first elder answered.

"We bring you food, though we have but little." The second elder pushed a bowl of rancid blubber toward Simon.

Simon moved out and sat on the ground in front of his door. "I would offer tea but I have none," he said simply.

"We thank you for your thought, Shaman," Nicholas Manaluk said. "But all we ask is that you help us with your thoughts. Since the, ah, misunderstanding." He stopped and cleared his throat. "Hunting and fishing has been very poor. We have come to realize that we have wronged our shaman. We ask your pardon."

As the two elders nodded in agreement to the umialik's words, Simon realized that this was a very hard thing for his older brother to do. The antipathy with which he had regarded his older sibling for all these years lessened just a small bit.

"I hold no grudges," Simon said, though it was not so. "I will be happy to use my powers for the village." His eyes squinted and his voice fell. "But I thought I was not needed."

"We are starving," the second elder said flatly. "Our lives are in your hands. If you will speak to the game and ask them to come back, we will give you a hunter's share."

"Caribou are moving this way, they walk on the edge of the Kukpuk." Simon nodded toward the river. He looked at his brother and said, "It would be well to put out nets at the mouth of the river. The whitefish are many."

Life evened out. The village grew prosperous and no one hungered. The short summer ended as the wind blew gusts of

269

snow across the wildflowers on the tundra. The village was well supplied. Winter creaked past, taking only two old ones and a deformed baby. One of the old ones was the wife of Solomon Manaluk, mother of an umialik and a shaman.

Spring returned and the whaling captain asked Simon to stand whale watch in that season, to be part of the cooperative effort the new Eskimo People's Republic was advocating. Everyone must do what they can.

So Simon Manaluk, troubled in spirit and mind, now took his place in the largest umiak to help his brother the umialik and his crew find the bowhead whale.

3

The pod slowed as the leviathans singlemindedly fed on the rich krill, seining tons of the minute animals from the sea water. Thinker slowly became aware of the toothed ones. They were still distant from him but closing on the outer ones of the pod.

A summons glowed across the far reaches of his awareness. Thinker stopped feeding as wonder raced through his neural system. There existed another mind in this universe! He had brushed it with his own! It was among the toothed ones. . . .

Curiosity overcame caution as Thinker's flukes propelled him toward the summons and the menace of which only he was aware.

Pain! Panic! The silent scream was almost a physical blow to him. The toothed ones had struck their first victim, while the rest of the pod continued with their leisurely feeding.

The toothed ones struck from above the world. Could he see them with his weak, deepset eyes if he pushed up into it? Propelling himself swiftly upward, Thinker broke out of the world and up into the thin life gas. His weight hit the top of the world and he sank into it once more. Frustration was new to him, another alien thing to ponder through time.

Thinker felt the summons again, stronger now, and closer.

His mind tingled with excitement. How could he communicate? How?

WE NEED YOUR FLESH, WE MUST TAKE YOUR FLESH TO LIVE. BE NOT AFRAID. YOUR INUA WILL BE RESPECTED. YOU MUST COME NOW.

Startled, Thinker angled down and violently fluked his way into the depths, away from the calm/assured/compelling/overwhelming/hungry presence. In fright and awe he hung motionless in the liquid of his world as his mind tried to grasp this reality.

Slowly, carefully, Thinker sent his mind up and touched a toothed one who rode the top of the world. Hunger/kill/warmth/mate/nurture/protect/hide. The mind was unaware of his presence. Thinker touched another toothed one.

WHAT! WHO ARE YOU? WHERE ARE YOU?

The thoughts came from Simon in a spasm of surprise. There had been alien wonder in his mind, a questing, a yearning for something undefined. Unknown tendrils had fingered through his mind. For him? The umiak rocked as the harpooner struck again at the breeching whale, announced by sealskin floats spiked into its flesh. Blood spread in large ponds of red on the blue sea.

The crew of the umiak paddled mightily, sliding the skin boat onto the back of the mortally wounded whale. Grabbing a third harpoon, the umialik leaped over the side of the boat and plunged it deeply into the massive head. The great mammal shuddered and stopped moving.

"Ee-yah!" Nicholas Manaluk spun around as he shouted his victory. He showed his crew with a wide smile, holding both fists above his head, stamping on the whale's back. "We eat well this day!"

The crew returned his smile, save one—the strange one, his brother the shaman, he stares into the water with wonder on his face! Is this a bad thing?

From the depths Thinker sent his mind into that of the toothed one's with a speed so great it cut easily through half-realized defenses. Images, knowledge, wonder, fear, pain, cold(?), and understanding of a sort were his. Visions of awe mixed with sudden dread. They do have reason, but they kill all, my, mine? They kill mine! They would kill me! This mind fears mine/me, this mind bites like a tooth, seeks not imponderables but our flesh! Why? Thinker filled his mind with the question, then sent it lancing into the toothed one.

Simon grabbed his head with both hands, trying to hold the presence still long enough to look at it. His fingers in mindless independence dragged down from his crown, leaving lines of sparkling blood in their wake. The insistence pulled at him, commanding, pleading, smothering his ability to respond.

"Wait!" he screamed, his eyes squeezed shut and fists grinding impotently into ears that hear no voice. "Let me answer you!"

Thinker let his mind relax and receive the melange of impressions that flowed from the toothed one. He circled his dead pod member and waited for reason to explain away his growing fear and anger.

Nicholas Manaluk stared at Simon, fear raising the hair on his neck and scalp. What is happening? The shaman has never injured himself before! Then he spied the great body circling around the kill on which he stood. He felt awe and exaltation, his brother has brought a second whale to them! What power this man has, there can be no others like him. How fortunate our village is! How proud our father and mother would be!

Nicholas's shout to the boat penetrated Simon's communications. "Another harpoon, quickly! This one comes to us!"

Simon tore his mind from the other's to stare at Nicholas as the umialik pulled the steel-tipped spear back in preparation to kill.

"No!" The hoarse scream skipped across the water. Men in other umiaks suddenly froze at their labors to stare at the shaman. "It thinks, it talks to me!"

Nicholas Manaluk's startled eyes flicked over the men in his boat and rested again on Simon. A vicious sadness swept over the umialik as pride died and anger blossomed. This was too much. His brother the shaman had finally walked on rotten ice.

"Bid it farewell, Simon," Nicholas said as he heaved the harpoon with all of his corded strength.

Thinker had stolen into Simon's mind. It was easier this time: he knew the way. He witnessed the confrontation between the two toothed ones and knew before Simon that the long tooth held by the other would bite. Thinker rolled and cut away from the threat, so the blow was not mortal.

The pain arrived, accompanied by realization and regret. Thinker allowed hate to spread in his mind, letting it feed on the regret and the realization that his kind would always be meat to the toothed ones. Nothing could change that. If the pod swimmers did not become food, the toothed ones would suffer for the lack. Their minds could only meet in mutual fear. Resolve was born.

Thinker swam under the drifting pod member and concentrated on the pain in his side. It, too, fed his growing hate. Thinker moved his flukes in swift arcs, singing a song of vengeance, straining upward . . .

Simon screamed, fighting the slithering, slippery presence in his head. His mind had followed the other into cool, pale greenish-blue vistas that invited. But the harpoon had sealed off access to that mindscape with pain and outrage, leaving hate for Simon and his kind.

Nicholas Manaluk began to take the few steps back to his umiak, knowing that there was something to fear here, not knowing exactly what—

The leviathan broke from the water, going impossibly up and up, blotting out the sun, towering over the suddenly small umiak filled with men, who first stared awestruck and then screamed at the hugeness now falling on them in unquenchable wrath.

273

Simon fought his way into the enraged mind of the whale and realized there was only one path to take if he was to live. He filled his lungs with air and dove away from the doomed boat. His heritage, his mind, his very soul rebelled at his choice, for the Real People did not swim.

Under the water Simon twisted about and saw the great body slamming the fracturing umiak and crew down into the frigid Chukchi Sea. Men he had known all his life screamed through the water at fate, at the whale, at Simon. Their air expended; they died. The whale slid across the drowning and crushed crew, pieces of wood frame and paddles buoyed to the surface behind the great body.

Simon cast about with his mind for the familiar aura of his brother. It was gone. Nicholas Manaluk with his disdain for his unmanly brother was no more. Simon felt a weight lift from his freezing shoulders.

He realized he was sinking. The numbing water had soaked his clothing. His mind raced as he fought to shed his parka. Panic confused his wooden fingers and he pulled at the wrong lashings.

A deep-set eye regarded him in his struggles.

An image of himself being held above water snapped into Simon's mind, a note of inquiry wafting about it.

YES! Simon's eyes bulged with the intensity of his desire.

Thinker rolled under the toothed one, noting the fear and panic that raced through the small, suddenly helpless creature's mind, and lifted it to the life gas.

4

Simon sat on the snow-covered beach wrapped in furs, his hands folded around a large mug of hot tea. Fragrant steam warmed his nostrils. But he didn't notice. He was already somewhere else.

ARE THERE ANY MORE LIKE YOU?

NO. YOURS WAS THE FIRST MIND TO TOUCH MINE.

I AM ALONE AMONG MY KIND ALSO. I HAVE NEVER LET THE REAL PEOPLE KNOW I COULD

SEE THEIR THOUGHTS. I FELT THEY WOULD KILL
ME.

KILL? THEY WOULD EAT YOU?

Thinker was perplexed. So many new things to understand,
including things happening in his own mind. He was seeing
his species from an entirely new perspective. These toothed
ones called themselves men. They knew so much about the
swimmers in the pods. Only because of their weaknesses had
the toothed ones/men not killed the pod off completely.

The people of the village were quietly packing. They would
follow the caribou like the Eskimo of the interior or else move
north to Point Barrow and live with their cousins. The surviving umiak crews had returned with a tale that would be told
for hundreds of generations.

The shaman that became an inua, and was returned to the
people in the form of a man, was obviously a witch. When the
witch called for warm furs and hot drink, he was accommo-
dated. That was the safest thing to do. But none looked him
in the face. And all retreated quickly after serving him.

Simon didn't even know when the people left Point Hope.
For the first time in over sixty thousand years, there was only
one human at the village site on the Chukchi Sea. None of
the Real People would ever return to that place, for a powerful witch lived there.

Early in the evening Simon became aware that he was hungry and tired beyond any point he had ever reached before.

I MUST FEED AND REST. WILL YOU BE IN THIS
PLACE WHEN I RETURN?

I WILL BE HERE.

Simon wondered at the lack of activity, the absence of villagers bustling about in daily chores. When he realized the
dogs were gone, a dreadful suspicion began to burn in his
mind. Rushing to the nearest house he stopped at the door
and called politely into the passageway.

"This one asks permission to enter."

His voice echoed off the bare walls. Simon walked from
house to house. Each empty dwelling pushed the barb of lone-

liness deeper into his mind until he suddenly sat down on the frozen ground, leaned against a wall, and sobbed.

WHY IS THERE EMPTINESS IN YOU?

THE REAL PEOPLE HAVE LEFT. THEY FEAR ME AND THEY HAVE LEFT ME.

WHY DO THEY FEAR YOU?

BECAUSE OF YOU.

Thinker grappled with the nuances surrounding the anguished statement and amid the pain and fear found resentment.

DO YOU WISH ME TO LEAVE?

NO! DON'T LEAVE ME! I WOULD DIE . . .

Simon realized he was screaming the words. What am I to do? I am not a hunter, I am not anything. Yet I have no wish to die, nor can I follow the Real People. They would kill me as soon as they saw me.

WHAT ARE YOUR NEEDS?

Good question, Simon mused. He began taking inventory of the abandoned village. The Real People had indeed left quickly. He found hides of caribou and musk oxen. A fish net with two small tears, a metal pot, fishhooks, and an old ivory-tipped spear piled up in front of his house as he wandered back and forth between the silent dwellings.

Finally Simon entered his own house and saw it with new eyes. What do I own? Through the years he had received many things as payment and gifts due a shaman. When his mother died he had not really cared what form payment for his services took. Now, suddenly, it all mattered.

Faint amazement at the discovery of a fine rifle, two pairs of sealskin boots, caribou jerky, and a wooden bowl of slightly rancid muktuk.

EAT NOT OF MY KIND.

The flat, even statement filled Simon's mind with tendrils of menace, salvation threatened, and immediate abandonment.

YOU WOULD HAVE ME STARVE?

SUSTENANCE?

276

Images of different fish species began to flick through Simon's mind. Most he did not recognize; some were swimming nightmares. Then other species of the sea: seals, walrus, eels, squid, crab, snails, even clams and mussels. Simon picked the creatures he knew to be of high food value, mentally nodded when their image was passed through him, then sat waiting when the images stopped.

THE POD FEEDS ALWAYS. YOU?

NO. I NEED BUT LITTLE BY YOUR STANDARDS. BUT I NEED FOOD EVERY DAY.

ALLOW ME SOME HEARTBEATS.

Simon wondered at the request as he wandered back to the shore. Of course; time. He sat on the pile of furs and watched the surface of the sea. Never in his life had he felt that he fit in with people. Then why did his abandonment cause him so much grief?

YOU ARE NOW UNABLE TO REPRODUCE? The query was its own answer.

I NEED A FEMALE OF MY KIND. Simon agreed.

I CANNOT HELP YOU, BUT I GIVE YOU THIS . . .

A terrified ring seal shot out of the water and landed almost at Simon's feet. The mammal slid to a halt and, seeing the human, began frantically to beat its flippers in an effort to regain the water.

Simon stared perplexed at the forty-pound animal. He had no weapon, not even a club, with which to dispatch it. The seal was moving quickly now, almost to the water. Simon rushed over and kicked it in the body, away from the shore. The blow almost broke his foot.

The pinniped snarled and gnashed its formidable teeth at the human. Simon kicked it in the head, using his other foot. The seal turned on the ice, rolling over partially and quivered vigorously. Simon thought he had killed it.

As Simon began to walk to his house for an ulu to butcher the animal, it convulsed and began moving toward the water again. He was enraged. He had fought it as best as he could; he had never needed physical strength before. In a flash of panic he looked through the creature's mind into its neural system and screamed at it to die. The seal convulsed once again and lay still.

Simon Manaluk seemed to step outside of himself and look down on the slight Eskimo watching the flippers quiver, watching the eyes change from a window of inner life to mere glassy flesh. He was elated and horrified at the same time. Never had he dreamt that he possessed such power!

"My life could have been so different . . ." he mumbled to the dead seal.

I GO TO FEED NOW. I FEEL NEEDS IN YOU THAT MUST BE MET. I WILL BE HERE WHEN YOU RETURN.

Suddenly Simon was truly alone, but he was too hungry and tired to care. He moved off in search of the knife that had belonged to his mother.

5

Spring passed quickly into summer and Simon spent most of his time on the beach. There was so much information for the two mammals to share, and try to understand. And, at times, understanding became a process of finding equivalences.

The human concepts of family and love were not alien to Thinker, but he could not fathom a village, or staying in one place all one's life. Thinker came to view the villages and towns of the humans as barnacles at the edge of the world. The idea of continents was completely impossible to visualize.

It took Simon some time to realize that Thinker's world was six times larger than his, and just as alien to Simon as his was to Thinker. Simon did not understand when Thinker told him it was time for departing from the Chukchi Sea.

WHY CAN YOU NOT STAY HERE WITH ME?

MY INUA BIDS ME LEAVE TO FIND MY OWN KIND.

BUT THEY CANNOT TALK TO YOU AS I DO, WHY MUST YOU GO?

IT IS TIME FOR ME TO SEEK MY OWN KIND a vision of two whales gamboling together deep in an ocean of serenity AND THE WORLD BECOMES STIFF WHERE THE LIFE GAS LIVES. I WOULD DIE HERE.

The image of a drowning whale, sinking slowly under a mantle of thick ice, faded from Simon's mind. A feeling of desperation washed over him.

WHAT WILL I DO? A human figure stands in the midst of a whiteout, lost in the middle of its world. HOW WILL I FIND SUSTENANCE? As Simon eats, his food fades from his hands, and he looks about in confusion. WHO WILL I TALK TO?! Simon holds his head in both hands, eyes clenched shut, corded jaw in a grimace of straining effort and tears pouring down his face.

Thinker was silent, equally confused at the psychological anguish that any human could have identified as guilt. This was totally unexpected. The concept had never before been considered and there seemed no way to ignore the mental needling.

YOU GO ALSO. A human figure swims, in a manner impossible to that species, next to a whale as a feeling of inner warmth suffuses both of them. WITH ME.

I WOULD DROWN, I CANNOT SWIM.

Both pondered the image of whale lifting man to air at their first meeting. The crushed umiak sliding down into the ever darker depths mocked at Simon.

A BOAT! I COULD GO WITH YOU IN A BOAT . . . WAIT, GIVE ME SOME HEARTBEATS. Simon began a quick search of the empty village. He was sure he had seen . . . yes! Behind, who had lived here? No matter, here were three kayaks stored carefully on a driftwood rack.

One was built in the old way using the skins of seals and coated with shark liver oil. The other two were twenty-first-century variations on the same theme. Simon had never be-

279

fore given the narrow boats much thought. Now he examined each with care.

Frames of lightweight metal tubing carefully lashed together were covered with a lightweight polymer skin born in the Great Technology Age of the recent past. Both boats appeared to be in perfect condition. The first kayak measured ten paces and had two circular openings from which paddlers could propel the craft through the water.

The second craft was much larger, and much stranger looking. Sixteen full paces long, one and a quarter paces wide in the fat, middle part. There were six circular holes for paddlers.

Simon entered the house looking for the equipment that was essential for the great boat's operation. There was a great pile of plastic domes, mast poles, paddles, air cushions, and objects that Simon could not decipher. He labored with his discovery for most of the day, figuring out what each part did and where it fit while being used and where it went when it wasn't in service.

As a child, Simon had learned from his uncle the rudiments of using a kayak. He had been a poor student, mostly because the instructions bored him in their repetition. He had understood the principles immediately and given more of a chance might even have become proficient. But poor students are not trusted with an uncle's only kayak.

Now he had the time, and the need. With the hand winch he found in the house it took him three days to work the boat to the beach and provision it. The next day the last human left Point Hope.

6

Three sails could be mounted on the boat, each with a large surface area that propelled the craft nimbly over the water. Simon learned to sail by trial and error as the man and the whale moved south. When Simon had to sleep, Thinker would stay near the strange boat and make sure it did not meet some hidden reef or rocky shore.

Thinker led the man straight south, veering slightly to avoid the Seward Peninsula. On the morning of the third day, land was visible to left and to the right. Simon was confused until he realized he was traversing the strait between Asia and America. In the old days it had been impossible for a man to travel through here without being intercepted by the ships of powerful nations.

But that was the past, and Simon ignored it as he sailed and paddled through the endless water. His boat was loaded with useful goods from the village. He had everything he needed. And he wasn't alone.

He sealed the hatches in the boat by means of plastic domes that fit into them snugly and were then made airtight by bicycle inner tubes inflated with a foot-operated airpump. The tubes were weathered but all held air.

The hatch configuration on the boat was one forward, two sets of two side by side amidships, and one aft. Simon spent most of his time in the forward opening, using the center hatches only when rigging the three sails. The weather remained clear and the Bering Sea uncommonly calm for five days.

The storm swept out of Siberia on the morning of the sixth day and found Simon dozing. Simon had slept whenever he felt like it: Thinker was with him and that was all the protection he needed.

The wind picked up and the soft lapping waves immediately changed into white-capped peaks that sent gallons of spray into the open cockpit in mere moments. Simon slid on his sprayskirt and hurriedly sealed it to the hatch rim. Pushing the rudder control with his feet, he changed course so the boat was running with the wind.

A snap brought his attention to the single sail that was still rigged and bellied out like an old man's gut. Simon knew the tubing would bend before the sail would tear, but he didn't want that to happen. The great kayak was shooting over the water, much too swiftly, racing with the storm front, trapped in that wave of icy cold air that heralds its master's presence.

He pulled down and out of the sprayskirt, then propped it up with an axe to keep the maximum amount of water out. As soon as he cleared the hatch he squirmed through his furs, clothing and other assorted possessions to the hatches by the sail. Pushing gear under the opposite hatch, he let air out of the tube until it lost its seal.

He caught the loosened dome and lowered it to the deck. Spray stung his face and hands as he forced the sail to give up its hoard of wind. Finally the sail collapsed against the mast. He pulled the long metal-and-wood mast out of its socket and lashed it to the deck.

The boat slowed a little. The true storm swept over him as he resealed the hatch and crawled forward. As he entered the sprayskirt he beheld the most frightening world he had ever seen or imagined.

Gray-green mountains of water rose and fell all around him. The top of each dissolved into rock-hard spray that bruised the man and beat a dinning tattoo on the boat. The boat pitched with an up-and-down circular motion that began to bother Simon's stomach. The wind shrieked at him. His eyes began to water and his body to chill.

WHY ARE YOU DISTRESSED? DO YOU SICKEN?

THE SEA IS TRYING TO KILL ME!

Simon was terrified. He had not foreseen this possibility. He was a man of the land who weathers storms inside a warm house. This was unbearable.

HOW MAY I HELP YOU?

A feeling of futility accompanied the question. Suddenly Simon laughed.

"What does it matter? If I don't die here I'll die somewhere else." He pulled down out of the skirt and then unfastened it and inserted the plastic dome. May as well do this in comfort, he thought. Simon pumped up the tube and watched the storm beat against the outside of the dome.

Time ceased to have meaning as he gripped the hatch bottom and kicked the rudder back and forth in an attempt to ride between the waves. Up, down, left, left again, right, the kayak traversed the endless range of whitecaps. Cold seeped through the hull of the boat and crept into his bones. He pulled the skin of a polar bear over his lap and legs and continued kicking the rudder.

Tired. He had never been this tired before in his entire life. His legs ached and his temples throbbed with pain. His hands were cramped from the effort of holding him away from the plastic dome and hatch combing. The boat was sealed airtight as well as watertight. Simon was close to unconsciousness when he decided that fresh air was a must, no matter how wet he got in the process.

Clumsy fingers worked long at the task. What's wrong with me? he wondered. With great deliberation he pushed the little stem down and the escaping air blew directly into his face. That helped. The hatch dropped down onto Simon's lap, water and wind pushing around it. He slid it across his legs and into the bottom of the boat.

The spray once again bruised his face with a steady needling, but the air felt so good in his lungs that he didn't care. There seemed to be a thunder rising above the sound of the storm. Simon grabbed the sprayskirt and pulled it on, and started snapping it down.

THE WORLD ENDS. I CANNOT FIND A WAY AROUND IT! ARE YOU ABLE TO CHANGE DIRECTION?

Simon laughed into the storm. Weather was the most difficult concept for the great mammal to grasp. "The world ends" was the whale's description for an island or a continent.

Simon pushed his mind through the storm ahead of him. Small glows of mental activity flickered out there but there was nothing he could learn from them. Grabbing the two-bladed paddle, Simon pulled hard to stay on the back of the mountainous wave that was lifting the boat higher and higher into the storm. A land mass darker than the air around it loomed in front of him. The air reverberated with the unceasing cacophony of surf colliding on immovable rock.

Suddenly there were no waves in front of him, just a wall of

283

heaving spray that danced on an unforgiving shore. The wave under the boat began to break apart and Simon realized that his velocity was much greater than he had thought.

The wave dropped away under him and the boat sailed through the wall of spray. Simon braced himself against the hatch as the boat angled downward, breaking out of the spray and slamming onto a wide rock shelf. The boat ground to an abrupt stop, Simon's head snapped forward; flesh split on contact with the hatch rim and consciousness vanished.

7

Thinker could not hear his friend. Never since the day they had first become aware of each other had they been this disconnected. Thinker could still feel Simon's life-force constant, but there was nothing in Simon's mind. When his friend had rested in the past, Thinker would feel his unconscious thoughts and emotions.

He had to wait. Thinker swam down and started building a bubble net. Fluking gently to one side, nothing strenuous, he emitted small burps that sent gentle walls of carbon dioxide streaming to the surface as he completed circle after circle. As the pressure eased on his body Thinker tightened the circle more and more, ever upward, sensing the minute life being herded together.

Minute life that offered sustenance, minute life that drove the great leviathan into faster and faster circles, building to a feeding frenzy that blotted out abstracts and focused on only one point: eat! The maw of the whale spread to its widest limit as the great beast shot into the air, water streaming through its baleen and trapping the krill for consumption.

The force of the life gas stunned Thinker. He had never before experienced this violent presence. Slowly he neared the surface again. The world was highly agitated here. His great body began to rock with the force of the liquid around it. He fluked sharply upward and breached into the heart of the storm.

The wind, aided by gravity, pushed him over sideways, slamming him into the world with incomprehensible power that gave him fear. The awareness of a force more powerful than himself was as close to the concept of a god as Thinker was ever to achieve.

He began to swim around the edge of the world where Simon was stranded. Many heartbeats later, Thinker decided he had gone the wrong way and reversed his course. He wanted to summon Simon again anyway.

Thinker asked the void and received no answer. Nothing moved around Simon, nothing threatened him that he had not already endured. Thinker swam on, skirting the edge of the world and becoming anxious. He didn't like the burning bubbly feeling in his guts, but he couldn't make it go away.

This edge of the world was too big. Thinker realized it would take too long to go around it, Simon might go somewhere. Simon might need him. He swam easily back to the place where Simon was.

Thinker relaxed. Now he sensed the dreams of the man. Simon must be sleeping now. The whale breached into the storm once more, blowing his last reserve of life gas through his blow hole, clearing his lungs of water. He didn't want to drown.

After filling his huge lungs with life gas, he fluked to the bottom and rested on the underwater slope of the mountain that was Saint Lawrence Island. Thinker drowsed in that state his species used in lieu of sleep. The storm rocked him gently even this far down.

8

"What is it, Mother?" The young woman squinted in the morning sun, trying to make sense of what she saw.

"My mother's mother would say it was a beast who died while eating a man. She was like that. I think it's some kinda boat and that man looks dead." The old woman removed the pipe from her worn white teeth and spat downwind.

"Shall we check, Mother?"

"Hell, Marilyn, you're the nurse, what d'you think?" The old woman cackled, put the pipe back in her mouth, and shuffled after her running daughter.

The pain mushroomed into a higher neural intensity with the advent of consciousness. Simon screamed.

YOUR PAIN IS MY PAIN. PLEASE MAKE IT STOP!

H-H-HOW?

LIKE THIS.

Simon's pain vanished and he gasped in surprise. For a few lengthy moments his mind assimilated knowledge it had had for millennia. He sensed his injury with new understanding, measuring the tears in his flesh, the microscopic network of cracks in his skull that radiated out from the arcing point of impact, and the hemorrhaging blood vessels spewing their pressurized load into spaces that threatened his existence.

Simon concentrated: weaving cell tissue and mending the torn vessels, fusing calcium cells and rebuilding the cracked skull, and lastly bringing life to the withered tissue of the cut —pushing the two sides together and closing the oozing gash. The skin hummed across the wound site and pulled tight. There wasn't even a scar.

The young woman's scream snapped Simon into immediate awareness. His eyes beheld two people. He smiled, he was genuinely glad to see people once again, obviously of his own race. He spoke the universal language to them.

"My name is Simon, I have been at sea for many days and I am glad to meet you."

"H-How, did you do that, uh, Simon?" The young woman was deeply agitated, carefully pointing a finger at the dried blood on his head.

Simon thought she was beautiful. "I'm a shaman," he said simply, and smiled at her again.

"Bullshit is what my mother would have called that. But what did she know?" The old woman regarded Simon through narrowed eyes. "We ain't had no shamans around here for a

286

long time. Not since the nineteen-nineties. How do we know you're not really a witch?"

Simon looked at her levelly. "You remind me very much of my mother. I'm no longer sure that is a good thing."

HOW DOES WITCH DIFFER FROM SHAMAN?

I WILL EXPLAIN LATER. I MUST TALK TO THESE PEOPLE NOW.

Simon tried to mask his irritation with the interruption and concentrated on the lovely young woman's voice.

"My mother," she said hurriedly, slowing her speech as his gaze met hers, "is only asking, uh, the same thing that other non-witnesses would ask."

"Non-witnesses?" Simon asked blankly.

"I saw your head heal. I know you're something, maybe even a shaman, and I don't even believe in them!"

Simon nearly laughed before he saw the tears in the corners of her wide, dark eyes. Almost involuntarily his mind embraced hers, carefully, probing and feeling. She was very frightened. She had just seen the impossible.

Simon nudged her mind and then her mother's. Both women blinked.

"For a minute there I thought your head was cut." The slim young woman's voice held an edge of fading hesitation. "But I guess not."

"No. I'm fine. Thank you for finding me."

Simon let his gaze wash over her full figure, which was superbly molded by the carefully sewn caribou skin dress. Someone on the mainland trades with these people, he thought. There was more than Aleut-Eskimo blood in her, maybe some Indian, or gusik. Her face was oval rather than round. However, she still had handsome, high, wide cheekbones. They strikingly set off her long-lashed, lustrous eyes and wide, generous mouth. He smiled at the beautiful face and concentrated on holding her curiosity at bay.

"You looked dead, I remember," the old woman said bluntly.

"Just resting, Mother." His smile was upon her and made it so in her mind.

"Who are you? Is this a boat or an old aircraft?" The young woman watched him out of the side of her face, like a bird studying a potential threat.

"I am Simon. Who are you?" His gesturing hand covered both of them. He noticed she was slightly taller than he was.

"I am Marilyn Oktuuna. This is my mother—"

"Don't you tell nobody my name!" the old woman snapped. "Only I have the right to do that and I don't want to."

Simon was amazed to discover that he could not find the old woman's name no matter how hard he searched through her mind. His amazement didn't get past his eyes, but the old woman saw it anyway.

"See! He almost had you telling him! I don't trust him, I got these feelings that I should like him and I got no reason to!" The old woman was so agitated that she bit the stem of her pipe in two.

He could settle here. He could have this woman Marilyn. Here was the life he had always wanted and he could make it work. He knew how. It was absurdly easy to change a person's attitude toward you.

But this old one, she had been a cynic for a long time. And keeping two minds in the shade was difficult. Could he manage a village?

He held them in thrall for a few moments while he probed for information. Twenty-two people lived in the village on Saint Lawrence Island—all that remained of the survivors of Gambell and Savoonga after the tsunamis of the Short War.

ANOTHER COMES.

Simon turned from the women and looked across the rocky beach to the sea. A one-man kayak was being propelled toward them by the smooth, strong strokes of its occupant. Simon quickly looked back at the women.

"Who comes?" He nodded toward the closing boat.

Marilyn shaded her eyes with a strong, steady hand and peered with squinted eyes.

"That looks like . . . yes, it is! That's Abraham Shugetuk. He is an honored hunter."

"How'd you know he was out there?" the old woman asked sharply. "He didn't make a sound."

"Perhaps my ears are younger than yours," Simon said politely to the woman. He turned to watch the man pull his kayak ashore, noticing the man's wide shoulders and light step as the hunter proceeded rapidly but casually up the beach toward the small group.

"What is that thing?" said Abraham, pointing at the great kayak and carefully studying Simon.

"It is a big kayak, built by gusiks long ago. I found it. My name is Simon. The storm stranded me on your island." The man's mind was like walls of ice. He was as difficult as the old woman.

"I am Abraham. From where did you sail this great kayak, Simon?"

As Abraham's eyes fastened on him, Simon thought of sled dog teeth on a caribou bone. With some misgivings, he reached toward the man's mind.

"I came from Point Hope, Abraham. And I am pleased to meet you." He concentrated on sending thoughts of friendship and brotherhood.

The hunter frowned.

"I heard this thing about Point Hope," he said slowly. "I heard that everyone who lived there had fled. There was a terrible witch that killed whale hunters and the people had to leave."

How fast the news had traveled! Simon was careful to keep his face frozen while he cast about for an answer.

"Yes! That is true. It was terrible. We all left to escape the witch." Simon pushed around the other's mind, seeking entrance, leverage. He found it.

He discovered that this man felt very strongly about Marilyn Oktuuna. There was almost an understanding between

289

them. Simon's heart sank. Should he look further for companionship? Then his resolve turned from cold water into firm ice.

Who knew how long it would take to find another village? Let alone another woman as handsome as this one! In exerting enough mental strength to subdue Abraham Shugetuk, he discovered his power was growing.

"How sad for you," Abraham said woodenly. "Welcome to our village." All three villagers smiled with twitching cheek muscles.

Simon understood so very much for the first time in his life! This would be so easy. After all those years of yearning, spying, humiliation, and rejection. He could finally have a woman. Two women!

YOU DESIRE TO REMAIN HERE?

YES, THERE ARE FEMALES OF MY KIND HERE THAT WOULD HAVE ME IN THE MATING.

DOES THE ANGER/FEAR COME FROM YOUR LACK OF KNOWLEDGE ABOUT YOUR SPECIES?

YES.

GOOD. IT FELT UNWELL. I MUST CONTINUE AFTER MY KIND. WILL YOU BE IN THIS PLACE WHEN THE WORLDS ARE JOINED AGAIN?

YES, WHEN THE ICE IS OUT I WILL STILL BE IN THIS PLACE.

EAT WELL. Thinker was gone.

For a moment Simon was anxious about being alone. Then he refocused on the beautiful young woman and knew that he wouldn't be alone much longer. He stood and stepped out of the great kayak.

"Take me to your village." His mental smile dazzled the three islanders.

9

Thinker moved rapidly south, swinging wide around the sick-making places. Toothed ones/men had flourished there once but now they were gone, leaving their death gases behind them. Thinker's mother had gone fatally close to one of the sick-making places, seeking the large krill that bred there, one accelerating generation after another.

The thought of his dead mother brought a familiar quickening to his heartbeat. His heart faltered for a moment as he realized that the feeling was the same as with the small "man."

Thinker had found the concept of "love" the most difficult to comprehend. Simon had been unable to clearly explain it other than to lament its elusiveness. Thinker had picked up intonations of mating desire mixed with Simon's incomplete attempts at explanation. Thinker had no urge to mate with the man, yet he felt a definite desire for Simon's presence. More than a desire; a definite need.

Pondering these things, he found himself entering unawares on a mortal drama unfolding nearby, which he sensed only when he was in the midst of it. A female of his species was trilling in pain and fear. For good reason; she was surrounded by a pod of Orca. The Killer Whale.

The Killer Whale had earned its name by preying on other cetacea. Thinker had witnessed the mindless savagery of the small, sleek, white and black torpedoes with exaggerated dorsal fins when he was still a nursing calf. The helplessness he had felt watching the bloodlust bloom into death for a pregnant cow came back to him in a wave of revulsion.

But now he knew what to do. He urgently summoned every porpoise he could contact to come to the aid of the already wounded female. Thinker had no concept of his mental range and was thrillingly surprised when over twenty of the intelligent sea mammals suddenly flashed past to ram into the Orcas at high speed.

When a two-hundred-pound porpoise bullets into the side of another creature, massive damage results. Internal organs are ruptured, bones are broken, hemorrhaging is immediate and often fatal. The six Killer Whales were totally overwhelmed. Two died immediately under the onslaught, two more drifted off jerking in mortal convulsions, and the remaining two survived only because they fled at once.

The female moved slowly, blood streaming from three wounds. She was in shock and in danger of sinking and drowning. Thinker moved to her side, nudging her upward, and sang songs of support and encouragement. She didn't seem to notice his presence, let alone hear his trilled urges. She sank lower.

Thinker worked into her mind, pushing aside the bone-hard door of fear and into the deadly depths of paralyzed inaction.

YOU MUST RISE TO THE LIFE GAS OR YOU WILL DIE!

Thinker waited for a response. Nothing. He pushed an explicit scene of a rotting whale carcass into her mind and noted the shudder of revulsion that followed.

IF YOU DO NOT RISE TO THE TOP OF THE WORLD YOU WILL TURN INTO THAT!

Finally the female showed awareness of life outside her terror-caged mind. She moved her flukes and the pain from her wounds caused her to shudder again. She paused for a moment and then churned into life, her massive tail pushing her rapidly upward to the life gas.

Side by side they floated on the top of the world, bathing in the life gas as the heat of the great eye warmed through their blubber and began to penetrate their massive bodies. The heat made Thinker sluggish. He drowsed on the gently rocking water.

Her nudge brought him instantly awake, and after a hesitant moment he followed her down into the depths. Her wounds had congealed, but still gave her pain. Small spasms marred the fluidity of her rhythmic movements. Despite these slight flaws, she still was a handsome thing in Thinker's eyes.

292

There was an appeal to her that he did not understand, but he did not hesitate to follow her lead. For the first time in his life he did not analyze the situation before he acted. Unbeknownst to him he was falling into a pattern older than conscious thought. Thinker was following the dictates of his genes and the command of racial continuity.

This was the first breeding season for both of them, and over the following weeks they lost track of everything but each other. Thinker found himself in a sensual gambol with the female that surpassed any physical euphoria that he had yet encountered in his existence.

Time after time he released dams that he hadn't known existed and each time he was awed by the closeness he felt with the female.

Then he slowly began to realize that while she was returning the physical overtures of mating she was not joining in the mental and emotional bonding that he was experiencing. The day that he understood that she was not capable of returning all that he felt necessary, he became despondent.

What had he expected? She was like the others of his kind; unknowing, unreasoning, and uncaring. She didn't even react when he suddenly ceased his constant attentions. Life simply continued on for her. Thinker suddenly realized that cognition might not be a gift, but a curse.

10

Abraham Shugetuk carefully kept his breathing even. A man had to be one with his prey, both to take its life and to honor its spirit. His right arm didn't even quiver as he held the spear cocked, ready to plunge into the breathing hole in front of him.

His eyes never left the pale, dried sliver of willow twig that served as his indicator. Abraham had found the breathing hole hours ago, scraped the snow from the top of the hole until it was very thin, and then set his twig carefully through the center. The seal would not be alarmed by such a small thing sticking down into his world.

A small thing that the animal could push up and out of its way with ease. And thus indicate its presence to the waiting hunter. Abraham let his imagination probe beyond the breathing hole.

He imagined a fat seal, full of fish, needing air . . . looking up and seeing this bright spot that promises air . . . muscles move the flippers and it rises through the water . . . The twig didn't move.

Abraham suddenly found himself thinking about Marilyn Oktuuna, and how her body moved. How she had been overwhelmed, possessed, by this newcomer. How she shared a lodge with him.

Abraham realized that his breathing was quickening. He concentrated on the willow twig to center himself. The twig was slowly moving upward.

With a strength fed on anger, his arm thrust the spear down through the center of the hole, past the twig, and into the neck and chest cavity of the seal. He quickly twisted the spear so the barbed point would hold the thrashing pinniped. Abraham frantically hacked at the air hole with a steel knife, enlarging it so he could pull the animal up onto the ice.

When finally he looked down on his kill stiffening on the ice, he apologized to it.

"I ask your pardon for using you as my heart's true target. I will treat you in the old way now." And while he brought his dog sled over and loaded his kill, Abraham carefully concentrated on his tasks, emptying his mind of all else.

But on the way back to the village he remembered the hostility he had felt toward Simon while he was out there, and then he thought about how the feelings changed when near Simon. His knuckles whitened as he squeezed the sled handles in frustration.

"Never before have I hunted an animal like this!"

The lead dog's ears twitched at her master's voice, but she did not slacken her stride. Something had to be done.

Marilyn Oktuuna was at her practiced best. Simon lay content as she bent over his nude body, kissing, licking, biting.

He enjoyed the sensation of her hair and breasts falling on him and pulling across his skin. But it was all empty.

She was the model of acquiescence. His silent bidding was followed to the smallest degree. But it was all his doing, his imagination, his lust. Not hers.

The other young women in the village were the same—sullen and unresponsive until he took hold of their minds and directed them in their actions. Holding twenty-two people in thrall was a wearisome thing.

At this moment all of the other villagers were asleep at Simon's command. Only he and Marilyn were awake, making love.

But were they? Were they really making love? Would she do these things to him of her own volition? He wished it so, therefore it was so. The more he thought about it the more important it became that her actions be voluntary.

If I lifted my mental shade from her mind, would she continue to love me? Continue to make love to me? He wanted that so much it made him ache.

The unfulfilled, feared, and fearful boy in him cried out for exorcism by love. She does love me. She must. She wouldn't do *all* of this with me if she didn't love me! And I love her!

Yes. I love her and I will take her from this place. We will sail off together and find love for each other. His head buzzed with the idea of her love. His soul demanded it. And he gave her mind back to her.

Marilyn sat back abruptly. Her eyes fought for focus. Her hair framed her handsome face and fell across her full breasts. Simon stared at her, holding his breath, a smile of joy waiting at the edge of his mouth for her acceptance.

She looked at him in his nakedness. Then she looked down at her own. When she looked back at him, her face had twisted into a rictus of rage.

"What have you done?" she screamed.

"I love you!" His voice was not loud enough to gain her attention.

"You are evil! You *are* a witch!" Her screams beat on him, they were unstoppable.

He closed his eyes and put his hands in front of his face palms outward, to ward off the loathing that emanated from her.

"I love you," he moaned. "I love you." He opened his eyes and dropped his hands. Just in time to see the glint of the fish knife arcing at him.

He reacted swiftly, automatically. The arc of the knife tightened and the blade plunged through the mass of her raven hair into her naked breast. He screamed with her.

"No!"

The echo of their united voices seemed to be trapped in his mind. He watched her eyes dilate in shock and begin to jell, and reached into her mind, only to recoil again as he discovered a perverse satisfaction in ushering her life force out of existence. Marilyn Oktuuna's hand still firmly clenched the knife handle as her lifeless body fell over backward.

Simon sprang off the bed and began pulling his clothes on. His voice issued forth in a thin, wordless scream. Her last thoughts would always haunt him, he knew. Simon finally began to loathe himself.

He let himself see the other villagers. And under the smiling, obliging, loving exteriors he had fabricated for them he could sense the total hate and fear.

He didn't want them that way. But before he had realized that he had already put them into the mental bonds that he now found so repulsive and unchangeable, Simon knew that if he released them they would kill him, quickly.

Just as Marilyn had tried to do.

The winter had been the longest he had ever endured. His sleep had been fitful with fear and his days engulfed in a constant mental stranglehold on the village.

296

From the first he had coupled with the young women. The release of flesh had been as wonderful and addictive as he had thought it might. Then he had fixated on Marilyn.

He held a bear by the tail in this place. He could not let go or the bear would take his life. Yet this final act of maintaining that hold sickened Simon to his very soul. He didn't want to do this thing anymore, but what choice did he have now?

Simon pulled on his mukluks and shrugged into his parka. His eyes carefully avoided the corpse on the bed as he pushed through the door. Once outside he drew in a lungful of the cold air.

I must get away from here. Where is Thinker?

Simon stared out at the fragmenting ice and felt it numb his mind. The white expanse was beginning to break up and the sight of water shining through the opening leads encouraged him greatly.

With an effort he returned his attention to the great kayak. His escape was ready. He had repaired the damage as soon as he could, and the boat was filled with the provisions he would need for a long voyage.

Now he walked to the boat and gave it an experimental shove. It was very heavy, but he could push it by himself. As he stared out at the distant, widening lead, he knew he had to do it alone.

He had discovered that his mental powers had limitations. If he was tired or ill, his range was reduced and more effort was required to maintain his grasp on the minds of the village. Concentration on any single other thing also weakened his mental fist. Like pushing a boat, for instance.

11

As Abraham approached Marilyn's house he felt the absence of the feeling of goodwill. While he puzzled over that absence he noticed her door standing open. Fear blossomed in his chest and he covered the last yards in an instant.

The sight of her corpse—the look on her face, the knife immovably clenched in her hand—told him at once that the witch from Point Hope had come to his village.

A growl formed deep in his throat. He looked out and saw the witch. So it thought to leave now, unpunished for this unspeakable act . . . Abraham ran into the center of the village. There was much to do, and quickly.

Abraham Shugetuk concentrated on being a seal. He had more practice being a seal than any other animal. He knew the witch could hear a man's thoughts and bend them back on themselves. But Abraham reasoned that with all the witch was doing now, it would ignore a seal.

He had rejected his .30-06 as a weapon, fearing that nonseal harmonics would accompany his slow approach over the ice toward the witch. Abraham was the best sling-wielder the village could boast. The sling was elemental and organic. Tied to his body beside the small bag of smooth stones, its walrus hide composition was one with the seal aura that Abraham was projecting.

The witch was still pushing the great kayak toward the opening in the ice a quarter mile distant. The men of the village coveted the kayak. He stopped that thought quickly. Abraham could not dwell on matters that would be foreign to the mammal he was pretending to be.

The witch either had not noted his slow, sliding approach or else was ignoring any nonthreatening element of its tightly controlled universe.

Abraham knew his roused fellow villagers watched through binoculars from a safe distance. They had discovered that the witch had limitations, and distance was one of them. Abraham snuffed at the ice under his gaze, just as he had seen seals do.

He inched closer, his arms stiff at his side mimicking flippers, his feet rigidly together in parody of the powerful tail of the seal. Abraham rolled slightly to his left and allowed his concentration to measure the distance to the witch. He was close enough. He could not miss.

Abraham Shugetuk pulled his sling free with one hand, palmed a stone, and was swinging the ancient weapon before he was fully on his feet. He concentrated on seallike thoughts of eating raw fish as he aimed and let fly the whirring stone. The witch didn't even look up.

12

Thinker recognized the edge of the world where he had left Simon and increased his speed as he swung around its edge. He probed ahead with his mind and was confused with the conflicting sensations he received. Much was not good here. Strife tainted the atmosphere, mixing with hate and fear.

Suddenly he perceived Simon's aura. The man was anxious, fearful, and hurried. Simon's mind seemed to be closed in on itself, hiding from . . . what? Carefully Thinker edged through the half-formed mental defenses. Pushing aside the frantic anxiety, he encountered guilt. Why would a thinking being lower itself to such a state?

Thinker probed one synapse further and found himself among Simon's memories. Tons of muscle shuddered involuntarily in revulsion. As the recent events ran at dizzying speed into Thinker's mind, a parallel questioning wonder at his deep feeling for the human began to surface.

Thinker was carefully formulating a greeting when a wave of intense pain/shock/fear burst out of Simon like the scream of a gull. The whale opened his senses to their maximum and found the attacker, now emboldened to the extent that he concentrated on his mission openly.

In an instant Thinker ascertained that Simon was injured to the point that he could not protect himself. The Abraham Shugetuk toothed one hated/feared Simon enough to kill him. Thinker ran questioning tendrils through Abraham's mind in search of the rationale for this act.

For the second time in his life, Thinker found himself in agreement with a member of a different species. Suddenly he saw Simon as Killer Whale with Abraham an avenging porpoise. The harmony of balance flowed over him like a current of warm water.

299

Abraham slowly advanced over the rocky beach toward the downed witch. Adrenaline hummed through his system. His first cast had been perfect.

He could see the blood from here, a one-shot kill! But wait! The witch moved, it wasn't dead yet! Abraham pulled another stone from his pouch. Once again the whirring sling began to orbit his clenched fist.

Simon's stunned mind was awash in conflicting thoughts. No matter how hard he tried he could not follow a single one to fruition. His mother stood in her familiar, hunched stance and nagged at him. Then she vanished, and it was his brother, Nicholas, peering down at him, showing his superior, mocking smile before also disappearing.

Memories ran through him with no more direction than water over a creek bed. Suddenly Marilyn stood there, arms held wide in invitation, the fish knife sticking out of her bloodied chest. Simon wanted to scream, but couldn't. Mercifully she vanished.

His motor responses were equally muddled and knotted. The basic prodding instinct of self-preservation got him to his knees once, but it lost impetus and he began to curl into a fetal position. His feet pushed at the heavy beach gravel in weak imitation of flippers.

His long-dead uncle informed him in his best teacher's voice that Simon would die if he did not do something very soon. Then the apparition laughed and faded. But the stone had done its work well. His brain was too damaged to function correctly.

He had to fix something; had to weave thought and concentration to make a tool. He could not. Fragments of death danced in the shards of his mind.

300

Thinker knew the hunter's purpose, and his motivation. He hesitated, sharing the man's rightful outrage at Simon's actions. Justice is not a cetacean concept, but by his own stated beliefs Simon was condemned to punishment of some sort.

The Abraham toothed one was swinging his killing skin over his head again. Thinker could feel the certainty of the kill screaming in the hunter's mind. A choice had to be made, now!

But new questions surged through him.

How would Abraham perceive Thinker? Could a rapport as complete as what he had with Simon be realized with this toothed one? Would he be welcomed by the other toothed ones on this rock? Could they fill the void that would appear with the death of Simon?

No. No. No.

These particular toothed ones would not even accept one of their own who was different!

Thinker slammed into the attacker's mind with such force that Abraham lost consciousness in midswing and collapsed in a heap. His question had answered itself.

In that single moment he had seen the truth. Abraham would have regarded Thinker not only as a witch but also as prey. Abraham was a toothed one adept at the tearing death.

Thinker registered the astonishment evoked from the hiding villagers by this turn of events. He also noted their hasty retreat as he reached into Simon's mind. As he repaired the damage in the human, he wondered if he might have been able to repair his own mother as well. Simon's aura coalesced slowly with the whale's help.

ARE YOU ABLE TO MOVE? CAN YOU LEAVE THIS PLACE NOW?

Simon swam up through a red mist as pain washed all around him. But he thrilled to the mental touch of the whale. With an effort he concentrated on the pounding pain in his head, closing the wound and soothing damaged tissue. Then he reached out.

MY FRIEND! I AM SO HAPPY YOU ARE HERE. YES, I CAN LEAVE THIS PLACE. I MUST LEAVE THIS PLACE . . .

301

Simon paused to collect his thoughts, to explain the haste in which he wished to leave. There was so much to communicate to the great mammal that he did not know where to begin.

THEN LET US LEAVE THIS PLACE AT ONCE.

Thinker could sense the villagers returning. They carried weapons that could reach farther than a sling.

With fear and joy powering his muscles, Simon pushed the great kayak out into the surf until the water was waist-deep, then he pulled himself aboard. A bullet buzzed past his ear. Simon lashed out with his mind, numbing those with weapons.

He could not chance the kayak being damaged now. His life was still at stake.

The sea grabbed the buoyant craft, pitching and rolling it about. Simon grabbed the mast and raised one of the sails. It bellied out and the boat was once more under his control. He was amazed at how quickly the island receded.

I HAVE LEARNED MUCH ABOUT LIFE, AND MY-SELF, SINCE WE PARTED. Simon paused, hating and needing to finish his thought. I HAVE DONE THINGS THAT SHAME ME, THINGS THAT ARE BENEATH ME.

Thinker sifted through the top layers of Simon's thoughts. The man's remorse and shame was something new to ponder, but his anguish struck a chord in him.

WE ARE VERY DIFFERENT FROM OTHERS OF OUR OWN KIND. YOU AND I ARE TRAPPED WITH OUR ABILITY TO COMMUNICATE, TO KNOW WHAT IS IN THE MINDS OF OTHERS WITHOUT THEIR KNOWLEDGE. OUR PERCEPTIONS ARE MORE COMPLETE THAN ANY OTHER CREA-TURE'S IN OUR WORLDS. WE ARE CURSED.

Simon steered the kayak absently, his mind going over the message from the whale. Thinker was right. They were cursed.

WHAT SHOULD WE DO? WHERE SHOULD WE GO? I DO NOT THINK I CAN FACE THE ICE TIME ALONE, THERE MUST BE OTHERS AROUND ME.

GO WHERE ICE IS NOT. The mental image of warm water and trees with large pointed leaves, of the sea teeming with abundant and colorful life, faded slowly and reluctantly.

IT ISN'T JUST THE ICE . . . BUT WE CAN GO THERE? Simon inquired.

Thinker felt a warm glow. The question had included both of them: not "I can go there?," but "*We* can go there?" YES, TURN TOWARD THE WARM EYE.

Would Simon be able to avoid entangling them both in trouble? Time to think about that later. They had far to go. There would be enough heartbeats to find answers.

Simon edged the tiller around until he was going southwest. The whale inquired why he could not travel in a straight line and Simon began to explain wind and basic sailing to a creature who had no need to be erratic in order to be precise. Saint Lawrence Island disappeared into the bluing mist behind them as they followed the setting arctic sun.

Here's an eloquent piece of work that creates a strong character and an unusual future society in enviably muscular, economical prose. Augustine Funnell is one of the newer names in the field, though his credits already include stories in Fantasy and Science Fiction, Isaac Asimov's, and assorted horror fiction magazines. He lives in Canada, and tells us no more about himself than that he owes passionate allegiance to the Boston Bruins. Why someone who lives north of the border would claim to live and die according to the fortunes of an American ice hockey team is in itself a subject suitable for fertile speculation; but it shows us, at least, that he has that knack for self-dislocation that seems to be essential to success in our field.

RIVER OF THE DYING

AUGUSTINE FUNNELL

What draws me to the river? I don't enjoy watching those wretched souls on the rafts drifting out of the city, nor am I at all fond of the Lord's Own Guards stationed at intervals to ensure that the diseased do not attempt to return. So what is it? Not the stink, not the hallucinogenic mists rising out of the infected river (for the mists move *with* the river, do not drift inland) and certainly not sight of the river itself, brown and brackish, contaminated with substances both natural and manufactured.

Is it the fear? you wonder. Some exquisitely honed emotion that impels me daily, morbid though it may be, to the place I fear more than any other? Perhaps. An attempt to brace myself against the future, when Nalynn joins the outcasts.

Yes. It is fear. That they'll find and take her, that I'll be alone; and in it I find what I need to be strong and cautious. The view, of brown buildings decaying beyond the fog, of other Lord's Own Guards stationed across the way, serves to reinforce that fear.

"Move along, Citizen. Or jump in."

I don't recognize this one, but they're virtually indistinguishable anyway, manufactured from a limited gene pool and grown to maturity in the Lord's Own Scientific Sanctuary, unleashed, with more brawn than brain, more cruelty than compassion, upon the citizenry. Which means he won't tell me twice, so I turn and start the long trek up the mossy steps, quickly enough to satisfy his brutish authority, slowly enough that I don't slip. Once, the steps were dry, the river clean and clear, and families came to spend afternoons flitting over the water. The Lord's Own Guards were more passive then, less obtrusive. But times have changed, they certainly have.

At the top I risk a glance over my shoulder to be sure he hasn't followed. He has lost interest, did not recognize me with my hood keeping my face in shadow, and is already scanning the bank for threats from the river. I stare for a moment as a pair of rafts, rotting bodies strewn atop, drift with the current. Even as I watch, a body topples over and sinks beneath the surface. Someone's father, or mother, child or sibling, once beloved but now a symbol of pain and fear, of all the things we hide from here in the city. Who reported? Who let fear battle love and win? Because the sickness is *not* contagious, I care not a damn for all reports to the contrary. It. Is. Not. Contagious. I have spent four months tending Nalynn, and I know it comes from the air, or the water, or the food. I know. As, I suspect, do Lord Early and his advisors, but they permit rumors to circulate and panic to spread because they feel it is to their future advantage. When the population has been decimated, when Lord Early has decided we have suffered enough for his mistakes, there will be issued a Palace decree advising all those not infected to present themselves at this clinic or that for inoculations. What joy there will be. What relief that the Lord's Own Medical and Research Corps has managed to manufacture vaccines for prevention of the disease. Support for Lord Early? By the Dead Christ, they'll lick his boots and forget there ever *was* a war, forget that the river flows through lands so deadly they glow in the daytime—in the God. Damn. Daytime!—and they'll wipe smooth brows and get on with the business of living, thankful that it was a loved one—or two, or five, or a dozen!—struck down, and not them. Oh yes, I know how it'll be. I do. Because I know my father very well, and I can see his hand of calculation in this as surely as I saw that dessicated wretch topple off the raft. (Father? Did I say my *father?* No. I could not have. Because he isn't. We have, perhaps, the same blood in our veins, and I may bear a strong resemblance to the Lord of the City of Perpetual Light, but my father? Those are words that incite, and I will rip the tongue from anyone who speaks them. I *could not* have said that. I *did* not.)

These narrow streets are nearly deserted, but no surprise that. The citizens cower behind their stones like frightened children, petrified by the mere thought of outside contact. As if they can wait it out, as if a truly contagious disease couldn't insinuate itself through the mortar. Few are the shopkeepers willing to sell their wares; rather the goods rot on shelves behind padlocked doors while citizens starve than a shopkeeper expose himself to danger. (Until the advent of the disease I had always thought greed the strongest of human concerns. Apparently I was wrong.)

A body blocks my way through a residential district, tossed from one of these doorways, or one of those windows above. Obviously diseased, discarded for the Lord's Own Mechanical Sanitation Corps to collect and take to the river. Which it will, once the message is received at Corps Headquarters. Undoubtedly whoever threw the body here has already done that, and now sits anxiously anticipating symptoms of the plague on his person.

She is young, perhaps fifteen, and her face is covered with blotches so fresh I can see them spreading even as I watch. I wonder if she was unconscious before they tossed her out, or if contact with the damp and unyielding stones has cracked her skull. No matter either way.

Briefly I consider taking her with me, but the sight of a healthy man carrying an infected girl would mean only that the healthy man would accompany her to the river; worse, they might track me and find Nalynn. But still, one is human, one wishes to exercise compassion whenever possible, and it goes against everything I cherish to leave this poor girl.

307

The decision is suddenly made for me. Grinding down the street comes one of the Lord's Own Mechanical Sanitation Corps robots to collect the debris. The ochre light in its faceplate gleams through the darkness, flickering briefly to red each time it passes an address, until it clicks to a halt beside us. Its scanners record my presence, but again my hood will prevent my face from being recognized at the Imperial Palace. Mechanical arms extrude, hoist the unconscious girl, retract to a load-effective length, and the robot lumbers down the narrow street, toward the river of the dying where at all hours the rafts wait, to be loaded slowly and methodically until full.

Good-bye, child.

The clicking of the robot has attracted watchers behind the curtains. I can feel their eyes upon me, and I am tempted to shout some reprimand, but there's nothing to be gained by that. This is a city populated by the crazed and the terrified, and there are more of them than there is of me.

A soft, cold rain begins. Soon there is wind whipping it through the street at an angle, making it sharp, needlelike. I push on, taking a route that forces me into the worst streets, through areas where the storm attacks most savagely. Since Lord Early still has people searching for me, I will take no chances. If they can track me through this, they deserve to find me. But they won't. They are motivated by fear of Lord Early, I by love of Nalynn. They want access to rewards— Lord Early's collection of alien mindjewels—I to save Nalynn from the rafts. They are *paid* to do what they do. I act as I choose.

On whom would *you* bet?

I never come here during the brown daylight, and anyone who sees me slip into the alleyway must suspect only that I am taking a shortcut through to the next street. Wrong. There's a doorway halfway down the alley, and even if someone can still see me in the darkness he will see only that I turned into it. He will not see me stand in the shadows, waiting to be certain there is no pursuit; nor, when I *am* certain, will he see me reach into the inky blackness above, grab the first of a series of rungs, and haul myself upward. Even in the daytime the space above the doorway is virtually invisible. At the eleventh and final rung there is a trap door, easily shoved open. There's a small platform, then a door, and as always, I knock softly before I enter.

Dim light from an outside illuminator filters through the single dirt-streaked window to fall on the bed where Nalynn rests—and has rested, almost every minute now—for over two months. She turns her blind eyes toward me, and the faintest of smiles flickers briefly across foamed lips. The reek of her is overwhelming; combined with the natural stuffiness of this hidden sanctuary it is almost enough to provoke vomiting. I gather my strength.

She has soiled herself again, unable to rise to use the chamberpot I provided. She grimaces as I touch her to begin the bathing, but no sound escapes her lips. I am finished in a few minutes, disposing of the rags and filth down a long-unused chimney. I have constructed a closure for the thing, but even so the smell intrudes. It must be at least half-full by now. Fortunately it vents two stories higher, so we'll attract no suspicious noses.

I risk opening the window a little, to let in some fresh air. She seems in control of herself tonight; sometimes she isn't, and she cries out, or groans, and I have to hold her head against my chest until she stops.

It perhaps seems strange to you that I enter and clean her and provide fresh air without speaking, but that has become our routine, agreed to without words. It permits her some humanity so that when we do talk, she is without embarrassment, as much like her old self as possible. Not that we speak much, or long, or of many things, for she tires easily. Especially these days, since the fungoids invaded her mouth and throat. Sometimes it is all she can do to say my name, or ask me to hold her.

This, I fear, is one of those times. "How are you feeling tonight, my love?"

Her mouth opens, flecks of foam bubble across her lips, and I can see the growths on her tongue. Still, after a moment she manages, "I'm tired, Auarja. So very tired." To punctuate this statement she sighs, a rattling thing that makes her cough softly.

She is painfully thin, much more so than she once desired. For she was a stocky woman, built low to the ground and broad through the shoulders, and I used to tease her that she could have wrestled carnivores in the Lord's Own Games if the rules had permitted women to do so. And though she did not like her shape, I did; it pains me to see her thus. Sometimes I'm almost glad she has lost her sight; it would do her no benefit to see how her condition affects me.

Selfish! Selfish!

I take her white hand in mine, and even though my body prevents light from the outside illuminator from falling on it, I see dark blue veins and cracked nails. There is barely enough strength for her to squeeze back, and even then I'm not sure she has.

"Lie with me awhile."

And this is why I detest those who've cast out their sick, who let fear win the war against love: the distinction that makes us human is the one that lets us make choices, that gives us the ability to weigh and decide. Animals act through instinct. They have no compassion. In humans, compassion must be given equal weight with instinct, and the decision reached must be the one that best combines the two. My instinct is to stay off the foul mattress, away from the rotting thing that is my love. My compassion tells me she is alone and she will die; it reminds me of the many things she has done for me, of the risks she has run to consort with a member of the Imperial Palace, and it demands that I do what I can to ease her torment. If that easing is the placing of my body beside hers, to hold her for a few moments and provide some small reassurance, can I justify acting on instinct?

I cannot.

We stretch out together, and I am careful not to hurt her. In her weakened condition the weight of my ribs across her arm might break a bone or dislocate a shoulder. I hold her lightly, although I am sure it must feel as though I am squeezing the life out of her. Still, she needs my strength, my reassurance, and she does not complain.

Outside, there are the unmistakable sounds of a robot rumbling through the street; hearing it, she shudders, and tries to burrow closer. It's not the robots *I* worry about, though; it's the people.

I can tell she doesn't wish to speak, nor be read to, not even be told about my day. She wants only to lie here with me beside her; it's a small-enough gift I give.

Are you getting all this? Do you understand?

I can't stay here indefinitely, of course, but I'll stay as long as I can. As the minutes pass I feel my eyelids drooping, and even though I know I shouldn't permit it, I let myself slip into a restless doze. Sensing this, Nalynn, too, lets herself sleep.

I have visions. Caused in part perhaps by the hallucinogenic vapors of the river, tendrils of mist that for some reason have not remained with the water. Or perhaps it's just my mind, playing tricks with itself to relieve the tension. Irrelevant.

. . . a monstrously huge Lord Early stands on a dais overlooking the city, watching the suffering, smiling. His advisors and sycophants play their respective roles, fly-speck small and unimportant save to serve the great man's ego. . . .

. . . the first time I catch Nalynn's eye, at an Imperial Palace reception for the first alien vanguard. She is serving food fresh and steaming from the kitchens, and I know at once she is no mere serving wench; or if she is, there is a mind behind those sparkling brown eyes that will soon lift her higher. . . .

. . . the Asunn, haughty and confident, permitting Lord Early and his court to fawn over them. They are curt with the staff, equally so with Junior and Senior Lords, only barely treating Lord Early and his immediate family as equals. They

311

are a proud race, tall and slender, with eyes the color of arctic
ice, thin-featured. . . .

But even in my dreams/visions I know you know all this.
I come awake/aware.

Nalynn snores softly beside me, grinding her teeth in the
darkness. She has always done this latter, relieving tensions
during sleep, and it has always annoyed me. I used to touch
her cheek roughly, perhaps hold her jaws together a moment
until she stopped, but now I can find neither the cruelty nor
the selfishness to do either. Her gums will be bleeding when
she awakes.

As gently as I can I disengage from her frail grasp. From
the nightstand, where the flowers I brought yesterday are
carefully arranged in a vase, I pluck a single bloom, and place
it in her fingers. She will understand.

It must be after midnight. I close the window, from the
side so as not to be seen from across the way, should anyone
be watching. I leave the door unlocked—what benefit to lock
it, should someone truly desire entry?—move across the platform to the rungs, and make my cautious way down to the
doorway. I carry the stink of the room and Nalynn with me,
and I cannot find it in my heart to wish otherwise.

Into the night, then, to observe the dying city, to record
with my eyes the barbarities we now permit ourselves because
of the treacherous Asunn. I wish I could stay with Nalynn as I
usually do, but this is more important. That doesn't mean I
like it.

This enormous square was—and someday will, I hope,
again be—a market. Fresh fruits and vegetables, artworks and
handicrafts, artifacts brought by the Asunn, and later, by the
D'sen'ji. Musicians played alien instruments, coaxing tortured
notes from devices that sounded at once bizarre and soothing
to human ears. The finest intoxicants, the most superb
aphrodisiacs. You could buy anything here. Sell anything too.
This was free ground, and political speeches of every stripe
were allowed. Encouraged, even. Lord Early felt opposition to
his rule to be a cancerous thing, but terminal only if sup-

pressed completely. Here was the forum that transformed the malignant into the benign. I myself spoke here a handful of times, and I listened a great many more. But always, as I'm sure you can appreciate, in disguise.

I exit from the market through the most darkly shadowed street. Not surprisingly, it is also the foulest. The Lord's Own Mechanical Sanitation Corps can only collect so much refuse in a given period, and first priority is given to the infected.

Why do I suddenly want to go back to the river? I've been there once tonight, already sated the fear that leads my footsteps. I will not go again. I will not.

Another body. And a few yards ahead, another. We're dying, make no mistake about it. But as much as I hate the Asunn for what they have done to us, I hate too those of us who turn from our sick. How much longer might the infected live if given warmth and comfort and concern from their loved ones? There are reports that indicate the average life span of an infected person to be three weeks. Three *weeks!* Yet Nalynn has been sick for four months. I know it is because I haven't abandoned her. I *know* it!

A year ago I would not have believed us capable of this. Despite rumblings of discontent with Lord Early and the Imperial family, despite my general cynicism, I would not have thought this possible.

I don't know what it is that first alerts me, but something in the back of my mind sends shivers down my spine. The noises I hear are not those of the Lord's Own Mechanical Sanitation Corps come to collect the human refuse. Oh, I can see that their shapes are the same, but there is a stealth to these movements that suggests they are mind-linked to Palace controllers, not preprogrammed and sent on mindless rounds.

It is so. I turn, prepare to take flight back the way I have come, but the passage is blocked. A doorway to my left. I pound on it, whispering for help. No one answers. I have but one option: let the robots get as close as I dare, then rush them and hope the controller is too slow to react.

There are three robots approaching from one direction, two

313

from the other. My chances are better with the latter, so I take a few casual steps that way, regarding the faceplates with forced geniality. My face, of course, is still hidden by the hood, but such things as heartbeats, physical shape, and outline remain constant, and these will already have been matched by the Palace computers. If I speak, my voice pattern will instantly be cross-matched, and my identity confirmed.

"Halt," issues from the speaker grille of the nearest robot. "Identify yourself."

I do not halt. I do not identify myself. Instead I take another step, and I am as close as I'm going to get—within two yards—without the controller extruding the robot's arms to block me. If I move now, I may yet escape.

I break. Too slow. An eternity too slow. The robot nearest me extrudes its arms, and as I leap over, the second robot releases an alloy-mesh net that brings me to the ground like a bird. I writhe and wriggle and scream and demand my release, but of course that is foolish. I barely feel the injection; I barely realize I have been injected before consciousness begins to fade; I barely manage to whisper, "Nalynn," before my strength ebbs; I barely . . .

Light.
Comfort.

I am in my bedchamber, in my very own bed. There, my Asunn mindjewel on the ledge below my shaving mirror. Over there my closet, filled with the Imperial robes befitting a firstborn. Sunlight streams through stained glass windows; I had forgotten that up here the brown city is something seen only if one wishes to look, that it is entirely possible to spend a lifetime ignoring the dirt and stink and death.

There are electrodes attached to my forehead, monitoring consciousness. I rip them away, but of course it is too late. I climb out of bed, am struck by sudden nausea . . . residual effects of the injection. I make it to the door, attempt to wrench it open, but naturally it is locked. I palm the release. Nothing. Keyed to another palm.

There is one escape: through the stained glass windows. But that is certain death, for my bedchamber is on the sixth floor of the Palace, and the fall to the rocks below will surely kill me. What *then* of Nalynn?

He has wasted no time. Informed by whoever was monitoring the equipment that I am conscious, my father—no! *not* my father!—Lord Early palms open the door, and stands in the doorway, outfitted in his most ostentatious robes. He is tall, handsome with dark hair graying at the temples, unwavering blue eyes, youthful even without regeneration treatments. He stares at me, expressionless. Have you seen enough of him? No? Unfortunate. I turn away.

"In almost half a year I've had not so much as a glimpse of my successor to the throne, and at our first meeting he turns from me."

His voice resonates with power, confidence. He is not accustomed to defiance. One would think his experience with the Asunn would have taught him something of humility. Apparently not.

"Nor does he deign to speak," Lord Early continues. He enters, and the door hisses shut behind him. When last I was here the doors made no noise.

"Your presence has cost me my favorite mindjewel," Lord Early tells me. He sits in my most comfortable chair, and sunlight glitters on his robes, his rubies. "I would think that alone entitles me to some civility, even if blood does not."

I can't help myself. "Civility!" I shriek. "Toward a murderer?"

He flinches, pained by my accusation. "I have killed no one."

"Directly, perhaps not. But you played games with the Asunn, with the D'sen'ji after them, and brought death to the realm."

"Death was making the journey in any event," he says, uncharacteristically philosophical. "At worst, I perhaps built a

315

bridge over a raging, but fordable, current. I played no games."

Is it possible he does not recognize his hand in this? No, it can't be. And yet, he is puzzled by my meaning.

"You played *all* the games," I tell him ruthlessly. "The Asunn came bearing gifts, and you accepted those gifts. You listened to their tales of war between Asunn and D'sen'ji, pledged them land for support bases in return for certain favors, and sent them on their way. Then the D'sen'ji came bearing more gifts, and you accepted those too, pledged them the same pledges you gave the Asunn. And you have the gall —or the stupidity—to be surprised when the Asunn retaliate with weapons and sicknesses? By the Dead Christ, surely you didn't believe the Asunn would give us the wonder of mindjewels, the ecstasy of 'disiacs, the security of their protection, then be content with treachery!"

"I thought . . ." He falters, sighs. "I thought it would be centuries until they returned. The emissaries told me they had been in deep sleep a thousand lifetimes. I thought they must return home first."

"It never occurred to you their colonization ships might number hundreds, that those hundreds *might* include warships?"

"No."

It's a simple denial, more galling for its simplicity. But it's also a long time past now, and there are more important things to worry about than dead lands and foolish promises.

"I grant you a mistake—stupid, perhaps, and deceitful, but legitimate in its way. I cannot grant you the right to let fear continue, when a single announcement that the infections are not contagious would calm everyone, and open the city to hope again."

"Not contagious?"

"Don't pretend you don't know." I can see by his involuntary facial reaction that I have guessed correctly. Even as his city dies he is scheming, hoping for the maximum benefit when he announces the manufacture of vaccines.

"How could you know they're not contagious?" His eyes narrow. He knows. "That slut from the kitchens. She's infected." He can't hide his satisfaction at this deduction, although to his credit he tries. And now I recognize the severity of my error. There will be no research for cures. He has hated Nalynn since the day he discovered I intended to court her, and now, now he can eliminate all that is precious to me. He has only to wait. He sees my understanding, and it revitalizes him.

"There are no vaccines, Auarja. Certainly no cure for those infected."

He is lying about the vaccines. He knows I know.

"You traded your rightful throne for a piece of common fluff to warm your bed. The exchange will prove unprofitable. I am sorry, but your consort will die. Without you."

He wasn't always like this. You must understand that. Although he ruled with absolute authority, and believed it his right, he took no pleasure in the nastier side of rule. He was a good man. Until the Asunn came. Blinded him with dreams. Rearranged his priorities. Introduced him to greed. Bedded him with promises.

"I suggest you resign yourself to facts, Auarja. As I recall, your mindjewel was among the most powerful of those we received. Use it. Calm yourself. Dream of a life free from these foolish whims."

My glance goes unwillingly to the ledge where the mindjewel is. They are wondrous things, mindjewels. A man has only to hold one, to daydream, and he has in his mind the feeling that those things wished for are so. You wish to be a king? Grasp the mindjewel and know the sensation of absolute power over life and death. There is a holo princess you would bed? The mindjewel can burn your loins with the heat of her. And afterward, you remember it as real, you *know* you were king, you *know* you penetrated beauty. It doesn't matter if fact is at odds with fantasy. For a while.

But again, you know all that.

I must have known I'd be back here. I must have known.

I walk across to the mirror, and see Lord Early's reflection watching me. Our reflected gazes meet. He nods. I reach toward the mindjewel, my body blocking my father's view. When I turn, I hold not the alien artifact, but one of their very own laser pistols. I taped it beneath the ledge a week before I departed the Imperial Palace. As I say, I must have known.

My father's expression goes from surprise to acceptance to amusement in the space of two heartbeats. "You won't kill your own father," he says. "Not with that."

He is wrong. He is very wrong. "I would kill a thousand of you to be with one Nalynn. And *especially* with this." But not under these circumstances. "But even if you're right, I *will* cripple you." I aim the weapon's snout at his knees. "Security could certainly break in, but the time it would take them would be an eternity for you. And I could make it even longer. You'd never be the same, even with regeneration."

What passes through his eyes shows he is convinced. His lips harden into a thin line, and I realize I have gone beyond any hope of redemption. Irrelevant, totally irrelevant.

"Very well," he says. "You are guaranteed safe passage from the Imperial Palace."

"Not enough. I want vaccine for myself, and treatments for Nalynn." I wave the laser in what I hope is a threatening gesture.

He shakes his head. "The vaccine you may have. As for the other, there *is* . . . *no* . . . *cure*. The sickness is an alien thing, Auarja, and we have made no progress in—"

"The vaccine, then." I am convinced there is no cure. I have always been able to tell when Lord Early is lying. I was supposed to learn to do it convincingly myself. Apparently it's one of the prerequisites for leadership. I never mastered it.

"Access," Lord Early says, "Medical Stores," and the communicator screen over my bureau flares from black to gray. In a few seconds some lackey has responded to his Lord's summons, and peers intently at his own screen. When he sees what is happening in my room, he is visibly worried.

"Yes, Lord Early."

"Deliver two vials of Asunn plague vaccine to my son's room at once. Also two syringes. Terminate."

The screen fades to black before the servant can acknowledge his lord's command.

"One injection may not be enough," Lord Early tells me, "and there've been complications with syringes used more than once, even by the same person, even when cleaned."

We remain silent until there is a soft buzzing at the entry panel. Lord Early palms open the door, and a member of the Lord's Own Guards stands there, a purple velvet cloth wrapped around his burden. All the while I keep the laser trained on Lord Early's knees.

"Set it in the doorway," I tell the Guardsman. He does, but only when Lord Early nods. "Go." Lord Early nods again, and the Guardsman disappears. I collect the velvet-wrapped package, slip it into a pocket of my cloak, then don the cloak. Lord Early's eyes are expressionless all this time. I prefer it that way. I set the laser on Maximum, wide-angle, hair-trigger. Lord Early turns to lead me out, and I press the snout into his spine.

"I *will* kill you if I have to," I whisper, and because I never mastered lying, he knows I speak the truth. He leads. I follow. Down the tapestried corridor, to the grav shaft. Lord Early accesses the communicator to the Guardroom, orders them not to interfere. We reach the main floor, exit to the nearly blinding glory of sunlight through crystal-lead domes, parqueted floors, alien ion-sculptures, and a mass of scowling Guardsmen who stand like statues, watching their Lord and Master herded through the Palace like a doomed steer.

Do you suspect treachery?

Nor do I.

I will take him outside, prod him toward the lower levels, and when I am certain there is no pursuit, I'll slip into an alleyway and be off. He has no chance of finding me; I've gone through the City of Perpetual Light ten thousand times

319

in the past four months, and Lord Early probably hasn't ventured outside his Palace since long before that.

(What I should do is parade him through the streets until he drops. Leave him in the filthiest part of the city, or bind him in the market square. But we are talking instinct and compassion once again, and I am cursed to favor the latter. I will simply slip away, let him walk awhile thinking I am behind him, then make his way back to the Palace once he discovers I am gone.)

There are five rafts in view, each crowded, each making its one-way journey into oblivion. The Lord's Own Guards are more numerous today, walking along with the rafts, alert to any attempt by the diseased to return. As if a single one of those doomed bastards could summon half the strength necessary.

I'll stay up here on the balustraded walkway, out of sight of the Guards, and watch for as long as I can stomach it. A while yet, I'm afraid. You can stand it. You aren't losing Nalynn; you don't need the strength.

Sometimes the darkness seems to take forever to settle. I think of Nalynn and I worry, I don't think of Nalynn and I worry. I wonder if—

What's *that? Nalynn!* I can feel her! We seemed always to have some sort of psychic bond, even across distances, so that when one of us hurt, the other knew. I know. She's dying.

Through the streets. Buildings a blur. Wisps of fog beginning to appear as they do every dusk. Nalynn!

How far? *You* keep track. I can only move as fast as I can, I have no time for anything else. Around this corner, down that alleyway onto the next street, across it and into the next alleyway. Thank the Dead Christ I know the streets of this city as well as I do. I don't even see the buildings.

This is the alleyway. Into it. The doorway. Can't wait to be sure it's safe. Up the rungs, no capuchin could do better, across the platform, no time to knock, wrench open the door.

320

She's writhing, shrieking in agony. Her cheeks are burning. And yes, she stinks. What did she think when I didn't come back? No, guilt changes nothing. Be thankful instead that I *did* get here before . . . before . . .

"Auarja . . ." But her voice is weak, and she can barely speak my name. "Hurts. . . ." She inhales, gathering strength to continue. "P—please don't . . . take me . . . to . . . the river."

I hold her, much more tightly than I should. Forgive me, Nalynn, for being so weak inside. She groans, but I hold her still. She lifts a hand to caress my cheek, and it is a coarse sensation, like a dead twig on parchment. "Not . . . the river."

The vaccines! In an instant I have released Nalynn, am fumbling through my cloak for the precious vials and syringes. "I'm still here, my love. Hold on. I have—" But I cannot tell her I may have a cure. It is too late for hope, too cruel to suggest it.

My hands tremble as I insert the needle into the first vial; withdraw the plunger until the chamber is full; depress it slightly to clear any air bubbles. Nalynn shivers as if freezing. I take her arm, turn it over; no time to cut her circulation and pump her arm. In the dimness I locate a vein, a thin pale line inside her elbow. I hold her arm still, babbling all the while, not even aware of my words.

There. It is done.

She slips almost at once into silence, the tension gone. Before my eyes she seems to shrivel, assumes a fetal position, and the suddenness of it stuns me. Only momentarily.

The treacherous bastards! What secret code did Lord Early speak while requesting the vials? For this cannot be a vaccine. It is instead a drug that produces unconsciousness, something Lord Early must have hoped I would inject soon after I left the Imperial Palace. He probably has mind-linked robots out searching for my slumbering body this very moment!

Her breathing is ragged, slow. But at least there is no pain. I watch her chest rise, fall, rise, fall, ri. . . . No! *No!*

Yes. She's gone. Gone, and I didn't even have a chance to say good-bye, tell her one more time I loved her.

It is *this* you wanted all along. I hate you.

It is a useless action, but I crunch the second vial underfoot, snap the other syringe into pieces. Shards of glass are imbedded in my thumb and forefinger; I don't feel a thing. Life stretches out like a vast, empty thing that can never be filled.

This, too, you wanted.

Now? I'll bury her. The river? *No!* I said I'd *bury* her. Not the river. Never the river. Not for you, not for the extra emotional impact, not for an iota of it! *No.* You have enough, you don't need any more. In fact, I insist that it end here. I will be alone with my grief, alone when I bury her.

No! Alone! I swear I'll slit my own throat if you insist on any more.

Good. You agree to go. I sense your animosity, but believe me: I don't care. I hate you; I hate your D'sen'ji masters. I hate the Asunn. Go back to your damned war and your filthy destruction. *Go!*

Very well.

I lie on the bed, careful not to touch Nalynn. I relax as well as I am able, and slowly, so very slowly, I feel the withdrawal of the alien thing that has attached itself to my brain. Tendrils of mist filter through my nostrils, my mouth, coalesce in the air above. Almost, I can see an image there, but it is something strange, repulsive, more so now that I know it has absorbed my experiences of the past two days.

It attempts to communicate with me, mind to mind, but I block it out. Go! I did what you wanted. I gave you the tour of our dying city, I let you record the death of my beloved. It was all I agreed to. Go. Take my memories and my pain, take it all to your masters so they can organize their propaganda campaign. It doesn't matter to me that support for the war effort is faltering, nor does it matter if the Asunn destroy you. I hope they do. And you them. Go.

It does. It drifts through the darkness, softly phosphorescent, out the doorway and back the way we came. An eyeblink in the tide of existence. When it is gone I turn to Nalynn, drape an arm across her unmoving shoulder, and make no effort to hold back the tears. We lie there in the hot, soft quiet, one empty, miserable life between us. But we will cheat the river. We will cheat the river.

There's plenty of snap, crackle, and pop in this fast-moving postapocalyptic fantasia, the work of a Maryland lawyer who's at the very beginning of what we suspect will be an auspicious writing career. His first story appeared in 1988 in Aboriginal Science Fiction; he has since sold a second to Interzone and this is his third. He reports he has also been a prize winner in the L. Ron Hubbard amateur writers' contest, but that won't happen again: he's lost his amateur status for good, by now.

I

THE BOOK OF ST. FARRIN

JAMIL
NASIR

I woke up on the concrete floor of a subbasement utility tunnel with the first syllables of the scum warning in my ears, and before I was awake, I was running. I had worn armor once, chased scums through the dark dirty places where they lived: I knew the surrender period after the bullhorn warning; I knew the dead silence when the hunt began; I knew that the ninth subbasement of the Utopia Luxury Apartment Complex was a place where you wouldn't risk taking scums alive.

I had slept in the utility tunnel because it opened on two unused stairwells. I dived down the urine-smelling blackness of the first—but too late. As I ran, a blinding pulse of violet light seared the concrete next to me.

I jumped the handrail, hit the flight below with my shoulder, jumped another rail, another. Bright light blossomed above me in the stairwell. I could hear the faint rush of a Black Angel's wings.

And then there were no more stairs, just a gray concrete wall at the extreme depth of the building with a foot-wide crack where the foundation of the Utopia Luxury Apartments had shifted. Concrete teeth tore at me as I rammed myself into it. Inside it widened. I hugged the ground as violet light flamed above me, breathed dust the Angel's hands made smashing the wall open. It was no good to him just to kill me—he had to take back one of my thumbs to get his bounty money.

I wormed blindly into the crack. Suddenly there was empty space under me and I pitched into blackness, tumbling in an avalanche of stones and dust. When I stopped I was half-buried in rubble.

I dragged myself up. The Angel's light moved somewhere far above me, showing a steep slope that a few pebbles rattled down. I stumbled down it, half sliding. At the bottom, a black tunnel opened. I plunged into it, turning on my own small light. Broken rock crunched under my feet. Cement dust stung my throat. I passed what might once have been a window, choked with concrete now, and facing downward.

After a while, cracked paving stones showed under the rubble of the floor. The ceiling receded into darkness. I turned a sharp corner, and my light showed windows, doorways, columns.

II

Everyone knew the City was built over an older city that had been destroyed in the Fire. The Ur, they called it, but no one ever went there—its radioactive ruin was hidden under a thick blanket of entombment concrete. I guessed that was the crumbling ceiling that arched out of reach of my light, held by concrete pillars like huge stalagmites. The massive buildings that stood partly crushed under it were made of brown stone, worn and pocked with age, with arched windows and doors. There were the remains of columns and fountains, carvings worn smooth in the stone. Pitch dark surrounded the beam of my light as I wandered, an aimless sightseer, chasing startled shadows. Silence lay everywhere like thick layers of dust.

326

My light was fading. I turned it off to save the battery, sat against a stone column. The darkness was dead, dry, still—but after a while I saw a flickering light, almost faint enough to be imaginary. I had never heard of Angels tracking scums through the Ur, but I moved silently behind the column, holding my breath.

Silence hissed in my ears. The light didn't get any closer. I crept along cracked paving stones toward it, until I could see that it came from a place in the middle of the street, like a window set in the ground. It flickered, changing colors, making the dead stone of the buildings seem to move, summoning ghostly faces to their windows.

It was a video screen, half buried in hard dirt, flashing silent static. I dug it out with my fingernails. It didn't come easily—there was nothing to show it hadn't been there for the hundreds of years since the Fire. Its casing was corroded metal thirty centimeters square by five thick, of strange design. There were strange buttons below the screen, with strange markings. I touched one of them.

The screen stopped flashing and a picture appeared. It was a picture of the building facing me on that street, a massive ruin with huge doors of rusted metal, and hollow, high windows. In the picture the building was dark, but not pitch-dark —maybe moonlight-behind-clouds dark—the metal doors were polished silver, the walls smooth and uncracked. The windows were dark but there was an air of life about the place, as if everybody was sleeping or had just gone away. Mist floated in the street. For a long time the picture stayed like that, and I watched it, wondering what it meant.

Then one of the polished metal doors swung open and somebody came out.

I dropped the screen, shone my light at the building. It was lifeless, doors rusted shut, windows blank, walls leaning.

I picked up the screen. The figure was coming toward me.

It was some ancient video recording, I told myself, maybe an archaeological find. Maybe I could sell it in the City. The thought helped me stand my ground.

The figure on the screen came close and looked into my eyes.

It was a beautiful dark-haired girl.

I knew she wasn't real, but I stared. Her eyes were large and luminous, somehow sad. She wore a long black gown. She put the palms of her hands together and raised them to her lips, as if in greeting.

"Toori protect me," I muttered, and passed my hand through the space in front of me where the girl would be if there was a girl. There was only dry, still air.

She smiled sadly and passed her hand through the air the same way I had.

"Toori protect me," I said. This had to be worth money in the City. Maybe enough to buy me a job authorization, a room in the apartment blocks, a wife. . . .

"Who are you?" I asked her. "An interactive simulation? Can you hear me?"

She touched her lips with two fingers and shook her head, as if telling me she didn't understand.

"Out," I said, gesturing furiously upward. "How do you get out?"

She shook her head.

"I live up there," I said, pounding myself on the chest. "Want to get out."

She studied me closely, then walked away from the screen.

"Wait! Come back!" I shouted in the dead air, banging on the screen. In a while she did, waving me to follow her.

Suddenly I got the idea. I walked along the street in the same direction she was going. On the screen, the street moved, and I was following her.

She walked quickly, glancing back now and then. On the screen, the buildings we passed were stately, well tended. Where I was, they were crumbling or tumbled into shattered heaps, plunged in blackness except where my light shone. On the screen, there were no people except the woman. Where I was, there was no one but me.

328   After a few hundred meters she stopped and pointed at a low doorway. I tilted the screen up to look at a tower, rising toward a dark sky heavy with clouds. In the beam of my light, the tower had a few stones missing, but was solid as far up as I

could see. The door was metal and took all my strength to open, with a loud squawking of hinges. A stone stairway spiraled into darkness.

I climbed a long way. At the top, my light showed rough foundation concrete—but there was a crack between concrete and stone. I slipped the ancient TV-thing into my jumpsuit, hoisted myself up, and after some hard scrambling came out in a cave that water had hollowed under a City street drain. I curled up in a dry corner and slept.

III

In dreams I carried the ancient TV-thing through the City, running from thieves, holding it high above the grasping hands of beggars, hiding from the police bribe-takers, resisting the electronically enhanced blandishments of prostitutes, running to the higher levels of the City, where the rich corporations lived—

I woke pawing blindly for it.

The cave was dark. Dim red light came through the drain grating from curfew warning holos that floated above the streets outside. I drank from a trickle of drain water and lay back down. Darkness and silence drove thoughts through my head; about how I had lost my job as a police bounty hunter to a younger, more aggressive recruit, become a scum—Socially Controlled Unproductive Member—how I had escaped from the indentured labor factory that made food for a world still poisoned and blackened, hidden in basements and condemned buildings, running now myself from the hunters. After a while I didn't want to think anymore. I propped the TV-thing on my chest and pushed the strange buttons until the screen glowed, lighting the cave walls dim gray.

I wondered if it would pick up a City channel, but it showed the underground building with the metal doors exactly as before—night-dark, misty, deserted. One of the doors swung open. The beautiful girl came out, came toward the

screen. Her eyes were searching and grave. Looking into them
I fell asleep again.

Slowly the night wore away.

But not before, groping painfully in dreams and looking
into her eyes on waking, I had recognized her.

I knew who she was. And I knew the TV-thing was going
to make me rich.

When day came, I pushed the drain grating up and crawled
out. The dim, crowded street smelled like smoke, garbage, and
sweat. Vendors called their wares from pushcarts. Between the
tops of the hundred-story buildings floated advertising holos,
sweet dreams you could buy if you had enough money. At the
corner two police Angels stood, black helmets swiveling.

A few blocks away I waited in line for a phone booth, and
when the plastic doors hummed shut behind me, took the
TV-thing from my jumpsuit and turned it on. I punched the
City's only free phone number. A simulated face appeared:
"Thank you for dialing the RAD Cola Corporation Neurolog-
ical Volunteers Line. We at RAD Cola—"

"Cut that." I held up the screen. By now the beautiful girl
was gazing out of it. "Take a look at this—have somebody
important look at it. I'll be back in touch. My name is Farrin."

I broke the connection, slipped the screen back into my
suit, left the booth. Cold, acrid rain was starting to fall. A few
blocks away, a warm, perfumed breeze caressed my face.

High between the buildings a RAD Cola ad-holo was forming, familiar logo shimmering. The faithful on the street were
kneeling. I leaned against a wall and let the psionic images
flow through me. A wide field appeared, filled with crystal
sunlight that could only have existed before the Fire. Tall
grass waved in a breeze. Birds sang and insects hummed.
Across the field, through a patch of tiny flowers, a figure ran,
long dress fluttering, dark eyes laughing, carrying two cans of
RAD Cola. The fragrance and electricity of her body en-
folded me as she handed me one of the icy cans and we drank,

the bubbly brown liquid impossibly tempting—even more, in that second, than the curve of her shoulders, her short, lustrous hair, her breasts pressing at the thin material of the dress, her eyes. Then it was over. The scene receded high into the air, collapsed into the red-and-white logo. People moaned, stumbled to their feet. RAD Cola was the richest corporation in the City—because of the psi advertising technology only it had, and because of the Holy Beloved, Toori Sith, the model who had starred in the ads for hundreds of years.

And whose face gazed from the screen of the ancient TV-thing I had found in the Ur.

IV

Across the street, people were crowding eagerly through the massive doors of a twenty-story concrete dome. Above the doors, red neon letters said CHURCH OF BEAUTY. In the entrance, a prostitute caressed me with implanted electrodes that sent shudders through my body.

Services were starting, the acres of concrete crowded with people facing a two-story dais. The Burning was in progress. Half a dozen figures hung above the dais, and a white-surpliced priest, brightly haloed with light from his electrochemical enhancers, was setting fire to them. The figures were ultraflammable plastic, and burst into flames that quickly consumed them. The first was a man nailed to a T-shaped piece of wood. Next a man in an orange robe, with a faint, inward smile. Then a bearded man with a sad, compassionate face. Then another robed man with only flames where his head and hands should be. As each of the figures was engulfed, the priest's voice boomed through the dome: "Death has overtaken you."

And ten thousand voices murmured the response: "Death has overtaken all."

Near me, a group of factory workers wore heavy plastic clothes and helmets covered with gray dust. An old man, probably almost fifty, leaned on a cane, face twitching with

331

some sickness. Two ragged, empty-faced children, holding hands. A man sleeping under a heap of rags on the floor. A half-naked girl with bruises on her face and arms. Faces gaunt and haunted, bodies thin.

The Burning over, the priest turned to the people with hands raised, enhancement auras crackling.

"Death has overtaken the world," he intoned.

"There is nothing left," the murmur welled up.

"The Fire has come."

"There is nothing left."

"Beauty has died."

A ritual sigh from ten thousand throats.

The priest effortlessly held a huge book open before him.

"I read from the Book of Saint Debbie, Chapter One.

" 'After the Great Fire the world was burned, and into it was born a baby, called Debbie. All around was the purple-sickness, and the buildings lay upon each other like slain creatures, but one man was wealthy: Alan, the father of Debbie. His Corporation had as much knowledge and riches as were then to be had.

" 'Alan said: "I will not let my daughter see this world, for such a world is not fit to be born into." So saying, he built a palace around her, filled with all the things that were Before, spending upon it as much as would sustain a million men. There were spacious halls and soft beds, greenhouses holographed like fields and woods. No people were let in except they were fed and washed, and skillful at telling beautiful stories of outside. Debbie ate only fresh milk and fruit and baked bread, bought for fortunes. She played in fields and forests, and had pet dogs, and at night lay in her bed watching the moon rise over the woods. Her father guarded her well; twenty thousand men labored to keep Debbie.

" 'Debbie grew to six years old knowing nothing of the Fire.

" 'So was Debbie saved.

" 'But outside, the Death Mother stalked the earth, embracing all that lived, and when she heard of Debbie she was jealous with wrath. So she called to Debbie in her dreams.

" 'In her dreams, all around were broken buildings, and people thin and gray, all the trees burned to ashes, the rivers black, and the sky dark. Her father and the others told her not to heed such foolish dreams, but one night she woke and crept to a door her father had told her never to open. She opened it, and there were all the things she had dreamed, and the Death Mother stalking over the earth. When she saw Debbie, she said: "Come here, pretty child." But Debbie ran from her through the broken buildings, and hid.

" 'The Death Mother seeks her still, walking over the earth, and so will she walk until she finds her. Only then, at the time of the End, will the world be healed.' "

There was rapt silence, and then the priest started to chant, his enhanced voice rich and melodious. The people answered in the same music, full of sorrow and ecstasy. As the chanting rose, the Images appeared above us: gigantic holographs of the earth ravaged and blackened, forests in cinders, cities turned to dust, rivers running with debris, the sky black and roiling, people blank-eyed, ragged, and skeletal, bodies in mass graves, the vacant upturned faces of starving children, then sprouting from all this the Fire itself, mushrooming sky-tall flame boiling into poison smoke. And finally, as the chanting reached its height, emerging from the flames along fashion-show catwalks or through the idealized landscapes of ad-holos, the Holy Ones themselves, sleek, stylish, and beautiful, and greatest of all, crew-cut and wearing a revealing leather dress, dark eyes smiling while the full lips sipped a can of RAD Cola, was Toori Sith.

The flames and smoke subsided around Her. The people raised their hands to Her, suddenly silent. Then the Image faded, and they began silently crowding toward the doors. The girl with the bruises was crying uncontrollably.

On the street, half a dozen big men in gray waterproofs were watching the people pour out of the church. As I passed, two started pushing through the crowd.

I tried to run. I heard the explosion, felt the pain. I cradled the TV-thing inside my jumpsuit as I fell. People's legs blurred around me, and then I could see only dirty water running over the concrete where I lay, and then even that blurred and went away.

V

I woke in a cubicle of glaring white, strapped to a table. Above me, a dozen robot arms held surgical instruments. My reflection in a blank video screen was unfamiliar: my ragged beard and hair had been shaved, my skin scrubbed clean.

The screen lit up, showing three men. Two were fleshy angels from before the Fire, tall and strong; one was old enough to have white hair, but his skin was pinkish, his eyes clear blue, teeth even and white. The third man looked more like a City dweller—small and thin, with gray skin and muddy eyes—but wearing an impossibly expensive suit.

The white-haired man turned on a speaker above my head. He smiled kindly.

"Welcome to the RAD Cola Corporation Central Compound, Mr. Farrin," he said. "I apologize for any inconvenience. I regret also that we can't talk face to face. We have the cleanest closed loop on the planet here, and we have to be very careful about outside contacts to maintain it.

"We want to talk to you about the simulation device our Field Operations people found on you this afternoon. We'd like to know who made it, and who hired you to approach us with it."

The three of them waited.

My voice cracked as I said: "I'll sell it to you."

"We're confident you'll sell it to us, Mr. Farrin," said the white-haired man. "We're not nearly as confident that our purchase will not be followed by further blackmail demands, either by your organization, using similar devices, or by others. I think you'll understand we can't allow that to happen."

"No one hired me," I said. "I found it."

The white-haired man was replaced on the screen by a man with a shaved head lying in a cubicle like mine. Robot arms approached him. A surgical saw cut into his head with a high-pitched whine. I shut my eyes.

"No blackmail," I rasped. "I found it in the Ur—"

"Toori Sith is unfortunately already part of the so-called Church of Beauty's liturgy," said the white-haired man. "An ancient-looking video screen showing her in the Ur could drive half the City wild in the belief that she is Debbie, the child who must die before the world can be healed."

I opened my eyes. The three men were back, watching me calmly.

"Whoever made the device knows that an uproar over Toori Sith could cost RAD Cola revenue. We can't allow that. So, again, Mr. Farrin: who hired you to sell us the device?"

"I found it. In the Ur. She showed me the way out—"

Liquid started to move through a transparent tube attached to my arm. Suddenly I was dizzy.

"Good night, Mr. Farrin," said the white-haired man.

I didn't wake up again until someone pulled the tube out of my arm. I felt sick for a minute. Then my eyes focused.

A Black Angel stood over me, filling the cubicle.

I screamed. The Angel's huge hands broke the straps holding me like rubber bands. Then it pulled off its helmet.

There was no one inside.

Someone had programmed it to come in and break me loose. And now a recorded message was coming from its hollow neck: "The Holy One has learned that you used to operate a suit like this. The Holy One sends this as a gift and bids you attend her on the 392nd floor. Go secretly and quickly. I am one willing to risk his life in the service of the Holy One."

I sat on the table and stared at the hollow Angel. When I was done staring I began to disassemble it. I worked as fast as I could.

Forty-five minutes later the suit and I were spliced as well as I could manage alone. It helped that my head was shaved, baring the electrode hookups and injector nozzles the Department had planted in my skull years ago. I hoped that not too many were rusted out. I hit a keypad inside the wrist: the suit hummed to life like a small nuclear plant. A soundlike buzz in an unobtrusive temporal synapse told me the batteries were fully charged. I checked through other sensory and parasensory inputs. There was static in some of the circuits—probably bad sockets on my side—but I could work with it.

Medium-range sensors swam up out of the babble of suit inputs. The building rippled away in all directions as a parasensory multi-D diagram. I was in a cell block on the 101st floor. The cells around me were empty. Three waking and two sleeping males (three quickly pulsing and two slowly pulsing green/hard/hot ciphers) were in a room down a hall, collocated with military hardware. An elevator shaft near them rose 294 more floors.

I lasered a circuit in my cubicle door, jumped down the hall, and nerve-gassed the guards before they could move.

No alarms were signaling anywhere that I could see/hear/smell.

The elevator car was on the 59th floor. I pried open the elevator doors, grabbed one of the metal guides in the shaft, and activated my thruster. I went up the shaft fast.

Halfway to 392, emergency logic was firing all around me. I didn't try to read it, went faster. Heavy grates were closing above, sealing off 392. I shot through in time, yanked open the elevator doors, and stepped out.

Into incinerating, white-hot pain.

Then it was gone; I was lying on a floor, still alive. An overload like that would take a military-grade microwave scrambler. Which apparently RAD Cola had. But somebody had turned it off.

I got up, got a visual. The wall opposite the elevator was three-meter-thick mirrored steel, coated ten centimeters deep with laser-refracting plastic. As I watched, it seamed and split apart. Security logic boiled and fumed nearby, suggesting a manual override. As I went through the opening in the wall a simulated polite voice told my audial sensors: "You are cleared for entry. Please be aware that the slightest activation of weapons circuits will precipitate an immediate preemptive strike by automated systems."

The wall clicked shut behind me. I was in a big space filled with unfamiliar inputs. A gemlike blue female cipher was static sixty meters away. I ate the distance with enhanced strides, stood in front of it.

I got a visual.

It was deep blue dusk. A few stars twinkled in the sky; I knew they were stars because I had seen pictures. There were plants too; not in environment tanks like at the Public Museum, but growing right out of the ground, crowding each other, some taller than a man. The Holy Beloved Toori Sith stood holding the thorny stem of a deep red flower, her eyes vague and dreamy. Wires were plugged into her head.

"Beautiful rose," she murmured. "She bloomed last night, in the dark. I smelled her while I was sleeping . . ." Her voice was soft as the breeze that stirred the plants.

"I'm here," I said. "But I only have about three minutes before I'll be gone again." My sensors picked up world-class firepower massing outside the metal walls of the garden.

The Angel's harsh voice seemed to hurt her, and she shivered, looked up at its helmet. "Take me to the place with the silver doors."

I ogled her with my locals.

"The place with the silver doors," she said again. "On the TV screen."

"I can't take you there. That place is poisoned, radioactive."

She looked back at the rose. "You prayed to me when you were in trouble . . ."

"Yes."

". . . did I help you?" She looked up again, her eyes more beautiful than anything in the world.

"Yes."

337

A massive disturbance in the garden's security circuitry activated sonic alarms.

"Help me," she whispered.

"I can't."

She closed her eyes and rubbed the flower against her face so that a thorn cut a deep gash at the corner of her mouth.

"Please," she whispered.

I hesitated, but then the Angel gently unplugged the leads in her head, picked her up effortlessly.

"Which way?" I transmitted.

She pointed.

I carried her to a wall. She put her hand on it, and three meters of metal slid aside. Beyond was a hall with windows, and beyond the windows, nothing—open air, night.

I shattered a pane of shatterproof glass. War machines were screaming down the hall, bellowing all-frequency warnings. I jumped out the window.

We fell fifty stories.

I keyed my wrist pad and the Angel's parawing came out. We sliced through night above lights, smoke, and giant holos. The City was an illuminated map under me. I wheeled around to head for the Utopia Luxury Apartment Complex tenement two sectors away, felt/watched it come closer on my display, one of its eight spokes collapsed into rubble.

Soon we were sailing between buildings. I brought the Angel down, then pulled the suit off as fast as I could, hiding the pieces under garbage that was piled up all around. The glowing, abstract spaces of the Angel collapsed into a smelly, murky alley that Toori Sith's short silver holo-dress faintly illuminated.

I took her hand and we ran, through empty streets under towering red curfew holos. Rain fell on a cold wind. At the edge of the Utopia's wrecked wing we crawled into a crack between tumbled slabs of concrete.

Toori Sith was shivering. She sat huddled against the concrete, hugging her beautiful legs against her chest. I watched her for a while.

Finally, I said: "Let me call them. Tell them where you are. They'll take you back."

She shook her head, rested it on her knees. A little blood-stained water ran down her chin.

I put my arms around her. She leaned against me, shivering. I felt the way you would expect to feel holding a goddess.

Then all that was gone.

I was standing on what, in antiquity, had been called a beach. It was wide and blinding white, ran up to thick green vegetation, down into water. The water stretched to the horizon, shades of transparent blue. A wave washed around my feet. The sun was hot, and graceful things with sweet, mewling voices wheeled high in the air.

It was deserted, except for Toori Sith. She wore a pair of shorts, her body slender, young, and brown, the breeze ruffling her short hair. She took my hand and we walked together.

"Is this an advertisement?" I asked after a while.

"This is my talent," she said. "I can bring people to these places."

"Not RAD Cola. You."

"The Corporation only records and amplifies. I bring."

"You have psi powers, then. You're a mutant."

She didn't say anything.

"Who are you really?"

"I don't know."

I waited for her to explain that.

"Eight days ago I had an anti-aging treatment. I don't remember much before that—disconnected images, dreams. The treatments do something to your brain."

She took my hands and put my fingers on the metal sockets under her hair. She lifted her arms, and there were sockets in her armpits. There were sockets in the soles of her feet.

"I heard about the video screen you brought from my informants in the Corporation, made them show it to me. When I turned it on, a girl came out of a building. She was exactly like me, except that she didn't have these." She showed tiny sockets in the fold of skin between thumb and forefinger. "She smiled at me and put her hands together, then went back into the building and closed the door. The screen went off, and they couldn't get it to go back on."

She knelt, drawing patterns in the sand until a wave washed them away, then drawing more patterns.

"I think I remember standing in front of that building a long, long time ago, dressed the way she was dressed. A long time ago, before RAD Cola and the anti-aging and the advertising . . ."

She was silent, gazing at the water.

"I have to see it," she said finally.

"But the City," I said, "is full of poison, radiation. Especially the Ur. Look at me." I held out gray, wrinkled hands that looked dead in the bright sunlight. Then, for a second, we were back in the City, huddled together in the concrete crevice, poison rain pouring down on a cold wind. When the beach returned, I went on: "It'll kill you, like the rest of us."

She didn't answer. She stood up and stretched, waded out and slipped into the waves. For a while I seemed to hear the sighing breath of the ocean, to see Toori Sith floating in its green depths, asleep. Then I was back in the City, she sleeping quietly against my chest.

I woke her a few hours later. The rain had stopped, but the red holos still hung angrily a hundred meters above the streets. She didn't seem to remember me, or where she was, but she wasn't scared.

"We better move now," I told her. "Dead time."

She nodded, wiping sleep from her eyes. I helped her up and we crept through rubble into the sagging hulk of the Utopia Luxury Apartments' wrecked wing, along a dark, mildewed hallway with peeling walls and holes in the ceiling that night sky showed through.

The bolt on a metal door was broken; it creaked open to show descending stairs. I used a small auxiliary light I had taken from the Angel. We went down nine levels, along a concrete passage dripping with water, then down a utility tunnel where dull yellow illumination tiles gave light. Then down another stairwell, until we were facing the crack that led to the Ur, torn wide open now by the Angel's smashing hands. There was a way to climb down if you were careful. We stumbled down the slope at the bottom, raising dust like ghosts around us, and faced the crumbling mouth of the Ur tunnel.

"Down there," I said.

She followed me, our feet crunching on shattered rock, our breath echoing like whispered voices, until the passage opened onto the ancient street. I couldn't remember which way to go, so we wandered, holding hands, shining the light at the buildings, she silent and intent.

Then, suddenly, we were there, the massive, leaning building with the metal doors looming before us.

"Here," I murmured, pointing at a square indentation in the hard dirt of the street.

But she wasn't listening. She was staring at the doors.

One of them was opening. It swung heavily, silently, just as on the TV-thing; but on the TV-thing the doors shone like silver—here they were dull gray, eaten by green oxides.

Out of the blackness beyond the door hobbled a hunched figure in ragged robes, a hood hiding its face. A pair of trembling, skeletal hands reached up to put the hood back.

It was an old, old woman, so old she had no hair, no eyes, so old that her blind stone-gray face was stretched over the skull like dry paper, pocked with the purple blotches of radiation sickness. A smell came from her like the smell of refrigerated dead things.

Toori Sith's hand was trembling. I couldn't move.

The ancient woman slowly reached out her hand.

Toori Sith's hand unlocked itself from mine. My feet were planted to the ground. I couldn't move even to look at her. I hissed: "Run!"

Then my mouth was stopped.

341

Toori Sith walked forward. She climbed the three small steps to the door, raised her slender white hand, and took the ancient woman's claw.

"Mother," she breathed, her voice soft and sweet in that dead place.

The ancient woman backed up, drawing her into darkness. The door swung slowly and heavily closed, shutting finally with a dull clang.

I stood for a long time, unable to move.

Hours later, when I stumbled from the Utopia Luxury Apartments' wrecked wing, squinting in the gray daylight, a flash of color caught my eye, a tiny jot of green against the gray. Through a crack in the sidewalk paving, a single leaf, tender and thin, thrust itself against the whole gray mass of the City. I knelt wonderingly to look at it.

Here, from France, is what may very well be the first science fiction story in the form of a computer game. Please bear in mind that we aren't saying that it *is* a computer game. It simply looks like one. But there's no way you can access it on your Macintosh. The only players of this game are its hapless characters—and you'll be glad of that, once you've read it.

"I was born on December 20, 1955," Francis Valéry tells us, "in a small city on the frontier line between France and Luxembourg. My eight great-grandmothers and fathers came from seven countries: France, Luxembourg, Germany, Italy, Spain, Scotland, and Ireland. So I am European!" Today he lives in Bordeaux. He has been a musician, a magazine editor, a bookseller, a literary critic, and a contributor of short stories to French small-press science fiction magazines and avant-garde mainstream publications—but since 1986 he has devoted himself entirely to writing, and at last word was putting the finishing touches to his fourth novel. This is his first professional appearance in English.

BUMPIE™

First of all we wish to congratulate you on your purchase. And to thank you for trusting us! BUMPIE™ is currently our most efficient program available, and we are sure that you will have no opportunity to regret your choice.

FRANCIS
VALÉRY

Before you try BUMPIE™, we suggest that you study the following guidelines most carefully.

You will be able to open a window and to call the main points on visual display at *any time* during the game. Use the functions keys *after* you have taken care of setting the system on pause. Remember that this operation should only be carried out as a *last resort*, as it may temporarily hide part of—or the whole of—a zone containing vital information.

BUMPIE™ operates along four levels of difficulty. When starting a new game, it is *absolutely* vital to use only the first level. Should you not respect this rule—for instance in order to break the security system—R.P.G. Inc. may not be held responsible, even partially, for the harm caused to the exploitation system, terminal, or reading heads. The same applies to the physical and mental integrity of the player, whatever the importance of the brain damage caused.

The following difficulty levels can't be

selected until a proposal has appeared on visual display at the beginning of a new game.

BUMPIE™ can operate along two chronological modes. We suggest you limit yourself to the INSTANT MODE, which corresponds to a factual chronology in conformity with the external timeline, called MAIN REFERENT. This mode allows a visual display consonant with the development of the program.

A second mode, called SEQUENTIAL MODE, enables an associate player to follow the progress of events from the point of view of the main player's internal chronology. This inner unfolding of time is called SECONDARY REFERENT.

All the subprograms are chained and numbered.

You may go from the MAIN REFERENT to the SECONDARY REFERENT at any time during the game. Look at the sequence number featured at the beginning of each subprogram, and use the "GOTO" at the end of each subprogram in order to break the standard chaining and insert (function key F7) to access the next sequence.

There is no need to come back to Disk Manager edition, as the insertion is automatic.

We encourage all players, whatever their level, to make the most of the REM notes so as to have referential elements at their disposal should the sequences appear in the same order again.

Nine messages in REM can be stored inside each subprogram. Should the system get stuck, a very explicit error message will appear at the bottom of the screen.

GOOD LUCK!

FIRST LEVEL

001 INSTANT 00—SEQUENCE 01

002 REM: "I have just swallowed the first piece of blotting paper dipped in Bumpie."

Such a simple gesture. Holding out your hand. Picking up the minute piece of wet paper. Then taking a long, slow look at it—a moment's hesitation before you lay it on the tip of your tongue—hardly biting into it.

No, this is no simple gesture. Rather, something like a mixture of anxiety and curiosity. For this is a scientific experiment, your alibi, or so you think, as pleasure slowly wells up. You are the only one to dare.

You will win—knowledge, or lose—everything. . . .

And then the fading light, eyes slowly closing, silence swelling, stifling the ultimate fears—those you thought to be the last. And your blood, pulsing between skin and bone, the tide of fear pressing against your skull, surging back like an immense breaker. A lump in your throat.

Now!

003 REM: "I have just swallowed . . ."

Just a few words hastily typed on the keyboard, or scribbled on the back of an envelope; ultimate will and testament.

Maybe I'll make it, thanks to the second piece of blotting paper, the one I dipped in the other product. It's my return ticket, synthesized only an hour ago. . . .

Imagine dozens of daring travelers mastering the bumper effect! The universe rebuilt, time remodeled, to suit our whims, into a symphony of differences. . . .

Our diverging dreams!

And then a sudden desire. If only it were tomorrow, if only you had already lived those two days. But right here, a few minutes ago, even before everything had begun. This is a childish wish, for we must create this future, or at least strengthen it, if we don't want to really doubt its existence, claiming that the project does exist. But when does life begin?

004 REM: "When does life begin?"

Why did I pick this out? Why did I write down this remark? All I feel is pain and fatigue. While the great concrete ribbon unrolls itself endlessly.

005 GOTO 160

110 INSTANT 11—SEQUENCE 03

What an unpleasant feeling this is. To know that you were right, that you suspected something before everybody else, as though history should unfailingly repeat itself again and again and forever.

—Hey! You fuckin' gophers!

There's an edge to Louis' voice. He sounds angry, just about to fly into a red-letter rage, as he will do on bad days, when everything goes wrong. When nothing works. Cold grub, warm beer days, when sun-rotted joints burst thirty miles away from the nearest garage, and you've got to push the bloody truck on the side of the highway and wait till the CHiPs come.

—You bunch of morons!

He comes up to me, sticky strands of hair over his specs, a fierce, nasty glint in his eyes.

—What the hell are we supposed to do with a five-kilo P.A.?

—Keep three of them to the front, five hundred on each side on the stage, and you keep the last one for footbaths! Easy!

But Louis is already gone.

111 REM: "Consider the last reply from the character named Louis as a statement and not as a real question. Don't take the main player's answer into account."

I watch him walk away, gesturing angrily at one of the organizers. I imagine his anger, swelling and vibrating, then unleashing itself onto the extra to crush him under tons of salted water, tanned surfers flying off the pearly peaks of the ocean.

112 REM: "Note that it is impossible to get out of the sequence without loading a second file beforehand."

I watch him walk away, gesturing angrily at one of the organizers. The man points out another person, in charge of the electrical equipment.
I hope they will sort this out eventually. It's true we can hardly play properly in such circumstances. Still I'm sure I had it specified on the contracts that we should be provided with at least a minimum of power.
I can't see my band. The truck hasn't arrived yet, and the drummer's station wagon is still parked behind the stage. He must be in the bar, on the other side of the stage, keeping company with the guitar player.

114 REM: "I'm trying to recapture the following sequence around three o'clock. I intend to position myself at the moment when Louis and I were getting out of L.A., heading for Santa Monica."

115 GOTO 170

150 INSTANT 15—SEQUENCE 5

349

151 REM: "Insertion is correct."

The Dart slowly slides northward, powerful and sleek through the dilapidated area situated west of Watts, while I try to imagine the sweet flavor of the Great River.

Every tiny street opening itself on our right ends up with a wall, memory crowned with glass shards, barbed wire, slash, scar, wound mirroring the white trash anxieties.

—Where are we?

—Not so far now. Go straight ahead for some fifteen miles and we'll come out onto one of the great avenues. Pico or Olympic, I guess.

A trail of cold composite concrete, mere slabs laid on raw sand, under the heavy leaden sky, and the occasional vehicle stranded in the night, the sad gleam of the whitish headlights, like a tunnel of light leading to . . .

152 FILE ALREADY EXISTS

153 REM: "I'm going too far ahead for the insertion. Remember to check the clock."

Louis holds out his hand to reach the radio and turns up the sound.

—You heard that?

—. . . .

—Riot in the South.

—So what? They're all the alarmist type on the radio. The same sons of bitches who cordoned Watts off, after the negros burned everything down.

—In '68?

—I don't remember. Maybe in the early seventies, well after Luther King died.

—And long before Jesse Jackson's act!

The FM is still spewing out its old anxiety, the sour funk which scares the Watts and Alamo Square areas shitless.

Beyond their differences, their problems and mutual hatreds, the two capitals have at least that one thing in common: they're scared stiff of those niggers who might fuck their daughters, rip all the Mr. Smiths' soft flesh, or even plough their kids' asses and stuff their heads and their veins with angel dust.

—I could do with a break.

—Gimme the wheel, and wake the kid up, he can roll us a joint. Is there any beer left?

The kid sits up, his weasel's voice comes from the back seat: "Almost nothing left!"

—Give it up, kid. If I boiled what's in the bottom of your pockets the brew would knock off a herd of elephants. . . . And there are at least 200 grams of grass in the truck, so you'll be able to fill up, son!

In the meantime on the FM:

— . . . but we haven't got the number of casualties. Violent fighting is reported downtown, near the Plaza. . . .

—Shit, it's more than a riot. You hear that?

But less than an earthquake, or Big Mama turning over in her sleep, or a storm washing down the hills' dirty skin on the other side of the bay, where the girls . . .

154 FILE NOT FOUND

155 REM: "I switch to pause and have a look into the catalog. The Bay Area topography isn't filed on the B-drive. Hence the impossibility of moving the action toward San Francisco within this subprogram. Don't forget that inserts are meant to allow you to leave the preceding subprogram under the SECONDARY REFERENT. Avoid the accident, and link again on sequence number 6."

And still on the FM:

— . . . reinforcements, by order of the governor. But we've been told that the National Guards have just fired on the demonstrators and . . . Can you hear me, Ronald? Ronald Bretnor, answer me if you can hear me? . . . er . . . Well, I think we have a small technical problem here. . . . Yes, I'm listening. . . . The San Diego line has been cut.

—What a fucking mess!

I don't like the expression of self-satisfied joy which disfigures Louis' face.

—Shut it up and drive!

—Oh come on. . . . It's none of our business!

The voice comes from behind.

—Just keep rolling your joint, will you? Are you two idiots or what? There's nothing funny here. Poor buggers getting gutted by the pigs. I was thirteen in '68 and I remember the Chicago convention and the four people they killed in Ohio. That's not what I call pleasant memories, believe me.

156 REM: "I have just understood that it is impossible to alter an already stored sequence without fucking the whole system up. I have corrected the first mistake when I prevented the accident. But God! What a mess there is everywhere else! I've decided to make an insertion so as to collect more information on those events.

157 GOTO 130

160 INSTANT 16—SEQUENCE 02

Meanwhile the slow ribbon of concrete unrolls itself, wide and endless, becoming a tunnel of light when we meet other vehicles. Four V-shaped headlights from an ancient convertible Chrysler. The blind globes of a battered pickup. Lovingly polished chrome, its muzzle sniffing the noxious trail of the exhaust fumes on the concrete, a low-rider from East L.A. that got lost at the upper end of Olympic Boulevard, drawn by the promise of a moonless night.

Louis is driving the Dart. I feel fine.

—You imagine it's just like that every weekend? An obsession.

—That's what I call a town. Just think that one day the whole planet will look like that. Real scary! Cold concrete everywhere, under a sky so heavy you could cry.

Sighing:

—Yes, I do.

161 REM: "Remember to edit the dialogues. Suppress repetitions. Don't forget that a character can't speak in the same way in a written dialogue. Check verisimilitude aloud, but polish it up a bit.

—Not even that! We won't even get the chance to see that!

I'm not sure that "chance" is the most appropriate word. In the sun-visor mirror, I can see the others, fast asleep on the seat, overwhelmed with fatigue.

—What time is it?

—Let's say around five. Must be a good guess.

—The truck must have arrived.

—You're kidding, aren't you? I hope it's been there for some time already. And that everything is ready.

162 REM: "Be careful about the time. Don't forget that the external chronology must be respected at all times. Above all, don't take the main character's assessments into account. Always use the same references. Don't hesitate to slip in indications in the source of the narrative. Maybe not in each sequence, but regularly."

—Maybe. We've been driving for some time, you know. Chances are that they've not arrived yet.

I wish I knew what really happened, if for nothing else than to understand the characters' reactions somewhat better. The spur of curiosity? I hope I will be able to insert at the right place.

165 GOTO 110

170 INSTANT . . . Error found—SEQUENCE . . . Error found

171 REM: "Insertion Error"

172 GOTO 180

180 INSTANT 18—SEQUENCE 04

181 REM: "Not so easy to understand what happened. An assessment error for the insertion. With an extra unknown factor on top of everything: will I be able to use INSTANT 170 again, or what's left of it? Obviously the machine counts any intrusion into the time zones, since I had to use two lines to get out of the subprogram."

—That was hearty, wasn't it?
—Yeah. In a way. But I can just see what Berthold will say. We'll have him breathing down our necks for weeks. I'd be surprised if we played tonight.
—You think so?
He turns around toward me, as if to get my approval. Only then do I notice the large bluish bruise swelling under the kid's eye.
Louis resumes:
—You're dreaming or what? You think Pat is going to be up to anything with a plastered arm?

182 REM: "Again check the transcription of the dialogues. Try to eliminate overgroupish vocabulary. Try to convey some of the characters' psychological features, speech mannerisms or repetitive expressions, but watch out for some redundancy.

Don't try to reproduce the conversation like a tape recorder. Too awkward. Use synonyms."

—You're kidding, or what? I hardly see Pat being up to anything with a plastered arm!

—You're overreacting, Louis. It's only a sprain. And the right wrist at that.

Then I see the guitar player coming back from the bar, looking furious.

—You bunch of idiots!

—Take it easy, it's no use shouting.

—If you lot want to fool around on the street, you just tell me before you start, OK? And you leave us in some joint somewhere. 'Cause I don't want to snuff it for your silly-assed sake!

183 REM: "Don't stress the fact that had he been the driver, he would probably have been the first to welcome a street machine atmosphere."

The best thing to do is to try and erase this sequence.

184 EXIT

185 CAN'T ACTION FROM THE EDITOR

186 REM: "I change to the direct mode and suggest another way out."

187 PROCEDURE NAME DOESN'T LIKE NAME AS INPUT

188 REM: "I check the procedure definition and suggest another way out. I carry on with another subprogram."

189 GOTO 150

END OF LEVEL ONE

ITINERARY:

Your departure point is San Diego.
Your arrival point is Santa Monica.
Your route includes two fixed points, one situated somewhere west of Watts (L.A.), the other at the administrative border between L.A. and Santa Monica—approximate reference: east of Lincoln Boulevard.
Two non-preferential byways: Pico Boulevard and Olympic Boulevard.

MAIN CHARACTERS:

Louis: predetermined function of road manager and chauffeur of private vehicle.
Pat: determined function of musician (lead guitar)
"The Kid": determined function of musician (drums)

SECONDARY CHARACTERS:

Berthold: undetermined function
Ronald Bretnor: suggested function Press/Radio

SCRIPT:

A touring band is going from San Diego to Santa Monica.
The main character has the power to travel in time, but only on an intellectual level on a SECONDARY REFERENT, his physical body being unable to escape from the MAIN REFERENT. His objective memory results from his experience in his SECONDARY REFERENT.
Violent events of an ill-determined nature, but with probable social undertones, break up in San Diego.

You have reached the end of the first scene, difficulty level one.

You have seven experience points at your disposal, and a life potential of 98%.

Do you wish to move on to the second scene, difficulty level two?

YES/Y—NO/N

SECOND LEVEL

050 INSTANT 05—SEQUENCE 07

I'm driving the Dart. Berthold is sitting beside me. I've decided to play this subprogram with brisk, precise dialogues.

—You explain that to me?

—The "San Diego Affair"? The last Earl Stanley Gardner novel or an old one by A. A. Fair?

—Sorry?

—Just kidding. You just gave me the second piece of Bumpie paper in San Diego, didn't you?

—When "just"?

—Oh well. . . . Hardly an hour ago according to the main chronology.

—In your system?

—In the program's, buddy, according to the external chronology, not the one you're running inside your head. Monday, 7 A.M., if accuracy still matters to you.

—But that's a subprogram I haven't integrated yet!

—So what? You don't generate time, kiddo. It does that on its own. . . . In my system, you gave me your junk with the directions for using it as a free gift. So I headed toward San Diego, to see how things were going. Funny, isn't it?

—Yeah. Go on.

—I know you would be there in the evening, so I waited for you to come with Erick, near the truck.

—What? Erick is in it too? But what's all this *shit* about?

357

—No, Fat Erick hasn't arrived. Well, not yet. Listen, you gotta give some other pieces of paper, for him, and give some to the others too.

—You're real crazy, aren't you? You think this script isn't complicated enough? You're all fucking crazy, that's what you are. I've been unable to control anything since you got into my game. At 6 P.M., we were in San Diego and . . .

—Tomorrow?

—Yes, tomorrow. And three hours later here we are, firing away at the CHiPs with thermolasers. But this stuff doesn't exist! It's a fucking fantasy. This program is supposed to propose nothing but realistic alternatives. And Sally—what the hell is she doing in this story? I created her all right, but that was in another game. . . .

—Listen, I don't know about Sally. It's your business anyway. And please, spare me the bit about realistic alternatives! You're the one who began the cheating when you took your dope at the beginning of the game. That wasn't in the rules, kiddo.

—Maybe, but this is the second level, and that wasn't in the rules either. I know the first level by heart, like the back of my hand, and I couldn't find anything else to get this fucking computer to accept the second level.

—Right, OK, listen: maybe that's what the second level is about, too. OK? Forget about Sally. If she comes from another script, she can't have enough consistency to hold on for a long time.

—But that is crazy, shit, crazy! She should never have been strong enough to get integrated this time.

—Unless she's on direct access on the inner drive. As long as the game is under way she'll be able to reappear and . . .

—And fuck everything up!

—Listen to me for a while, will you? You've got a big mouth but you don't understand shit about shit. We're not playing anymore. You hear me? *It ain't a game now.* Get it? We're fighting for our skins now, not for our characters.

—I won't listen to that bullshit. You're crazy.

—OK. Try and kick me out of this subprogram.

— . . .

—Just try!

051 EXIT

052 THIS FILE IS WRITE PROTECTED

053 AGAIN EXIT

054 DISK IS WRITE PROTECTED

055 AGAIN EXIT; CUT / CUT / CUT / C

056 PROCEDURE-NAME DIDN'T OUTPUT

057 AGAIN CAN; STOP; STOP; STOP; GOTO 050

058 DISK IS FULL

—Are you going to stop that, you bloody fool? You'll get us stuck in this subprogram!

—But it's only a game, shit, a game!

—Can't you see that he's talking bullshit. He's just trying to get you to waste your ways out and to get you stuck in a sequence. The trick about the REM which can be used again is a con. If you take the same way twice you go straight into a trap. And no way to off the system. Get it? You're the one who wanted to live his fantasies, weren't you? You're the one who synthesized the Bumpie. Nobody told you to do it, is that correct? Now it exists. Trying to save your ass by getting out of the system won't change *nothing!* This crap is completely out of control. All the ghosts are programmed to prevent you from taking over, and you won't be able to get out until you have. . . .

— . . .

359

—And right now, San Diego has been completely eaten up! You get that? It's only a kind of magma, formless matter without identity, crushed up, laminated mudlike matter. No, not even mud, it's beyond mud, undefined matter, do you understand?

—So what do you suggest?

—Nothing. We just go on, that's all. You may go out of this subprogram, if you link it somewhere else. That's all you can do. No playing on your own, kiddo. As long as you were the only one in the game you didn't freak out, did you? So you go on like that. You've got to know what you want, don't you?

—Right. We fix up a meeting somewhere?

—We don't need to. We'll meet. . . . Just one thing: don't insert anything on the first sequences. Let's keep them for contacts if anything really important happens.

059 GOTO 173

130 INSTANT 13—SEQUENCE 06

The comments from the radio are comforting insofar as they exaggerate everything. Riot means incident. A horde of demonstrators is a peaceful meeting. A violent confrontation implies a black eye and a crushed toe. . . . And this exquisite high medium crackling they call listening comfort, subtle harmonics from a brand new string brushed on an acoustic Martin. And the sun-gorged bell of a sparkling cymbal, radiating kilowatts of molten gold, deep fleshy bass notes, full and yet firm to the touch, warm . . .

Why should it be any different today? A skull exploding because a tear gas grenade has struck it at the end of its crazed —accurate?—run. Shattered jaws, smashed-in ribs, while the pigs start firing at the black—multicolored?—tide.

Bullets make no choices. Some are lost, but not for everyone. Watch out if you meet them.

Three hours for the boys. Same with me. Why was it that the clocks synchronized to such an extent? Coincidence maybe. Side effects of the Bumper effect, a subtlety from the program setting all the clocks on cue?

Three hours, and everything was normal. Three hours, and hell is set loose, blood freezes, and there's pain in your stomach.

—Faster!

The Dart rushes into the Safeway parking lot. The shock absorbers cushion in. The back of the car scrapes the ground.

—We'll have to change the shocks.

—Drive on!

A slight bump on the front wing: the overturned shopping cart crashes into the department store window. Louis goes faster, changing gears manually. The car turns down an alley which opens on a small side street.

—Again!

Before it comes out onto another boulevard.

—Turn on the radio.

— . . .

—It's dead. All wavelengths.

The kid fishes into his bag, takes out a magnificent pearl. But the Beast closes his toothless jaws, pinning down the dauntless swimmer's leg. Like in a bad serial. I have to dive, before the sharks come, before my lungs burst. . . .

131 I CAN'T FIND THAT DRIVE

132 REM: "Impossible to insert. I have to go on with this subprogram."

The kid fishes in his bag, takes out a . . . small battery-powered radio and begins to bully it about.

—I can't find anything either!

—Louis, slow down and try to get out of town. We have to try and meet the truck.

133 REM: "Pause accepted. I switch to search and let the subprogram run on, until the two vehicles reach their meeting

point. Note that there will be a free sequence available, but of undetermined length."

134 FOUND

—Oh!

I wake up with a start. I can hardly speak.

—What's the matter?

—We've just passed the truck.

—They saw you?

—Hard to say. Anyway they were parked along the embankment, with at least two police cars and two motorcycles for company.

—The Highway Patrol?

—By the look of the bikes, yes, probably.

—You turn round, and you park behind them. Slowly.

I shouldn't have dozed off. I just hope nothing important happened. We are part of a vast flood of vehicles, all heading in the same direction. Louis takes the outermost lane, slows down and turns into the opposite lanes, almost empty of traffic by now.

—Look! Here they are.

Never get out of a parked vehicle under the CHiPs' noses —even slowly, even with an idiot harmless expression on your face. One of the cops comes up to us:

—Move along!

—We're together, the two of us, and the guys in the truck. Have they broken down?

He steps back, slowly, takes his weapon out and aims its big muzzle at me.

—Get out calmly, and with your hands up.

While the two other pigs run toward us, stroking their machine guns.

—Put your hands on the hood. And spread out your legs! Louis is edgy.

—Is it all right like that? I want a lawyer!

362

—Shut up, Louis. . . . I whisper, but not fast enough for the cop.

—Shut it up, asshole!

135 I'M HAVING TROUBLE WITH THE DISK

136 REM: "Disk access error. I try to insert again."

137 I'M HAVING TROUBLE WITH THE DISK

138 REM: "No way to get out of the subprogram."

And I've only got one possibility left for a GOTO. I decide to carry on inside the MAIN REFERENT.

—Shut it up, asshole!
And still the same pain in the pit of my stomach.
—Bugger off!
I know that voice. . . . I look up toward the top of the embankment. Surprise, surprise . . . Berthold is shouting at us from the top of the hill. The CHiPs turn round, and then collapse, pierced open, emptied out by Sally's thermolaser.

Sally, oh God, and Charlie! King and Queen of armored division attacks. Sally, most beautiful fox of Texas, queen of the Bronx hot nights, princess of the North Dakota snows— Sally in her Indian squaw costume, wreathed in the mists of Venice, while behind her the giant wheels of the aquarium city resume their crazy spinning—as if nothing has changed. And Sally in the Gondolas. Sally in the sky with diamonds. Sally of the quicksands, coming out of the mirror like womb. Sally gone away to die on the rhythm of her mother's womb. Sally, in love with her own death . . .

—Sally!
A grenade explodes under one of the black Chevrolets, set- 363 ting it ablaze in a single fiery kiss.
—Get out of here! Berthold screams, while this message, coming from God knows where, appears on the screen.

—San Diego, yesterday evening, around 8 A.M. I'll meet you there.

130 GOTO 050

173 INSTANT 17b—SEQUENCE 8

174 REM: "Second attempt to integrate this subprogram. I have stored Berthold's warning about a possible trap effect."

What I feel is of little importance, and of little use. I am not surprised to suspect, at this point, a crack in the program, a breach of continuity demonstrated by the fact that at this very moment I should be sitting on the soft rear seat of the Dart. I could also decide that I am now at the center of this rift; an extreme explanation. A more reassuring temptation is to admit that the past isn't frozen, not even the already integrated sequences. As if my contribution to the script, my choices, the decisions I took, couldn't guarantee that reality has been sufficiently impregnated to be accepted, once and for all.

This is easily acceptable, this discontinuity of the MAIN REFERENT. But how horrible to understand that I can't trust my own memory, or even taped observations: this reality I have helped to build, to mold, gives way under my feet, behind my back.

Any remodeling of the far past modifies the . . .

Not taking into account a foreseeable increase of this kind of open situation.

—Who are you?

I turn around, abruptly.

—Don't move!

As if it was sensible to do anything else, with this first weapon aimed at me. Open situations . . . but singularly repetitive ones.

—Listen, I'm not from here.

Wrong reply. I can imagine the system, nibbling a few decimals off my life potential.

I add:

—Maybe you could . . .

—I'm the one who asks the questions here. Which group do you belong to?

I found it difficult to analyze the landscape displayed on the screen, in the background. "Masses of disorganized matter," Berthold said. Primeval matter.

—Which group of Irregulars? Answer me!

—I really don't understand your question. I can hardly imagine who these Irregulars can be. Where are we?

The girl doesn't answer, but looks at me carefully.

—I have no weapon, if that's what you're looking for.

—Do you know what the Bumpie is?

—Oh, the Bumpie. . . . Well, let's say it's a kind of very powerful drug, whose primary effect is to induce. . . . It's as if the user could travel in time. Yes. It's a way to explain the phenomenon.

She lowers her weapon, satisfied with my answer.

—And which isn't really up to scratch, is it?

I nod.

—All right. I'll take you to headquarters. This is San Diego, or what's left of it.

A message superimposed onscreen: YOU WIN TWO EXPERIENCE POINTS AND 3% LIFE POTENTIAL.

—This is . . . San Diego?

—Used to be. Now it's a fragment of the Bumper Universe. Don't ask me to explain what it's . . . watch out!

She grabs me by the sleeve and pushes me into a shadowy corner. A dark mass appears in the street. A massive tank—about ten meters long, four or five meters wide—crushing everything under its tracks.

175 REM: "Memorize description of the machine."

176 IDENTIFICATION?

177 FILE NOT FOUND

—What is it?

—Haven't got the faintest idea. They appeared a few hours ago, well after the confrontation with the National Guard. And there are more and more of them. They're after something.

—Something?

—Or somebody. You, maybe. . . .

—I'm sorry, but I don't find this funny.

—It's all right. It didn't spot us.

I wish she could tell me more about all this, but all of a sudden I get the feeling that she is as helpless as I am.

—Take me to Berthold.

—You know Berthold?

—Quite well.

— . . .

—Well, no. . . . Listen to me. Tell him that you saw me. I am the Player. And tell him too that I have to go at once if I don't want to be carried away into the next moment.

—The next moment?

—He'll understand. Tell him that I have already integrated the following moment—for me it's the fourth sequence. You'll remember? Fourth sequence and the instant number is eighteen. Berthold will understand all this.

—Don't worry. Instant number eighteen, fourth sequence. Anything else?

—Yes, something. I'll be waiting for him in sequence number . . . No, I'll be waiting Monday at 2 P.M. He'll find the insertion by himself. I must be off now.

—Tell me. . . .

—Yes?

—Are you really the Player?

—I'm supposed to be.

—Well . . . good luck then.
170 GOTO 010

END OF LEVEL TWO

ITINERARY:

No further information.

MAIN CHARACTERS:

Berthold: Masters the Bumper effect as well as the main player. He organized a body of fighters in San Diego, called "The Irregulars."
No further information on the other characters.

SECONDARY CHARACTERS:

Ronald Bretnor: Erased.
Sally: A ghost only available on direct access from the inner drive. Undetermined function. Character coming from a previous game.
The Girl: A member of the Irregulars. No information available.

SCRIPT:

The violent events that took place in San Diego have led a third force to intervene. No information available apart from the use of heavy war vehicles such as armored tanks.
A secondary effect of Bumpie seems to have caused the slow but steady decay of the background landscape, turning everything into a kind of undefined, incoherent matter.
It appears that the police are looking for the musicians. For unknown reasons. The character named Berthold becomes more and more important and leads part of the game.

367

You have reached the end of the second scene, difficulty level two.

You have nine experience points at your disposal, and a life potential of 91%.

Do you wish to move on to the third scene, difficulty level number three?

YES/Y—NO/N

THIRD LEVEL

010 INSTANT 01—SEQUENCE 09

Berthold pushes the door open.

—Are you in?

—Come in. And this time you explain everything to me, all right?

—I ain't got much to explain, kiddo. I don't know much more than you do.

—Well, I still wish I knew a bit more about your character. And then . . . Let's say I'd like to be sure that we are on the same side! I'm coming from San Diego, but my insertion was aimed at Santa Monica. Or at least Los Angeles.

—Third level. You weren't obliged to accept!

—Except that you told me that I wouldn't be able to get out of the system unless I had taken over control of the Bumpie, didn't you?

—Problem is that the map doesn't really match the territory anymore. You can't use this fixed itinerary, with its mandatory passage points, its departure and arrival points, and all these landmarks. This is the third level, and you must define a new route. And take the zones one must avoid into account.

—Like San Diego?

—For instance!

—So why did I find myself there when I intended to make an insertion somewhere else?

—Because this is the third level! . . . Shit! And you're also playing against the system. Last time we met I pointed out to you that it was blocking your ways out with false messages, "file full," "no file," "wrong drive," and so on and so forth. It's up to you to get him to accept your insertions!

—And in the meantime I find myself in San Diego, in front of a nutty girl ready to cut me up into slices!

—I know. She told me. You were safe?!

—Maybe. But I can no longer get out of the subprogram just like that, you see, fade away as soon as things are getting a bit hot.

—Correct. But it's up to you to lose your bad habits. At the third level you must expect to be confronted with any kind of situation. Right. Listen, I haven't got that much time to give you. You can't insert into L.A.: any attempt to get out will take you to San Diego.

—But what the hell do you want me to do in that cocked-up place?!

—Fight! With useful information: there are hundreds of Bumpie users now. That's what's fucking everything up! Everybody is trying to consolidate their own environment. There are two consequences to this. On the one hand, all matter is losing its coherence. It reverts to a kind of neutral state to resist contradictory demands. . . . On the other hand, time's running away too. . . .

—Time?

—That's more difficult to explain. Time structure has broken up. On your way you may stumble on bits and pieces of past or future: bubbles of your own time, fragments of universe—familiar ones since you're responsible for them. But they're jostled about, burst into and burst open by shards coming from other realities. By fragments as "real" as they are, from other characters' points of view.

—But this is crazy! Who let those people use Bumpie?

—Not me. But I'm as interested as you are in the answer.

—Still, it could be you, or me, in a past that's been modified since?

—Or in a future we haven't explored yet.

—And it would modify the past?

—Definitely. Past, future, it's all the same. . . .

—But there's a catch, you see. I find it funny that you should explain all that to me in such a detached way, somewhere between academic speech and polite small talk. As if . . .

—As if nothing, kiddo. The only sensible behavior is to let things be. Every intervention entails one more fucked-up touch to the background, one more unforeseen detail. Plus the risk to have to deal with the consequences. Amplified, twisted-up consequences. At any time. . . . And that's how you freak up on your own.

—Easy.

—Realistic! Besides, the Bumpie which has been passed around is much less powerful than yours. Which means that on the short run the users will disappear.

—Like Sally. To come back out of the blue.

—Sally is a different case. She's been saved on the inner drive, while a small charge, punctually validated and followed by a quit editing, will wipe all these characters away.

—And set the counter back to zero, maybe.

—Certainly not.

—There's one thing. . . . The girl from San Diego was quite conscious of the changes that were taking place under her eyes. As aware as I was. I can tell you that at that time she was as real as me.

—In your system. Because she was fifty centimeters from you.

—The tank wasn't. It was as real as this table, and fifty meters away. Just like the cops on the highway.

—They were real.

—All right. The tank was a ghost. Like the ruins it was crushing? Hell, I wish you had been there. This thing was real scary.

—I've got to go. Keep the morning for contacts. You're going to have a guest. In a few minutes. It should be Erick.

He should get out of a subprogram parallel to what will be your sequence thirteen. And he will make his insertion here, now, in sequence fourteen.

—But I'm only in sequence nine!

—I know. You must insert to switch on sequence ten, but don't forget to relink immediately after you're out of thirteen.

—Same level?

—I don't know. Listen. Somebody is knocking on the door. . . .

011 GOTO 060

040 INSTANT 04—SEQUENCE 11

041 REM: "This is like slow, meticulous restoration work, an accurate link-up of all the fragments I wish to save. But what a mess! How am I going to sort everything out? This slow, painstaking progress looks more like crude mending. Don't forget to get the subprograms as close to each other as you can. Like this for instance:

Useless dialogue:

I think they should be here soon. Listen: you'll tell them that I went to get some Bumpie. Berthold will understand. The meeting place will be this café right in front of us, on the other side of the square, in fifteen minutes' time.

042 REM: "A minimum of changes, I must make three pieces of Bumpie paper, those I handed around, in their future. . . ."

Later:

—You got them?

—Yes. But they've already been passed around, a short while ago, in another future sequence. I've just synthesized them, just to . . . well . . . to justify all this, validate my memories.

—What about this sequence where Louis wrecks the Dart?

371

—I don't know. For the first time I've lived through a kind of nullification of the script, but inside the same subprogram. I was about to find out HFAC's identity. . . .

—So?

—Nothing. Everything was erased. The characters disappeared, dissolved within seconds. And the Dart was rebuilt in the same way, when Louis had smashed it against a concrete street lamp base. In Santa Monica, on a pedestrian mall.

—Have you noticed how everything is going faster?

043 GOTO 070

070 INSTA /////////////////////// ERROR FOUND ERROR

070 INST ////////////////////// ERROR FOUND ERROR FOUND

". . . . . This program is definitely fucked up."

045 REM: "And I was about to forget about this fucking middle sequence."

060 INSTANT 06—SEQUENCE 10

061 REM: "The first thing I note is that there seems to have been a few changes since I first came here. I'm using the word "seems" on purpose because now I know that horror may appear at each turn of the road. The background is familiar to me. We are right in the heart of Santa Monica. Behind us the ocean is roaring. The Dart is parked on the right-hand side of a large avenue, like a good girl, its massive radiator grill pointing at L.A., toward a crossroads I know well."

I open the door of the car.

A draft of fresh air peppers my hair with light. The pavement is as stable as . . .

This is ludicrous. There I am, testing the solidity of a pavement with the tip of my boots.

The town is quiet, overwhelmed by the late afternoon sun. . . .

062 SOURCE AND DESTINATION DISKETTES DIFFER

The town is quiet at this early morning hour.

I'm progressing slowly toward the pedestrian mall. Remembering happy moments of life in Venice. My father used to take us—Mom and me—to the spaceport, to see the massive iridescent metal ships. Remembering how I hoped to get into the Space Academy, a hope shattered by a visual deficiency. . . . For a long time the space vessels had only my regrets to take away. I can still see the huge Galaxy station wagon, its fins, its reactors. . . .Then my father bought a green Cadillac 1959. Of course it was the plainest one on the lot, a mere coupé, without any chrome or optional devices. And yet a wealth of fantasies. The tailfins' wild line, again the promise of stars so close one could stroke them. The Cad' was second-hand but in perfect condition. And my father managed to get a customized plate which shouted "FINS 4 LA" to whoever wanted to see it . . .

FINS 4 LA . . . No more fins for Los Angeles . . .

A draft of fresh air peppers my hair with bitterness.
The town is quiet at this early morning hour.
I'm slowly walking down the av . . .

—Get in! Fast!

The Dart springs forward; Louis grabs my arm. Our speed presses me against the seat. I catch a glimpse of the tank in the mirror. It's blocking the way behind us. It appeared out of Ocean Boulevard to cut our retreat.

All of a sudden Louis brakes hard, tires squealing, as the Dart weaves its way between the street lamps of the pedestrian mall. A shock, a shattering sound, and I am thrown against the window. Blood flows.

—I'm all right, go on!

—I wipe my bruised lips with my shirt cuffs and fasten the safety belt. I remember the cart crashing into the window of the Safeway.

—Hold on!

Louis strikes the concrete cradle, the front of the car is lifted up before it strikes the street lamp. Smoke billows up from the disemboweled radiator, the wounded car is wailing, and I see, under the hood opened by the shock, its throbbing heart.

Strict, black uniforms. White boots. Black helmets. Ludicrous.

—Get out, and follow us without resisting.

I show no reaction.

—Don't force us to use our weapons. Please get out.

The uniform takes us toward one of the tanks. Surprise, surprise. I can see Erick standing between two mute creeps.

—So you're here too?

—So what? By the way, have you some?

—Some what?

—Oh, you can talk in front of them. They're completely tone deaf. Real machines. They stay still between orders. As long as we don't try to hop off, they won't react. So? You got some?

—Some what?

—Some Bumpie! Berthold said that you had made some for us.

063 REM: "Berthold told me to make some and to give it to the others, but that was such a long time ago!"

I fish hesitantly into my pocket, pick up the small pieces of blotting paper.

—Yes, I've got them, but don't ask me where they come from!

—Is it good, or is it the same crap the kids in San Diego have?

—It must be good.

A sudden flash of inspiration.

—Since I synthesized it.

—Give me one. I don't feel like staying longer.

—First tell me who those people are.

—The creeps? Why bother? HFAC troops, I guess.

—HFAC?

—Anyway, they don't mean us any harm.

I run my tongue over my aching lips, taste the sweet tang of blood.

—Have you seen what they did to my car?

—It's Louis who smashed up the Dart, kiddo.

—Shit. I'm fed up with this patronizing, calling me kiddo all the time. Am I the Player or am I not? Why are you here?

—Because you called me, kid . . . well, nothing. I came with Berthold. He must be waiting for you in the café opposite.

—The café in front of us?

—You gave him the appointment, didn't you? Just before you went to get the paper. OK, I must be off.

And before I can move, Erick swallows one of the pieces of bumpie paper and fades out from the screen.

I turn around. The square is empty. The Dart is carefully parked along a stretch of pavement.

—I must be off, but where to, for God's sake! As if I wasn't supposed to go somewhere too. I'm the Player. Do you hear me? I AM THE PLAYER.

060 GOTO 040

070 INSTANT 07—SEQUENCE 12

—Where are we?

—You're wasting your time, kiddo. This guy is going to tell you that . . .

—I'm not allowed to answer your questions.

—Isn't it amazing!

—Follow me, please.

—And perfectly self-confident, see. . . . Let's follow him, let's follow him. This corridor may get us somewhere eventually.

What a strange corridor. . . . We walk among piles of litter, through a forest of metallic structures occasionally jutting from cracked, dislocated blocks of concrete, heavy tombs under which lie the corpses of hundreds of fighters. Blietzkrieg, instant war, and unexpected death have turned Our Lady of Angels into Our Lady of Darkness. The arrogant capital of the South has been erased and turned into magma. I remember the doomsday landscapes described by the survivors of the terrible fire that destroyed San Francisco a long time ago. The heavy, fantastic pages that loomed up from the magic books of Babel. The image of a Maltese falcon, etched on a ring, the ring sliding from a dead man's finger as the red plague swept over the town.

Our Lady of Darkness . . .

Old Jack's ghosts haunting the city's corroded arteries. Ruins . . . Another image prevails, shoving the others aside, beyond the borders of the night: the Bumper Universe.

—Please, follow me.

The uniform steps back, and gestures toward the wide open door:

—Please, gentlemen, do come in.

—You may escape, but only for a while. I suggest you come in without any more fuss. The situation is under our control, as you well know it. Our men are everywhere, behind each time bubble, protected by our black ships. Everywhere I tell you, omnipresent. We rule over all realities.

He traces out a vague memory.

—We can find you wherever and whenever we want to. And always faster, can't we?

—I think I'm in no position to negotiate.

—Not in the least. Come in, your friends may wait in this room. You and I should have a word together, don't you think so?

071 REM: "It's useless to try and put him on the track. And I'm sure that the man I'm talking to knows very well that there's nothing I want more. With the mad hope that I'll be able to ask the questions I'm dying to ask. . . . And to hear the answers that will quench my curiosity."

—I'm listening.

—Fine. Let's talk Bumpie then, for starters. We want the formula.

—You've got it.

—No, you are mistaken. We own something very much like it, but infinitely less sophisticated, less subtle. Less efficient, I should say. We want your trade secret.

—What do you have to offer in exchange?

—I like you. What about your life? Is that enough?

—There's nothing you can do to me. It would be useless to kill me and it wouldn't give you the formula anyway.

—True. But it would at least prevent our enemies from laying their hands on it one of these days.

—Since you're so well-informed, you should know that I can get out of this subprogram on my own. And if I have observed what's going on around me carefully enough, the universe is falling to pieces much too fast for you to have a grip on it. If I were you, if I had the means to do it, I would try and stop this shit! If you're not doing it, it's because you are unable to do it. Is that correct?

—In part. It's true that the situation is evolving faster than we thought. But it is also true that you're playing with your life. If we delay you a little bit longer, you will be thrown into a subprogram you have already explored. Do you think you could exist twice at the same place . . . at the same time?

—"At the same time"—it doesn't mean anything, and you know it very well.

—Are you ready to take the risk?

—Why do you create all those alterations?

—I'm going to surprise you there. We do create some of them, but not all of them. As a matter of fact we have nothing to do with the most . . . spectacular ones! You are responsible for them.

—You're kidding, aren't you?

—You *are* the Player. We are here only to resist you, in a perfectly normal way. We are the pitfalls, the dead ends, we set up the traps. So it goes. It's . . . our function, our reason for being there, or for disappearing, if you are able to outwit us.

—So if you're just pawns in the game, meant to test my reactions, or to spice up the game, why do you want the formula?

—You'll find out if you reach the fourth level, my dear friend.

—And what about those armored buildings on tracks? Am I responsible for them too?

—Ah, what you call our "ships"? They're just service vehicles, adapted to their environment, immune to the Bumper effect.

—Listen, I don't understand what you're up to. But I'm certainly not going to give you the formula. There are many things I don't get, all right, but now I'm convinced that the only way I can win this game and break up this fucking system is to regain control over the Bumpie.

— . . .

—So if you haven't got anything else to tell me . . . This time I'm the one who is in a hurry, and I'm expected somewhere else.

END OF THIRD LEVEL

ITINERARY:

No further information.

MAIN CHARACTERS:

Berthold: enough information to place this character on the player's side.

HFAC: main enemy. Has enormous technical means at his disposal. Important staff.

SECONDARY CHARACTERS:

No further information.

SCRIPT:

The Bumper effect has spread to the whole of Southern California. We know that the cities of San Diego, Los Angeles, and Santa Monica have been destroyed. There is not sufficient information to speculate on the situation in other cities. The aim of the game has not been clearly defined yet. The player's survival may be the main goal. The entity called HFAC may maneuver to obtain the formula of the Bumpie only to prevent the player from regaining control over the situation. If neither side masters the Bumper effect, it may become an element susceptible to annihilate one of the two competing sides.

You have reached the end of the third scene, difficulty level three.

You have twenty-three experience points at your disposal, and a life potential of 58 percent.

Do you wish to move on the fourth scene, difficulty level four?

YES/Y—NO/N

FOURTH LEVEL?

Somehow their features are familiar to me, but the overall shape of their bodies hardly recalls that of human beings. They are dark vultures, messengers from the deep night, pellucid and yet thick-winged bats. Parchment, I mean. No, there used to be some in our house when . . . a drum's skin. An old brass band drum, with this fake tanned parchment, thick and uneven, circled with metal eyelets, stretched over a multicolored wooden box. Carefully braided straps hold the skin in place, which you can wring to regulate tension. . . . I can't remember it very well. It would always become unstretched, and I wedged used electric batteries between the cords and the side of the box so as to tighten the flabby skin.

Their wings feel like the beat of that drum, laborious, a soft, reboundless belly, and they wear long black tunics. They are bad-quality caricatures of angels, of the kind one meets in the harlequins' cemetery. I am not afraid. Maybe I should be frightened but I'm not.

Oh, now I'm not sure what they looked like. Their faces fade away, and it's not so important anyway.

I open my eyes. I recognize my body, even if I can't see it. Guess it's mine, actually, but it really is. Look, it's me, this row of screens, those blinking lights, those diagrams and sinusoids. And the tinkling. Why did they bind me?

I hear: "Problem" and then "reanimate." "Incident" again, and then "we almost."

The completed sentence must have been, "We almost had a problem when we reanimated him," or something of the kind.

I close my eyes again, for a short while. Sally's face appears above mine. She has changed her haircut. My throat hurts.

Feels burnt. I wish I could cough, spit, or clear my throat, but I'm not strong enough yet.

And Sally asks:

—You smoke a lot?

—Yes. A whisper . . .

Somebody comes up to me, rolling another table against mine. The kid hasn't woken up yet, tosses and turns in his sleep.

Sally leans over him:

—It's all over now. Come on . . . it's over. You must wake up now.

Then, only for my sake:

—You all right?

—I guess so. . . . The silky rustling of her blouse. She unplugs something.

—We'll take you back to your room.

—Is it finished?

—Yes!

She smiles.

—Everything's fine. You took some time to wake up.

—My throat hurts.

—It's normal. It will pass. Keep your arm still.

I catch a glimpse of the drip, a thin snake of nourishing plastic. And light at last. This bitter taste in my mouth must be the tube they placed, aching throat . . . and the over-whelming light tumbling from the ceiling. And the mask . . .

—I can't remember anything.

—It's the anesthesia. It'll get better. See, keep your arm stretched on the edge. We're taking you back to your room.

—Is this the fourth level?

Berthold is looking at me with an amused glint in his eyes.

—What fourth level?

I hesitate:

—Where are we?

—You must rest. That was quite a shock you had, kiddo. But it'll be all right.

—I've seen Sally again.

I remember now. Fear crawling under the rough sheets, stroking the ribs, creeping up. A whiff of anxiety.

—What the hell am I doing here, Berthold? Where are the others?

—Everything's fine, you just believe me. No problem, you just stay here a few hours to get some rest and we'll talk about all this when you wake up. You just take my word. Everything went fine. Within two or three days you'll be home safe and you'll start writing again as soon as you feel like it. A few weeks' holiday! Me, I rather like that, you see, it's been a long time since I've had any holidays.

—All right. We keep the morning sequences for contacts?

— . . . as you like it. It's up to you. Well, I must be off now. Try and get some sleep!

—May I have a word with you, Mr. Berthold?

—Of course, doctor. The nurse told me everything went all right now. . . .

—This is delicate. The operation went satisfactorily, and your friend is safe, but . . . please come in.

On the screen, I can see Berthold walking into the study, followed by the surgeon, who adds genially:

—Please, do sit down.

Before he also settles himself in a deep armchair. . . .

—You're musicians, aren't you?

—My friends are. I deal with the organization of the shows, relations with the press, and so on.

—Were you with them when the accident took place?

—No, I wasn't. But I wasn't far. I was already there, and I saw the car coming.

—There were four people in the car, weren't there?

—Yes. The driver, two of the musicians in the rear seat, and him. . . .

—What happened?

— . . . One of those stupid accidents. Maybe the car was going too fast, and then a kid ran out of the parking lot, pushing an empty shopping cart. Louis braked. I think the kid got scared, he let the cart go, or maybe the car hit him first, I didn't see very well. And then it swerved to the other side of the road, and crashed against the concrete base of a street lamp.

—So that's it. But the shock wasn't too violent?

—Not at all. We've always had big cars to drive, for comfort and for the musicians' image too. Those big cars are kind of reassuring.

—We ran a few tests on your friends, but they're perfectly all right. Except for some rather peculiar substances our analyses traced.

—It's not a habit of theirs, you know . . . and . . .

—It's none of my business, Mr. Berthold. I'm not a policeman. But we do have a problem with your friend, or at least something unusual.

—But he looks fine, doesn't he?

—On a physical level, yes he does. When we checked him in, he was unconscious.

—Comatose?

—No, no, let's not use big words. He passed out. A hardly surprising loss of consciousness, caused by the shock. Nothing alarming. A few nice bruises, superficial cuts that didn't even call for stitches.

—So where's the catch?

—We don't know, Mr. Berthold. It appears that your friend has ingested a sizable quantity of a noxious and rare new drug which has been around for a while. But a strong one, whose effects we don't know very well yet.

—The Bumpie?

—Yes. The name is quite evocative of the feelings the users must experience: the impression of being jostled around in time, sent from one place to another. It induces a kind of partial loss of consciousness. The user recalls events from his past randomly, jumping from one place to another, and feels

383

as though he were reliving particular moments of his life. There's a kind of feedback between memories and what the person perceives of the outside world. He is stimulated by those elements from the outside world: a noise, a light, conversation being held around him, or the sound of the radio, for instance, comments from a journalist, or a song's lyrics. Everything whirls around inside his head. The user sorts this out, selects what he is interested in, the element he can integrate into his delirious thoughts. Have you already used this product, Mr. Berthold?

—No, I haven't.

—Don't. That's my advice to you. It's real crap. I'm sorry. . . . Much more dangerous than heroin, or crack, even.

—And as for . . .

—As far as his body is concerned, there's no problem. I told you: there was no surgical intervention. He was just reanimated and we had him eliminate all the drug. But mentally . . .

—He is delirious?

—That is not the appropriate word. What he says is rather coherent, as if he were still under the influence of the product. I wish I could reassure you, Mr. Berthold, but I'm afraid that your friend will suffer from some side effects after this experience. Maybe have trouble assessing events, a kind of schizophrenia, not permanent but. . . . Tell me, is your friend a musician?

—Yes, he is.

—No other activities?

—He publishes novels and short stories from time to time. Is that important?

—It may be. Do you know what he was working on lately?

—He's just finished a novel. I've found the proofs on the floor, next to the front seat.

384

—You read them?

—I read the manuscript.

—Interesting?

—Some sort of computer game. You don't quite know

whether the character is real or part of the program. I think
he wanted to address the problem of consciousness, the solidity of reality. To show that a fictional character endowed with
a kind of electronic memory, created by a computer, could
very well not doubt his existence inside his environment. See
what I mean? As long as there is a creator, his creatures have
no reason whatsoever to challenge their own existence, to
have existential problems.

—What if they do?

—I think that's what the book is about.

*

??? REM: "I have reached the fourth level. Sally plays the
part of a nurse. I have seen Berthold. Everything's fine. The
situation is under control. I can have some rest now. That's a
hell of a good game. . . ."

From a first-time writer whose professional background includes such fascinating odds and ends as a stint in numismatics, a year spent conducting tours of the Louisiana bayous, and a season of professional table-tennis (!) comes this light and airy satirical view of what's just around the corner in the world of marital discord, told with verve and gloss reminiscent of the lively old days of Horace Gold's classic magazine Galaxy.

386

"What do you mean we can't get a divorce?" Thurgood demanded, his poured-acrylic suit shining blue in the office spots.

"Yes, what do you mean?" echoed Sylvia in the very tone of voice that had originally driven Thurgood to seek an end to their eight-year-old marriage.

The bald severance counselor smiled apologetically across the teak vastness of her desk.

"I'm terribly sorry," she said. "You just don't qualify."

"But we've had the prerequisite number of fights documented on video," Sylvia sputtered. "We've worked hard for this divorce. Practiced. Saved for it."

Thurgood nodded vigorously. "You must be mistaken," he said, in the voice that had moved more than one family to buy a bigger, more expensive car than it needed. "Besides, I've already arranged for Sylvia's replacement. She's due in on Monday from Oslo."

"I suggest you have her flight delayed," the counselor said.

Was it his imagination, or did Sylvia repress a smile?

Thurgood cleared his throat.

"I don't think you understand. . . ."

"It is you who misunderstand, Mr. Dalkins." The counselor stared at him severely until Thurgood lowered his eyes. "I repeat that you do not qualify for divorce at this time. Since the passage of the Family Preservation Act last year, our requirements have changed."

LOVE IS A DRUG

LEAH
ALPERT

"But it's all there," he said helplessly. "The letters from our creditors. The contract. Signed affidavits from our employers. . . ."

"What more do you want?" Sylvia asked, her voice silky. Thurgood recognized it as her precoital oral mode, and for a moment lusted guiltily after his soon-to-be ex-wife.

The counselor, too, seemed snared by Sylvia's seductive tones. She gave her a frankly appraising look which left Thurgood resentful and possessive. That was his almost-ex-wife that that dyke was undressing with her eyes. And Sylvia seemed to be enjoying the attention, the bitch.

For a moment, nobody spoke.

Sylvia took advantage of the pause to lean toward the counselor. She'd worn her second-favorite black spandex suit, very low-cut, and her bounteous bosom seemed to tremble on the brink of full exposure. The counselor's eyes were glued to that spandex threshold.

"Isn't there anything we can do?" Sylvia asked throatily. She took a deep, deep breath and slowly let it out.

Beads of perspiration gleamed gently on the counselor's tanned head.

"Uh, well, there is drug therapy," she said, raising her eyes to meet Sylvia's.

"Drug? What kind of drug?" Thurgood said. Both women ignored him.

"Is there?" Sylvia purred. She stretched like a cat awakening from a nap, tawny hair cascading down her back, chest rising until Thurgood thought her nipples would pop out from beneath their taut black cover.

His wife swept golden strands of hair back from her forehead in an imperious gesture which Thurgood had once found thrilling but now thought aggressive and even somewhat mannered.

388

The counselor stared, open-mouthed. Then her gaze met Thurgood's. He glared. Her cheeks reddened. She sat back in her chair and attempted to recover her composure.

"Yes. Yes, there is," she said. "You could probably qualify

for a divorce once you'd satisfied the drug-bonding therapy requirements. Anybody who fails that test proves their marriage is irreconcilable."

"We'll do anything," Thurgood said. "How soon can we sign up? Can we finish by this weekend?"

"I don't know. You need to see Dr. Regnan in Section J. Of course, it's lunchtime now. But he'll be back by two o'clock, probably." She turned off her deskscreen. "Thank you for coming by. We'll bill you."

Thurgood rose, nodding. It was one-thirty. With luck, they'd be finished with this drug therapy nonsense by four o'clock. Take some pills, maybe a hypo or two, and hello Oslo!

Sylvia remained sitting in the green leather chair.

"Are you coming?" he asked.

"In a minute. I want to ask the counselor something. Privately." She gave him a cool look with her deep blue eyes, a look which alternately boiled and froze his blood.

"Fine. I'll meet you at Section J."

He was glad he was divorcing her. Eight years had been too long, by half. He slammed the door behind him.

At two-thirty, Section J reopened from lunch break.

At two forty-five, Thurgood began pacing the mirrored reception room, accompanied by his reflection. He stopped for a moment and studied himself: dark hairpiece in place, square jaw, white teeth capable of a ferocious grin. That plastic surgery had certainly been worth it. Thurgood flexed a carefully sculpted bicep before he remembered that he was annoyed, and began pacing again.

At three-fifteen, Sylvia strolled in, touching up her fuchsia lipstick.

"Nice of you to make it," Thurgood snapped. "Did you just lose your way or was it a temporary attack of amnesia?"

Sylvia smiled vaguely. Her eyes seemed unfocused.

"Sorry I'm late."

Thurgood recognized that dreamy, postorgasmic look only too well. It made him want to shake her.

"Don't be so angry, hon," she cooed. "At least we won't have to worry about that bill now. Besides, I've always wanted to do it with a bald woman."

"Couldn't you have waited until after the divorce?"

She stopped smiling. "Couldn't you have waited until after the divorce to buy Oslo a ticket?"

So she had been nettled by that little disclosure, Thurgood thought. Well, good. He *had* meant to tell her. And at least he knew that she still cared. It would make the ending even more satisfying.

"Good afternoon, folks."

Thurgood spun around, but the beige-carpeted reception area was empty.

"Oh, don't be confused. I'm not here," said the tenor voice cheerily. "One can't be too careful, you know. People on all kinds of medication come in here."

"Where are you?" Sylvia asked politely.

"In my office," the voice said. "Dr. Regnan at your service." The monitor hanging from the ceiling showed a thin man with a long nose, a drooping mustache and a headful of curly black hair. He grinned. "And I believe that you are the Dalniks?"

"Dalkins."

"Oh, right. Sorry. Cynthia said you might be coming by. So you're interested in drug-bonding therapy, are you? Seems like everybody is these days, now that the law's changed. They've really made divorce as difficult as possible, haven't they?" The doctor giggled. "When would you like to get started?"

"As soon as possible," Thurgood said.

"Then take the second door on your right. The one with the 'better living through chemicals' sticker. I'll be waiting."

Thurgood grabbed his wife's arm and propelled her through the door. A long corridor led them to a red-carpeted room with a table, two white plastic chairs, and a sign that said OPEN WIDE. Dr. Regnan stood by the table, clad in a long blue smock. He was very short, barely clearing Thurgood's shoulder.

"Ah, Mr. and Mrs. Dalcourt . . ."

"Dalkins!" Thurgood snapped.

"Of course. Sorry. Would you press your palms against this screen?"

"What for?"

"Identification." Dr. Regnan nodded happily as Sylvia complied. "Splendid! And now you, Mr. Dal—kins."

Sighing, Thurgood pressed his hand against the screen, and wished that Dr. Pixie here would get on with it.

"Wonderful. Now please be seated." Dr. Regnan paused. "You realize that once you've completed drug therapy, there should be no obstacle to your qualifying for a divorce, if you still want one."

"Oh, we'll still want one," Thurgood said.

Sylvia glared at him. He remembered that he'd had to work long and hard to convince her that a divorce was really in their best interests. Well, she'd agreed, hadn't she? Even if it had taken a year of arguments and threats to convince her.

"How long does this therapy take, doctor?"

"Thirty days."

"What?" Thurgood was out of his chair and across the room.

"Mr. Dalkins, I must request that you release my arm," Dr. Regnan said pleasantly.

"Thurgood, let go of him." Sylvia's tone was playful. Her kick was not.

"Ouch!"

Thurgood dropped the doctor's arm and began rubbing his own.

The cool sting of a hypo on his neck made him gasp.

"Easy, now," the doctor said. "Just sit down here. You may feel dizzy for a few minutes. Some people do."

Thurgood's world revolved like midnight tri-d video. He was vaguely aware that Sylvia had also received her shot, but that awareness was swamped in the tide of kaleidoscopic images washing over him. The red carpet became a panting tongue eager to swallow him, the white chairs were huge fangs, impaling him and his wife. The doctor's face swam before him, eyes elongated, nose melting. Thurgood tore at his collar; he was dripping with sweat. And freezing.

"T-H-U-R-G-O-O-D?"

Sylvia called his name in a long, slow yodel. It took her about a week to get through all the letters.

Thurgood closed his eyes, feeling the bile beginning to rise from stomach to throat. He fought back the urge to vomit all over his expensive blue eel boots. The blood roared in his ears. Just when he thought he could take no more, the sound receded. Timidly, he opened his eyes.

The room had stopped spinning. Dr. Regnan stood by the door, smiling encouragingly. Thurgood wanted to punch him.

"Is that all?" a shrill voice queried.

It made the hair on the back of Thurgood's neck stand up. Irritated, he turned.

The owner of that awful voice was his wife. He'd never noticed how screechy she was before. And that hair; it looked like somebody had left a bowl of whipped egg whites on her head, streaked with yellow and purple food coloring. And that ridiculous getup she wore; it was at least two sizes too small. Maybe she needed to go on a diet.

"Well, after thirty days, come back and see me," Dr. Regnan said.

Sylvia looked at Thurgood. Her horrified expression indicated that she found him less than appealing. He bristled. How dare she stare at him that way? His suit had cost twelve hundred dollars.

"Mr. Dalkins? Mrs. Dalkins?" The smile vanished from Dr. Regnan's face. "Hmm, this is most irregular. You should be billing and cooing by now." He looked at his watch, then shrugged. "Oh well, give it time. Everybody's physiology is different, and these drugs don't always work immediately."

Then his smile reappeared. "I'll just leave you two to adjust. You know the way out. And I'll see you in thirty days. We'll bill you."

With a wave, he was gone.

Teeth gritted in mutual antagonism, Thurgood and Sylvia gathered themselves up.

On the ride back to the condo, Sylvia corrected his driving three times, criticized the color of the car—and she'd selected that very shade of purple herself—and told him she thought he needed a face lift, even if he was only thirty-nine. Every jibe, every slur, was delivered in that same grating tone of voice. How had he ever survived eight years of it? Thurgood despised her, from the split ends of her overprocessed hair to the acrylic tips of her orange toenails. He couldn't wait to divorce her. He'd call Oslo as soon as they got home and explain the delay.

The first day they spent as far away from each other as possible, he in his study, she in the bedroom, each sulking.

On day two, she made him flan for dessert, which he loved (and which was strictly off his diet) but neglected to tell him she'd spiced it with habanera chilis.

On day seven, he epoxied her amethyst contact lenses (the expensive faceted ones) to their lapis lazuli case.

On day sixteen, she poured full-strength aphrodisiac into his orange juice, lured him into the bedroom, tied him to the waterbed frame with silver cords, and left him there, throbbing in tumescent agony, for forty-eight hours.

On day twenty-two, he strangled her poodle.

On day twenty-five, she microwaved his toupee after first marinating it in green salsa.

On day twenty-eight, he called the stock brokerage where she worked and insulted her boss, his boss, and her boss.

On day twenty-nine, they both called Dr. Regnan.

"Mr. and Mrs. Dalkut . . ."

"Dalkins!"

"Good to see you." The doctor's smile was the same. His blue smock was the same. The only thing that had changed was Thurgood's attitude. Now he wanted to kill the doctor.

"And how are we doing?"

"We are just about five minutes away from committing homicide," Sylvia said sweetly.

The doctor blinked. "Beg pardon?"

"If we hated each other before, it's nothing compared to what we've been feeling over the past month," she explained.

"Real hatred," Thurgood added. "Pure. Undiluted."

"I don't understand," the doctor said. "You say you haven't felt warm or affectionate? Haven't spent long hours in bed, cuddling? No love? No bonding?"

"Try poodle-strangling."

"How odd. Let me check something." The doctor leaned over the deskscreen, muttered to himself, pushed a key, muttered some more. When he turned back, his smile was slightly less incandescent.

"Folks, it's simple," he said. "A case of an honest mistake. I gave you the Agony instead of the Ecstasy."

"What?"

The doctor shrugged. "We keep them on the same shelf, you see, and occasionally this happens. . . ."

"I'll sue!" Thurgood thundered. "I'll own this clinic!" A cool sting at the neck cut him off in mid-howl. A glowing warmth was spreading through his body. Suddenly, he felt better. Much, much better. He didn't want to sue the little doctor. He wanted to hug him. He was a wonderful human being. Thurgood knew it instinctively.

"There we go," Doctor Regnan chirped. "An improvement, yes?"

Thurgood smiled beatifically.

"What's going on here?" Sylvia demanded. She sounded cross, and Thurgood felt his stomach knotting in dread. Then he heard her yelp as the doctor gave her an injection too. A moment later, she was gazing, dewy-eyed, at her husband.

Thurgood thought she looked especially fetching in her red latex dress with the black studs. In fact, it was his favorite out of her entire wardrobe.

"I'll just leave you two alone," the doctor said tactfully. "See you in thirty days."

Neither Thurgood nor Sylvia heard him, so absorbed were they, each in the wonders of the other.

"Oh, Thurgood," she sighed. "Green is such a good color on you. And I'm so glad we decided to get your nose fixed." She gave him a dazzling smile. Her voice was soft, melodic. He felt his heart expand with love.

"Yes, my sweet," he murmured, kissing her hand. "Your taste is exquisite. And I'm so glad you agreed to that breast enhancement. In fact, you look glorious. Let's go home and . . . enjoy each other."

Without another word, they hurried out of the office.

They spent the first day in bed.

They spent the second, third, and fourth days there, too.

On the fifth day, they got up, showered, went out for Polish/Vietnamese sausages, then rushed home and went back to bed.

On the fifteenth day, Thurgood thought that perhaps they ought to call in at their offices, but Sylvia began licking him in that special place again and he forgot what he'd been talking about.

On the twentieth day, Thurgood decided that he needed a depilatory chin treatment, and after all, maybe a little time away from each other was a good idea. Sylvia agreed, and made an appointment for a body facial. Freshly depilatated, Thurgood returned to the condo before his wife and found a message from Oslo blinking on the deskscreen in his study. Guiltily he remembered that in ten days he and Sylvia would be divorced. Maybe he'd better talk to her about cleaning out her dresser . . . but he'd worry about that later. He could hear her at the front door. He hurried to the bedroom to greet her properly.

On the thirtieth day, they were awakened by the door buzzer. Groggily, Thurgood wrapped a black sheet around his waist and opened the door. Dr. Regnan stood on the welcome mat, eyes twinkling, grinning his pixie grin.

"I thought so," he said with satisfaction.

"What are you doing here?" Thurgood asked.

"Just a little house call." Regnan stepped inside. "May I come in?"

"House call?"

Regnan winked. "For special clients only. I see that the bonding drug has been a big hit." He rummaged in a silver pouch hanging from his belt. "Not unusual. Most people like Ecstasy. It works on all but the toughest cases."

"Uh, doctor, about that divorce . . ."

"Oh, you don't talk to me about that part," Dr. Regnan said happily. "That's Section P. I'm just here to give you the antidote."

Thurgood drew back, clutching the silken sheet. "Antidote? What if I don't want it?"

"Thurgood?" Sylvia called from the bedroom. "Poopsie? Who is it?"

"Now just relax, Mr. Dalkins. Nobody *wants* the antidote."

"Then why give it?"

Dr. Regnan chuckled. "Why? First, because nobody would do any work. Everything would come to a grinding halt as we all sat around, lost in the wonder of our significant others. More importantly, the drug is unstable in the long term and slow to metabolize out of your system. After thirty days, it can start to affect your serotonin levels. Give you a lifetime of migraines. We don't want that, now, do we?"

With a smile, Dr. Regnan placed a hypo against Thurgood's neck. There was the familiar sting. Thurgood waited. And waited. After five minutes, he felt absolutely no other effect. No chills. No sweats. No paranoia about slavering monsters waiting in the pantry to nibble him as hors d'oeuvres. Even Dr. Regnan's nose looked the same.

"Shouldn't I feel some change?" Thurgood asked.

"It's very subtle," Regnan said. "You'll just feel more inclined to get back to work, start taking care of the rest of your business. Now, where's your lovely wife?"

Thurgood sat by the bedside, watching Sylvia sleep. She had started yawning right after Dr. Regnan administered the antidote to her.

Fondly Thurgood watched her snore in the yellow glow of the bedside clock.

I'll tell her I don't want the divorce tomorrow, he thought. What a good idea the drug-bonding therapy was.

Happily, he crawled into bed beside his beloved.

When he awoke, he was alone. The clock read nine-thirty.

"Sylvia?"

Silence.

He wandered groggily into the study. She'd left him a message: *Left early for work. Didn't want to wake you. See you tonight.*

Good, he thought. Back on schedule. And it's time for a shower.

The needles of the waterspray felt exhilarating on his back. Drying off, Thurgood admired himself in the mirror. Muscle tone was still good. He could pass for thirty-five, easy.

He selected a silver-gray suit and, feeling daring, a teal tie to set off the yellow shirt.

When he got to the car lot, his redheaded secretary greeted him with a relieved smile.

"Mr. Dalkins! I thought you were still on vacation."

"What's wrong, Greta?"

She wrinkled her freckled nose at him.

"We're swamped. Mr. Thomas is in the hospital with Rudolf Bing syndrome."

"Again?" Thurgood shook his head. "How many psychotics did he marry this time?"

"Fourteen, before they caught him." Greta's green eyes twinkled. She scanned her deskscreen. "I've relayed the most important messages to your memo board."

"Thanks." He turned toward his office.

"Oh, Mr. Dalkins?"

"Yes?"

"We've been receiving urgent messages for you from somebody in Oslo."

Thurgood felt his cheeks burning. "Uh, tell her I'm dead. No, wait. Just tell her I'm in a meeting and I'll return her call as soon as I can. Then kill the memo."

Greta looked confused. She squinted at him. "You mean you don't want to receive any of these messages?"

"Right."

"Whatever you say, Mr. D." She winked. "You're the boss."

Wearily, Thurgood pressed his hand against the door lock. The door sprang open and he slumped into the house. First day back at work, and already he was exhausted.

"There you are," Sylvia said. She flounced by him in a ruffled orange minidress. "Listen, the movers are coming in fifteen minutes."

"Movers?" Thurgood sat down hard in the red chair by the door.

"Come on," she said irritably. "Don't play games with me. I've arranged for another place to live until the divorce is final."

"Final? Wait a minute," Thurgood said. "I wanted to talk to you about that."

Sylvia paused, hands full of clothing. "Look, we've been through it all before. It's too bad the drug therapy delayed our plans, but maybe that was a blessing anyway. It gave me time to find a place."

"Where?"

"I'll be staying with Don Parker."

"Your boss?"

Sylvia smiled. "Sure. Why not?"

"But he's almost fifty!"

"There's something to be said for maturity," she said, and disappeared into the bedroom.

Desperately, Thurgood followed her.

"But the drug therapy," he said. "Didn't it change you? Don't you feel better?"

"Of course," she said, folding shirts and putting them into a suitcase. "I feel like I've been on vacation for a month."

"That's not what I mean," Thurgood said. "Look, if it's a matter of a few gray hairs, I can get a new toupee. A silver one."

"Don't be ridiculous." Sylvia laughed. "You wanted the divorce. You brow-beat me into it. Now you've gotten what you asked for. You should be happy." She sealed the suitcase. "Don't forget, you've got my replacement on ice in Oslo."

"The hell with Oslo," Thurgood cried. "I want you, Sylvia. I'll do whatever you want. You like old? I'll get old? You like bald? I'll have the rest of my head depilatated. You like women? I'll get a sex change. . . ."

"Thurgood, you're getting hysterical."

The doorbell rang.

"That must be the movers," she said.

Thurgood followed her to the door. Two burly women in yellow overalls were waiting outside.

"Mrs. Dalkins?" said the bigger of the two.

"Come in, ladies."

With sinking heart, Thurgood watched his wife designate which pieces of furniture were to be moved. In an hour, the condo was half-empty. Numbly, he watched Sylvia prepare to leave. She was golden, beautiful. She was going.

"Thurgood, it's been fun." She hugged him once. "Call me sometime."

"Sylvia—!"

Blowing a kiss from her purple acrylic fingertips, she waved fondly and closed the door behind her. The only woman he would ever really love was gone.

He sat, slumped, in the darkened room. The phone light began to blink on his screen. Oslo calling, he thought. After a very long while he leaned forward and said hello.

If, as purists like to maintain, one of science fiction's prime roles is to plunge its readers into strange and challenging new terrains of the imagination, then K. Hernández-Brun has provided a classic example of the art—which will catapult you, without benefit of roadmap or Baedeker, into an astonishingly visualized and tantalizing realm of the utterly strange.

Its author, who has spent much time in England and currently lives in the Basque country of northern Spain, was born in Colombia in 1947, and has degrees in anthropology, linguistics, and social studies. This is his first published science fiction story, though he reports that he is at work on a sequence of other stories set in the same mysterious and wondrous era.

K.
HERNÁNDEZ-BRUN

He was a short colored man. He was a very degenerate man; yes. So short that he could have been mistaken for an hocateris, an untouchipes. Nonetheless he was undoubtedly one of them: Ociranthropos: Ordipes. More precisely, he was an hovioris: hair bordering on the color of aubergine, but with unmistakable violet eyes. He belonged to the lowest, the last of the seven castes of Ordipes: Zasipes, the most tyrannical and despotic of the Ordipes. The caste which supplies the lowest ranks in the command chains, such as foremen, section heads and patrol commanders in the SEPIS—the "sepes" as people call them. But that defective was very degenerate, to tell the truth.

He had one complete arm . . . the right one, and the other was cut off a little above the elbow.

As soon as he saw me coming, he approached me very purposefully while trying to reach a paper bag he was carrying under the armpit of his severed limb.

When I was about to tell him, "Sorry, I can't" (I thought he was going to ask me for some money), he quickly returned to the place where he had been lurking. Turning his back he picked up something from the ground, which from his movements I suspected he was struggling to put in his mouth.

I could not tell with absolute certainty whether the rest of the severed arm was in that bundle of newspapers tied across his chest like a VIP's sash. It could be that I clearly noticed it when he approached me, or that I only suspected it then, and later on I corroborated it. It also could have been that when he turned his back to me revealing the string that crossed his back diagonally, pressing the short-sleeved robe against his purple skin, I thought it then, and now I state it as a matter of fact. Neither could I explain why, instead of speeding up and getting away, I just stood on the pavement looking at what seemed to be a pub (OS-JIM's), in which several rows of customers could be seen amusing themselves in front of individual TVs. Some of them were rather desperately and others very calmly sucking a red liquid which contained small crystal balls (or they could have been bubbles) coming through a complicated system of connected rods to a twisted crystal straw.

Because of the bicolored rhombus on the sign, anyone could tell it was one of our places, for Sustipes, although its owner was for sure an hoberoris or a musmiris, fourth along the command chains and responsible for the entertainment of the populace. The customers were all Ocaris, that is, hocarades and muargadis, most probably servants in Distribution Centers or subordinates in the Points of Command in the sector. A few Ocarrise (carrying bags in which they take belongings and lunch to their workplaces) clustered around the screens. They were only watching, of course.

What drew my attention was that as some customers sucked the liquid they turned a dusky red while others changed intermittently from a brilliant blue to greengreenishyellowishpurple. Apart from Ocarrise, the rest seemed quite content.

The only employee in sight, a cashier, was pedaling while pissing himself with laughter as he operated a small computer, a commonplace computer to tell the truth, which received the orders, passed the bills to each customer and regulated the amount of liquid passing through the straws.

Just as I wondered if there could be any link between the programs the customers were watching or the games they were playing and the color they were acquiring (or was it due to what they were drinking?), the small pale purple man with the bandolier-like strapped arm caught up with me again.

"One of these for one thousand and the two for one thousand and five hundred," he said, emptying out at an astonishing speed the contents of the paper bag onto the palm of his hand which, contrary to what one would expect, was a completely normal hand although slightly discolored.

He executed four movements, but so rapidly that they seemed to be one. First, he took the bag from under his armpit, and with his teeth (more exactly, two bony arches encrusted in his gums but not separated like teeth), he held the bag from underneath, then he emptied its contents onto the palm of his hand and immediately, in a precise swing of his head, he righted the empty bag to its original place. I would've liked the time to have watched this sequence in reverse, but I gave up the chance. I shook my head, reinforcing it with a "no, thanks," and quickened my pace to indicate my total disinterest in his offer.

To tell the truth, I was getting nervous. The sepes of the SXI were hunting the unlicensed pavement sellers like mad (to claim the twenty-five bonds in reward given by the Distributive Association for Popular Benefit-PES for each illegal seller killed). Also it was highly probable that someone who knew me had passed by and seen me in deals with an individual who, instead of being cautious, seemed more interested in being labeled a rat (speaking in a deliberately suspicious manner and showing me his hand against his stomach, not to conceal his actions but in such a way as to attract the attention of passersby so that they could see what he was offering me).

The hovioris, however, as though he had been fully informed about what I had gone to buy, did not give up with that triple negative but speeded up his pace till he finally caught up with me again. Then, at the same time as he addressed me very aggressively, "Make an offer!," he thrust out a hand, in the hollow of which he softly held a pair of indigo eyes: Ocindoris' eyes.

403

I acted as though it had nothing to do with me and kept on going. But the little man, without dropping behind, attacked me again with a string of short but clever sales chatter:

"Take them! Hold them in your own hands and look at them without any obligation! . . . They are real eyes, see for yourself! . . . I plucked them out myself less than half an hour ago. They are still warm: touch them and you'll see. . . . They are eyes of muinadis: muniris'. They belonged to a muiniris who was walking along with her daughter. . . . I plucked them out without damaging them in the least. They have not the slightest scratch, hocinis. Look at them! . . . They are fresh eyes! . . . I'm selling two for the price of one! . . . If you buy them, I'll tell you the place where they are regenerated, assembled and connected for only five hundred. . . ." Immediately, as if he were dealing with someone from the other side of the wall, he lowered his voice to say, "They are muniris', hociris' women, Ordipes!" Then nudging me with his elbow, he emphasized their color. "Eyes of muinadis, hocinis . . . Ocindoris!"

"Sorry, hovis, I have no money," I repeated, shrugging and holding up my hands to emphasize my refusal. I quickened my pace and zigzagged across the pavement, intending to lose myself in the current of the crowd. I took advantage of a traffic jam caused by a trafrob that had gone out of control, and crossed the road. I continued walking on the other side without slowing down till making sure I had left the hovioris completely far behind. However, I still continued running so fast (not exactly run-running but more like jog-trotting) that I ran over one of those alkalivores of permanent smile who though it is true they no longer upset Ordipes (especially Tipes and Zasipes) and do not break the Lir anymore, they have certainly become an obstacle for pedestrians; like that lot of nerels getting entangled in one's feet and tearing themselves to pieces everywhere for a bond or a scrap of food from the rubbish bins (but the alkalivores, what are they going to ask for?). A dolled-up muamiris throwing out her hand to pin a badge on my shirt (SAVE A CAT) was left, as people say, spinning like a top.

To regain my breath, and glancing behind to check whether the hovioris was still after me, I stopped by a small group of people who because of their genial air and also the cause they were promoting (NO TO TREATMENT WITH MEGOCREPA FOR GRIPES-A, DISAFFECTED AND MILITANTS), I knew immediately they were students of the Jesuitic University.

Most of them were Ocadamis, and around them, forever in attendance, were three or four ociranthropos from the highest caste: Ocrussoris. That is, Ordipes from the first caste, Tipes, the only caste entitled to wear, besides their own color, garments of the color of the Ocadamis, with skin and hair as white as snow, as people say.

I put my hand in my pocket with the serious intention of giving them a contribution (a modest one, to tell the truth) but an inixia, with a complexion so white-white that it seemed to be of replastic, deigned to tell me with her crystalline smile:

"We are not asking for contributions, hocinis; it's just to spread disquiet." Next, graciously moving her head while fixing back her long white hair into a delicate cat-tail, she added by way of explanation, ". . . we are students of sophilopesics."

I immediately seized the opportunity to impress an inixia who was also a student at the Jesuitic. So, making the obligatory bow, I asked permission to talk and said:

"Who am I but an hocaris, to address myself to Ocadamis and Ocrussoris. . . ." and pointing at the banner, I added, ". . . but the wording after gripes-a is a tautology."

At this, she cast her eyes over me searchingly. Then, looking at the banner and with chin held high, she looked at me contemplatively, smiling a half smile.

At the age of almost twenty years, I had never before been close to or talked with iociris or with iniris, much less looked at from so near or spoken out to an inixia of the Archetipes. But she was the most beautiful inixia I could ever have imag-

405

ined. She was between fifteen and seventeen. Her eyes were like two of the purest brilliants. Crystallines. And if that was not enough, she smiled at me. Even so, I was really scared and I began to think I had tried to be too smart.

Three Ocrussoris (two hocrusades and one mugiris) also came closer and began to stare at me quizzically. But no matter how friendly and smiling two hocrusades might be, who, how should I say, do they not make afraid? Because of the heat, or their white robes, the redness of their skin was enhanced. Only their brilliance made the eyes distinguishable. But the hair over the white robes blazed. As if on fire.

"A tautology? Is that the same as saying a petitio principae?"

I felt myself, I do not know how to describe it, between fear and elation. Satisfied. I'm not sure. I only knew I had scored a point and that I was very excited. It even occurred to me that there might be a patrol around getting uneasy because I was too close to an inixia. However, as one sometimes does, instead of giving her a straight answer, I bowed my head and, withdrawing, I said:

"There I leave you that disquiet."

Such arrogance could well have cost me my head. But I was jubilant. I had been less than a couple of feet from an inixia, an Archetipes. She had talked to me, smiled at me, and even . . . well, perhaps I should not say. No one would ever believe me. The worst or the best of it is that, as Ar-Rob says, only the Lir, the height, color of skin, eyes, blood and hair, the castes and the sepes, differentiate us. For the rest, we are all equal. But maybe the legend is true, that before the Great Fire (from which ashes still sometimes fall), all races of ociranthropos mixed freely, including with the Ocateris. However, because muniris and even munixadis preferred to pair with hocatades (from which latter mix, the legend says, all we sustipes descend, including the discolored Ocarrise employed in domestic service and glasshouses), the hociris, led by the hocrusades, declared war on the hocatades. Though it might have been possible for the Ocateris to win that war had it not been for the profitless treachery of the Azurboris. But having been defeated, they were expelled to the tercalx where, if not killed by droughts, heat or untimely snowfalls, rats and flying cockroaches would exterminate them. Since then, apart from capturing them for the Circus (in truth, for throwing them to the beasts) and as forced labor in the mines, any kind of contact with Ocateris is punished with the suppression of life, and this applies to us, sustipes, excluded forever from positions of leadership or command. And if we were not also expelled to the tercalx, it was because the Ociranthropos needed someone to keep their machines and businesses going and to do their dirty work. But the Azurboris came off worst. While appearing to be neutral, they had made a secret pact with the hociris and had, themselves, been the main instigators of the War of the Muniris, which I think was the name given to that war.

Azurboris had planned for Ociranthropos and Ocateris to exterminate, or at least decimate, each other so as to make it easy for them to gain absolute supremacy in the SEPI. As had existed before the Great Fire.

But their plans backfired, because after expelling the hocatades together with their muatadis, the hociris turned against their former allies ("Once a traitor, always a traitor," OCTer), using the same argument that the Azurboris, masters in sophistry, had employed in persuading them to fight the War of the Muniris: the Defense of the Lir, or "the Darraga," which is the name given by the populace.

They were fine ones to talk! Azurboris (hozurbades and muzuradis) who, according to the legend, were incapable of bringing before the Radamis a sole hozurboris or muzuriris who was not mixed race. Pure. Male or female purebred.

Strange beings, the Azurboris. People say that any of them might have had hair like that of the Ocateris, Ocamoris or Ocarrise; eyes like those of the Ocurdoris or Osmaroris; and the red skin of the Ocrussoris. (Although most of them had skin midway between the color of the Ocadamis and that of the Ocrussoris, but with eyes which could have belonged to any or no caste at all, so infinitely were they mixed.)

All of them were exterminated in defense of the Lir, or "the darraga," as the populace call it.

The punishment inflicted on the Ocadamis, ancestral guards of the Lir, was not of a lesser kind. They kept their titles—and yet reign, but do not govern. The worst is that they were . . . but then, how do they reproduce themselves if their hocades are impotent and their munixadis frigid and sterile? For they do exist. There are only a few hocades and a few munixadis, yes. But there they are. And the munixadis are so beautiful!

When I turned my head, the inixia under the banner was still looking at me, or trying not to lose sight of me. Did I disquiet her?

Suddenly, an avalanche of tramps and adnerelabs separated us for good (sun and chemistry create them, and they give me . . .). Almost all were one-armed, one-legged and perhaps earless (one couldn't tell because of their long hair). Some of them had no arms, legs or hands at all. They were helped by their companions. One of the tramps was pulling a platform of a little more than a meter in length with ball-bearing wheels, creaking under the load of the platform trundling along a few centimeters above the ground. The load: a human trunk with only the head, but eyeless and earless. The mouth was wide open, screaming for something. One of the tramps, a woman heavily covered in rags despite the heat, approached the oddity with a bottle. When the tramp holding the rope caught sight of me looking at the platform, he made an obscene gesture and shouted something vulgar, but straightaway changed his demeanor and held out his hand, begging for money. He was an horioris. Or more precisely, he had once been an horioris of the third caste: Hipes, third in the command chains and responsible for printing and controlling the bonds. But now, together with his companions, all of them ordipes, they were nothing more than remnants of ociranthropos begging from an hocaris. I pretended not to see his outstretched hand, but I felt a shiver and I suddenly remembered the insistent hovioris chasing after me with those two eyes in. . . . Or perhaps what made me grow cold was to remember Ar-Vic, as I watched the tramp's eye socket dripping horribly. . . . And to think that because he is Ocamoris he can live fifty years longer than me, for so it is ordained in the Lir. Even if I had been loaded with bonds, I would not have given him one!

I do not know why the thought crossed my mind to see the small hovioris come my way again. To tell the truth, I was not thinking of making him an offer. For I had only two hundred and fifty bonds, and had I offered this, for just one eye, he certainly would've insulted me, and there is not a thing you can do because with those kind of people you get nowhere.

The color of the eye was not a problem. As everybody knows, in the year 506 the Rebellion of the ClimbSights obtained some concessions in that respect. The Ocarrise, it is well known, won the right to have a violet eye. We, the Ocaris, up to one indigo, and if we could afford it, the two of them violet. But dress in those colors, no! The Lir expressly prohibits it. Only ociranthropos, that is, Ordipes, are entitled to exhibit the color of a caste lower than its own. The color of a higher caste, no. Unless he or she is Ocrussoris, licensed also to wear white (though they can never be transplanted with crystalline eyes like those of the Ocadamis). That is the Lir. But we, Ocaris, who do not belong to any caste, what inferior color are we to exhibit? The dark color of the Ocarrise? And for the Ocarrise, which one? Only the Ocateris are lower, and they are colorless. Unless carbon and night have color. Besides, the Ocateris wear hardly any clothes. They go almost naked in the tercalx, wearing rat's fur around the loins during the day, and at night they are numbed by the cold wind or buried under a sudden snowfall. And who would want an Ocateris' eye, colorless? A sightless eye, yes!!! More than one Ocarrise in domestic service, who work and save a lifetime to afford a real Ovioris' eye (or at least a Barraquer with incorporated myoptisensor), end up with an artificial one. Or with two light brown eyes that only enable them to work in Production Units or workshops where the owners do not accept sustipes with darker eyes or skin, even though they could not be accused of having the slightest bit of Ocateris in them. A sightless eye would also be acceptable to those ocaris supporters of the ClimbSights who to affiliate with the party must have at least one real violet eye and the other artificial; or one indigo, completely useless but colorful. Also, those of the iociris and iniris who are such rebels that . . . And what if I had bought one of the eyes from the hovioris and it turned out to be an imitation, and worse, an imitation made by the NIID? I would have lost my bonds like a fool. Because one cannot say to those little people, "Right, I'll buy them, but first let's get them examined by someone who knows." Or perhaps they agree and take us to an accomplice who immediately certifies the eyes are real when they are not (as happened in the case of Op-Pach-Pich with that brain transplant which now keeps him talking . . . well, why add to the gossip). But the truth is that I noticed several suspicious details: in the first place, I am sure that the eyes had not belonged to the same person. Although they had been roughly washed or dusted with some sort of powder with the deliberate intention of disguising the difference, one, it is true, was an ocindoris' eye, or of a muinadis, but the other seemed to be an Ovioris'. Yes, it was an eye of Ovioris. And now I even think they were different in size! The hovioris mentioned, among other things, an inanis walking along with her mother, or a mother with her daughter, which amounts to the same thing, and it could be that an eye came from each of them (though there are inanis with large eyes and muiniris with small eyes), but that is very unlikely because surely . . . well, it could've been that he had already sold the other two. . . . No, no! In any event it's not possible, for a muiniris must only pair with an hociris of her own cast, unless she wants to be eliminated along with her mate. How is it then that being a muiniris, she was able to produce a violet-eyed inivis? An inanis, yes. But an inivis— impossible! In any event, one thing is true: whatever color

410

those eyes might have been, that hovioris intended to cheat me. He said that he had removed them less than an hour before. And that couldn't be true! The bag in which they were, although damp (maybe from his own perspiration) bore no fresh bloodstains, nor dry blood anywhere, neither did the eyes. However, there were many more signs suggesting that the small man intended to cheat me at all costs. For instance, that hovioris could use only one hand because his other arm was hanging, completely useless, across his chest, and neither in the stump, which I could clearly see, nor at either end of the bundle was there any screw, rivet or anything else indicating that he could've assembled it himself had he needed to use it. . . . Besides, it was feasible that the wrapped arm was not his but stolen, and the reason he was carrying it was precisely to give the impression that it was his, thereby taking advantage of the circumstance that he had one arm missing. How then was he able to remove those eyes—with only one hand? Impossible! Supposing, for example, he had taken the knife in one hand, or rather, with *the* hand (because the idea of plucking them out with his fingers is revolting), how was he then to immobilize his victims? (Like the nigladis do after toppling their contenders, or in the way of the ratback-riders in the Circus?) Or it could be that they were unconscious, yes, because the eyes he showed me were not damaged or scratched or anything and it was clear they had been cleanly removed. Or maybe it was that he had accomplices. But there still remains the difficulty in removing someone's eyes with only one hand and without damaging them . . . with a spoon perhaps? But in which case one of the victims at least . . . or both of them forcibly would've had . . .

I stopped thinking on the subject when I realized I was only rationalizing the fact that I hadn't offered the hovioris the two hundred and fifty bonds in my possession for at least one of the eyes (Make an offer! Make an offer! he insisted, beginning to get angry while trying to put them into my . . . my . . .). Because the truth is that I only need . . . But no . . . but how did he know? How could that little man have guessed that I was just on my way to buy Ar-Vic an eye as last week he had been assaulted, and because he had no money on him (he's always broke), well, he got stabbed. "I've been knifed," he said on arriving home and pressing the gash with his two hands, which looked as if they were encased in molten lead, covered as they were in coagulated blood.

"This will teach you not to go around with an empty money bag, you sonovawhore." Ar-Vic recounted the muggers' threat uttered while they cut off his ears as if he were a rat in the Circus. On top of that they tore out one of his eyes!

Fortunately, he had no tail; otherwise he would've been finished off completely. Because take him around the arena they did . . . and how they took him around! They not only robbed him of his clothes and NID, leaving him naked, unprotected, and without the knowledge of who he was, but also abused him from top to bottom, kicked him inside and out and pissed upon him—just to be vicious—because what resistance would Ar-Vic put up, when he is a pacifist, an ultrapacifist? He is a threefold OV. He's one of those who are "out and out opposed to any form of violence." Which is why they're attacked from all sides. For understandably, they are against the hunting of unlicensed pavement sellers, the beatings at the uneven hours, and Circus spectacles ending only when one of the contenders is killed. Likewise it is even understandable why they would oppose the nigladis, incited by the Militants, occasionally striking down a single sepes. But they carry their pacifism to far. How could they expect the populace to support them when it is obvious that they want to shut down the Circus, without saying so, of course? But is this not their intention when opposing safari expeditions in search of rats and nigladis for the spectacles? And I also think they go too far when they oppose the trapping of hocatades and muatadis for working in the mines and transporting the minerals to the city walls. Crossing hundreds of kilometers of charred land, black as the skin of the ocateris, where there is no shelter from the sun, a sudden snowfall or an electric tempest. And where there is no escape from packs of starving rats, or a cloud of flying cockroaches capable of devouring a six-hundred-kilogram rat in minutes (as told by the hopades returning from the obligatory service in the Sepes). For it's a fact: If there are no Ocateris to work in the mines, then the first who have to do it are the hopades; after them, us. It has always been so. First, the Ocateris: hocatades and muatadis without distinction of sex, then, Ocarrise; and after them, us —Ocaris. I'd like to see Op-Tognign or Ar-Magn or Op-Guev, sword in hand, facing a seven-hundred-kilogram rat in the Circus. And what does Ar-Vic think the rats should be fed on? For I suspect that he is for sure going around pinning on badges in favor of the cats. It was because of his idiocies that he lost his eye and ears. And he would've lost more things but for the luck of a taxi driver passing by who, bar in hand, drove the pests away before they finished him off. Because Ar-Vic himself prompted them to rob him of more parts. How on earth could he have been so naive to tell them (beg them) to remove a foot instead of the eye? Only because he thought he could conceal its loss with an artificial foot if not a real one, since anyway it's difficult to tell the difference. Does he not know that you cannot bargain with those kind of people, because they immediately lop off what they can . . . and gouge out the rest, for being such an idiot? With the scrambling for organs there is today . . .

"We're leaving you one eye," the muggers told him. "For what there is to see, one eye is enough."

Thinking on these matters, I reached the first quadrangle where distribution-acquisition businesses take place. Just at that moment a patrol of sepes of the S-XVI, exhibiting their smart seven-striped uniforms, were lining up the jobless, leftelectuals, climbsights and other gripes from the Sector to present them with the beatings which announced that it was three o'clock in the afternoon.

Holding my Normalized Identity Document and passes for Quadrangles, Sectors and Subsectors in my hand (although I'm not a gripes and carry no distinction or mark of one, nor do I have eyes or colors that I'm not entitled to—it's better to be safe than sorry), marching to the sound and beat of the knocks and blows, I quickly passed where the usual recitation of the Major Code is repeated, on every uneven hour with the floggings ("The Lir is P. P ES. The Lir is SEP. P is P of Ocadamis. Ocadamis uphold the Lir. Ocadamis are Archetipes. The castes are seven. Seven and only seven castes there are. Castes are Ordipes. Ocrussoris are Tipes. Ocanoris are Bipes. Ocamoris are Hipes. Osmaroris are Lipes. Ocurdoris are Bosipes. Ocindoris are Sipes. Ovioris are Zasipes. The Lir is P. P ES. The Lir is. . . . Ocadamis are all of the Ociranthropos and none of the Ociranthropos. Ocadamis, of crystalline eyes, and white skin, blood and hair, are the SEPI and from before the SEPI. Ocrussoris, of red blood, skin, hair and eyes, are first in the SEPI. Ocanoris, of . . . Ovioris, of violet blood, skin, hair and eyes, are seventh and last in the SEPI. Who is not in the SEPI serves the SEPI. Who is not in the SEPI is not purebred. The unpure race has no place in the SEPI. The SEP is the Lir. The Lir is P. P ES. The Lir is: White is for Ocadamis; thou shalt not wear white. Red is for Ocrussoris; thou shalt not wear red. Between Ocadamis and Ocrussoris there is no caste nor race nor color. Orange is for Ocanoris; thou shalt not wear orange. Between Ocrussoris and Ocanoris there is no caste nor race nor color. Yellow is for Ocamoris; thou shalt not wear yellow. Between Ocanoris and Ocamoris there is no caste nor race nor color. Green is for . . . Ocadamis shall live out their natural life. Thou shalt not curtail the life of an hozuoris nor of a munixis before their natural time. Ocrussoris shall live for one hundred and ten years. Thou shalt not end the life of an hogoris nor of a mugiris before its allotted time. Ocanoris shall live one hundred years. Thou shalt not end the life of an holaoris nor of a muliris before its allotted time. Ocamoris shall live ninety years. Thou shalt not end the life of an horioris nor of a muamiris before its allotted time. Osmaroris shall live eighty years. Thou shalt not end the life of an hoberoris nor of a musmiris before its allotted time. Ocurdoris shall live seventy years. Thou shalt not end the life of an hourdinoris nor of a muriris before its allotted time. Ocindoris shall live sixty years. Thou shalt not end the life of an hoindoris nor of a muiniris before its al—").

Without checking my pace, I bypassed the small semimobile businesses with their junk displayed on crates, carts and normalized walls. I next passed the subsector with its immobile businesses of the same kind, property of the vepes S, T and G, and finally, I came to that interminable subsector with garments and human parts that are, who knows, second- . . . or third-hand.

At first I entered the shops, inquiring as though only casually interested, but after visiting a few places I got straight to the point, as I was beginning to get nervous. It's true I had all the obligatory passes with me, but the one for the Multicolor Zone was due to expire at seven, and to get back to my zone I would have to cross the V sector, unless I hired a taxi to make a detour. For I had almost certainly missed the last "subca," and I didn't want problems with the Ultras, least of all with the hourus of the Pure Party. It is not that I'm afraid of them, only that I don't want any problems. Not even the hogus and hovious, the most fanatical among the "pepes," have ever scared me, no sir. But neither did I have a coat with me for when it would get cold. Last night and the night before, the temperature dropped below zero, and if I was still out there by the time it got late . . .

It was almost six-thirty and I was still going into distriacquis. I probably went into more than a thousand of those businesses where, if you don't find what you're looking for, it is because what you're looking for no longer exists. The problem was not that I found no eyes, but that the money I had was not enough to buy even an eyelash, as was put to me by a shop assistant.

Prices are the same everywhere; from small businesses specializing in the matter to the huge multistory distriacquis buildings occupying almost an entire block. And not only were the distribution prices fixed, but so were the payments for acquisitions (covered by a "redistribution pact"), as I

415

proved when pretending I wanted to pawn a finger (the mere thought of parting with an eye terrifies me).

It was as if all the loan sharks (some of them displaying pianists' hands, covered in gold rings with precious stones and held in place by original assembling mechanisms) had come to some sort of agreement, or had a price list learned by heart. And they also had the same excuses for not offering any discount: taxes, unfair competition from clinics, eye banks and pirate businesses of the same kind which transplant onto the client parts stolen from himself and bought, back door, from organ traffickers . . . big business, excuses about harassment from the sepes of Section XVI, who threaten to seize *the merchandise*, "leaving us with no means of working," the cut they had to hand over to the seven-striped ones who, according to the pawnbrokers, seem to be partners in the business, though without contributing anything, of course. And on and on went the excuses for not giving me a single bond discount. And between complaint and complaint, they hit out against the "unfair competition" and the "sonsovarat of the Section sixteen."

I decided to set off for my zone having acquired only the two ears (slightly large; informer's type ears. Anyway . . .). My balls were beginning to hurt from so much walking around. However, passing through the Multicolor Zone, I found the solution to the problem of the eye. Out of curiosity I looked at the stalls of the GRIPES-A of positive reaction who, satisfactorily normalized, exhibiting their own colors and natural eyes corresponding to skin and hair color, and also equipped with their respective licenses, now dedicate themselves to distribute home-produced crafts and imitation jewelry, both original and that copied by the NIID. They, naturally, also distribute barraquer eyes; imitations, of course, but so good that it is difficult to distinguish them from the originals, as they have a dirm-op-sensor which enables the false eye to follow the movements of the real eye. Ar-Vic, I thought, is so fatuous that he will not mind at all if I get him a false eye only good for covering the hole left by the muggers. And no sooner will he have obtained his new NID (for which purpose we have already contacted the appropriate intermediary), he'll return to work displaying that subordinate false smile, his imitation AR-Trox gray robe and the infinite vacuiti of the hocaris. Providing the zasipes, the surly zasipes in charge of his section, with no grounds for accusing him of being a Climb-Sight sympathizer. Neither could any of the conceited muargadis in the office nor iniris in the street possibly say that he has only one eye or any physical defect in sight.

For sure, I thought, he'll be more displeased with the teasing of Op-Pant and Vi-Har when they discover, or I tell them, that he has been given a woman's eye, albeit an Ordipes eye. Moreover, I thought too, why highlight the matter further, since from all points of view and whichever way you look at it, the muggers were right: For what there is to see, one eye is enough.

Damian Kilby was born in Enugu, Nigeria, in 1961, but has lived in the United States most of his life. During his college days he planned to become a psychotherapist, but that vocational plan seems to have gone by the boards in favor of a career in writing.

He says that this sleekly written tale of life in alien captivity is his first published story. That seems hard to believe, considering its accomplished craftsmanship, but it seems only courteous to take his claim at face value. It'll be interesting to see what sort of fiction he's able to turn out once he's had a little experience at it.

1

DANIEL'S LABYRINTH

DAMIAN
KILBY

A snapshot. A wordless moment filed in my memory. Marie—my wife—is facedown on the street, her legs stiff, her arms twisted awkwardly. Her right hand still clutches at the revolver. Look, the lighting is dark gray. The grainy fall of snow is heavy. Look closely and see the darker shadows around Marie's head. I know this is blood staining the gray snow. And I am in the picture too. Daniel, the husband. My head is thrown back and my mouth is stretched open. I am probably howling into the surrounding silence, cursing nonsense into the sky.

Some memories work this way. My mind recreates only a single frame of action, leaving me to figure out the context and emotions or make up dialogue if I want to. Sometimes memory lets me down, holding back too many details from my own life. Other times one snapshot is all I can take.

There are some details worth noting while I still have this particular picture out. One: it is snowing but the scene takes place in Virginia, USA, near the end of August. Two: the snow is very dirty before it touches the ground. Three: the .38 in Marie's fist is my gun.

I can only guess the nuances of feeling I experienced standing over her body. What I do know is that I betrayed Marie in more ways than one.

2

Here is another snapshot from later the same day. The small figure in the foreground is me. I believe I have been running aimlessly for a long time. But now I am stopped, staring at the lights glaring through the nearly black snowstorm—the lights which fill most of this picture.

Surely I could not have guessed at what those lights meant. Did I realize that something huge was hovering up in the sky or did I imagine it to be an outpost of surviving civilization, electric power somehow intact?

This is the last picture from a sequence. A moment later the planetary probe scooped me up, rendered me unconscious and swept me away from planet Earth. But those are facts I put together much later. I was thirty-one years old then. Years have since passed, though I can't be sure how many. Five? Ten? Fifteen?

Looking closer at my image, I see I was holding the revolver which I must have pried from Marie's fingers. Was I thinking of killing myself or defending myself? Had I, at this point, given up hope?

3

I betrayed my wife just a few hours before the end of the world. I came home that evening still sticky with the scent of another woman but Marie didn't seem to notice. My excuse —that I'd stayed late phoning the company's West Coast sales reps—was all prepared. She remained curled up on the couch with a mystery novel, the TV ignored, flickering and babbling over in the far corner. She often slipped deep into her reading and that night she barely lifted her head for a hello. The part of me that was waiting for her to ask questions just kept waiting.

The emergency broadcast blared from the tube, warning against panic. Then the sirens started. We heard distant explosions as we climbed down into our basement. I carried a jug of cider and a loaf of bread grabbed from the fridge. Marie clung to a bottle of grapefruit juice and her novel. All the lights winked out.

I remember Marie whispering, "Thank God we never had children."

We sat in the dark and listened. The sirens went dead with the lights. I thought I could hear the murmur of humanity for miles around. Then the wind came. We listened to it batter through the walls above. We heard all the objects that had filled our life clatter and smash. Finally the whole house collapsed. A section of the basement ceiling caved in, kicking up plenty of dust and pelting us with debris.

The wind passed on and we pressed close, waiting in the dark. For a good while a single thought—that I should have taken a shower before coming home to Marie—circled persistently around the inside of my head.

4

I didn't know I was on board a giant spaceship. I didn't know the radiation was being washed from my body, sick cells replaced, all germs and disease expelled. There was nothing for me to see, hear or smell. Time was endless and motionless. I did feel slight movements against my flesh but there was no frame of reference for me to interpret these events. I imagine it was like a flashback to the beginning of life, inside a womb.

Time began anew when the things that had been molded to my body lifted away. Still all my experiences were out of any context. I stood, bare feet pressed into a soft floor, blinking into shades of red and blue light, breathing heavily against a thick atmosphere. I caught sight of slinky-armed machines receding from me, sinking into far-off walls. The walls sealed up, now revealing only a seamless blue facade.

I was in a damn big room, at least the size of a high school gym. The red ceiling looked three stories high. At the far end of the chamber I spied two green pillars, except I understood they couldn't be pillars since they were moving to and fro and swaying slightly. I might have guessed that these were living creatures, especially when I saw one thrust out a spindly five-jointed arm and touch one of the walls.

I heard a faraway voice say, "You are whole now," but a moment later I had trouble believing I'd heard anything.

The green pillar-things left the room. I couldn't tell how. They vanished through one of the walls.

There was a pile of white clothes on the dull red-colored floor in front of me. Here was something I could understand. Without pause I began to get dressed. Trousers, shirt and thin-soled shoes. They all fit well, though the material felt slick and alien against my skin.

Numb, following the logic of dreams, I began a stroll around the empty room, running my fingers along the smooth, lukewarm surface of the wall. The wall's blueness looked milky, as if there was a liquid, slowly flowing upward, under the surface.

Then I found an exit leading down, with just enough headroom for a human. I had no idea what else to do so I followed it into the maze of hallways I would come to call the hive.

5

The hive is made up of nothing but corridors. At first I probably stuck to the main, hexagonal-shaped hallways, where the walls were gray-blue, the floor a soft red. Then I poked into the gray-lined tunnels looping off at odd angles and the boxy metallic-blue passages where I had to stoop down to walk through. Wherever one travels here a crisp light, coming from all sides, keeps the world free of shadows.

The only thing to do was to keep moving. To stop was to force myself inward. There were just too many memories I didn't want to look at. I had to stay one step ahead.

I have to stretch myself to imagine the confusion, even terror, I felt when first wandering through this now familiar territory. Pieces of memory surface in no logical order, the edges blurred, part of the seamless backdrop of the life to which I have become accustomed.

Eventually I discovered the dispenser indentations which occur occasionally in the walls. Each has two taps and a fold, out of which pop wide-mouthed chalk-color cups. Out of one tap comes a clear, bittersweet fluid and from the other a thick goop with the consistency of oatmeal. I must have paused a long time before taking my first meal, wondering if it would kill me slowly or in an instant.

There was the first encounter with a cleaning beetle, a creature or machine I now take for granted. First I heard a rising-falling buzz. I edged around to face the noise. In a moment a blue-domed thing came around a bend, gliding down the corridor at a steady pace. There was a white glow ringing its base and its blue surface was broken up by a pattern of black blotches.

"Who are you?" I asked with faint hope.

There was no answer. The beetle didn't slow as it came closer to me. I had to press to one side as it skimmed past. It was waist-high and roughly five feet in diameter.

After it went by me, the rhythm of the buzz slowed and the beetle came to a stop. A clear liquid sprayed out from several of the black spots. It soaked me. I sputtered and cursed the fluid's bitter taste.

The beetle moved forward, resuming its regular pace. I jogged after it for a while but it just glided on and on, so I eventually gave up.

Every time I met up with a beetle (for a long time I was sure it was always the same individual busy persecuting me), I got soaked. At one early encounter I tried to wrestle with the creature. I got a grip under its rim, tried to tip it up, but

423

found that the beetle had become an immovable object. Its buzzing chided me patiently.

In time I figured out that the beetles cleaned the hive, sucking waste and debris up under their shells and spraying their fluids. The bitter showers did seem to clear away the worst of my sweaty grime (though there was no way to get a shave). Still, the beetles never ceased to be something of a nuisance if they showed up when I was sleeping or, later on, when I was busy making love. . . .

6

Marie and I managed to cope with hunger. It was thirst, when there was no more juice to portion out, that drove me to force a way up out of the wreckage. We estimated three days had passed.

Most of the neighborhood was flattened. A layer of snow powdered the landscape, forming a blank mask over the carnage. We moved slowly as if this was all a bad dream. She stood still at the edge of the house, perhaps waiting to wake up from it all.

"There must be something left to drink," I said, kicking at the debris of the kitchen, trying to summon more strength.

"Maybe," Marie replied.

I managed to push back a section of wall and dig up a dented can of ginger ale. We carefully shared its contents.

"No signs of life," Marie said. "I don't see or hear anyone else."

7

I could pick over the memories of my last days with Marie, sew them all together and stretch them into a story. What is really in my head, though, are shades of old emotions, a swirl of voices, the taste of a desperate kiss, the bite of the cold and the ache of that desire to survive.

Here are some details I remember:

We found bodies everywhere. I believe most people died from some very hard radiation. I figured we'd escaped the worst of it during our three days in the basement; that by now most of the radiation had blown away or dissipated or done whatever radiation does when it has finished killing. I had hope that our chances for survival were pretty high. At times I entertained a vague idea that we could be the new Adam and Eve, eventually repopulating the planet.

The snow started up again and never stopped falling.

Marie screamed each time she stumbled over a body hidden in the drifts. At one point she sat down in the snow and blubbered about everything being all over. I had to drag her onward. We were headed for the commercial strip, where I planned to salvage food and winter camping gear.

We forged ahead. I had hope and I tortured her with it.

Here is a clear little snapshot: I am bending over a cop in the parking lot of the shopping center. I am tugging at the cop's gun. Marie is standing to one side, shouting, her hands pulling at her hair.

She said something like, "Not a gun, Daniel! It's too awful. All this . . . and now you want a weapon."

I explained, "We might need it for protection."

She pulled on her hair and clumps came out in her hands. Then she wept while I swore I would always protect her.

8

I sighted a meaty middle-aged man, with the beginnings of a sparse beard, standing in the gray mouth of one of the smaller tunnels. The first human being I'd come across in the hive. He stared as I rushed forward.

"Damn, it's good to see you," I said. I moved to face him and I saw another human figure lurking back by the first bend in the tunnel.

The man facing me smiled silently. He hunched down so that he was looking up at me. I paused, wondering what was the most appropriate thing to say.

"What is this place?" I blurted. "Where are we?"

"A long way from home." The man's eyes drooped and his lips became rubbery, barely managing to pronounce the words. "This? This is the rocket ship. Destination: moon. Stars our destination! The galaxy's a heart beat caught in my little fist."

"That's enough, Rover!" The second person, a hatchet-faced younger man, hurried up to the tunnel's edge.

"Rover?" I said.

"He's such a bad boy," Hatchet Face said. He grabbed at a strip of cloth around the older man's neck and tugged, dragging the man back like a dog on leash. A second savage jerk brought Rover to his knees. "He's a bad boy but he's a pretty pet." Hatchet Face patted Rover's head and straightened out a few locks of hair. "Such a pretty baby; I end up forgiving him every time."

"Our mission to explore," Rover spouted. The cruel yanking on the leash didn't stop him. "Flying saucer rock and roll. One thousand stars by sunrise. Black hole bowling."

"I'm afraid he hasn't been paper-trained. Dumb animal!" Hatchet Face smacked the top of his companion's head. "Rover, quiet. It's teatime. How about a little drink? Just a little one." Rover mumbled inaudibly. Hatchet Face turned to me. "You'll excuse us now. It is teatime. Do come again."

He dragged Rover to the dispenser indentation across the corridor and began filling two cups. They both ignored me, even when I pounded against the wall with my fist.

"Tea is an import product," Rover declared.

I ran away from them and didn't slow up for a long time.

My wandering was insistent, interrupted only by fitful periods of sleep on the soft floors. Movement the very stuff of existence.

9

Marie wouldn't talk to me much. I did the talking. About how I loved her. How we would build a house all on our own. How I would hunt for food.

Trooping about, we came across two survivors. The first ran from us. We had one glimpse of a face and then he ran around the side of a building. I called after him and even tried to follow for a minute. The second person wouldn't stop laughing. Her face was covered with blotches. She staggered and fell in the snow. I reached to help her up. Her hands felt frozen. I propped her up against a wall with one of our down sleeping bags wrapped around her shoulders. Still she laughed and laughed. In the end we fled the scene.

Marie and I weakened noticeably over the course of a few days. And our hair was falling out and pieces of skin were coming loose and sometimes we couldn't hold down dinner. . . .

And it was hopeless, right?

Giving up wasn't in me. Hope felt like a feature of my essential self. I wasn't ready to let go.

10

The green pillar things in the chambers above the hive were living creatures. They called themselves eurides. When I came upon one of those exit ramps, I'd sometimes followed them up out of the hive and drift through giant, empty rooms, occasionally seeing one or two of these eurides. Generally they weren't interested in conversation but by activating a device in the wall they could speak clear English. I took to shouting questions at them, while keeping my distance.

"Where am I?" I'd call out. Or, "What is this place?"

"Lifesphere," was the answer.

The Lifesphere, I learned was "a vessel . . . traveling between the stars."

"How did I get here?"

"One of our planetary probes collected you." The eurides spoke with toneless flat voices which issued from all sides of the room.

"When are we going back to Earth?"

"Never."

I usually headed back down after a short while. The deeper I ventured into the Lifesphere, the weaker gravity became and the more disorienting the varied shapes of the chambers. At least down in the hive the ceilings fit human proportions and there was food to eat.

11

The final straw for Marie had to be the little gunfight I got into while we were poking around in a dark ValueShop Supermarket.

"Don't touch my food," a voice croaked at us from across the next aisle. Then we heard the blast of a gunshot and the ricochet of a bullet off to the right.

I pushed Marie to the floor and dragged my pistol out. I emptied all six chambers and one of my shots connected. We heard a gurgling noise and then some thrashing about. When that silenced, I crept over for a look and Marie followed. It was an elderly man and he'd caught a bullet in the neck. He clutched a rifle to his chest. The floor was slick with blood.

Marie ran out of the store and I followed, leaving behind our collection of canned goods but still hanging on to that .38. She told me that we were murderers. The whole world was destroyed and still we were murderers!

After that she never spoke to me again.

I guess it was then she decided to bring it all to a true end. That night she slipped away with my gun.

12

How do I explain Andrea?

Twisting and turning my way through the hive, eating hundreds of desolate meals, I finally stumbled upon a woman.

The only woman, for all I knew. It felt like love.

I can call up this picture of Andrea from that first moment I sighted her. Her arms and legs are long. Her hair is a tangle hinting at orange and gold. Her face is an almost pure white

428

and I can read there a sensitivity—vulnerability and need. The whole snapshot has an emotional sheen that makes Andrea seem blindingly beautiful. Especially beautiful is the pain expressed in her face. I thought that I knew exactly how she felt.

After I rounded a bend and we saw each other we stood still, then we approached one another carefully and silently. We touched each other's face—it seemed to me we each expected to find that the other was a ghostly figment. We kissed —pushing lips, greedy tongues—probing for life. When we spoke it was babble, a relieved torrent. I was thankful we both spoke English, though the actual words weren't important.

In those moments sex was an immensely powerful force. We ripped away our sterile uniforms, locked together, pushed against the wall, slid to the floor, grinding into each other. At first I noticed the way the floor gave slightly to the rhythm of our movement but our union soon melted back the walls and the ceiling. I felt I was plunging into a world outside the hive. The transition from barren, unrelenting aloneness to the unity of two flesh-and-blood lovers had the quality of a miracle.

"We're dead and exiled in Hell," Andrea explained later, leaning into my chest. "This is the land of emptiness . . . like the coils of blank space inside our minds. But now I've found you. Now we can have love."

"I love you," I said, unrestrained. I was sure it was true. How could it be otherwise?

To embrace, to touch, that was what Andrea and I lived for. At first we were horrified at the idea of letting go at all. We had to keep the link, some bit of flesh to flesh, even while eating or making our toilets. We called the passage of time between bouts of lovemaking a day and the days flew by rapidly.

13

First there was a sense of beauty, then sadness, and then a hollow feeling. My love was a lie—to myself and Andrea. I loved her body. Loved her need for love. Her raw humanity. Anyway, at that time she was *Woman*.

I committed myself. We murmured about love all the time. Just a word. More than a word. It loaded me with a sense of responsibility.

She was centered around the single idea that we were experiencing the afterlife. Eternal damnation. Our only escape was love. Nothing else even had a chance of existing in the void of perdition.

What was there between us? Just this need and a great void to be filled. Powerful emotions without substance to sustain full-time love. I told myself I loved her. Tried to believe we were true lovers trapped together for eternity. But my feet got itchy—I couldn't stand to sit around forever and constantly face my own promises.

Andrea adjusted to my tendency to wander off. She said, "Wherever you go, the coils of Hell will bring you back to me."

I marched away for what must have been weeks and months, tottering along some edge in my mind.

14

A small section of the hive came to be more and more populated. Here was a place where Spanish and English were spoken. Where thirty or forty shell-shocked survivors of "the end of the world and other indignities" gained a feeling of solace and security through proximity to each other. Most often this area was called Settlement. At first this name was almost a joke since there was just a bunch of individuals and couples drifting about in similar orbits, perhaps circling in tighter to intersect each other with greater frequency. Then a lot of them slowed up and took to hanging out in the same corridors, sleeping just inside the more narrow tunnels and developing a loose network of relationships. And in that area I was called Seeker. "What are you looking for?" these now-settled folks liked to ask when I marched by. But I wasn't looking for anything. I wasn't much of a seeker.

For all my wandering, I always circled back to Andrea and my desire to be in love. As time wore on, I had wandered so much that there were areas where I knew configurations of intersections and turns by heart—and could thus often keep my bearings. Out beyond the margins of Settlement was where I usually found Andrea. She generally walked about naked, staring into space. Her face lit up when she sighted me returning, conjuring up that initial snapshot of her which I carried around in my head.

Some crazies lingered, like reluctant satellites, out here along the fringes of Settlement. Our most frequent encounters were with the man known as Mr. Plenty. He traveled a regular circuit, spouting cheerful greetings. He had lines like, "Welcome to the Land of Plenty. Milk and honey on tap. Never a cloud in the sky and you can sleep all day." He once assured me, "Red and blue are the two most perfect colors created by God." He was sure we were all among the blessed.

Andrea ignored Mr. Plenty. Several times I spoke of moving closer into Settlement but she became nervous at the suggestion. "I don't like to be around so many phantoms. You and I have substance. You know we're stranded in the desert, caught in one final loop of time."

15

In a high-ceilinged but relatively narrow chamber I came upon a euride who granted me an unusually long audience. When I approached, the alien seemed to be watching shapes pinwheel through the interior of a series of fat tubes which swelled out of the wall. After a time it moved closer to me. I could make out the fibrous texture of its green hide and the tiny wrinkles which shifted with each swaying motion.

I sucked in my breath, then demanded, "Where are you taking us? To some planet—where humanity can start over?"

"No," the euride answered. "Humans will travel with us. You will remain in Lifesphere."

"Just like that," I said. "Don't we have a choice?"

"The simplest translation: humans are property."

"Like animals! Like slaves?"

"Slaves," the euride said. "Yes. The analogy is close enough."

"What about our rights?" I snapped. "What about justice?"

"Earth humanity is an extinct species."

"But," I stammered, "slavery is evil. An abomination."

The faceless creature lost interest in me. One of its usually hidden arms reached out to touch the wall. Shapes began to flash past inside the blue tubes.

I wasn't in the mood to ask any more questions anyway. I slunk through the narrow exits which cut into the thick walls, heading down to the hive. Once again, ready to return to Andrea's arms.

16

Somehow I hadn't heard about her till Mr. Plenty told me, "You should talk to Scholar."

"Who's that?"

"Scholar said she'd like to hear your adventures. She talks to everyone," Mr. Plenty said.

"Why?"

"She wants to know every wonderful detail. And you, Seeker, have been to so many places! She wants the blessing of knowledge."

"Don't listen to him, Daniel," Andrea said. She began massaging my shoulders.

"See how nice and warm it is today." Mr. Plenty started to move on along his appointed course. "And Scholar, she wants to know how the weather stays so temperate. How, why, when, where . . ."

Andrea was relieved when he passed from sight. She

reached under my shirt, tracing lines around my chest. She kissed up and down the side of my neck. I forgot about the whole conversation for a while.

But later I went to Scholar and she sat with me for a long time, urging me to describe in detail everything I could remember seeing since my awakening aboard this Lifesphere.

17

I led Scholar up from the hive, through gargantuan euride chambers, to the narrow chamber with the vertical pipes bulging from the wall. Apparently I was the only one who'd ventured up to face the eurides more than once. She had shown great interest in these tubes when I told her my stories—even more than in the disturbing conversation that occurred in the same room. Well, it was probably the very same room, I wasn't sure, but there was the bulging wall and that was most important.

Scholar ran her small hands along as much of the tubing as she could reach and then carefully explored the flat parts of the wall. Something caught her interest higher up. I served as stepladder. She wobbled about, up on my shoulders. I gripped her ankles firmly while she pressed a spot on the wall with both hands. "The blue thickens here, into a kind of blotch," she explained.

"You did it," I said. I helped her down to the floor, my hands steady on her slim hips.

The liquid blue in the tubes started to flow noticeably faster. Shapes bubbled forth and spun by so that we saw each one from all sides. Forms such as a cube studded with cones were simple enough, but others were hard to follow with the eye, full of undulating curves and weaving ridges.

Scholar smiled. Then she chewed on her lower lip, intently watching each shape spin past.

433

"The progression repeats itself," she said after a while. "This is all going to be very interesting, someday, when we make sense of it."

Then she climbed back up onto my shoulders and pressed another spot which she was sure hadn't been there before.

I watched Scholar. And she patiently watched the next sequence roll by, trying to commit every detail to memory.

On the way back to the hive she said, "After all you've told me about your life, Daniel, you should call me by name. Rachel. Not Scholar. I'm actually a real human being."

"Sure. Rachel," I said, running my fingers through my beard. "Tell me who you were, before you became Scholar."

18

I remember I was holding Andrea's hand as we drifted through some silent corridors. Then at the intersection with a tunnel I heard the scrabbling noise of strange feet. Something colored in silver and polished browns leaped out at us and clamped its four stubby legs around Andrea's calf. Between those legs was just a small disk of a body with no visible head.

"It's biting me!" Andrea screamed. She beat at it with both fists. I grabbed onto two of its legs and peeled the thing off her. It left behind a deep gash in her calf. On its underside, clicking angrily, was a mouth made up of three beaklike sections, each streaked with Andrea's blood. It thrust out a thin worm of a tongue. I threw the nasty thing against the wall.

Three more of these creatures scurried toward us. If it hadn't been for my state of panic I might have laughed at the stiff-legged walk of these knee-high beasties. They made me think of ugly pieces of furniture brought to life through some clumsy means of animation. But I was panicked, especially by the slurpy clicking noises they made. I rushed at one and sent it flying with a high kick. It bounced off the ceiling and dropped to the floor. The other two reversed direction, still clicking as they ran away.

434

"Evil boogers," Andrea moaned.

The booger that had bitten her was showing signs of reviving. Its beaks opened and shut and the legs twitched. I picked it up by one leg and spun it down the tunnel after the others.

I bandaged Andrea's calf with my shirt. "Hold me, hold me," she said. I wrapped my arms around her.

The one I had kicked seemed dead. We hurried away so we wouldn't have to look at it any longer.

19

Ideas were important, worth exploring. Rachel—Scholar—had many theories, especially about this inside-out world we found ourselves in:

That the eurides left us to our own devices so that they could observe how we adapt to an unfamiliar environment—to watch the development of our social structures. This would give them one last chance to study humanity. We serve as a little footnote at the very end of Earth's history.

That other creatures in the Lifesphere, such as boogers and even the cleaning beetles, were survivors of other holocausts. The eurides might be collectors of rare species from around the galaxy. Or they might be survivors of a holocaust of their own.

Or that we and the other creatures served specific functions, which we cannot easily discern, within the Lifesphere. Much like microbes in our own digestive tracts. The eurides, too, might be part of this greater whole.

What Rachel believed and lived by was the idea that we could come to understand the Lifesphere and our situation in it. And out of understanding we might shape a destiny, become more than just a footnote. Understanding was a long way off and to get there every detail had to be carefully considered.

Here are some details about Scholar which stuck in my mind:

Rachel was slight, almost delicate. Her dark hair curled close around her face. Sometimes she made people angry when she laughed at the funny-sad parts of their stories. She adopted a very level and persistent tone of voice when she asked her many questions.

She told me, "I bummed around for years. I got a kick from quitting one job after another. Then I worked in a hospital and decided there really was something I wanted to do. It wasn't easy getting in but I was very excited. My second year of med school was about to start when the end of the world came."

Her memory, she claimed, was nearly photographic. She was storing up every detail reported to her, reviewing it all for patterns or missing pieces. With enough patience she was sure things would fit together.

When Rachel looked at me I felt she was staring through the layers, seeing the multitude of my selves and, I hoped, seeing something solid underneath.

20

"I have something to show you." Rachel grabbed my hand and led me down one of the low, narrow, squared-off tunnels. "Old Scholar has done some exploring of her own," she said.

We came to an exit leading downward to a blank wall. Rachel pressed at a spot near the top of the wall and it slid away, the passage continuing down. The walls pulled farther and farther apart as we moved on, till it was hard to see them where they curved away into the distance. The ceiling was so low we had to continue on our hands and knees.

"Don't worry," Rachel said, "I really do know where I'm going."

"It doesn't matter," I said. "I go anywhere and everywhere."

She laughed. "You're a little crazy—but pretty brave." Then she said, "We're here."

I felt sandwiched between red ceiling and red floor. Rachel ran her hands over an area of the ceiling and her fingers found something. The spot turned dark under her touch. Then the floor disappeared out from under us.

For a moment I was sure I was falling into the blackness spread before me. I saw stars—faint, faraway beacons. I spread my arms out, running my fingers along the floor which was, after all, still holding us up.

"We are lying against the hull of the Lifesphere," Rachel said, her voice soft and close by. "I discovered that it can turn transparent. The vacuum all around us and out there the stars . . . here we can have nighttime at last."

In silence we stretched out on the invisible floor. I adjusted my senses to the vastness of this night. Cold, yet so complete compared to the thin, unchanging day of the hive. The view changed with the sphere's spin. A dusty river of light that had to be the Milky Way cut across a corner of our field of vision. I imagined that our galaxy glistened with countless possibilities. Slowly, slowly it rolled past like the foaming crest of a breaking wave.

Gradually the sound of Rachel's breathing eased inside my awareness. I moved my arm and it brushed against her. She slid her fingers between mine.

As we made love I felt a flood of relief coming from suddenly knowing my own feelings. Apart from all else, the joy was in knowing it was Rachel I was with. First times with someone you discover you truly love can take on a mythic quality even as the action is taking place. Again I felt I was falling into the stars, but very slowly. Floating into night's ocean.

"Maybe," she said, as we lay still again, watching the Milky Way slip out of view, "we can keep this place our secret for a while. Come here when we want to be alone and when we want the night."

21

Back in the red and blue daylight of the hive my feelings of elation did a flip-flop and sank to become a heavy weight in my gut. Rachel was wonderful but I was forced to think of Andrea, who still needed—and claimed—my love. In turn my thoughts slipped back to Marie and those "other women"—

437

all just bones buried under the ashes of planet Earth. What was I doing still alive?

I began pacing up and down a length of hallway. Mental pictures, of the sort I couldn't stand looking at, kept rising up before me. They all meshed together to form a very ugly pattern.

My answer was to slink out of Settlement and keep on moving, headed nowhere. The plan was to blank Rachel, Andrea and the memory of women from my mind. Each step would take me farther from responsibility for their feelings and for my own.

22

I had gone a long way and hadn't seen more than a single cleaning beetle, so the torrent of boogers hurrying past at an intersection was startling. I stood stock-still while what must have been a thousand of the gleaming silver and brown creatures scrabbled past. Their chattering clicking filled the corridors with an ocean of sound. They paid no attention to me in their hurried march. If one slowed down, others crawled right over it in their haste.

When the end of the horde passed, I followed, setting to a steady jog to keep up. The boogers were a swarm of nightmare beasties but they were real. Yeah, that thought returned me to Rachel. She always wanted to look at the reality of the situation even if it wasn't easy. She held out hope. Now I had her on my mind. I thought of her asking questions. Where were the boogers going? What was their purpose?

I couldn't find out the answers. I grew tired and the boogers didn't. But thinking about Rachel and dealing with reality had me feeling foolish over this urge to wander aimlessly forever.

So I headed back in the direction of Settlement. I'd tell Rachel how I loved her. I'd live life the way I wanted.

23

Andrea was sprawled out naked by a food dispenser. When she saw me she sat up.

"Daniel, come to me." She held up a pale breast in each hand and pouted.

"I'm moving to Settlement. Permanently," I said. "I want to be with the woman called Scholar."

"You love me!"

"No, Andrea. Not the way I thought I did."

For a while she refused to understand my message. When it sank in, she moaned about death and damnation. She ran away from me, down the corridor, screaming. I caught up after she fell to the floor and beat her fist against the wall. She pushed her head against my shoulder and I put my arms around her.

"There's no way out," Andrea said.

"I have a life I want to live." After a pause I added, "Maybe you can move into Settlement too. Maybe you aren't in Hell after all. You could start a life of your own."

"No, no!" Andrea pulled away. "Go to the phantoms and demons—but don't make me watch."

She tuned me out after that. The best I could do was force her into some clothes. I hoped it might help her avoid getting raped by some crazy. Maybe I could avoid having that on my conscience.

24

Settlement was gradually becoming more closely knit. Sometimes a good number of people would take interest in Rachel's projects. I tried to concentrate on her optimistic plans, to block out my own restless lines of thought.

Five of us finally managed to tip a cleaning beetle over onto its rounded back. Its blue-black underside was warm to the touch and interspersed with soft bulges and ventlike rows of openings.

439

First the beetle's buzzing died away. Then the light around the edge of its shell faded and the underside grew cold. Some said it had died of starvation. Others thought its battery had run low.

We spent a lot of time puzzling over how we might dissect it. Knocking it against the walls just barely dented the shell. We smashed some cups from the food dispenser but the fragments were too soft to even scratch the surface of our specimen.

Finally we pushed the beetle back right side up, just in case it might come back to life. It didn't. From then on we had to squeeze around it to get through that corridor.

Rachel assured us the project had been worthwhile. We now knew more than we did before, even if we couldn't do much with that information right away.

25

Another of my scenes of death. I wish this one was just a single frame. Andrea's red, torn body stretched out on the floor of a tunnel, her face looking up at me. But memory doesn't stop there. I step toward her. Mr. Plenty—for once speechless—and Rachel stand still behind me. Two boogers with bloodstained silver legs get up and wobble away from the corpse. I scream at them. I grab one by the leg and smash smash smash it against the wall while the other scurries away. Kneeling down beside Andrea, I run my fingers over her blotchy, cold cheeks. . . .

Minutes later Mr. Plenty found his voice. He said, "She's happy now, Seeker, wherever she's gone."

I told him to shut up.

Two boogers weren't enough to kill a grown woman. I thought of my encounter with the rushing hoard of boogers climbing over each other. I pictured them swarming all over unhappy Andrea when they found her in their path. Then . . . Then I flashed to snapshots of gray drifts of snow piling up on Marie's corpse back on Earth.

Rachel said my name several times. She must have seen some horrible new expression fall over my face. I didn't respond to her.

I headed down the tunnel in the direction the second booger had taken, the dead one still dangling from my hand.

"Wait. We need you," Rachel called. She seemed to have guessed my intentions. "Please don't go, Daniel. I need you."

I couldn't stop. In fact I had to go faster. Were all the landmarks of my life women? Each leading to a betrayal? All on a winding course to insanity? I ran away, chasing demons. Leaving Rachel far behind.

26

I got to know the boogers very well. The subtle shades of silver running up their legs. The bumpy edges of their flat bodies and the soft spots where the shiny brown hide grew dull. I could feel the life vibrating through the cold leg of a booger and I could tell when that life had fled. I can still hear the constant clicking of hundreds of those three-way beaks— sometimes a dry, angry sound and other times a wet, greedy noise.

Despite vivid recall of those details, the actual time I spent chasing boogers through the endless threads of the hive is a blur of violence. I think I swooped down on five or six different hordes—or they may have been parts of some greater swarm. The pace was relentless. The main body of a booger horde never slowed much. Whenever I pulled back from one of my frenzied attacks, all but a few stragglers were drawn on by some insistent call.

I was driven too. My mind and body were united in the single task of pursuit, only resting when my legs couldn't keep going. I might have been trying to atone for the guilt wedged inside me, but at the time I felt beyond atonement. The only thing was to keep moving. Keep chasing death.

I killed boogers. I threw them against the walls. I kicked,

stomped, mashed and gouged. I clubbed them with the stiff bodies of their dead brothers.

27

It can't be a real memory.

I see myself wading into the knee-high stream of boogers. They begin to crawl over each other, trying to get around me. They are piling up around my waist. Soon they are attempting to scramble over me too. More and more swarm across my body, nipping at me as they pass, some biting deep. The weight presses me down. I begin to thrash my arms and legs but I can't get up. The boogers stream on and on.

I couldn't have survived this kind of experience.

This might be the way Andrea died.

28

The images of battle pass and end in a stillness. I found myself sitting on the floor, my back to the corridor wall. Crumpled and twisted corpses spread out from me for a long way down the hall. Blood oozed from wounds all across my body. I felt incredibly weak. The weakness slowed my thoughts, the rage fizzling out for the first time since Andrea's death. I felt a sense of relief at the thought that I was edging up to my own death; this suddenly struck me as being the purpose behind my war with the boogers.

I sat there waiting. All was silent around me. Fully conscious only occasionally, yet I always had the sense of sitting and waiting. Sometimes forgetting where I was and how I'd come to be here.

After a long time I understood I wasn't coming closer to death. Survival was apparently only a matter of getting up and going to the food dispenser.

My thoughts: I'd come to the end of the run. The boogers hadn't killed me and I didn't have whatever it takes to do it myself. My grief was run out, drained away along with all the violence. The drive to nowhere was over. I should have died but I didn't. And somewhere hope flickered.

I dragged my carcass over to the food dispenser.

29

Of course, my life—my story—doesn't end at any one conclusion.

I drifted down a corridor with the sensation that I'd been reborn into a new skin. When my path intersected with a swarm of boogers, I backed up to the wall and let them pass, swatting away the few strays who took an interest in me. I trotted along in their wake, the long habit of movement taking hold, no desire for violence left, my mind feeling clear and fresh.

Wandering peacefully, I tagged behind swarms here and there, admiring their relentless pace. Would they die if they stayed still too long? I experienced brief flashes where it seemed they were an extension of myself spreading throughout the hive. I liked to wonder if the boogers were looking for something but didn't know what it was yet. Theories about boogers were one way to occupy my mind. Maybe they had once been a highly intelligent species who went insane trying to find a way out of the Lifesphere. Still, it was hard to imagine them as truly intelligent. I more easily saw them as creatures bred for racing, bets laid on them at some alien racetrack.

Many times my thoughts settled on Rachel. What projects was she working on now and did she ever think about me? I had deserted her, chased after madness and fled from her struggle for the future. I considered going back to her but I had no idea what I could say. "I'm sorry" didn't sound nearly good enough.

It seemed I traveled deeper and deeper into a sort of booger zone—though I realized that the boundaries of such a territory would have to be ever shifting. Even when there weren't

443

any in sight, waves of chittering, scrabbling booger sounds rolled down the tunnels and passageways.

30

A key scene. At the intersection of a main corridor and a gray-lined tunnel. I'd passed thousands upon thousands such junctions during my time in the hive. Now I froze, watching three boogers at this intersection: one slumped against a wall, another staggered and weaved aimlessly, and a third was climbing out of a dark crevice—where they should have joined together, the intersecting walls had parted, leaving a distinct gap.

It was as if a seam had popped in the fabric of the hive.

The third booger dropped out to the corridor floor and began a meandering, slow-motion drunkard's walk. Two of its legs buckled and it toppled over.

I broke from my daze and rushed up to the gap. It was too dark inside to see much. I turned sideways and slipped through, fumbling and feeling my way along with my hands. The material coating these inner walls was cool and hard with occasional warm spots. First there was a long stretch of smoothness, then the wall felt covered with ridges and blisters. A fist-sized bubble moved under my fingers, buzzing just like a cleaning beetle. When I gave this wall beetle a nudge it zipped up, zoomed across the low ceiling, then buzzed back and forth along the opposite wall before coming to a halt and falling silent.

My eyes were adjusting to the dark. Some sections of this inner chamber were lit by a faint glow, as if light was seeping through from the corridors on the other sides of the walls. Other points were much darker, usually where the walls swelled inward with odd-shaped bulges. Scattered here and there I made out the shapes of over a dozen dead-still boogers. I could only guess that they'd wandered in here by accident and in some way ran out of energy in the gloom.

Eventually I discovered the looping series of tubes which

made up the back side of a food dispenser. I recognized it by
the stack of familiar wide-mouthed cups poking up out of a
slot. They pressed against a flap in the wall, which was letting
a good deal of light seep in. I tugged on the flap, allowing a
bright shaft of light to cut into the darkness. Four or five wall
beetles zipped around angrily but they were unable to stop me
from jamming a fragment of broken cup into the flap.

With the added light I had a vivid impression of being
caught inside the workings of alien machinery. The surfaces
were all a deep purple-gray—shadowy symbols floating within
—ribbed by curving ridges here, pimples in V-shaped patterns
there. The walls flexed in and out unevenly, liquid shapes
frozen in motion. When I pressed my palm to a blotch on the
wall, the food dispenser started to gurgle. A wall beetle
whisked over and perched over the spot until the gurgling
silenced.

A different noise caught my attention. A booger near my
foot was twitching one of its legs. I scooped it up, carried it
back to the opening, set it down on the red corridor floor. The
booger twitched some more, then wriggled its legs in a weak
pantomime of walking.

Ah yes . . .

I ran my fingers up along the edges of the parted hive walls.
My mind stirred with deliberate thoughts and new resolve.
Something had come of all the wandering after all. I hadn't
known what I was looking for but here it was.

31

It was a long march; I had plenty of time to think things
through. How, exactly, would I approach Rachel? I hoped she
didn't have a new man but that wasn't under my control. I
mulled over a million different explanations I could give her
and tossed each away in turn.

I started to bump into crazies with familiar faces, which
meant I was approaching Settlement.

A medium-sized horde of boogers stormed through a pas-

445

sage I wanted to cross. Watching them recede down the corri
dor I realized they were headed straight into Settlement. I
started to chase after them, worried about the people who'd
get caught in the swarm's path. But there was no way I could
run long and hard enough to catch up, not to mention slip
ahead to warn everyone. Still I raced on—it was important
not to give up.

When I limped into Settlement the horde had already
passed. Settlement dwellers were busy smashing stragglen
boogers against the walls. There were at least two dead, others
wounded. I could have told them to press up against the walls,
shown them how to shrug away boogers with minimal movements. I pushed aside this line of thought—I was now a man
in the process of forgiving himself. Next time Settlement
would be prepared.

I found Rachel bent over one of the wounded. She heard
me approach and turned to face me. She stared for a long
moment.

"It's Seeker," I said, thinking I might be hard to recognize
with my clothes down to a few stained ribbons and my body
laced with fresh scars.

"Daniel." She jumped forward and threw her arms around
me.

We pulled apart and she looked at me again, as if trying to
appraise my sanity.

"I've come back." Turning from her, I strode to a nearby
intersection. I ran my hands up the seam where the blue wall
met the gray one. High up, to either side, I found cold spots
and I pressed down on these. The seam opened like the parting of two lips. I waved my hand into the dark chamber beyond the burst seams in this blank-faced labyrinth of ours.

I said, "Rachel, I have something to show you."

32

Picture my face when Rachel told me she was going to have
a baby.

At the time I stood just inside the mouth of an inner chamber, wearing a shirt and trousers recently produced by one of the behind-the-scenes devices we've begun to master. I was working with two members of my mapping team, adding on another sector to our ongoing hive map. Using sections of booger leg, we carefully etched out white lines onto a smooth portion of inner wall, all the while swatting away the endlessly persistent wall beetles.

I jumped out into the corridor and shot a glance at Ruy—the medicoman—standing behind Rachel. He nodded, saying "Yes, she is pregnant. Approaching the second trimester, I believe. And she's in fine health." Ruy had already successfully delivered a healthy baby girl into the community.

Rachel and I snuck away to our secret chamber beneath the hive and let the star-misted night revolve around us. She slipped off her clothes and I rested my hands on her belly, trying to feel the life expanding inside her.

"We'll be measuring time again, when we watch our children grow," I said.

Rachel put a hand on her own abdomen and said, "Children and then grandchildren. They'll understand so many of the things that are mysteries to us."

33

I come out a narrow circular entry into a sort of shelf or ridge halfway up a wall inside a roughly U-shaped chamber. Gravity is weak. The air coats my mouth with a metallic film. At one end of the chamber spontaneous glimmers of light appear in midair and then dissipate. A euride is working its arms up and down along the wall opposite me. Dark geometries appear under the surface, one following the other as the alien touches them. I observe the quick movements of its arms, the gentle sway of its body and the shifting configurations it manipulates.

Now I definitely am the Seeker—my habit of wandering a proven agent in humankind's uphill struggle. Settlement is

447

expanding, and at the same time, we become ever more tightly knit. I see the shape of my life inside a larger pattern of human history. My key find—the inner chambers of the hive—has yielded up clues useful in several areas. Scholar is at the center of the essential project of decoding the symbols— language, we hope—floating within the Lifesphere machinery. Mastery of the numerical system may already be ours. We are fairly confident of our estimate that the whole sphere is twelve miles in diameter. The hive probably covers roughly 450 square miles; the sphere's total space is more than enough to keep our generation busy exploring.

This is unusual: the euride moves toward me. It hasn't actually turned around but I feel it is looking at me now. The top of its stalk is near my eye level. Where are its eyes? The arms have disappeared. What would we find if we dissected one?

While I have its attention I ought to think up some questions. Overeager, I shout, "What is your name?" Well, at least it's one I haven't asked before.

A pause. Hesitation? Now it reaches for the wall. "Eurides do not have the kind of individual identity you refer to."

"Then how do you identify each individual?" I call back quickly. I've found a talkative one.

"Individuals have coordinates describing a relationship to other eurides in Lifesphere."

"Your goals," I say. "Maybe you eurides would like to settle down someday—around a star, on a planet."

"No. Lifesphere is our habitat." It moves back from me. Have my questions disappointed it?

I shout forcefully: "What are your plans, then? Where do eurides come from. Tell me where the Lifesphere is headed."

"There is no destination."

"What are your intentions for us humans? Over the long term."

The alien moves farther away. Its swaying quickens.

"Are you—are eurides happy?" I call out, "I don't suppose you know much about love."

448

There is no answer. The alien is back at the wall playing out another sequence.

Okay, Mr. Euride, be mysterious if you like. Do you know everything we humans are up to? Maybe we have a secret or two of our own. Someday my children's children will know all your secrets and you just might wish you'd taken a little more interest in us.

I mutter my last question once more, then resume observing the chamber, taking mental photographs of all the significant details.

BANTAM SPECTRA
SPECIAL EDITIONS

*A program dedicated to masterful works of fantastic fiction
by many of today's most visionary writers.*

☐ **Synners by Pat Cadigan**
(28254-9 * $4.95/$5.95 in Canada)
Synners create computer generated realities for art and entertainment, but when they inadvertently create a deadly virus spreading through the computer network, its up to them to stop it.

☐ **Winterlong by Elizabeth Hand**
(28772-9 * $4.95/$5.95 in Canada)
In the ruins of a post-Apocalypse Washington D.C., twins who were separated in childhood approach a reunion that could reshape human history.

☐ **Points of Departure by Pat Murphy**
(28615-3 * $3.95/$4.95 in Canada)
An outstanding collection of the short fiction of Pat Murphy, including the Nebula Award-winning "Rachel In Love" and an introduction by Kate Wilhelm.

☐ **Phases of Gravity by Dan Simmons**
(27764-2 * $4.50/$5.50 in Canada)
An ex-astronaut searches for the meaning in his life, guided by a mysterious woman who leads him through his personal "places of power." "Earth , air, fire, water: Dan Simmons. Warily, in awe, we watch him and marvel."--Harlan Ellison